MAD LOVE

"I'd rather be the submissive queen of an honorable king than the ruler of a crumbling kingdom."
-Kinsley Hayes

Lynessa Layne

USA TODAY BESTSELLING AUTHOR

By Lynessa Layne

The Don't Close Your Eyes Series

Killer Kiss — a novelette

Don't Close Your Eyes

Complicated Moonlight

Mad Love

Dangerous Games

Hostile Takeover

Target Acquired

Point Blank

The Hitman's Girl - Eric's Story
featured in The Hitman Anthology

Short Stories

The Getaway

Winter in Roatan

Whispers Through the Trees

The Crow's Nest

Magazine Articles

The Villains of Romantic Suspense

To anyone ensnared by temptation, destroyed reputation, swayed during inebriation, worked through devastation, been victim of objectification, underestimation, overspeculation, used for recreation,
endured excommunication, generalization, defamation,
fought manipulation, deterioration, exploitation.

Push through consternation with determination. Your transformation brings reformation exempt from all future evaluations of your limitations.

The best proclamation, retaliation and retribution is to let them see they failed to bring about your decimation.

Love, Lynessa Layne

Cast of Characters

- **Klive Henley King** – anti-villain./hero also known as Complicated Moonlight and Kinsley's pirate. Enforcer of crime syndicate, Nightshade, leading double life

- **Henley** – Klive's alter ego for pulling hit jobs and undercover stings

- **Kinsley Fallon Hayes** – Protagonist. Bartender, college student, renowned sprinter known as Micro Machine

- **Andy and Clairice Hayes** – Kinsley's parents

- **Ben** – Andy Hayes' co-worker, Klive's friend

- **Jase Michael Taylor** – Navy SEAL,Navy SEAL, lead singer of Rock-N-Awe, lifeguard, Kinsley's longtime crush

- **Tyndall Taylor** – Jase's little sister, Kinsley's best friend

- **Mike and Bianca Taylor** – Jase and Tyndall's parents

- **Rustin Keane** – Jase's childhood best friend, combat veteran, cop

- **Nightshade** – crime syndicate

- **Joey** – Klive's personal security detail, private investigator

- **Eric** – Klive's Nightshade lieutenant

- **Christophe** – Klive's private investigator, Joey's employer

- **Marcus** – Kinsley's manager, Nightshade member

- **Gustav & Jarrell** – bouncers at the bar Kinsley works at, Nightshade members

•**Bayleigh & Garrett** – Kinsley's co-workers

•**Constance Marie** – Kinsley's friend, Jase's co-lead for the band Rock-N-Awe

•**Antoine (Sweetness)** – Constance's cousin, Gustav's brother, Kinsley's hairstylist, military spec-ops, has worked with Jase

•**Inferno** – biker gang crime syndicate comprised of dishonest firefighters. Rivals of Nightshade.

•**Ray Castille** – Inferno's disgraced leader, Fire Marshal

•**Pat Connor** – Inferno biker

•**Sara Scott** – Kinsley's co-worker, Patrick Scott's widow

•**Adrian Miller** – Kinsley's art professor

•**Ian Walton** – Kinsley's personal trainer and track coach

•**Eliza, Lindsay, Julie** – Kinsley's track relay team

•**(Looney) Lucy** – Kinsley's track manager and biggest fan

•**Brayden** – who Kinsley dubs Frat Toy, has huge crush on her

•**Shay** – Kinsley's alternate/replacement on the track team

•**Nolan and Devon** – Jase's buddies from high school

•**Matt** – lifeguard who works with Jase

•**Angela Ansley** – Kinsley's high school nemesis

•**Detective William Bartlet** – worked Sara Scott's murder, saddled with training Rustin

•**Sheriff Ansley** – William Bartlet's boss, Angela Ansley's father

Character Point of View

♂ = Klive King

♀ = Kinsley Hayes

MAD LOVE

Lynessa Layne

USA TODAY BESTSELLING AUTHOR

1 | ♀

I STIRRED AT THE sound of Klive's accent.

"Fifteen minutes, please. Keep a low profile. I'm about to rouse my wife. We will meet you down the street outside the gate. Thank you."

My heavy eyes unglued when Klive's finger traced my profile and tapped my nose. I blinked several times as his face took form before me.

"I heard you talking, I think," I mumbled, my voice distorted as half my face pressed into the pillow. "Was I dreaming?" Suddenly, I jerked up in alarm. "Did I wake you up? Was I sleepwalking?"

He shook his head. "I wasn't aware I needed to worry about you walking out the door in the middle of the night."

I fell back into the nest of pillows with relief, then looked at him. "Something wrong? It's still dark."

"Love, nothing is wrong, aside from what brought us together in this room. We've shaken our tail for now, but if we don't get back to Tampa before they know we're gone, we may lose our edge. I'll drive. You'll sleep."

"Bummer. I was so hoping to trick you into wearing a banana hammock on the beach to torture my friends."

Klive laughed out loud and shook his head in disapproval. "All right, naughty girl. Your friends have the luxury of drinking their days away on the beach. You and I operate under different circumstances. Here, I pulled your track pants from your duffel and packed the few effects you took from it. I'll give you a moment to dress and use the restroom, then meet me on the balcony."

I nodded and shoved the heavenly cloud of blankets aside. In a stupor I did as he said, then pulled the door to the room closed at my back once I stepped onto the balcony. Klive leaned over the railing and peered down at the deserted cobble stone streets below. I couldn't help memorizing him this way and wanting to somehow preserve the man before me. Instinctively, I knew he was to vaporize with the responsibility life doled. I replayed what I could recall from the phone call he'd made before he'd awakened me. Klive called me his *wife*.

What would that be like? To see him this way and saunter over to run my nails over his back the way my mother did to my father? I'd never pondered the intimacy and permission of such gestures until this moment when I wasn't allowed to without being weird. *Did Klive even like to be touched that way? How did he like his back scratched if at all? Hard, soft? Barely grazing?*

"Oh, good. You're ready?" he asked as he turned to find me watching him. I nodded and chewed my lower lip. "What's wrong, love?"

"Klive, if I wrap my hands behind my back, will you kiss me one more time before this all vanishes? Is that too inappropriate to ask?"

He smiled though the look in his eyes was strained and sad; aching like my own. His hands wrapped behind his back as he dipped his face to mine. My hands clasped tight behind my back, as tight as I wished to hold to him. *Oh, Klive King ... what you do to me!* His kiss was so ... *consuming.* The world around us melted under the warmth of his mouth, taste of his breath, the tingles racing up the back of my neck as my desire climbed and reached for more against the abrasion of his five o'clock shadow.

He pulled away like he sensed my urgency, kissed the tip of my nose, my forehead for a lingering moment, and unclasped his hands to offer one to me. I sighed, took his fingers and allowed him to lead the way downstairs around the corner to the gates of the city.

A white Tesla idled silently with an obedient bellhop standing beside a valet. Klive tipped them both, walked me around to the passenger side, opened the door, and helped me inside. The door closed. He got into the driver's seat a moment later.

"I was right about your car, sir. I deserve another kiss."

He leaned across the console to peck my lips the way a normal couple does. Nothing about Klive said any relationship with him would be normal. How could one be normal when he delivered surges through my skin at every touch, butterflies through minuscule side-glances, intensity that said he was always calculating different outcomes to keep you on your toes?

Klive decided to take the A1A back to the I-4 so I could enjoy the scenery of moonbeams against the East coast waves along with the beautiful mansions that dotted the beach front properties. To be honest, I thought he was prettier than the view. So was his hand he held my fingers in. His thumb brushed my knuckles every so often. My heart clenched hard. Longing constricted the air in my throat. I looked out the passenger side until I fell asleep, exhausted from the perpetual wishes tormenting my mind.

When the car stopped, the door opened. Klive leaned in, wrapped his arms around me and lifted me from the seat. I tried to rouse myself enough to walk, but surrendered to his gentle, "Shhh ... I've got you, Kinsley."

"Yes, you do." I nestled into his neck as my fingers laced beneath his hair. I was too sleepy to care about walking. Klive carried me until I heard the beep of a key card in a door, the slam a moment later. More beeps. Another door. Another soft bed with heavenly blankets.

3

"Sweet dreams, say your prayers, love." Klive kissed my forehead, and I whimpered in protest. I reached up and pulled him down until he kissed me the way I wanted.

"You are the dream, Klive. I want you."

"So are you, Kinsley, and I want nothing more."

Hours later, harsh beeping of an unfamiliar alarm clock jerked me from my dreams. My eyes opened to bright light outlining heavy curtains above a humming air conditioning unit. The jarring sound had my fingers fumbling around the unfamiliar nightstand until the damn thing silenced. The red digits blurred and focused.

Holy crap! Ten-thirty!

I jumped out of the bed and yanked the curtains back. Blinding sunlight glittered against the white caps of Tampa Bay from about five stories up. At the shock of light, I squinted while blinking back spots as I peered into the dark cave of the hotel room I'd slept in. A note rested on the nightstand. Took me a few moments before the words appeared without glowing green orbs blocking them.

Morning, love. Brunch downstairs before parting ways to appear as though we happened upon one another? St. Augustine our little secret. X-Complicated.

He had very elegant handwriting. Mom would've appreciated his technique. I wasn't sure how I felt about him not signing the note. Eh, at least he'd more than confirmed he'd sent all those roses. I folded the note to keep and went into the bathroom.

"Our little secret?" I asked my reflection while unwrapping a toothbrush and mini toothpaste offered by the hotel.

Damn. *Why hadn't I considered this?*

My eyes didn't look offended, nor did the glow of my skin. I wasn't offended at all. Intrigued was more apt. If I went home like this, my parents would think I'd gotten laid for all the natural flush in my cheeks and light in my eyes. Bayleigh always had this glow after a good romp. So, what did that say about Klive and my magnetism toward him if he didn't touch me and lit me up this way?

I found my duffel bag on top of the chest of drawers. A billowy sun dress with a strapless fitted bodice hung on a hanger in the tiny closet. Well, hell. Klive was a passive brat. I tapped my chin just imagining his evil grin. I couldn't wear a bra with this dress, and I wasn't packing pasties in my track duffel. Loved how he refused to get me out of my clothes when I begged yet chose this to enjoy my lack of certain clothing in his own mind. Wicked man. I smiled with a little chuckle when I looked at the floor and noticed a brand-new pair of heels to go with the dress. The same ones I'd tested with Constance, but they were in red rather than gold. Guess Miranda, the salesclerk, had gotten his other request after all.

"Of course, heels and a dress, Mr. King." I had half a mind to wear my jeans and tacky tee out of this refined establishment to blow a hole in his plans. Crazy, though; *how had this man managed this when he'd been up all night? Or had he brought these things to St. Augustine when he'd packed his own bag? Maybe he'd planned to take me out today but had to shift his plans when those guys chased me?* My heart ached at the mystery and stolen potential date.

I freshened up and dressed, finger-combed my hair since I didn't have my brush. Thank God for a modest padding! I adjusted the bodice firmly over the girls, stepped inches taller into the heels. *Remarkable how well everything fit,* I thought, as I buckled the straps. In the full-length mirror in the room I whistled at what these heels did for my calves. No wonder Constance was in love with them. For good measure, I took a few laps around the room to get my balance right. No public fails for me today, thank you.

I tucked Klive's shirt and my track pants inside my duffel. "Holy shit!" My keys tumbled in the bag! The Honda key was gone from my Civic's key chain, a neon tag with a number and the name of the hotel in its place.

"What the hell?" I left my car at the bar because Jase had taken me home Thursday night. Do I even want to know how the magic man performs his tricks?

"No," I answered my thoughts as I checked the room to be sure nothing was left.

Did Klive not want to be seen taking me home if he went out of his way to have my car brought here? Klive hadn't slept in here. *Had he gotten himself a room, or gone home with plans of running into me here? Should I stay or go? If I stay, was that a silent agreement to creating secret rendezvous? If I left, would he come looking or wonder where I was? Maybe he'd feel stiffed the way I'd made Jase feel after standing him up?*

My mean girl conscious popped up and said the only fair option to Jase was that I leave Klive. How could I be so offended at Jase's desire when I'd felt the same toward the man rejecting me last night? Yeah. I needed to leave. Just because I wanted Klive didn't mean I was giving away my self-esteem.

I stepped into a long hallway, counted the paisleys on the carpet as I walked with my track duffel slung over my shoulder. A little awkward with my heels and the weight of the bag, but I worked the look with more confidence in each determined step to leave this foolishness behind. I exited the elevator downstairs while studying the valet tag. Outside, I passed the ticket over and waited for the valet to bring my car. There, like a perfectly directed play I had no idea I starred in, Klive appeared from the corner of my eye with two other men. All of them wore light colored suits and spoke of fishing. Klive was laughing at something one of his company was saying when he faltered as though genuine at the sight of me. *Maybe he realized I was leaving?*

"Upon my word, gentlemen. You've seen the runner from the paper, yes?" he asked. "It is you, is it not?" he asked me as though barely acquainted with me.

I swallowed and nodded, then remembered to smile. The valet parked my vehicle at the curb while I pretended I wasn't stupefied as to how my Civic got here.

"I am the runner, yes, sir. Glad to know someone read the article," I said. "In fact, I just came off a meet last night." I gestured to the heavy bag resting against my hip.

"Kinsley!" My father's colleague, Ben, jogged out from the parking garage. "What a pleasure running into you here," he said with a great smile. Ben took me by the hands and kissed my cheek. Klive wore surprise in his eyes. Before any of the men said anything, Ben turned and greeted them, then asked if they minded whether I joined them for brunch.

Klive and Ben knew one another? Had brunch together? Small world.

"Oh, Kinsley, I guess I should've asked if you were free first. I hope you will join us," Ben said. "It's delightful and my friend, here, is buying. I'm almost positive he wouldn't mind one more."

Klive said, "By all means. Would be our pleasure to have you join."

"What do you say? Hungry?" Ben asked. "You look beautiful, by the way. Those are killer heels."

"Thank you," I said. "I suppose I could join as long as it really isn't too much trouble. Y'all can be my alibi for missing family yard work," I teased. The valet placed the bag in the backseat of the car when I told him I'd be back after brunch.

"Kinsley is Andrew Hayes' daughter." Ben filled the others in while we headed back into the hotel. Apparently, these men worked in the same building.

I couldn't help my fascination with Klive in this capacity. He was way too distracting in a white suit like the hero rather than the dangerous rogue I sensed. Funny thing was, in this capacity, with these men, he was like another personality altogether. If I'd worn white, I'd be a magnet for strawberry jam mishaps. I bet Klive would walk out of here looking as spotless as he did sauntering in.

I ripped my eyes from his smooth complexion as he pulled the door open for me, gestured I go ahead of them much the way he had when we'd been enemies in the elevator. He switched characters between last night and this morning just as he had two years ago after asking me out, then doling an insult for my refusal.

"Thank you, sir." I walked through, Ben and the others behind me while Klive fell in back. I pulled the door for the restaurant. Each man tried to refuse my hospitality, but I arched an eyebrow and told them to go on. Until I came to Klive, that is. I didn't give him the chance to insist I go ahead of him. I released the handle and followed the others before he caught the door and stepped through. He chuckled to himself at my back while flutters filled my belly, more so as I fought to look like we didn't know each other.

"Her father's been going crazy with worry over her," Ben was saying. "She didn't make things easy at the office this past week. Just for that, Kins, you owe me a lunch date to pay for your mistake."

I laughed too loud and slapped Ben's arm. "Not a chance. You can have brunch, but I'm dating another man, Ben."

Klive swallowed and appeared ruffled. He said his name to the hostess before she led the way. Klive motioned I go before them. I noticed the hostess glanced back at me, then looked beyond at him.

"Dating another man, huh?" Ben asked. "No wonder your dad is up in arms," Ben muttered. "Is that why you were MIA? By the way, you look badass with all these designs on your leg and hands. I bet he'd flip his lid if he saw you, though."

"Thank you, sir. I've been missing in action because I was with friends doing college things that college girls do before I grow up and graduate. One of my friends painted this on my body. Yes, I'm sure he'll flip when I see him."

"Graduation?" one of the men asked. Ben filled in the blanks while he ushered me into a chair he pulled away from a table for me.

"Thank you." I scooted closer to the white tablecloth and unfolded the linen napkin to lay across my lap. Suddenly, all my mother's drills on table manners rushed through my mind as I tried to pretend to belong with these men. Elbows off the table. Work from the outside in. Crossed ankles, not legs. Knees together. Sit up straight. Shoulders back.

"Very impressive," one of the men stated. I blinked up at him and took a sec to realize he was speaking about my major, not my manners. "I hear diabetes is the silent crisis growing bigger than global warming and at a faster pace."

"Yes," I said with a bright smile. *Someone knew!*

"Well, Kinsley, it's a shame your father couldn't join us. Although he may give us all grief for stealing a moment to have mimosas with his daughter." One winked.

Ben chuckled. "I promise this moment is more pleasant than what you go home to."

"Yikes. I believe you are right, Ben." I couldn't help my genuine smile, even if I worried about my father the more Ben seemed to. "Bring on the champagne and orange juice, STAT!"

We all laughed while Ben signaled the waiter to order our drinks. The waiter rushed like a man on a mission. Good.

"Where are my manners?" Ben asked and introduced the others, in one ear out the other, before landing on their noticeably quiet host. "Kinsley, this is Klive King. Don't be offended by his silence. He's not as rude as he comes off. Girls scare him," Ben teased. "Klive meet Kinsley Hayes."

"Hi, Klive," I said with a blush and placed my hand in his. No different than the way I had the others, but Klive's touch was charged.

The waiter returned with crystal glasses filled with our pretty cocktails. When he left, I picked back up. "Nice to meet you. All of you. And thank you for inviting me to brunch. I've not had the pleasure. To be honest, I never considered coming into a hotel to eat without having slept in it the night before." *Shit. Stop talking.*

"Ms. Hayes, the pleasure's all mine," Klive said. He unfolded his linen napkin with deft grace and laid the cloth over his lap. His fingers wrapped the stem of his crystal glass. "Girls don't scare me. I find most women think I'm off-putting for not putting up with their bullshit. The ones that don't find me off-putting, I'm put off by." Klive's eyes lit while his lips smirked. His company gaped at his audacity while I chuckled. No way I put him off. That much was evident by our back and forth liaisons. I wouldn't be surprised if half his smirk was due to the fact that he knew I wore no bra.

"I'll gladly drink to that." I lifted my mimosa. His brows shot up in pleasant surprise to clink glasses with me. The others, not expecting my reaction, lifted their glasses in agreement.

"I'd never fault you for your honesty, Mr. King," I said. "We share a common thread. Most women find me off-putting, which works since I'm put off by most of them as well. Perhaps we should hang out to keep them at bay?"

The group laughed as I took a sip of my orange juice and champagne. The men asked about my sprint, my average times, what events I ran, then surmised why other women probably found me off-putting.

Klive's foot bumped mine beneath the table. I swallowed the thrill with more mimosa.

"So, gentlemen, do we order from a menu, or partake of the buffet?" I asked, looking around.

"Anything you want, love," Klive said. "I prefer the menu. Not a fan of the shared serving spoons and others breathing on my food."

Ah, the germaphobe. "You don't mince words, do you, Mr. King?" I grinned and opened the menu.

"Ms. Hayes, please, call me Klive."

"Well, Klive, you may call me Ms. Hayes." I fought a flirty smile as Klive pulled the menu down so his eyes grinned over the edge. I lifted my chin, shoulders back like a proper lady. I cleared my throat. "Having been in the food service industry for some years, should I spoil everything with wondering when the last time they disinfected their menus was? Or whether they used a dirty cloth to do so?"

"Oh, ma'am, we wouldn't dare," the waiter rushed in alarm, giving his eavesdropping away. "All of our facilities are given the utmost care and attention for maximum customer satisfaction."

I quirked my eyebrows while his very defensiveness and guilty blush confirmed my theory. Ben chuckled to himself, the other men seemed amused as well.

I turned my faux snobby charm on the ruffled waiter. "In that case, may I have the Eggs Benedict with the Hollandaise on the side, please?" I handed my menu over. The waiter nodded and took Klive's order. The others said they weren't afraid of germs and willing to brave the buffet. Klive rolled his eyes and produced his phone. I grabbed my mimosa and took a long drink to hide my contempt at this ultimate dating pet-peeve.

"Pull yours too, love. If I ignored my phone for you, these gossip whores would have a field day. We are being studied. If I don't look at my phone, one may accuse me of infatuation for being unable to rip my eyes from your shoulders and collarbones in that dress. The way your pulse beats in your throat. The dry swallow that belies my effect on you ...."

"Holy shit," I whispered. "My phone is in my duffel bag. What the hell do you want me to look at instead of the way your jaw muscle jumps when I get under your skin, sir? That little twitch in your lips when you try not to smile?"

11

His eyes shot to mine, stunned that I paid him as much mind as he apparently did me.

"Seems we are both wretched poker players," he mused and texted like I didn't exist.

"Indeed. Know what my father taught me about poker?" I asked.

"What's that?" he asked without looking at me.

"Be willing to quit while you're ahead. No sense losing everything you've gained to bluff on a hand you can't win with." I stood, downed the last of my mimosa, set the glass back down. "Give my meal to a homeless person."

Klive's phone laid on the table. "What are you saying?"

"I'm saying there are safer bets I'm willing to make. No bluffs or secrecy necessary. Thanks for everything, Mr. King."

His jaw muscle jumped while his eyes turned to stone. I sauntered toward Ben to kiss his cheek and tell him I got a call from a friend and needed to leave.

"May I walk you to the valet?" Ben asked.

"I'd like that. Thank you." I took the arm he held out as if we were together. Ben told the guys he'd be back. I smiled over my shoulder and waved at them, but my eyes flared at Klive before shifting to neutral. There was a difference in secret rendezvous together in a hotel room versus shame in public with others. Klive needed to learn the distinction. I was no one's girl coming or going by the back door.

When I handed the valet my ticket, Ben studied me in a different way than I ever recalled in all the years he and my father worked together.

"What is it, Ben?"

He shrugged. "I don't know exactly. Something seemed ... *there*."

"With?"

"I've never seen him check anyone out. He skimmed you. Twice."

"Who?"

"Klive. Then again, I've never seen him approach someone in passing. He read about you and approached you like he was a fan."

"It happens from time to time," I told him.

"He called you *love*. I've never heard him call any woman that. *Dear*, maybe. *Miss. Ma'am*, but of course it sounds like mom, which is pretty funny, but never *love*."

"Oookay ..." I trailed like Ben was crazy. "I'm pretty sure Brits say that often. Easy endearment," I offered.

"He shook your hand, Kins. He'll shake hands if he has to, but he hates contact."

"Ben, maybe he just didn't want to make me feel uncomfortable. You're reading too much into that back there. Trust me, as a bartender I come across all types. People do strange things sometimes."

Ben laughed and shook his head. "Kinsley, Klive King does *not* go out of his way to make women feel more comfortable. You heard him. He's put off by them, therefore he never does anything to draw anyone. As long as I've known him, he actively repels them. I guess I thought he was a closet gay. I just— hell, I don't know. The way he looked at you. *Not gay.* But he didn't only look at you like you're hot in the heels. He ...." Ben tilted his head like the right word might fall from his ear.

My car came down the ramp of the parking garage into the bright sun. The light glared off the windshield into our eyes. We squinted at one another.

"Ben, I'm flattered. He's attractive, but like I said, I'm dating someone. So, if you're trying to set us up or someth—"

"Admiration!" His fingers snapped. "Kinsley, he admires you. That's what it is." Ben dismissed me altogether, shook his head at his own thoughts. "Damn, girl, you've got the magic touch. I've never had more respect for you or him. Enviable, Kinsley. His respect is hard to earn."

I thanked the valet as he passed me my keys. Ben gave a tiny wave and walked back inside as if he'd had an epiphany.

I shrugged, tipped the valet and drove away from an odd experience more confused about Klive's enigma than before.

2 | ♀

THE SPIRAL SAILED THROUGH **the air** as Daddy kicked sand to run fast enough to catch the football. Mom sat in her lounger beneath the shade of my beach umbrella, slathered in sunscreen barely whiter than her very fair skin. She cheered for him when he pulled the pigskin from the air and turned to pass the ball back to me in the manner he'd taught me. I dodged other beach-goers and hurdled a sand castle as Daddy threw harder than he had the other times. Yep. Being a brat while he pretending to be happy that I'd invited him for a daddy-daughter date. That's okay. He wasn't the only one playing passive-aggressive games.

We tossed our football only one lifeguard tower away from Jase's after I'd confessed our fight to Tyndall. She wasn't mad at me for putting him in his promiscuous place. "I'd be disappointed in you if you just gave in to him," she'd told me. "Why don't you have a date with your father? I'll find out which stand Jase is working, and you can kill two birds with one stone."

"You're brilliant, Tyndall. Thank you!"

"You're welcome. This way the quarterback gets a taste of the talent he's up against," she'd snickered. Tyndall used to come to the beach with my family. She didn't like football but loved to sit with my mother and cheer while Daddy and I pushed one another further with each throw. "I only wish I could come watch Jase twisting in the ocean breeze."

"You think he'll even notice?"

"He'll notice. If he doesn't, the other lifeguards will tell him. Go have fun. Text me later with updates. Can't wait," she'd said.

"You're getting sloppy!" Daddy shouted over the thundering waves.

"Coach told me I shouldn't be running! What do you expect?" I asked him as I fought the surf. Daddy joined to help before the waves carried the football out to sea.

"There are a lot of things we tell you not to do that you do anyway, Kinsley Fallon!"

"What do you want me to do, Daddy? You both tell me to grow up and get ready to leave. I loosen my grip on your safety net and you have a conniption." The ball eluded both of us. He shot me a look like the loss was all my fault. I shrugged. "You can keep staring at me like I'm the worst child in the world, but that won't make it true. I know I'm better behaved than most, trust me, you're lucky. I think you know it."

Some kid grabbed our ball and ran. Again, my father shot the silent blame. We both chuckled when the kid tripped in the sand, lost the ball, and the waves took our pigskin again.

"There's still a chance," Daddy said.

"Yup, and that kid right there is the perfect example of things you didn't have to put up with from me. I may have let my friend draw designs all over me, but at least I'm not a thief."

His eyes fought to stay stern. He looked back at the water and grabbed my hand so we could fight the waves together.

"You know it's a lot easier and faster if we walk the sand to chase the ball," I said.

"Yeah, I know," he answered. "But the salt water is erasing the henna and the longer we are in here, the more I see my little girl coming back into her own pretty skin. No tattoos necessary. Not to mention, this is good for you. Walton said you've been working out on the beach so often he hasn't had you in the gym for resistance training. So, here you go."

"I don't need to pull weights like a sled dog when I can run in the loose sand, Daddy. Walton should come out here with me."

"Negotiate with your coach on your own time," he told me. "Pick up the pace. You can do better than that. Come on!" Daddy fought the waves faster until I struggled against the churning current far worse than any belt Walton placed around my waist, undertow stronger than a large weight dragging on the ground behind me. This was a full-bodied effort.

"Is it me or does it seem like you want to do more than condition me? Maybe switches from the weeping willow at home would be better and faster than drowning or a shark attack?"

Finally, my dad's hard-ass gave way to a laugh. *Oh, thank the Lord!* "Nah, the shark attack would be way faster than drowning or the switches. You'd have to get a ladder, then I'd have to listen to you whine about your fear of heights!"

I gave Daddy a smart-ass smile. The joy was short-lived as I heard the unmistakable sound of a whistle blow long and loud. The lifeguard sprinted down the ramp of his tower while those playing in the water made a clearing and ran out of the water like a shark was spotted. He dove into the waves while I looked in alarm for someone struggling in the emerald surf. Daddy hurried us onshore and we watched while he realized. He pinched the bridge of his nose.

"Kinsley Fallon. Tell me Mike's boy didn't just ruin everyone's fun to save our football."

My eyes were wide with trepidation as that was *exactly* what Jase had done! Everyone watched and waited with bated breath for a victim that didn't exist. Jase held our football over his head as he waded through the water like the guy who never lost a ball in battle. The crowd laughed and clapped while he took a bow and brandished a bright smile. His whistle pipped. He waved everyone back to having fun.

"Yours, I believe, sweet Kins?" Jase held the ball while my eyes rose up his legs, dripping shorts, drenched torso, private grin enjoying his sexy inside joke like before we ever crossed the line from friendship.

What the hell? Where was his anger, attitude, angst?

Where was mine?

"Thank you." I took the ball with a bashful blush. His hands ran through his wet hair to squeeze excess water like an audition for the next cover of *Men's Health.*

Damn, Jase was effing hot. So was the knowing in his eyes before they flashed kind and indifferent toward my father.

"Afternoon, Mr. Hayes," Jase said. "You have an amazing arm! Did you play ball?"

Jase knew the key to a man's ego, did he not? Daddy thawed and clapped a hand against Jase's bicep. "Thanks, son. Played in Tennessee on scholarship. Gave up the draft to make a life with this little lady's mother. However, all the flattery in the world won't save you from answering for how you behaved with my daughter the other night."

My eyes bugged behind sunglasses. Jase tucked his smile away and asked for a word with my father from the privacy of his watch tower. My father quirked his eyebrows in smug delight. My tongue traveled against my cheek, arms crossed over my chest.

"He's braver than I thought, Kinsley. You go back to your mother. I'll be along."

"Jase," I said. The ball lifted in my hand. "Thanks, again." Could he sense the only brief apology I might offer before he sold me out to my father?

"You're most welcome, baby. Go have fun."

"Fun. Right. You, too."

Daddy looked ready to flay Jase's sexy flesh for dinner to keep me from ever having a taste. I swallowed a lump of nervousness and walked back down the shore playing I-Spy as I searched for my umbrella and mama in the colorful crowds.

"Where's your father?" she asked as I trudged up and tossed the ball into a bucket.

"Having a heart-to-heart with the man-child I booted out of my apartment the other night." I sank into my beach chair. My toes dug into the sand. The henna was now a faded hint of the rebel I'd been for a few days. My defiance washed away just the same, though a little petulance remained. Mom watched me as I watched the waves. "Mom, I hope you guys know I didn't sleep with him. He wanted to, but I wouldn't do that so soon, and I damn sure wouldn't do it with Daddy watching out the window."

"I tried to tell your father that it shouldn't matter if you did. Morals aside, you aren't fifteen. You're about to be twenty-five. Your decisions and business are your own. Same as the consequences." She sighed and stared at the waves, too. "I'm impressed you held out. Proud of you. Jase's reputation precedes him with the ladies. I've heard good things about how naughty he is." She clucked her tongue while I bit mine. "I also heard you had your first run-in with Angela Ansley since high school." She leaned over to dig two cans of Summer Shandy from the Styrofoam cooler. I winced when she tossed one on my bare legs. Our pop-tops snapped open, booze fizzled inside. "Cheers to you fighting like a lady even if you did shamelessly use Bianca's son to get the job done. Only fair he was invited in for a little kissing as a reward."

My can froze between us as my jaw dropped. "Mother! I can't believe you!"

She clinked hers against mine and downed a gulp. A pretty pageant smile branded her lips. "You disappointed in me rather than being grateful that I'm *not* disappointed in you?"

"It's not like that. I didn't use him. How did you even know about that?"

"Bianca called me when your daddy went to their house to order Mike to produce his son. Andy wanted to question Jase about the whereabouts of his daughter."

"Holy crap!" I slapped my forehead. "How embarrassing! Damn. I'll never run away from home ever again, jeez. Are they mad at me now, too?"

"Nah. Mike and Bianca weren't upset. Your daddy wasn't disrespectful toward them. Mad at Jase, maybe, but he wasn't available at the time, so I'm sure Jase is getting quite the ear-full now. Bianca also let it drop that Jase came to their pool house late Thursday night in a grieved stupor. Told her about your mixed messages and torture, not to mention Sweet Kinsley's hidden mean streak. He said you used him for body shots against Angela Ansley, he thought he was in the green, then you threw a red light when he ticked you off."

My lips pursed as I fought a guilty thrill at ruffling Player Taylor's feathers.

"Look," I said, "I won't deny there's something there, and it's been there for years. Maybe this is it, Mom. Like *the one*. Now I'm on the run like a bride with cold feet leaving the groom at the alter before he's even proposed. I don't even know if he's the marrying kind."

"Jase being the groom in this picture?" she asked. "I just need to be sure I've got the right guy since there's more than one. For all I know, Jase is the one you're using to run from the proverbial alter ... I mean, Bianca did say Jase was mighty miffed about your flirtation with a handsome British bachelor."

My face flushed while my eyes went wide. "How do you know he's a bachelor?"

She chuckled. "How do *you* not? Guess you've succeeded at keeping your head in this sand for a long while."

My tongue traveled over my teeth. "You know I avoid social media and the news. I'm not a fan of gossip. That's your world, mother. I can't handle the negativity. People make up their minds and run with assumptions. If I paused to listen, I wouldn't be where I am today. It's toxic."

"Uh, huh. Well, you may need to bury your head deeper if the rumors keep growing. Ben called your father after you had mimosas with his friends, one of which was a very awed Klive King who seemed a smitten fool over Ben's boss's daughter. His company agreed. A big game you've got going."

"Is nothing secret? Ben's like a big brother worse than Jase. Freaking tattletale."

"Oh, Ben wasn't calling to tell on you. He wanted your father to know you were alive and well in case Andy hadn't yet heard from you. You just told on yourself by confirming there's a secret there. I told your daddy if he didn't lay off about that man, you'd keep secrets. Guess I get to say I was right."

"Good grief! Everyone is making this seem way more than it really is. Ben included. If anyone seemed awed, it was him."

"For good reason, Kinsley Fallon. Ben said Mr. King was enamored with you, but he didn't say anything about you returning the sentiment during brunch. In fact, Ben said you told him not to try setting you two up because you were dating someone. If I were on the run from the alter, I'd throw the one I wanted off by pretending to be involved with someone else ...."

She took another long drink. I followed her lead. *Yes, more alcohol, please.*

"Mom ... I'm not using Jase. I'd never do that to a man I really cared about. He's too important to be a pawn in stupid love games. If I were gonna shamelessly use anyone, it would be Rustin Keane. That guy has zero qualms about who he bangs. He's a happy pawn, too flirty to be offended."

She grinned. "Jase's cop friend?"

"Yeah."

"You confessing to using him?"

"Hell no. He wishes. I'm just making a point."

"Know what I love about all of this?" She twisted in her chair to lie on her hip, her legs tucking beneath her like a perfect pin-up in her bikini.

"My wriggling discomfort?" I said like an ass.

"Nope. You've been your father's daughter for the better part of a decade, but all of this proves you may have turned into a tomboy under his guidance, but you paid attention to your mother in the ways of women. Dusting off those dresses, skills in heels, who knows, maybe other things will come out of the closet you swore you'd never wear again."

"Don't hold your breath. I'm never putting on a pair of ballet *pointes* again if that's what you're getting at. When I'm done, I'm done."

"Mm-hmm ...." She trailed with a lingering look I didn't give attention. "Keep running, Kinsley. He who runs the hardest deserves to catch you if he can. Your daddy was the MVP in more ways than one, young lady."

"You mocking Jase?" My eyes met hers. She tilted her head in confusion. "Never mind. You mean to tell me you made Daddy chase you?"

"I didn't make him. He did it all on his own. I just enjoyed the fun before I gave in. If I told you he was the only one running after me, I'd be lying. Maybe your daddy is scared because he sees too much of *himself* in all this. Too much of *me* in *you* ...."

I snorted. "I'm nothing as sweet as you. I don't have your grace under pressure, perfect manners, poise. As much as I wished to be just like you, I'm a clumsy mess with an attitude problem who puts her foot in her mouth and ass at once. It's quite a talent. Amazing I'm able to run like that, eh?"

She snorted a laugh this time. "Little lady, you've listened to your daddy's love stories like he didn't have a checkered time of catching me. When parents tell you how they met, they want you to believe that sex only happened after marriage, that they were virgins so you'll stay as such. Like we were born saved from the sins we supposedly never committed in our youth. The truth is, we're terrified of our children running into who we were before they existed to tame us down. I wasn't always who you make me out to be. Although I'm glad for your compliments, I was clumsy, too. Ballet doesn't teach grace in everything."

"I thought you and Daddy met and fell in love on a blind date. He said his bestie was your date, another girl was his. You both dumped them for each other. The rest is history."

"Indeed, that's how we met. Love came much later. Your Uncle Edwin will always tease I was the one who got away. Your father will always joke that someone can't steal from Edwin what never belonged to him."

"I have a hard time imagining that." I took a sip. "Uncle Edwin still coming to visit soon?"

"As far as I know. Timmy said his dad is in talks with a company here to remodel a new franchise Edwin's funding. Wants to flip a failing food chain as this year's hobby. That man has more money than he knows what to do with."

"Wishing you traded in Daddy for Edwin?" I snickered.

She beamed at my naughtiness. "Do I need to spank your little bottom in front of everyone here, Kinsley Fallon?"

"You didn't deny."

"Can't put a price on your father. You have no idea the hell I put him through to prove his love for me. No money in the world would've changed my heart or mind. You're very blessed, Kinsley. I couldn't have asked for a better man to raise our child."

"That's really sweet, Mom. Edwin's done pretty well raising Timmy, too, though. Not often you meet such a devoted single father."

"Yeah, well, who needs to marry Edwin when he lavishes his generosity every time he visits? Is that why you're excited he's coming to town, child?"

We laughed together, but I shook my head. "You know better. Money doesn't matter to me."

"It will when you move out. But that's a discussion for another time."

I sighed. "They've been talking for a while. You think Jase will still be interested after this?"

She shrugged. "Guess we will know by the look on your father's face when he eventually returns to us. Kins, do me a favor?" she asked.

I realized I'd lost count of how many times friends and family asked me to do them favors in the last week alone.

Hell, could I remember everything I'd agreed to?

"What, Mama?"

"When you need something other than your daddy's arms on the porch swing, *I'm* here, too. I know you avoid me because you think I'm gonna pressure you about braving your *pointe* shoes again. I'll never deny that the ballet studio would offer you a great release, even you can't deny that it used to. But give me more credit as your mother. I know and empathize with your plight more than you realize. There may be times like this past week when you alienate your father for reasons he may not understand, but don't forget that I might offer what he cannot. If things get too hard to navigate, just give me a chance."

Jeez. *Had I been so hard on my mom?* I wasn't sure what to say, so I just said, "Yes, ma'am."

3 | ♀

MOM AND I WATCHED **my father** trudge through the loose sand wearing an unreadable expression. He bent to kiss Mom and rose with a snicker at my disgusted groan.

"That boy has it bad for our Kins," he told her. I gave an inward sigh of relief.

"Uh, huh. So do others, Andrew," Mom said.

"Keep an open mind," I said like a smart ass, "Or else your Kins will pick someone other than the guy you want out of sheer teen-aged rebellion. After all, she's right here and going off the rails." I flailed my hands in pretend panic.

Daddy ruffled my hair. "All right, kiddo. Whatever you do, don't choose that lifeguard. He's bad news. My very last choice. I choose that guy over there." He pointed to some old guy in Hawaiian shorts and black socks in flip flops. Mom and I laughed.

His hands held his hips as he fought a smile.

"Way to sell it, Dad." I stood up and adjusted the bottoms of the bikini Rustin had bought me. I stole the football. "I'm gonna go work my magic on the one you chose for me because I'd rather end your speculations. Life's too short to remain single forever."

He snorted and took my vacated chair. I grinned to myself when I caught his jaw drop from the corner of my eye as I walked toward the man's position. The man had to be at least seventy-five. I aimed my football for the waves just out of his splash zone, then I took off running toward the ball and flounced into the old guy's periphery. I chased the ball into the water and apologized for disrupting his view. His smile was worth the play. So was my father's back under our umbrella when the old guy captured my toy as a wave washed the ball ashore.

"Oh, gosh you didn't have to do that, sir! You got your socks all wet," I told him with an empathetic smile. Dammit, now I felt guilty for playing.

"If I don't want wet socks, I shouldn't walk near the water," he reasoned then squinted. "Hey! You're the runner!"

"No, sir, I just look like her. People ask me that all the time."

"Young lady, are you pulling an old man's leg? I recognize that smile from your picture in the paper."

"Alright, you got me," I said. My sunglasses went onto my head to give him eye-contact. I threw in the victory smile as a bonus confirmation.

"Well, what a pleasure to meet you. Don't you let that one from Gainesville get you down. Heard you didn't run yesterday for undisclosed reasons."

"Don't you worry, sir. Call it a psychological operation." I tapped my temple. "Gotta let the steepest competition get too cocky before I remind her whose boss when we meet again."

"I like your style." He tapped his own temple.

"Thanks for getting my ball. I told my father to choose any man from this beach for me to marry. He chose you. Maybe I'll give you a call for a date sometime."

His eyes crinkled as he chuckled and slapped the football. "You trying to give me a heart attack, Micro Machine? Besides, there's a lifeguard lookin' like he's waiting his turn in line." He peered over my shoulder. I chose not to look.

"Psh, that guy? He's got nothin' on you."

Jase overheard our convo and laughed as he walked up with a polite greeting.

"She toss this ball into your area, too?" he asked the old guy. When the man nodded, Jase shook his head. "I saved it from the undertow about twenty minutes ago," Jase told him. "Didn't realize I was being played until now, though." He pinched my ribs to make me laugh.

"You keep her on her toes, boy. She's got to keep her times. I've got money riding on her, so I don't want her lying down on the job, if ya get my drift."

Oh, dang! Jase and I gave surprised smiles.

"Don't you worry, sir," I said. "No way I'm slowing down to walk an aisle when I'm way too busy running lanes, and I dang sure ain't lying down any time soon."

"See?" Jase gestured. "I'm already keeping her on her toes running away from aisles, so will that do? Unless you two have something planned?"

"That'll do for me," the old man said. "Already have three ex-wives. I can't afford to remarry a girl like you with all the alimony." He winked. "Y'all have a good day."

We chuckled and told the man to have a good day.

"Fetch, boy!" I tossed the ball. Jase shot off like lightning. My daddy also lunged from the lounger to intercept. The two of them ended up crashing into a sandcastle.

"Man, I'm still in uniform." Jase dusted sand off his shorts. "Now they're gonna report the lifeguard for ruining their kid's fun."

My dad walked away with the ball, chuckling all the way. A miffed mother held to her hips. Jase apologized and jogged back to the kid to show him how to dig up periwinkles then hide them in a little puddle he'd created. *Awww!* My hand rested on my chest.

"Think fast!" Daddy ordered and tossed the ball to dispel my girly moment. I barely caught the ball. Before I could run, Jase lifted me by my hips while I had a laugh attack at his tickle torture.

"I still caught the ball! It counts!" Jase shouted back at my father. Daddy tipped the ball from my fingers and jogged back to my mother. Jase set me on my feet so I could catch my breath. "You're out of shape, sweet Kins. Guess I haven't been keeping you on your toes enough...." He beamed his winning smile like he could look as wholesome as Rustin if he tried hard. I shook my head. We walked apart toward my parents. Jase threw his arm across my shoulders to pull us together. "Baby, I was an asshole, you were a bitch. Truce in the name of evading another lecture from your pops?"

I smiled up at him. My fingers wended through his at my bicep. "Truce."

"Hot damn, sweet Kins." Jase whistled as we walked up. "You know what they say about daughters and their mamas. Looks like I'd better go down on one knee now so I can bag the younger version."

My father's head tossed in laughter; a finger waved at my naughty love interest. My mother cast her gorgeous grin up at us, but I cringed as that smile took on different intent.

"Thank you, Jase," she said. "Can we expect to be seeing you around for good?"

"If Kinsley ages like you, you're damn right, Mrs. Hayes."

I slapped Jase's belly.

"Ha! He ain't gonna live past twenty-eight if he keeps coming on to all the women in my life," Daddy joked.

"What can I say? I've always been attracted to danger," Jase said like a smooth player. "Mrs. Hayes, for as long as your husband doesn't kill me and your daughter will have me, I'll be around."

"You know," my dad said, "my daughter will only have you around for as long as you ask for."

"Daddy!" I reached out and popped his arm.

"Yes, I was just remarking to Kinsley about how I was younger than she was when I had her."

My eyes bugged. *She most certainly hadn't mentioned a damn thing about that!*

"Speaking of babies." Dad grinned. "Jase, I've been friends with your father since you were a baby, before you guys moved away for a bit there. You might play, but I happen to think you're a very honorable man, I respect what you've done for our country. My Kins would be lucky to have you and you her. You have my full blessing when the time comes."

That didn't just happen! I couldn't look at Jase because I was too busy gaping. So was my mother, to my ultimate shock. We both stared at my very smug father while he downed what was left of my Summer Shandy.

"Need a drink, Claire?" Daddy asked. "Your mouth looks dry. Kins, I'd offer you another, but I told Jase how fond you are of golf. He said there's a putt putt course he'd love to stomp you on. I figured if you've got a shot at someone marrying you, you have to give a man a chance to be tougher than you at something. Much better than you showing him up at football, honey. You don't want to scare him away."

"Hayden Andrew!" my mother said, but her smile was far too bright to hold the heat she tried to bring.

"Maybe you should reschedule, Jase," Daddy feigned concern. "She looks sick. Doesn't she look sick, Claire? You need some water or something, Kins?"

My mom shook her head and pursed her lips, big smiling eyes up at me.

"Jase, maybe we should invite my parents so that I am armed with a golf club for the remainder of this humiliation?" I cheesed at Jase, but my smile morphed into an adoring one at the actual blush in Mr. Player Taylor's cheeks.

Jase cleared his throat, bashful grin crossing his speechless mouth. He nodded at my father, shook his hand. "Thanks, Mr. Hayes. All jokes aside, I'm honored."

"You're welcome, boy. Y'all get out of here. This is my date with your mama now, Kins. You go have your own. Hope Jase has his own ball-retriever."

"Hayden Andrew Hayes!" I said his full name on an incredulous smile. "You are in so much trouble, mister. Now get your ass off my sarong, sir. Oh, yeah. I cursed." I held my fists at my hips. He reached beneath himself and tossed the red cotton my way.

I blew them kisses while we left them there to gossip and speculate on my love life. Jase and I walked up to the sidewalk. *What to say to someone who'd just gotten permission to marry me after we'd just been joking with that old man?* I dropped my flip flops to the concrete and stepped into them. Jase cleared his throat, but I held my hand up.

"Jase, you don't have to say a word. There's absolutely no pressure in this coming from me, and now I owe you a real apology because it seems our parents have teamed up."

"What if I asked him permission he didn't give until just now?" His words rushed from his mouth as if he'd been holding his breath too long.

"Whoa!" The breath rushed from my lips. "Let's play golf and see if you still want to marry me after my sore loser streak comes out." I was only half-joking.

He chuckled. "Good point. I appreciate the offer to test the waters before I dive into something I can't get out of."

"Oh, sir, you need to behave!" I beamed and smacked his abs. He caught my hand and pulled me against his sun-warm skin. My parents weren't watching us, but a dark thrill went through me at possibly getting caught with our skin-on-skin contact. The same skin I'd been longing to touch after he'd retrieved my ball.

"What if I'm tired of behaving, sweet Kins?" Jase bit his lip in that way that his teeth dragged slow enough to conjure memories of him doing the same to my own lip. Now the breath whistled through my parted lips for different reasons.

My hands traveled his biceps, the fingers on my right hand traced the dragon's scales. *Maybe I test the waters with what makes him afraid?*

"So, Jase, you saying you want to make me your wife and have pretty babies with me while I grow to look just like my mama?"

"In a nutshell, baby." He bent to seduce me with the flavor of his smile.

"Hmmmm ...." I hummed against his mouth when he parted our lips. He wasn't afraid at all. I was. I broke our kiss to peer up at his eyes. "When did you ask my dad?"

"Before I sent you flowers. He said he needed to see some effort, because if he'd had no idea I was in love with you, you probably didn't either."

Air eluded my brain. I felt light-headed. There was no more wondering whether Jase was the marrying type. I'd never looked at him that way before because he didn't look like that type, but I guess I was wrong. Daddy told me not to close my eyes. *Well, congrats, Big Papa, they're wide open now.*

"You know, we don't have to walk down any aisles to practice beforehand ...." he trailed in temptation.

"I'll let you keep kissing me, sir, but this is unofficial. I mean, I'm not even your girlfriend and already you're proposing? I knew you were fast, but ...."

He smothered my words to kiss the ever-loving sense outta me like a single melting moment might talk me into saying yes to anything he asked.

"Damn, if you keep kissing me like that for the rest of my life, I may have to concede," I said as he had my knees mighty weak.

"I guess I'll have to knock you off your toes to really show you what you could have for the rest of your life."

"Playing with fire so close to my parentals, Jase? Is that a good idea?"

"If I never test the boundaries, I'll never know my limits or how to break them down."

"Damn! No shame?"

"No, ma'am. One thing I've learned the hard way about Kinsley Hayes. She may be a sweetie pie on the surface, but she's attracted to risk. No good boy is gonna get the job done." Jase winked like a chef holding a super-secret recipe. Something delicious was certainly simmering in his mind if the heat in his eyes said anything.

Was he right? Jack Carter had been the best guy and I'd been with him for years. Nate ... I wasn't sure what category Nate fell into. I wasn't sure I had a type or really knew my type. I knew that I cared about Jase so much that he deserved a fair chance to show me his whole person. The old lady from the beach had told me to take what he gave and not press for more. That I was a vacation destination of sorts. The allure of vacation was seeing only the pretty parts. You didn't stay long enough to learn the ugliness on the edges. How to go about learning this guy beyond the crush on-stage without both of us revealing those ugly places we'd hinted at during our first fight

....

He batted my dangling hand between us the way he had the morning of our last date. "Ready to go meet your future in-laws for some fun?"

"Your parents are coming?" I asked in pleasant surprise.

"Yeah. I played ball with your father. Only fair you have to golf with mine. Don't worry, my dad is nowhere near as good as I am. You two can compete for last place. Mom taught me how to swing a club, so don't count on any mercy from her."

34

4 | ♀

"**MY PARENTS ARE GONNA be thrilled to see you,**" Jase said. He turned the truck into the parking lot of the putt putt place with a large pirate ship out front. "Baby, you cool with us getting closer? Like for real, I can't get to know the inside if you don't let me in, and I really can't get *inside* unless I know you."

"I guess that's fair." I unbuckled my seat belt. We got out of the truck. I adjusted the sarong and the wife-beater he lent me. The large tank that fit his muscles hung loose on me and covered my bottom. I tied a knot at my back to pull the material tight.

When I looked up, Jase was watching like a gaga fool. "This is a good look for you, Player Taylor. Don't make a big deal of everything, k? Just let it all happen as it happens."

"Ditto."

"I hate that word."

"So I've been told."

My jaw dropped. "By whom?" I asked with attitude like this was more locker talk.

He grinned. "Tyndall, duh. You're so easy to rile."

"Jase M—"

He cut me off at the mouth with his. "Every time you give me lip, I'm just gonna kiss you so you can't finish a single negative sentence."

"Even in front of your parents?" I asked and looked around the parking lot.

"Especially in front of my parents. Dad will be so proud of me for finally moving in on you instead of watching and wishing. Why do you look around like you're afraid someone will see us this way? You ashamed of me?"

"Absolutely not, Jase. Quite the opposite. I'm just not used to public affection."

"Well, I'll have to work on that, baby. How else will I stake a public claim without open affection?" He took my hand and held our intertwined fingers like a display.

"Michael!" Bianca shouted when we walked up. "Look who it is outside of church, in the flesh, holding our son's hand!"

I smiled as Mike stood up from chattering to the baby alligators in the small pond below the golf course where the decorative ship docked.

"Well, well, well. Kinsley Hayes. Damn, son. About time you grew a set and grabbed her before someone else did." His dad patted Jase on the back and beamed with pride. Seeing Jase as an adult standing beside his father was an odd experience. They used to perform together at the bar some years back, but beneath dim lighting the similarities weren't near as glaring. Mike ruffled Jase's hair. Jase released my hand to ruffle his dad's hair with both hands. *Adorable!* They both shoved their hair back, tried fixing the messes together.

"If you face one another, you may be able to go off the reflection," I offered. My lips spread into a cheesy smile.

"She's right, son. Here." Mike faced Jase and they fixed one another's hair. They looked at me once more to evaluate. Bianca giggled and shook her head while I nodded. They'd both screwed each other's hair worse than before. Neither cared to fix the issue.

"Guess I can see what I have to look forward to if I marry you, eh, Jase?" I winked like the player who'd come onto my mom. Jase tickled my ribs.

"Nah, sweet Kins. I look better than him. I get it from my mama, too," Jase said. We all laughed since the only thing he'd gotten from his mother was her olive skin and hazel brown eyes. Tyndall, on the other hand, looked as Cuban as her mother, but with Mike's ocean eyes, height and light brown hair. Jase tucked his mom beneath his left arm, me beneath the right. He kissed us each on the head before his father lifted his phone.

"Glad you got a picture of us," Jase told his father, "before we put a golf club into Kinsley's hands. She might accidentally bust my nose instead of the ball."

We all laughed.

"Actually, I was thinking of busting more than one ball," I teased.

"Jase, this is living proof of God's miracles in your life," Mike joked.

"Yeah, our son, like his father, needs a ball-buster to keep him humble, so this is a perfect recipe," Bianca said.

Mike and Jase chuckled while Mike handed me a golf club with a pink handle usually reserved for kids. Bianca rolled her eyes as he gave her one the same size. "Miniature clubs for miniature ladies with big tempers. These don't reach as far."

"Oh, dang. That's right," I said. "Guess your boy cried in his mom's arms over what a meanie Sweet Kins is, huh?"

Jase gaped at his mom like she was a traitor. She seemed just as surprised. I stood after missing my first ball, put my hand on my hip while leaning on my club like a cane.

"Jase, your father just spelled out your mother has a bad temper. Do you really want to give her a hard time for gossiping with my mother? Grand kids are on the line, doncha know?"

Bianca laughed. I jumped when she swatted my bottom, Spanish muttering followed. Jase and Mike held both their clubs like beefy bodyguards hiding pleased expressions.

"Young lady, it's been too long," Bianca told me.

"Indeed," I told Bianca. "My Spanish is a mite rusty, so I'm gonna pretend I have no idea what a little brat you just called me." I grinned, earned another slap on the bottom. Jase shook his head at my courage, but the full smile warming his face warmed my heart for him. "I'm not sure what you're smiling about. Guess if we end up together, you're gonna have to learn French to translate my bitching at you in another language like your mom does you guys. That's the secret to your successful marriage, right, Bianca?"

They all laughed. Mike put his arm around my shoulder, gave a little squeeze. "Sure have missed times like this. I know Tyndall does. I agree with my wife. It's been far too long since we've enjoyed your feisty spirit, sweet Kins."

"I missed hanging with y'all outside of church, too," I admitted. For a moment in time, I entertained the insane idea of these two babysitting a baby of my own, Jase a proud parent. Would having a child replace that certain light Jase's eyes had lost over time?

Jase knocked his ball in the first hole on one try, bragged in fluent Spanish, then bitched about the impossible woman he loved, gestured to his parents about how he was risking his life by having to sleep with me to give them children with my pretty green eyes. "And, with my luck, they'll have her attitude problem, too," he finished in English.

"You give me way too much credit," I told him. "Although, if you have a little girl, Jase, you're gonna be mighty happy if she has an attitude problem. Ain't that right, Mike? Tyndall certainly got Bianca's."

"I'd lift a beer to that, indeed," Mike agreed.

"Guess the men in this family love punishment," Jase muttered.

I busted his chops over the course of the next seven holes until we went into a cave. Jase was on par while I had thirty-two points already. I missed a hole that went around a bend. Jase walked around the side to help me find another ball, but I grabbed his head and glued my mouth to his for the hottest, fastest kiss that might mend the pretend pain I enjoyed inflicting with my digs on him.

"What was that for?" he asked, breathless.

"Think of it as a Band-aid for your poor ego." I winked and grabbed my ball, content to write down a six for that hole.

We trekked behind Mike and Bianca to the next hole, up some stairs near a waterfall.

"Maybe you're trying to bandage your own ego, sweet Kins?" Jase asked from behind me as I walked up the steps. His lips brushed my bare shoulder. Tingles engulfed my whole body.

"Whatever do you mean, sir?" I looked over my shoulder again so he could kiss my lips this time. He grabbed my hips as we stood in wait of his parents to finish putting.

"This is a good position. I have stairs at home. Could recreate this to create the baby you keep talking about."

"Holy crap, Jase!" my breath hissed. "I'm just playing around."

"Are you because you know what they say about jokes being half jokes. I think part of you wants to have my babies, too."

He scooped my hair away from my neck to trail kisses along the back. I arched in too much sensation, my speech winded. "Jase, you want me to admit to dreaming at times, sure. But maybe we do something normal first before we end up eloping and knocked up?" I cursed when his lips traveled.

"Mmmm ... what normal thing did you have in mind?" he whispered against too sensitive skin never-before kissed!

"I can't breathe when you do that. I can't ... can't ...."

"Can't deny me for too much longer? Is that what you meant to say?"

"Your parents are gonna wonder where we are if we don't catch up."

"You gonna run to my daddy since yours isn't here to be your buffer, baby?"

I mustered all strength to face him even though I could've caved into much more. "Jase, there's no way in hell I'm going to bed with you after one date."

"How about we make a bet. I win, you go out with me on a second date later tonight. You win, you choose how I proceed."

"I choose how you proceed anyway. You can pretend to hold the power, but you don't pass go without my saying so."

He hummed and pulled my belly against his. "I love a good power play," he said.

"Mmhmm ... sir, you're trying to trip me up and trap me because I'm losing so bad right now, there's no way I won't be going on your date."

"I'll take that as a hard yes to going out later, sweet Kins. Now let's finish whipping that ass so I can take it out in something sexy later."

"What did you have in mind?"

"Nuh, uh. You have to finish. You can't be using this as an excuse to bow out before we see just how awful you are at this." He gave the most adorable victory grin.

"Fine." I stuck a pouty little lip out just for him to bite softly in that way that drove me nuts.

Even though we caught up to his parents, we ended up hiding in several alcoves of the putt putt golf course to kiss for longer. Every kiss thawed any lingering awkwardness from our fight.

I'd make up issues just to make him hold his promise to kiss me anytime I said something negative. After about thirty minutes of doing this off and on, he told me if we kept up he was almost certain someone told him kissing too much also caused pregnancy.

I laughed like a dang fool and he smothered that, too. When I disentangled, I said, "I wasn't even doing anything wrong. Why'd you kiss me?"

"Positive reinforcement, baby. If I never reward you for good behavior, I'm gonna have the biggest brat on my hands. Last hole. Now, let me show you how to hold this club properly. Stand just like this," he told me. His parents stood by with adoring looks on their faces while Jase wrapped his arms around mine, his body at my back while we lined up my ball.

"This is not a kid-friendly game at all," I joked. "Of course, you'd wait till the very end to teach me how to do this. Guess you were too afraid I'd smoke you in this, too."

He snickered when we swung. My ball missed four times even with his help. He shook his head in disapproval.

"Know what that means, don't you?" Jase asked like 'aw shucks'. "You've missed fourteen out of eighteen holes. I have twenty points. You have sixty-four, Kins. Time to pay up."

"Because we didn't know that was going to happen."

"Aw, but Mike came in a close second to last," Bianca offered, held his card up. "Forty-seven."

Mike chuckled while I glared at her, though I could never truly give her a mean look. Even if she loved to bitch about me *en español*, hee hee.

"What time do I need to be ready?" I asked in Spanish. They grinned while Jase answered in Spanish.

"I'll pick you up at nine. Club doesn't have last call till three."

We hugged his parents when we walked out to our vehicles. Jase opened the door to his truck and helped me into the passenger side. Bianca opened their car door beside me.

"Does this mean we will see you both at church in the morning?" she asked. Her eyes lit on her son's panicked face. My turn to snicker.

I cleared my smile. "You want me to pretend I might be there if he's planning to keep us out till the middle of the night? I won't. However, I'll make a deal with your son. I'll go out with him on a third date if he agrees to come to church with me next time."

Bianca's eyebrows rose. Mike leaned on his forearms above the passenger side of their late model Mustang. Jase shifted from one foot to the other.

Mike spoke up. "The girl you want to have your children asked you to go on another date and church, son. I say if you're willing to put a baby in her belly, you'd better be man enough to nourish her soul first. If you aren't ready to do that, you dang sure ain't ready to go to the alter where you want her to join you. How you gonna stand in front of the church for vows when you're unwilling to walk inside?"

Yikes! I gulped at his dad's ass-chewing, but wisely kept my mouth shut because I agreed with his point, even if I did feel bad for the public scrutiny.

"Welp, Kinsley Hayes." Jase sent me a defeated sigh. "Guess I gotta cancel my deal with the devil if I'm gonna save my ass from charring in church."

Bianca sighed like Jase had just flushed all their fun. Mike smiled at me, said he'd see me on the Sunday of my choice. "I'll bring the extinguisher just in case," he finished.

I pursed a huge smile at his smart-ass humor. Bianca shook her head and shut herself inside the car. Started the engine with a roar much like her child was fond of doing. Jase cursed and knocked on his mom's window. She rolled the tinted glass from between them, stared up at him like more Spanish ass-chewing was on his horizon.

"Don't be mad, Mom." He pecked her cheek. "I'm sorry. *Te amo.*"

She gave him a whispered piece of her Cuban hot head I had a hard time hearing. Mike walked over to me to say another goodbye before shutting me inside Jase's truck like he needed to protect my sensitive ears from the awful things Bianca might say. As Bianca's voice rose, Mike grabbed his son's biceps to steer him away from their car.

Jase opened the driver's side door. I heard Mike talking over the rumble of the Shelby's idle. "Jase. You have a date, but I have my own, and your attitude better not get in the way of my getting laid, boy."

Jase shook his dad off and jumped inside the truck. He slammed the door and rubbed his hands over his face like he could scrub the image of his parents in bed away from his mind.

"Don't say anything," he said through his fingers.

"Oh, did you think I was gonna apologize? Because I'm not sorry."

His hands dragged down to his chin; eyes narrowed while I smiled huge. Bianca shifted into reverse. I waved before noting Jase got his driving technique from his mother when she sped away.

"Guess papa's gonna get his fill of angry sex," I joked. Jase growled.

"If you aren't careful, so am I, *sweet* Kins." He enunciated the T.

"Ooh, lala. Maybe one day."

"Do you have to look so happy?"

"Yes, because I *am* so happy. Now, let's go. Too bad we aren't in your car because your mom's driving makes me hungry for more donuts." He reversed as I pumped my fist when he finally cracked a smile. "Victorious," I cheered.

We drove over his mother's tire marks. "You're killing me, Kins."

"Not yet, but I'm sure I can arrange something," I said.

He surrendered to a silly grin, the inside joke lighting his eyes before his shades fell over them. "I'm sure you could," he said to himself. "Guess I'd better get my shit together before you order a hit on me."

"Damn right, Mr. Taylor."

5 | ♀

JASE SANG ALONG TO **loud music** to drown any further smart-ass humor from my mouth. To make me feel better, he held my hand over the console while our hair tossed in the wind as we sped toward my house. About ten minutes away, he turned the music down.

"Pack an overnight bag, baby. Your dad gave me permission to take you out and let you stay over at my place after if we stay out too late. I just have to abide by your rules. I could tell he had an awfully hard time not laying down his own rules, but he's giving you room to make your own decisions. I told him Rustin will be there, too, so it's extra protection."

"Protection?" The only protection I assumed my father would've been concerned with was the type that prevented babies.

"Yeah, he's your dad, Kins. Of course he's gonna worry about you. But Rustin and I agreed. We want you to have fun without worrying about some dick drugging you, dammit. This is my turf. Anyone stupid enough to try shit there is gonna have a death wish."

"Whoa, please tell me you didn't say anything to my dad about me being drugged?"

"No way, but after you being gone without a word, I think he's just worried about you disappearing for good. I could tell he was rattled. Hell, if he was more worried about *that* than me trying to sleep with you? Yeah ...."

"Touché. So, Mr. Friday Night Lights, when you gonna visit my track? It's only fair if I've agreed to visit your turf tonight."

"Oh, is this the date before church?" he asked.

"Nope. This all to even the playing field."

"Hmm, maybe we should take this to a physical field, sweet Kins. The regulars at the bar were begging for a real game after we went back and forth Thursday night. You've got the arm and the speed, but if I don't take you down behind closed doors soon, I'm gonna need to take you down however I can, even if it means you walk away with scraped knees and grass stains."

"Ohhh!" I held my fist over my mouth like a dude. "Don't tempt me to take you up on that."

"Brave words, baby. When's your next home meet?" he asked.

"Two weeks."

"I'll be there. In case you wondered why I haven't come so far, it's hard for me to travel outside the area because of lifeguard duty. Seems a smalltime job, but it could mean the difference between life and death. Fun turns to tragedy in a flash if the undertow takes someone. I have a hard time saying no when I'm called in, because I know if something happens when I could've been there to prevent it ...."

"Say no more. I totally understand. I love your devotion to saving lives," I told him. "Let me give you a hint, Jase. What you just did? That was a great communication. I'm not a mind reader and my mind goes haywire with scenarios when there's no explanation. Kind of what happened the other night," I admitted.

"How so?"

"Our fight? Locker talk. I had no idea when you two could've talked about me or why I would've come up. My mind went crazy with the mystery and embarrassment."

He sighed as we slowed for the highway exit. He glanced at me for a beat like he didn't want to confess. We stopped behind the line of traffic at the red light.

"King bailed me out of jail after I beat the shit out of the fool who drugged you. I didn't go to the station to give a statement. I was arrested along with that prick because the cops couldn't differentiate when they were trying to keep the peace for these high-rollers hosting the party."

"You didn't ask for Delia or Avery to get you out of trouble? They would've vouched for you. Hell, they were glad you taught him a lesson."

"Nah. No sense pulling either of them from their event. Besides, I knew King was good for it. He may have allowed me to sit and stew for a while, but just like I was grateful to him for saving your ass from a full dose, I knew he would be grateful enough to bail me out for beating the shit out of someone he'd have like to hurt for the same reasons. Mutual respect. Twisted, I know. It's a guy thing."

"Wow ...." I digested that night with new eyes, then assessed his face while he turned right. "If you two share mutual respect, when did the locker talk come up? Y'all bond over my bullshit?" I couldn't help the edge in my tone.

"Easy, baby. King didn't outright say any names or brag. It wasn't like what you overheard between me and Rusty. When King came close, I smelled pussy. Yours is the only one I know he wants. I called him on it."

I gasped and blushed deep red with humiliation. He did a double take. We turned into the community. Jase steered us through the esplanades of Sago palms and tropical flowers, past the various home sections of different styles and price-tags.

"I didn't allow him beneath my clothes," I said more to myself. "It couldn't have been me ...."

Jase laughed, but I was ready to cry as this was just awful. Seeing Jase dancing with other women, the redhead all over him; I expected that from him. Klive, not so much, especially when he kept turning me down. The shame of his not claiming me in public this morning lit my cheeks anew.

"Kins, quit looking that way. Man, why do you set me up to fail? Dude doesn't have to go underneath clothing to smell like sex if his hands were in the right places. I just told you yours was the only one he's interested in." He shook his head while we turned into the housing section my parents lived in. "Kinsley Hayes, only *you* could make me defend another man having his hand in my cookie jar."

"*Your* cookie jar?" I sat back near the window to take him in with a lot of attitude.

"You gonna snap your fingers like Constance now? Bob your head while you're at it?" He grinned. "Yeah. Mine. We already discussed this. You're my girl, he knows it too. When I called his shit, he just said *she has the best moan.* I think he was crabby about not staying with you. Can't say I blame him. I'm surprised he didn't wait till the morning to get me out, but maybe he didn't trust himself to behave. Sucks to defend him, but I have to be fair since we weren't technically together yet. Damn, it's so hard when it comes to you, though."

We turned into the circle drive. My parents were still out on their date. Maybe Jase's parents should meet up with mine to booze about their children causing chaos.

"Jase, you're so confusing." I sat for a sobered moment. Before I got pissy with him for no good reason, I focused on the good. "Damn, Jase. You were *arrested* ... and after I said actions—"

"Hey, baby. We both apologized. No big thing, remember. Let's leave it all in the past. Can't change what happened, but we can change how we go forward. I promise I'll try harder to be an open communicator. Not gonna lie, it's not my strong suit."

"Mine either." I unbuckled to lean across and kiss his cheek. "Thank you for beating that guy's ass for me."

"If I'm getting bonus points for beating ass in your honor, I also punched Klive for saying that about you."

My mouth dropped. "Where?!" *Klive didn't have a scratch on him....*

"Stomach. He punched me back, though. Right now, we stand even. What can I say? I'm hoping tonight I gain more points that have nothing to do with punching anyone."

"Jase, you have a very thick skull. Only *you* would continue antics that got you kicked out of my apartment." I shook my head and bit my lip. "You are a brave son-of-a-bitch. Klive doesn't look like he plays nice with anyone who pisses him off."

"Yeah, but Klive's smart enough to take a hit he knows he's earned. I think he *wanted* me to hit him. He wants to see if I'll defend my girl and draw lines he can't cross."

I snorted in bitter amusement. That asshole. I was glad Jase hit him.

"Jase, I know we flirted with some heavy artillery today concerning marriage and babies, but until I'm officially your girl, *I* draw the lines, got it?" He nodded. "Thanks for everything you did for me. Just because I have a hard time accepting your chivalry doesn't mean I don't appreciate it. Just gonna take some getting used to. I hope you understand?"

"Yes, I get what you're saying, Miss Independent. Should you decide you need assistance, I'll be here."

I grinned and kissed his smile. "Good boyee." I ruffled his hair and slammed the door on his laughter.

6 | ♀

HOURS LATER, I WAS **on the porch** with my father having confession without really confessing much at all. I needed to give him time with me since I never thought about how awful this week must've been for him. Mom was gone to have drinks with a miffed Bianca. Mike was supposed to come over and hang with my dad in a bit.

"A club, huh?" Daddy asked. "What if someone unties that shirt?"

"I double-knotted," I said. My fingers played in the tie at my waist where my wrap shirt tied together. "At least it covers my bottom, eh?"

"Barely," he muttered in petulance. "Could stand to cover more on top...maybe add an undershirt?"

"Ha! Not happening. Daddy, you said you wanted transparency. A club, yes. There will be cleavage a-plenty not including my own. Booze and dancing, probably sex in the bathroom. Drugs. A fight or two. Guys who want to untie my shirt that won't have a shot in hell. A parent's worst nightmare. But, what if I told you I've gone clubbin' multiple times without you knowing and I'm here to tell the tale, drug free" — *no way in hell I'm telling him about my recent scare—* "not pregnant or an alcoholic, no wardrobe malfunctions."

Daddy gave a long sigh. "I'm glad you wore pants, even if they are a leather second skin."

"Exactly. If I have to fight these on for ten minutes, imagine how much harder they'll be to take off when I'm hot and sweaty from dancing. There's no easy access. You're welcome."

"Ha! Alright you little monster."

The Charger's engine stole my father's attention as we heard Jase coming long before he rumbled into the driveway. Rustin and Jase got out of the muscle car, Rustin like the preppy good boy in his white polo, Jase like his opposite in a fitted black muscle shirt. Rustin pulled his seat up and Mike got out with a twelve pack of beer.

"Figured I could hitch a ride with my boy so I can hitch another ride with my wife when the night's through," Mike told my dad.

"Good plan." Daddy lifted my feet off his lap.

My heels with the ankle support were on the porch, so I worked on strapping myself in while my dad strode out to the drive to greet everyone and appreciate the Charger's sleek black paint and chrome engine block beneath the street lights. As I walked up, I looked to the ground when I caught Jase appreciating my attire the way my dad appraised the car.

"She's beautiful," my dad said.

"Yes, she is." Rustin grinned.

Mike shot them a warning glance, then winked at me. Jase fought a smile.

"Thank you, sir. I've put a *lot* of hard work into her," Jase told him but stared at me. Mike chuckled and clapped his son's shoulder, no mussing his James Dean hair tonight. I noticed Jase shook my dad's hand with his right even though he was a leftie. The leather band cuffed his wrist that lifted in a wave when he finished escorting me into the passenger seat. Rustin sat in the back. We waved at our dads who sat on the porch steps popping tops to their cans. They waved back.

"Damn, you're lookin' mighty fine this evening, Mizz Hayes." Rustin leaned forward from the middle. Jase's black shirt stretched with his bicep as he shifted gears with caution not to wake the neighborhood this time around. The car was still too loud to skirt by. Wonder if he was behaving because of his dad?

"I agree, you look hot," Jase said once we were on open road. I noticed he kept glancing from my face to the lace hem of the top adorning my amplified cleavage. Yeah, I may have dusted off the push-up for this occasion. Rather than wear a dress like I had the other night, I wanted back in my own skin. If these pants had made Klive a smitten fool who'd thought of me two years later, I knew they were guaranteed to punish Jase for wicked thoughts. Even if we'd smoothed things over, we were playing on his turf. I wasn't going down without a fight.

"Thank you, both. Y'all look nice— well, as nice as bad boys can look," I amended. He and Jase scoffed in unison.

"Speak for yourself, little miss. Showing all that skin," Rustin said.

"I second that," Jase said. "But I'm not complaining."

"Did I sound like I was complaining, because I wasn't," Rustin said. I smiled to myself as they gave each other knuckles.

We cruised down to a bay-side club with a line down the street. Several cliques and squads I recognized from the bar stood in wait. When we parked, I stood outside the car while the guys primped in the rear-view mirrors. Jase pulled a comb from the glove compartment and ran the tines through his hair, slicked then tousled in the front. Classic like Delia had mused. He passed the comb to Rustin who straightened his spikes in the mirror and smoothed the sides. Rustin checked his teeth, then came up and grinned like I was a test subject. I rolled my eyes but smiled while they got out of the car.

"You ready?" Rustin asked.

I looked at my invisible watch. "Are y'all? I'm running about ten minutes late."

"After watching you running a football in a bikini, I'm ready to make you ten months late," Jase teased. "Territory marked."

"No fair!" Rustin grabbed one of my hands. "I miss everything."

Jase grabbed the other hand to stop me from slapping Rustin.

"I wasn't talking about me marking my territory, baby. I was talking about you marking me on Thursday night. Unless you were just using me to settle an old score with Angela?"

"Mmhmm ... would that upset you?" I tilted my chin up and bat my eyelashes.

He grinned. "Nah. Feel free to use me anytime, but if you adhere to that golden rule, all I ask is the same liberty."

Touché. My smile flat-lined. Maybe I understood more about Jase than I cared to admit. Thank God for darkness and the opportunity to calm myself without them noticing my pissy pout. I watched the parking lot and my feet like I needed to be sure not to trip.

Jase ignored the line at the club the way a king walks into his own palace. I wasn't even stopped for my ID as the bouncer stepped aside and greeted him by name.

"Hey, Taylor, you lining out a football game? Everyone's talking about it."

"Oh, yeah," Jase confirmed. "After she threw a public gauntlet, I have to deliver. Make her put her trash talking mouth to work."

"You're gonna let her play?" the bouncer asked and took me in like I was a cute little toy.

"Trust me. She's got the skills. Gives me extra chances to take her down," Jase joked. I slapped his stomach as he laughed. Several in the line called his attention about Rock-N-Awe. "Hey man, you mind if I pull some fans?"

"Not at all."

Jase lifted his chin and gestured to the ones begging with their eyes to be near the lead singer and his backup. If there weren't both male and female in this group, I'd have balked. Playing at chill around his fan base was harder than I'd expected. On one hand, I saw this as a blessing where my own fan base came in. Then again, the men at my meets weren't dressed like hookers ready to pleasure me at the crook of a finger. The women clamoring to be seen with us, well, with the guys, were dressed and ready to be on their knees with no price tag. They also tried to pretend I wasn't in the way.

"It's Mackenzie, right?" one asked as we walked through the door.

"It's *Kinsley*," Jase corrected her and squeezed my hand. "Y'all have fun. See you at the next show?" He waited with eye-contact so they didn't feel rejected. They agreed. His lips dipped to mine for a second long enough to give them the hint. Flutters in my belly released endorphins of victory. *I'd passed the test!* Well, at least this one. If Jase expected me to remain neutral to the attention, surely he'd reciprocate rather than beating up every man who wanted a photo with me?

He'd punched Klive ... crazy! Glad he didn't mar Klive's pretty skin, hee hee. Klive punched him back. Pretty ballsy. Both fools.

Jase took us to the bar for drinks. Three mojitos later, I stared at the dance floor feeling a little tired of sitting, but maybe too dizzy to stand straight. This place may as well have been Rock-N-Awe's home base. I listened to band lingo, then came the soldiers. Not wanting to disrupt their military jargon, I politely smiled. Their dismissive courtesy reeked as bad as the competing perfumes and colognes floating in and out of the bar area. I was reduced to a civilian outcast who had chosen to stay spoiled on home soil while they'd been courageous to fight overseas for my ignorant bliss.

When a female 'he-lo' pilot who'd flown in Afghanistan joined, I grew irritated and intimidated. This was worse than the women buffing my mom's nails while talking smack to her face in their native language. The haloed helicopter pilot made her way beside me. "Bored?" she asked and told the bartender to make me another.

"No, that's okay, I probably shouldn't," I insisted. "I've had too much."

"A lightweight, eh? With Dragula? Jase must love you're so cheap." She giggled. I knew she was playing, but she weaseled under my currently irritated skin. "That's his call sign, ya know? Jase's a legend. Combo of Dragon and Dracula. Got that fire power and thirst for blood. Shame what happened. Oh, hold on." She answered a text while I gaped at the huge diamond solitaire on her left hand. Every beautiful tooth beamed from her smile when she noticed me noticing. Coral lips, olive skin, itsy waist with voluptuous curves. A veritable bad ass brick house telling me, "Don't worry. I'm off the market. And he's not my type. Too full of himself. So am I. There can only be room for one ego in any relationship, don't you think?"

Damn. Blunt. I wanted to ask her what the shame was in Jase's life, but my brain was on slow-motion-Attention Deficit Ooh Shiny and the ego thing.

The fresh mojito arrived. I lifted the cup up in a toast like I agreed, then downed more than I should've.

A man walked up and kissed the woman whose name went in and out of my ears. The men around the group greeted him like he was higher ranking and they were in trouble. She got off on their intimidation and grinned at me again. "He's retired. Twenty years older, but he's done things Dragula looks up to. So sexy, especially since he is so plain. You'd never know." Her lips almost touched my ear so he couldn't hear her. The music was too loud to hear normal conversation anyway. I found myself inspecting the retired Commander when she wrapped her arm around my waist and led me to the dance floor. I hated that I had to lean on her support. "What do you think?" she asked. "About older guys, I mean. Jase is older than you, right? You look like you shouldn't even be in here. They check your ID?"

"Are you a cop?" I asked. My body numb, I swayed without caring how close she was or what her angle might be.

She tossed her long black hair and wrapped her other hand around my waist to pull me closer.

"Not a cop. Wouldn't be surprised if Jase got chicks in here without legal IDs is all. You're pretty. That ego thing ... you might be too pretty for him. See, I feel cool to dance with you this way because I know I don't have to worry about you hitting on me because we are both pretty."

This chick made zero egotistical sense. A wonder her head fit through the door.

"If I look like a pretty kid, you look like an over-aged predator, yeah?" *Shit.* No filter.

"Oh! And she's got claws! I like her, Jase," she said over my head. Jase closed in at my back and nuzzled my ear. When his hot breath met my skin, I tilted my head against his chest.

"I like her, too," he told her against my skin. Oh. Damn. I wanted too many bad things as he got into the groove with the music and allowed his hands to roam. Mine captured his to still them, and the woman's left my body, thank God. I was glad that she'd been there to keep me just uncomfortable enough to keep Jase in line. He must've felt me relax, because he asked, "Homophobic, baby?"

I turned around to face him, my brows knit. "Don't give me that politically correct bullshit. Maybe, one: I'm not gay or bi-sexual. Two: I don't want to be felt up by *anyone* unless I invited them to do so. Boundaries. Get it?" I snapped my fingers.

"Excuse me?"

I jumped at the sound of the Aussie accent. Chad's roguish smirk shone like a mind reader with perfect timing.

"I'm on break and noticed you were quite bored at the bar. May I have a dance? Unless—" He paused and glanced at Jase like he was asking him permission as well. "You're otherwise occupied?"

I fought a smile at Jase's glare. We all knew what Chad was doing, but there was no legit way for Jase to call him out without looking like a total dick.

"Jase, may I?" I asked. "Your comrades are still at the bar, so you've got plenty to keep you occupied."

I wasn't really asking. I grabbed Chad's hand and carried his offer to the center of all the warm bodies sweating in a fatigue of hormones. The song shifted without a club-style remix to Hey Violet.

"*Queen of the Night*," Chad said. "Like you."

"Awww!" My frustration melted with my whole expression.

His gleam was gone. He grabbed my waist, left one hand dangling by his side as he closed the space between us. We began to sway, and I placed one hand behind his neck.

"Are you gay, Chad?"

"No."

"Are you coming onto me?"

"No."

"What is this?"

"You needed saving. Now, dance with me." He grabbed my free hand with his and pulled my palm to join the other behind his neck. His palms ran from my waist to the middle of my back, urging me against him to slow dance, our bodies finding a chemistry that had to look like more to the other couples around us. His hands slowly dragged down to the base of my spine and laced together. "Relax. Just one friend rescuing another. I'm safe," he said at my temple. "You're drunk. He's not. Neither was she. Rustin's bothered, too. After the shit that went down at Delia's, it's hard not to worry."

"Shhh ...." I leaned back, one finger covering his lips, staring at him for a while in a moment that may have been romantic if we were like that. There was something incredibly beautiful I couldn't not appreciate. Something wonderful about my innocence in such a setting with a man that made Jase's dragon coil with his fist. Chad's lips parted on a smile, well aware of the intimacy-envelope-pushing in the maneuver.

"Admit it, you enjoy pissing him off." He took my hand from his mouth and took proper form.

"Not as much as you do." I grinned. His nod was barely perceptible as he increased our sway and play. "He's not bad to me, Chad."

"He's not good for you, either," he told me and dipped me enough to make me giggle.

My smile faded as he lifted me up. "Look around us, Chad. Is anyone good for me?"

"Probably not. At least not in this place. You're pliable. Maybe we could go to another club together sometime. Like dance to something completely different?"

I smiled up at him a tad confused. "Different how? Like a date?"

"A friend date. Different, as in how do you feel about Rockabilly? Swing?"

"Sure!" I choked on my excitement and looked down in alarm. As Rena Lovelis sang about something bringing her to life, Klive came into view. I hated lingering on someone I needed to turn my back on. I tucked my face into the crook of Chad's neck to hide from the emotional toil.

7 | ♀

CHAD NOTICED MY SUDDEN **shift.** "Hey. You alright, love?"

My eyes closed as I swallowed hard. "Please don't call me that," I said. Chad never once called me love before. *Why now? Why did that word bother me too much?* As if the endearment belonged to one person. *One love. From one accent.* "Use my name. You know I love it." I tried to lighten up real fast so maybe he'd not catch onto the response I hadn't anticipated.

He chuckled and hummed against my temple. "Hmm. You're beautiful tonight, *Kinsley*."

"Your accent is beautiful, Chad."

"Isn't it just?"

"You're not so bad yourself," I said. We settled into the song and one another's arms, but I sagged against him to hold to every second of emotional hide-and-seek I could get.

Klive wasn't looking at me when I saw him. He was with Jase at a table. *Had Jase invited him? Why would he do that if he'd asked me on a date? Was he rubbing me into Klive's face somehow? Ugh! One man was too ashamed to be seen with me in public, the other too immature not to show me off to gain a one-up. What the hell was with the guys in my life?*

Around Klive sat men from the military group, the band, and some I didn't recognize. The women clung to their guys like the most beautiful accessories, not a single one of their guys ashamed to be

61

seen with them. Rustin stood opposite, his only accessory the brew in his hand. He watched the floor while nodding at conversation. He shifted in and out of sight with the bodies around us. I knew Rustin's view of me was obstructed by Chad's face, the way Chad's chin turned so his cheek tucked me in the way I wanted. Rustin looked nice enough, but Chad was right. He had the stare of a bodyguard whose charge was close to danger. *For himself or for Jase? Was he my babysitter?* The thought made me angry.

The song changed, my mood changed, and Chad grabbed my hand to move us through the crowds that packed the floor with the *Edge of Seventeen.* Laser lights and mirror ball reflections darted among the throng on the floor who moved more like a single writhing creature as the beat picked up with Stevie Nicks' iconic lyrics. No way Rustin kept track. I wondered if that was Chad's point. After all, he had been able to see him the whole time.

"You have a ride home?" Chad shouted to be heard. I nodded. He did too and signaled two fingers to a passing server with a tray over her head. He traded her cash for the shot glasses we tossed back. As I did so, I noticed cages above us suspended from the ceiling. Women inside held to the bars working their curves to the bend of the song's retro beat. "You want some alone time?" he asked. I realized his point, grinned, but shook my head, suddenly shy. "Ah, come on. The guys can't hover over you if you're hovering over them. You've got the moves. I got all your favorite songs."

"So, I find freedom by getting inside of a cage? I like your style, sir, but I'm not dressed like them."

He laughed full and loud. "You may not be rocking a thong beneath a dress, but you haven't seen your ass in those pants. Trust me, you'll torment them. Besides, there's one other chick wearing pants up there. You'll be great!"

He had a point that clicked in this fuzzy moment ... too many fuzzy moments in recent history for my liking ... too many uncertainties developing that I didn't like at all. My nervous eyes shifted to Chad's daring gaze. No one in here was good for me. Chad seemed like he hated me in this place and wanted to put me in a cage to keep me from bad places, but those ladies weren't dancing like ladies at all. How was that bad place any better than the one surrounding me now?

He checked his watch while my tongue traveled the inside of my cheek.

"Fine. How do I get up there?" I asked.

"Easy." He signaled someone else. I watched as one of the cages lowered to the edge of the floor. He led the way, holding my hand in his warm grip while the woman who got out fanned herself and beelined for the bar, mouthing a thank-you to Chad. He winked at her and gestured I hop in once we stood before my free prison. "I'll be right there when you're ready. Just signal."

I nodded and stepped inside with uncertainty, but a frisson of rebellious adventure lifted with the cage. Holding to the bars, I beamed at Chad as he called I have fun and stared up in a way that made me grateful I wasn't wearing a dress.

I gulped as my fear of heights added sweat to my palms. Before looking out over the floor, I looked across at the other women dancing at my level. A dynamo in hip-hugging bell bottom jeans and a crop top threw a big smile and her hands toward me, waving me on like this was a vintage game of *Mortal Kombat.* At the same time, Chad took his post on an elevated corner glowing with black lights illuminating the white stripe on his shirt. His lips kissed my way as he mixed the beats to eventually fade into Ice Cube's *You Can Do It.*

I cackled at his intended encouragement blending with the naughty dancing he wanted to draw at the same time. I checked the chick across the way. She pointed to her eyes then ran that hand over hips that seemed to have a mind of their own. Two other women in the cages at each corner of the floor seemed to do their own thing but fed off one another. I stood like the uncertain prude offering no inspiration. They came to their bars to evaluate me. One gestured in a way that told me to ignore everything but them. We were on our own plane. Just the four of us in hoochie wear with a dirty soundtrack. The people below didn't exist, only their heat and the dare to keep up or surpass.

My hands ran over my rolling body and folded behind my head. I closed my eyes. Everything vanished and nature took over. Soon, I didn't care about scandal. I ran my hands over my thighs as I swiveled to changed levels. The woman across the way nodded and watched like I'd tossed her a snack. I held to the bars while I relished the chance to use the secret belly-dancing classes I'd been taking for years behind my parents' backs. The body will do what the mind wills. My mind listened to the words telling me to put my back and ass into the music, so I did. My hands held to the movements in my abs to appreciate the sensuality I was tired of pretending to ignore. I wanted to be as sexy as the accessories on the arms of every badass bitch at Jase's table. *Was there one around Klive? A woman holding to him that he wasn't ashamed of like I was a bad idea because I was too sweet? Too kind? Too good? Was that why he refused to sleep with me? Refused to compromise my morals as if I were too moral for his touch? Just because I valued the gesture didn't mean I wasn't resentful during the buzz of alcohol-laced reasoning. I was so tired of being good!*

When I opened my eyes, money littered the floor beneath my feet. *You Keep Me Hangin' On* blended next like Chad foretelling a future filled with iffy choices that changed with Klive King's ever-shifting desires. Maybe Chad spied from his high perch the torment Klive put me through? If so, that meant Jase and Rustin could too, and I was shitty at pretending. *Was Chad trying to warn me? Maybe he wasn't even indicating Klive but Jase since they had friction?*

My hips swirled, dipped while my hands ran everywhere with drunken whims competing to destroy the good girl image I'd worked so hard to maintain. I was above this, but right now I just got off on how I was above a crowd that looked up to watch me. Every movement, the feel of my hair loose, spilling down my spine, chest, between my bulging breasts, through my fingers to shove the tresses back, so much sensation and self-awareness, nothing else. Just my body and the music like my secret self wanted out of the apartment. The naughty ballerina belly dancer who loved classic rock and club at once. My hands traveled like they belonged to the man who'd inspired dirty dreams since he'd grabbed me in the elevator.

The people didn't watch me like I was some under-aged girl who couldn't hack real life; like the 'kid' in the parking garage told she was too sweet and wanted different things than someone of his level. Real men like that one watched my ass in these pants as though the women grinding against them weren't nearly naked in places. I bit my lip and looked away from the truth of the power I possessed.

My eyes connected with Chad's. He danced with a hand to his ear and played with a sound board, but he watched, too, not so friendly in this capacity. The one who pissed Jase off for real while I believed what my naïve mind wanted about even good men. Alcohol told a truth my sober mind usually rejected: good men, like good women, could be bad. I'd never seen everyone around me in such a way as I did now. Drunk goggles made the hippy hipster across the way so sexy, but in the way that I wanted to put my arms around her to make the helicopter pilot inferior.

A guy in an Inferno vest walked beneath my cage. *Had I ever been on a bike? I needed an asshole to protect me.* I rolled my eyes at the memory of Pat Connor's words about men and motorcycles.

Pat Connor's prick of a friend was dead. I'd been on a bike. *Had an asshole aside from Jase come to my defense?* Klive's words were so vague about Pat. *How did that ripple through their community? Why was I thinking about this in the lusty here and now?*

Because no one could be an asshole like the one who'd seen Patrick Scott last.

Finally, I spun and swiveled to face the table where they sat, seeking the gray seductive eyes on my mind. Up here Jase, Rustin, Chad, no one could touch me. They couldn't be close and read my face to determine the thoughts I supposedly wore in the open. The men at the table hadn't moved, but the women gathered and laughed like new friends. Jase watched a sexy server prancing past.

Chills broke out over my skin, not in jealousy. Klive's fingers rested around his mouth. His eyes locked on my cage like a man as tormented as I was, longing to be locked in my prison. *Good. See what you chose not to take, you dick!* I ran my middle finger up my body, over my breasts, up my neck to my lips. I kissed the tip and touched my ass. His eyes narrowed. The others seemed in motion, distracted, while Klive had no shame in staring like my every move ratcheted up the anger I compounded with my calling his shit this morning. A look like that, yeah... The bottles on that table could easily be knocked to the floor before he lunged over the wood to rip the cage down. I bit my smirking lip and held to the bars as I worked my hips and shoulders, daring him to watch as if I could punish him.

He said something and grinned before craning his neck to the person speaking to him.

Ice hardened the heat in my blood.

Angela Ansley!

Was he trying to piss me off at my own game?!

A straw between her fingers stirred the drink in her other hand. She was talking through a smile. Even if they were at least three feet apart, three miles wouldn't have been far enough. The others laughed around her and smiled at him the same way she did.

Well, Mr. King, you arrogant asshole. Aren't you charming?

I glared and signaled a passing server. A minute later I lowered to the level of the rest of the realm.

8 | ♂

JASE PEELED THE LABELS from the half-empty, sweating bottles before him. When one label came off, he crumpled the paper and tossed the remnants into a glass across the table. The underlying anger ticked a box on my checklist of requirements.

"I don't talk cash until I have confirmation," I told him.

"I understand what you're saying, King." Jase nodded from my right, stared through the mirrored starbursts of color lighting the dance floor. Crissy and Molly worked their ways into user's hands throughout the club. Nightshade tucked bills into their clips. However important the cash flow, I found my gaze glued on the woman in the same black leather pants that enslaved me two years ago. She danced in ways that shouted at the sex I'd refused, touched her body like I had at Delia's. The sexy heels extending the line of her legs, the stretch of those pants on her ass, the shirt that wrapped her swollen breasts like a present I needed to rip the bow from, heavy makeup on her go-to-hell glare, all of this exhausted my libido. So did the tossed hair, every sensual push away from her face or flip of long bangs from her eyes. Peeks of the curve at the tops of her hips and midriff as she lost herself without care of how provocative she presented her normally casual package. Her hands held the flesh of her bottom like she may be imagining they weren't her hands at all.

Jase watched like an angry cat ready to break into the cockatoo's cage, pluck her feathers and devour every tasty morsel. *Or, was that me?*

"No biggie," Jase stated. "Not too sure it's for me, King."

I scoffed and chuckled to myself. *What a crock of shit!* He wanted in almost more than he wanted his pretty bird. The truth shone in his eyes, but I wasn't positive his motives were pure, though no one's motives were pure if they were being considered for a Nightshade position, now were they?

"If you're having doubts, not sure I blame you, mate. She's very sexy," I offered.

"You know it." He grinned. Rustin downed a swig of a beer as he studied her in obvious desire from where she danced as though paid to do so. The woman knew how to work that pretty body of hers in ways that I was certain took sex to an entirely different level. *Had Jase discovered that level with her yet?* She hadn't let on, but why would she? Especially if she were trying to tempt me to sleep with her. Jase appeared too tormented to be satisfied. His eyes sought alternative options as they breezed past with bouncing breasts ready to nurse his every ache.

Was he strong enough to hold out and wait for his prey, or would he settle for fast food?

"Taylor, do you know the difference between starving and fasting?"

He nodded like a deaf man, then snapped out of his own thoughts. "The difference between starving and fasting? You mean like Monks and Christians do?" he asked, eyebrow arched.

I nodded. "Sure. It's not wholly for religious purposes, though."

"Okay ...? What?"

I assessed his expression and wondered when the last time I may have enjoyed such ignorance was. "The difference is discipline. Starving is a forced decision or even done against your will. Fasting is suffering for a greater purpose to open the mind during weakness. This I know you may understand, even if you've never fasted. You've suffered for a greater purpose."

"I have. Not sure what your point is, King. You talking about suffering for Nightshade?"

I shook my head, disappointed in how he knew so much sacrifice yet couldn't understand applying that to his lust for the good Christian in the cage going bad to win this foolish boy's attention like she needed to behave the way his other groupies did. For her sake, I took satisfaction in that I couldn't say I hadn't tried.

Then again, perhaps I was too harsh on him. He was only a man. Not a single heterosexual male in this place watched that redhead in this rare element without becoming aroused, including the deejay. Chad Patel, also the bloody reporter that stalked my every social move, flirted with her as he mixed music he knew would challenge her to compete with the other caged birds in the most enticing ways.

I licked my lips and arched my eyebrow at Taylor. "She officially yours?"

"How so?" He studied me now like I was the fool. "You asking because you're interested, King?"

"Taylor, I don't have time for bullshit. Relationships included. Meaningful shagging, that sort of lot," I offered with a gesture of my hand. "Fooling around is one thing. Shagging, completely different. You don't shag *her* once and you don't leave with your soul if you do."

"Damn. Guess I should welcome you to the club now," he joked. "I agree. Shagging her once, as you say, not possible. She's too ... I dunno the exact word ... I just settle for sweet, but sweet isn't it."

"Chaste, virtuous, wholesome perhaps?"

Jase laughed. "When she's not drinking, maybe." He shook his head, smile fell. A blind man would see the conflict. He wore the inner debate like a cross around his neck; equally convicted and handcuffed by the good girl amid corruption. I longed to inquire whether he'd ever seen this side of his sweetheart before.

Chad mixed older songs into newer, back and forth. I watched him dancing and watching her as he played songs like his own Kinsley experiment. This guy knew her, knew how to draw her. He picked a classic song that made me wonder if he was experimenting with the men watching her as well, that little prat. If Chad saw my affinity for her so clearly, so did anyone. Not like I'd done my best or even *minimal* to appear complacent to her, *but shit! Did he think we were all playing games with her? Was he protective of her, or one of the men in this misery?*

My hand settled around my mouth just as Kinsley spun on her toes enough to make her hair fly and land around her face. She ran a hand through the tresses. I imagined doing the same before pulling enough to tilt her head for access to taste her beautiful throat, hear her moan my name one more time.

Her eyes landed on mine like a guilty woman tired of hiding matching thoughts. I expected her to look away, expected Jase to bitch about this, but he was distracted by a passing waitress who watched him like she may be a regular source of sex.

Even as her boyfriend's eyes strayed, Kinsley narrowed her eyes on me like *I'd* done something wrong. I held her eye contact with mutual frustration. She dragged her finger like pointing out all the places I was no longer allowed to touch because I hadn't publicly claimed her. My smile hid beneath my hand when she kissed her finger and placed the tip to the ass I wanted to spank so bad. Pants included. She drizzled slow and seductive down the bars she held to, a proverbial siren tempting a man to her cage to kill him.

Go on, love, bleed me dry, but do start at the concentration of blood hammering the pulse of the song— shit, I needed a distraction!

"You gonna watch, or you gonna go out on the floor, Mr. King?"

I grinned a silent thanks for the very distraction that'd cool my veins.

My head tilted toward the exaggerated Southern drawl of Angela Ansley. The ever-present annoyance with this little twit mingled with vindictive satisfaction for Kinsley's unfair anger toward me. The torment she made me suffer day in and out compounded my insatiable desire with every toss of hair, cackle, dirty look from innocent eyes. I couldn't handle much more without snapping, but which side would be the one to take her? White collar or criminal? The woman in that cage was no different from the one who danced to dirty music in her undergarments when alone in her apartment. She'd let the naughty secret out to play in public. Bitchy Bonny playing dangerous games, testing my patience and trigger finger.

"Are you a wallflower who has no fun of his own?" Angela asked.

The blood drained from down under with each passing second this kiss-ass patronized me. One glance at Eric and he stepped in to invite Angela to the dance floor. When I looked back at Kinsley, the cage was gone. The song ended and bled into another. Jase cursed and thanked his God as though unable to withstand another word of Angela's or another dance from caged Kinsley.

I chuckled. "So, if you sign, Taylor, what're your plans for your girl? Certainly, you hold no illusions of being involved in Nightshade whilst trying to live happily ever after?"

Who'd win? Kinsley or Nightshade?

"The exact reason I told you this may not be for me. When we first started talking about all of this, she was still the untouchable bartender. Suddenly, she's open to me? Not sure what the hell to do, King. She's ...." His words faded as he lost sight of her.

Rustin grunted as his beer found a place on the wood he never looked down at. He ducked into the masses and traveled like a rogue cowboy caught in Kinsley's lasso. As Jase watched him go, he ran a hand through his hair as though he'd pissed Rustin off. Odd.

Especially given that when he re-appeared, Rustin glued to Kinsley on floor within our view. The way Rustin gripped and maneuvered her seemed geared to upset Taylor, but Taylor seemed upset for the wrong reason, a reason I couldn't pin. Hmm ... were they running their own game? My mind flashed back on the locker talk convo Kinsley divulged to me at the beach bar before I'd helped her escape on my bike. Maybe she needed another escape ....

"You seem awfully liberal with her." I no longer held back my possessive stare. "Taylor, she isn't peanut butter for your mate's toast. Something you eat and spread to the hungry men around you."

He blinked and glanced over, took an alarmed double-take. "Whoa, King, ease up. You've got the wrong idea. Kins and I ...." He searched for the right words, but grimaced as he would around a lemon in his mouth. "We aren't exactly together yet, so I can't just go out there and tell her she can't dance with anyone else. Use what happened at Delia's as exhibit A. I put my foot down to protect her, she basically tells me to shove my possessive foot up my ass. It's not only that. I confess, I like to watch the way other men handle her, but ultimately, it's the way she handles them that I like the most. Watching them turn to pathetic pussies because they want hers helps me to see she didn't torture me in particular, but that I'm part of an entire race. Case-in-point." He gestured to me, then Rustin, up at Chad.

I sat back as I nodded in understanding. Made sense, but there was more to the pain and longing in his eyes. He was in love with her, and I loathed his feelings.

"Rustin's pissed at me. Where our business is concerned." He gestured between us. "He thinks there's no contest."

We watched for a few beats the way Rustin's fingers dug into her hips just beneath the hem of her shirt, how close his smiling lips came to hers as he spoke to disarm her. She tilted her face up to hear him better and read his lips, then laughed and slapped his arm. He grabbed her hands and pulled them over her head, turned her, and wrapped them over her belly so he could pull her against him to grind right up against her ass.

Jase and I sighed in unison, his deflated, mine a near growl.

"Thing is, King, she scares me."

My hand scrubbed over my mouth as my jaw clenched. I spun to face him so I'd stop looking.

"Oh?" I asked. To seem casual, my fist wrapped around the leftover Captain and Coke to toss the liquid back and snag a cherry. I toyed with the remaining stem remembering Kinsley stealing mine before I'd made her cry.

"Yeah. She's too clean, educated, driven. I'm a fucked-up mess whose drive was left in Afghanistan with my guys. I don't deserve her."

"You're bothered by her education?" I was stunned. "Don't you have your G.I. bill or some lot?"

Instead of cheering him up and pointing out options, I should've been storming onto the dance floor and snatching Kinsley by the elbow, hauling her away from Rustin to replace rationality into her nonsensical inebriated brain. She could tell me to put my foot up my own ass, I didn't care, because she may argue, but we knew who'd win. As my candidate, Jase needed to learn to put his foot down even when the thing he went softest for bucked his authority.

"Klive, you hear about those men who can't handle strong women, and you think what pussies, but what happens when you become one because of your own stupid shit without realizing it? She's a lot of woman to handle, and what happens if I don't handle her correctly?" he asked and turned to me as well. I saw a man in fear. Genuine fear. So, this was why he debated joining Nightshade rather than just throwing his heart to her?

Dammit! I didn't want to like him! I wanted her for myself, and here lay a perfect opportunity to use my silver tongue for my benefit, however, I remained silent. Why?

Because she loved him.

Or did she?

Bloody madness! I was tired of thinking, staying patient, pretending I didn't know what she needed. *Should I take her before he damages her beyond repair?*

"Come on, King. You think she's gonna be affiliated with someone involved in some crime syndicate? She'd be ashamed, disgusted. Look around us. Girls like her don't mix with men like us, King. Well, like you're offering me to be."

Oh, that's right ... I can't claim her because of the bloody syndicate.

I scoffed in bitterness. "Well, don't get your hopes up anyhow, Jase. Not too certain you're the man I'm looking for. A Nightshade position isn't for the soft. It's a hard sacrifice with alternative rewards." His immediate regret was a thing of manipulative beauty. "Taylor, look at it this way; you're still free to marry your princess and move into your castle without becoming a villain." My eyes met his, and they weren't kind.

He'd insulted me, and he knew.

I'd pissed him off, and I knew.

"If you think *I'm* soft maybe you're right to look elsewhere. I've handled my shit well because I channel my softness for *her* into what I'm doing. For example, when I saw a woman being stoned to death in Afghanistan, Kinsley became that woman. The men doing the stoning died in two seconds, two bullets. You dismiss me as a pathetic romantic, the loss is yours."

In other words, don't mistake his love for weakness.

Hmm ... was this part of why he was now back on home soil?

Before I could ask, Jase jumped up bent on sudden escape.

I glanced over to see a giggling Angela Ansley aimed straight for us again. Jase darted to the dance floor. I launched toward the restroom, then snaked around the line to a discreet alcove I watched from. I nodded at Eric as he sauntered toward me and passed a roll of cash that I shoved in my pocket. He continued as though we weren't acquainted.

Kinsley and Rustin danced hot and heavy. She was every bit as wanton in reality as in her dream state. My undeniable distraction, the possessive mixing with protective, the avoidance of every other woman; I was tethered and jealous. We had thick chemistry, but I wasn't alone in that. I hated that she appeared to connect with others so easily, even if she was drunk. *Who was the sober winner?*

When Jase and Rustin sandwiched her between them, Kinsley ducked out and hastened to the nearby invitation of the woman in the bell-bottoms from the cage earlier.

Another of my men sauntered by and passed money. I pocketed the bills and watched Kinsley working her body with the other woman in a way that had me ready to eat my balls for lunch. I needed to get the hell out of here, but Jase and I hadn't finished our business. Rather than dismiss him as I'd considered for brief seconds, I now wondered if Kinsley was the key to everything I needed from Taylor. She unlocked his menace.

He and Rustin went back to the table. I made my way toward them after buying them more drinks and deciding to liven them back up. This shit was far too heavy. Jase needed fun.

"Shit!" I muttered as I spotted Angela and no Eric to keep her away. Too late to turn back now. She was at the table, bent over the edge, one of her spike-heeled feet kicked up as she rested on her elbow and laughed at something Rustin said to Jase. They were trying to keep from being rude while not giving her the attention she was intentionally drawing toward herself as her skirt rose high. Several men appeared ready to pull the hem while she bent that way. She knew what she was doing. I sneered in disgust as her dilated pupils scanned mine in askance. I shook my head with an exaggerated irritation. *No, I don't want a blow job in exchange for increasing your fix.*

Her lip popped a bit in a pout. She turned her slutty attention back to the man that she knew, without a doubt, was off-limits where Kinsley was concerned. All the bullshit kissing ass and phony conversation I'd eavesdropped on between she and Kinsley Thursday night was for show. Angela Ansley was officially on my radar. While she smiled at Jase, I watched her sidle onto Rustin's lap. She licked her fingertip before running a pointed nail across his lips. *Was she aiming to get him fired?*

Rustin sighed, but her finger entered his mouth. She moaned with a lusty smile. He looked away on a grin and bit the tip of her finger like a playful warning.

"Ms. Ansley, we work together, your father is my boss, and Kinsley—"

"What about that bitch?" Her finger yanked away to point in his face. *Hard to maintain the fake facade when you're high, eh?* "You know that's what she is, right, Jase? She may have you fooled, but her true colors will come through, and you'll see. All of you. She plays innocent and sweet, but behind closed doors—"

"Oh, what, so you've fucked her, then?" Rustin fired like she'd insulted him. "Because I can't see what else you could possibly mean about her behind closed doors."

"Would you like that, Officer?" she giggled.

"Dep-u-teee." Rustin shook his head and shoved her off his lap with offended disgust.

She stumbled against me and gripped my shirt to catch her balance. I locked rigid with rage as she fisted my shirt and drew her lips toward mine like she'd never get another chance. My hands cupped her arms to pry her away. Without thinking, I shoved her toward Jase, because, "*He's* far more liberal than I am."

"Shit, man!" Jase caught her and glared. We all snapped at the sour side of Kinsley when she shouted. Gone was the sweet little temptress, replaced by one seething pissed young woman.

I lunged to stop her, but she wielded her fury with a stunningly sharp slap to my face before she homed in on Angela. I cursed and held my cheek, baffled by her ferocity and speed. She would need every ounce in order to have a shot against Angela the High Giant. This wasn't looking good.

9 | ♀

THE BITCH. SHE JUST couldn't "Stop touching my things!" I shouted the rest of my thought.

Klive reached for me. Without thought, my palm slashed a red print across that pretty skin for his role in this. I'd have relished the joy, but Angela. *Just Angela.* Jase grappled for control over Angela Ansley's tentacle-like hands suctioned to personal places that seemed to multiply before my blurry rage. The very last ounce of control I'd exercised for this bitch crumbled like a sugar cube in my clenched fist wrapped around her hair.

"Ow!" Her head snapped back, her body plunked to the floor, and she looked around in stunned fury just in time to feel my hand smack the shock off her face. I formed a fist and punched her where I slapped her.

"Ohhh! Yessss!" *The satisfaction!*

People pushed out of our way. Shouts and chants became white noise as I focused my sights on a long-awaited target.

Her claws came out. *Good!* "Bring it, bitch!"

Damn Chad began playing The Prodigy's *Smack My Bitch Up.* The people around us seemed to *promote* this!

She grabbed my hair, my beautiful hair, fueling my fire. When she jerked, I pulled against her grip and all but lifted her from the floor by her hold. She shuffled in front of me with a stinging slap to my cheek. I kicked a leg out against hers to knock her off balance, then kicked her in the stomach. As she doubled over, I thrust my weight against her to knock her to floor. Her arms came up, but I aimed my knees to pin her biceps to the floor and sank down onto her stomach to deliver hook after hook after hook to that freaking beauty queen face, not giving a damn about my fists or risking broken knuckles. Nate, my boxer ex, would be disappointed in my fighting dirty, but proud of how I kept the upper hand and used the momentum for all the spare seconds they lasted. *I was done with her shit!*

All those years she spent ruining my life, convincing me I wasn't good enough, pretty enough, poaching my talents, stealing my glory for the sake of her ego!

I groaned in sadistic satisfaction when I felt her nose crack. She freed one of her pinned arms to reach between us and deliver a crushing hit to my cheek bone I knew was going to bruise. She swung her long legs up and wrapped them around me enough to knock me aside. We went rolling across the floor in a fit of slaps, punching, screaming, and hair pulling. She rolled me beneath her to have a turn on my belly. Her weight was heavy on my ribs while she swung her balled fist toward my eye, but I blocked and thrust the heel of my hand between us to connect with her jaw before I bucked her off me and scrambled to my feet. Every obscenity I knew flew from my mouth as I grabbed her hair to pull her face down to punch her again, but she thrust a foot at me. I dodged, but she grabbed my hair, too, and she kicked a hard blow to my ribs that stole my breath and made me want to puke.

This girl just didn't go down, did she?! Actually, I'd bet that's all she's good at!

I rammed her away from me so hard, she lost her footing and stumbled back against a table. Some of my hair went with her. Pitchers of beer and shot glasses pitched to the floor. More spectators scattered to give us room. She gripped the edge of the table while she caught her breath and looked around us. I held to my ribs for a second, the wind knocked out of me.

"Come on, Angela! I'm just getting started, you fucking slut!"

When her glare settled on me, I shrugged off my nausea in the name of the pleasure derived from beating her ass. *Who knew when I'd get another shot?* All in.

I shoved my crazy hair out of my face, felt my lip was bleeding, so I wiped my mouth to confirm while shaking my head at her in renewed rage. I spit blood before I shoved the belted cuffs off my ankles with the heel of my shoe, no care whether they tore in this moment. Her chest heaved as she felt herself to check she was intact.

"What's the matter, Angela? You think I might've popped an implant?"

"You wish these were fake," she said, fury rebuilding with her faster breathing and flare of her bleeding nostrils.

"Everything else is!" Finally, the second cuff lost the grip on my ankle and I kicked off my heels. The movement caught her eye. I took the shot and fanned my leg in such a beautiful high kick, the ball of my ankle snapped her glare toward the table where this all started at. "That's for ballet!" I gracefully pulled my foot down. "For the scissors!" Hitch kick straight to her chin. "For my stolen crowns!" Kicked her in the stomach so she doubled over. I grabbed her by the back of the head in her stupor and leaned near her ear. "For touching *him*!" I was right about to nail her face with my knee when I felt myself being lifted by strong arms around my waist.

"Let me go!" I shrieked. "Not yet! I'm not done! Put me down!" I flailed and struggled to get back to her. I dove and tangled my fingers in her hair to support her head so I could deliver a hard slap, but the tips of my nails were all that connected while I was yanked away.

"Stay away from my guys or else next time I'll fuck you up way worse!"

She lifted her head and smeared blood over her mouth with her hand as she screamed at me and chased for more. Jase blocked her path and took a hook to the face. He spun her to pin her elbows behind her back.

I laughed an evil villain laugh as I watched from Rustin's arms. "I bet that's not how you planned on having him pin you, huh, bitch! Face it, I am the one they want, not you! If he wasn't holding me back, I'd bend over for you to kiss my ass because this is one fuckin' thing you will not take from me!"

When Jase and Rustin wrestled us outside, I managed a maneuver and slipped out of Rustin's grasp before he could stop me. I jumped at the chance to deliver another kick to her stomach while Jase had her arms pinned. Dirty, sure. Who the hell cared? Had she cared about suffering any consequences without her father always keeping her out of trouble?

The crowded 'oooohed' at the kick and the hook that was now headed for her left eye. She wouldn't look pretty again for a long time. No, she wouldn't forget me. My fist connected blissfully with her cheek bone and brow. Singing pain shot from my knuckles through my elbow, up my shoulder, but pleasure numbed the aftermath.

That is, until Rustin tackled me to the sidewalk with one of his cop holds and trapped my arms behind my back. The breath whooshed from my lungs. My cheek scraped against the concrete while he bent my hand forward on itself in an agonizing torture.

"Ow! Rustin, you're *hurting* me! Let go! I'll stop!" I heard sirens in the distance. "Shit. Rustin, please don't let them arrest me! Please! I've never been in trouble before! I didn't mean to! Well, I meant to. I mean, I meant *everything*! But I don't want to go to jail! Oh, God!"

"Shut the hell up, Kinsley! Stop talking before you make this worse and incriminate yourself. I promise to do my best, but you just went all TKO on my boss's daughter! *Shit!*"

When I struggled, razor sharp pain shot up my arm. Jase shook his head, his expression serious, but I spied the faintest glimmer of amusement dancing in his eyes, tugging at the corners of his mouth before he cleared his throat and expression again. Rustin was right; Angela sagged limp in Jase's arms. Fresh anger sizzled to life at him holding her.

Then sobriety.

Damn, I hoped charges wouldn't be pressed against me; her face was really bloody. *Was mine?*

Almost everyone in the line had their phones out recording. I realized I was in a world of trouble. Rustin knew I was coming off of the adrenaline and alcohol as I filled with impending doom. He was right. My mouth would implicate me in their videos.

Tears slid down my nose, over my cheek mixing with blood before hitting the concrete. *This effin sucks!*

"Kins, we're rounding up witnesses that confirm she was all over your boyfriend. I'm gonna try to get you out of trouble as best I can," Rustin said, "but, I'm still so new here I don't think I have enough say to be much help just yet."

My parents and coach crawled through my mind. I closed my eyes to more tears. They'd be so ashamed. Walton would have no choice but to suspend me from at least one meet. I'd be lucky if that were the case, but realistically, I was looking at two or three for this, especially if Angela pressed charges.

Wait.

If she pressed charges, I was looking at losing the remainder of my running career before graduation! Fines! Jail time! A record!

No! This bitch couldn't steal this life too! No! No! No!

Maybe if I apologized? But, was I sorry for what I'd done? Despite the consequences I faced?

A cop car screeched to a halt at the curb. I saw the feet of two cops, car doors slamming, their steps into our space stopping right before my face resting against the sidewalk. A paramedic arrived while one deputy ordered Rustin to, "Get her on her feet. Let's see the damage."

"Long night?" Rustin asked him.

The deputy nodded. "Sixth bar fight in our precinct tonight. Hate Spring Break. Although, this is the first cat fight."

Rustin got me to my feet while I winced against the hand he still bent in on itself. The deputy whistled and tilted my chin. "Lot of blood." His partner placed zip-tie cuffs over my wrists and pulled them tight. The one examining my face glanced at my chest, then at his partner as we saw Angela coming to. "Shit. She got into it with *Ansley's* daughter? This is bad."

"Yeah, but can you blame her?" the partner muttered behind me. "If I were a chick I'd have gone at her a long time ago."

"Careful, man, Daddy's home," his partner said.

On cue, Angela's father in uniform stormed out of another vehicle and stalked over to where the paramedic beamed a light into her eyes. Jase still held her arms. Was that necessary now that her father was here?

Mr. Ansley looked through Jase, ordered the paramedic out of his way as he examined her face himself, then he *yelled* at her. *Her!*

I cringed and averted my gaze, landing right on the smirking grin-non-grin of Klive King. He stood beside Jase like the casual king of everything. Despite his front row view of Angela's ass-chewing, he wasn't looking at them. He studied me, his hands in his pockets. I blame the alcohol for how I stared back without flinching. *Are you happy now?* I narrowed my eyes and relished the pink spot on his cheek. He licked his lips. Without breaking our staring contest, he leaned over to speak to the Sheriff. The Sheriff shook his head, glanced at me, back to Klive's unwavering stare, asked a question, and Klive nodded. So did the Sheriff before he jerked his daughter from Jase's grip to the cop car parked behind his own. He strode up. Klive held my eyes like he'd cut the zip-ties, hold my hand, and massage the ache in my wrists if I asked. *Yes, please!*

"Put her in the back of my cruiser," Mr. Ansley barked.

10 | ♀

Tears of fear filled **my eyes** as Rustin spun me toward the Sheriff's Suburban. He marched my dragging feet to a place I'd never been before.

"Russssteee, please, do I have to be here? I'm sorry not sorry. I've never been in trouble!" Rustin slammed the door on my desperate protests. I shook my hair loose. The matted waves hung around my face as several in line snapped pictures and video of Micro Machine being arrested. "This is *bullshit*!" I shouted and kicked the seat in front of me. "That bitch bullies me for years and *I'm* the one going to jail?!"

Peeking through strands, I saw deputies come out of the club with notes the Sheriff read over before he came to open the door beside me. He knelt and looked at my face. "At least she fought back," he muttered. "Ms. Hayes, you nailed my daughter pretty damn bad. Tell me why I shouldn't press charges against you."

My chin trembled like the rumble before a volcanic eruption. Tears spilled first, then all emotional contents under pressure spewed from my mouth about what a bitch his daughter had always been to me, how she had acted tonight. I saw his face flinch when I told him about her threatening me with a pair of scissors. The time she hid my clothing when I showered after swim practice. How she tagged the restroom stalls with my name so I got in trouble for graffiti, then told the school I was sleeping with the math teacher in charge of detention. Detention she'd earned for me! The math teacher almost lost his job while I'd been interrogated by the staff. On and on I went through so much bullshit! Unfiltered insults rained out in an uncontrollable flood, much of my blunt terminology too bold and disrespectful in my drunkenness.

Finally, I sniffled and hiccupped, "After *all* of that, how could I remain chill? I love that man, and she could tell, and she was trying to mack all up on him! She doesn't care about him like I do!" My freaking crunk self was talking ratchet, but whatev. "She wants the D because the D is *mine*! She can have anyone else's, *not* mine!"

He gestured I lower the volume. I choked on a few deep breaths and apologized. "I'm sorry. I don't mean to disrespect you, sir. You don't deserve my attitude. My daddy is gonna whip my ass for the first time ever! I wish you'd whipped hers—"

"Enough," he interrupted and looked around us at the commotion. "Love that man? Which one? Jase Taylor?"

"Huh?"

He waved away my confusion. "Ms. Hayes, I'll level with you. My wife, Jeannine, has been friends with your mother for a long time. Jeannine may have mentioned some issues to me over the years, but never let on the true extent. We should've done something sooner, so it is I who should apologize to you. Now, I'd rather tell her that our daughter was involved in a car accident. If you don't mind laying low for a few days until this blows over, I won't tell your parents since you're an adult. And I am not going to arrest you. *This* time."

Yay! And yikes!

"Seems you have friends in high places. Don't waste their favors."

What?

"You won't have trouble with Angela from here on out." From nowhere, a wry smile crossed his face. "Guess dynamite really does come in small packages. Your father might want to whip your ass, but he'd be proud you know how to defend yourself. A handy asset given the company you keep. Not so sure he'd be happy about that. I'm glad my deputy got you off her when he did. We may have had to press charges because she'd have been hospitalized." His friendly facade hardened to a degree that scared the hell out of me. "This is your one and only warning. Kinsley Hayes, I get another call about you, I will arrest you no matter who comes to your defense. Got it?"

His unblinking blue eyes traveled between mine. All the white showed around his irises. Talk about bi-polar. *Lips zipped! Don't speak that!*

I shuddered. "Yes, sir. Never again. This isn't me. I'm a good girl and plan to stay that way."

"Wish that was the case for everyone," he muttered, then stood to help me out of the SUV. He cut the zip-tie cuffs.

"Thanks." I rubbed the raw skin and minor bleeding from where the sharp plastic cut into my wrists.

The Sheriff nodded and jerked his daughter from the other cruiser. He didn't bother removing her cuffs. She glowered and stumbled as he held her elbow and shoved her into the seat I'd just come from. Her eyes darted over my shoulder, then back to mine with a mean, vengeful smile on her blood-caked lips. Before the SUV pulled away from the curb, Angela mouthed, 'Bye, bitch'.

"You have got to be kidding!" This wasn't over. I already wished I'd have put her in the hospital. I mean, what the hell would make her stop? "She's a freakin' psycho."

When I turned to face the amassed audience, I saw the bouncer gawking. Those in line snapped photos and filmed. Against my temper's wishes, I dismissed them and looked for the guys, but I didn't see them. *What the hell?*

"That bloody Taylor guy is getting his car." Klive sauntered over, a silent heat in his gaze. "Rustin was ordered to the station to type up the report since he was a witness. Sheriff's a mite angry one of his deputies was on location and allowed his precious princess to take so much abuse before stopping it. Here." To my shock, he pulled the expensive shirt over his head and ordered me not to move my arms while he pulled the fabric over my head, his fingers stretching the collar to avoid touching my face. My protest died as I looked down and gasped. My top was ripped wide open; my white push-up bra on full display and spattered in blood.

"Ooh! Guess I have a souvenir," I said to myself with a little smile. "Maybe I'll give my bra to a voodoo priestess since it's got the whore's blood."

Klive sighed while I shoved my arms through the sleeves. Pain sliced through my left ribs.

"I told you not to move, Kinsley. You should've allowed the paramedics to look you over." He pulled the cotton over my torso until the hem rested above my knees. I wore a halo of heavenly cologne. Lewd comments called from the line about him stealing their view. "Bloody perverts," he muttered.

"I'd have allowed the paramedics to check me over if they'd offered," I shot back.

"They did."

"What?" I stared, baffled. He shook his head.

"How much have you had to drink tonight, young lady?"

"Don't call me that, sir."

"Don't call me sir."

I hated that he made me smile when I wanted to be mad at him. Without thought, I reached up and ran a finger along the softness of his cheek. "I'm glad I slapped you." He grinned and my fingers trailed down to trace his mouth. "I missed our battles."

"It's been twelve hours, love."

"Feels like *forever*." I sighed.

"You're far too kind when you've been drinking." He licked his lips. My finger got wet. He chuckled when I yanked my hand.

"As evidenced by the blood."

"Affirmative." His mood shifted, suddenly serious, frustrated, deep. His fingers walked beneath the shirt up my left side in a clinical curiosity. Fire breathed from my lips when he crossed over two. "Easy, love. Don't know that you'll be running for a bit. Think they're fractured. You were very impressive. That was a hell of a kick you took. Can't believe you didn't go down. She has big feet."

My anger faded at the pleasure of his compliment and insult to Angela. I smiled a little, reluctant, staring at the ground and our feet. His in Doc Martens seemed twice the length of my bare feet so tiny by comparison. My eyes dragged up his blue jeans, belt, abs. I jerked back realizing I stood too close to his bare chest. He grabbed me for stability. Not his. Mine. Drunk. That's right.

"You're really tall when I have no shoes on and you do."

"Let's collect your effects from inside, shall we?"

"Klive ... Klive ...."

"Yes, love?"

"Am I ugly now?" Tears filled my eyes.

He sighed and tucked my hair behind my ear. "Kinsley, you're—"

"Kinsley, you ready, baby? We need to get you checked out." Jase walked to my side. His car rumbled at the curb in the background. He looked me over, then at Klive. "Hey, thanks for covering her. You mind watching her for a minute while I grab her stuff?"

"Not at all."

"I bet. Oh, hold on." Jase grinned before he pulled his own shirt off and passed the tee to Klive. "So you don't get a draft." He relished in the cheering of the women in line while Klive laughed. Phones snapped more pics of all of us. I just wanted to be away. Jase flexed both arms and peacocked like a macho idiot into the club. Klive folded Jase's shirt. He placed the cloth in my hand. His fingers went to the small of my back to guide me to the idling muscle car.

"In you go."

"Do I have to? It's so loud." I reached up and massaged my temples. Klive captured me when I wavered. I snorted a giggle. "Did you do that on purpose, sir?" I examined him thinking of our first interlude.

He chuckled. I relished any hint of kindness. "Did *you?*" he asked.

"Did I?" I asked. "You, me and honesty? Maybe. Yeah. You're really hot without the costume. And clothes. No woman in that line would blame me. But she might hate me. After that she'd better keep her hands to herself, too." I giggled again, then whined when pain stung my lips.

"Shhh. You shouldn't say such things. Your pretty smile just opened the split in your lip again."

I sagged in sudden exhaustion. There, against the warmth of his bare chest, wearing his shirt, I closed my eyes and held to what I could, not giving mind to the scandal. He opened the car door and ruined all my happiness.

"Come now. You don't want your boyfriend to feel you're cheating."

"I hate that word."

"No arguments, love."

"I like that word." The leather bucket seat hugged my angry ribs as I peered up through the open window once Klive eased the door shut. His hands held to the frame, a silver ring on his left hand. Defined shoulder muscles, collar bones, smooth skin, tight nipples and abs. "Klive. You said you weren't married."

"I'm not."

"Good." I made my finger a number one. "*One love*, Klive. Understand me?"

His head cocked, but Jase's voice stole his attention. Klive's voice told Jase *your girlfriend might have a set of fractured ribs on her left side.*

"There's that word again," Jase jested and thanked him. I heard the name of a hospital. Great. More public. His driver's door slammed like a hammer against my temples.

Klive and the club vanished. The droning engine shouted at my folly while I held my head. Jase rested a hand on my thigh while his car rumbled onto the highway toward the hospital against my wishes.

11 | ♀

COACH WALTON RANTED INSIDE the curtain dividing my space from other beds in the ER.

"Dislocated collar bone. Two bruised ribs. A right ankle that's already taken strain. Look at your face! For Chrisssake, I barely recognize you! Did you get into it with a damned hyena? Twenty-nine videos of you fighting, saying words I can't repeat. Four videos of you knocking out the same woman while she was held by this behemoth, who's what? Your boyfriend? And what about those other pictures and videos of you with some guy who gave you his shirt? Isn't that the same one who gave you the rose at the meet? I can't even keep this bullshit straight!"

I sighed. "My collar bone is scheduled to be reset anytime now. Bruises fade. And the ankle was never as bad as you made it seem. Emergency rooms aren't sound-proofed, Coach. No one asked you to come, and I didn't write you down as my emergency contact," I said quietly. My temples pounded at the same pulse rate as the swollen contusions on my cheek and lips. The knuckles on both hands were caked with dried blood I dug my index fingernail against. The other index finger rested between a clamp with a wire reading my pulse oxygen levels.

The TV in the upper corner played on mute while a needle in my arm pumped fluids from a bag on my left. Klive's shirt folded on top of my ripped shirt and leather pants on the floor beside the chair I'd placed them in. As soon as Walton had yanked back the curtain, he'd moved my clothing to the floor and sat, but jerked to his feet to pace through the audible math problem I'd created with my behavior.

Jase frowned beside my bed. His hand gripped one of the side rails. He had enough wisdom to stay silent for the moment and feigned interest in my vitals ticking across the monitor behind the bed.

"You didn't have to write me down, because I didn't need a call." Coach cursed and yanked the ball cap off his head, gripped the brim to point at me. "There I was cruising updates on social media, enjoying a beer and a break, *me* time after giving you girls your time in St. Augustine. Therapy for a stressed coach whose star sprinter may be unable to bring her normal heat. Suddenly, videos tagged with our area popped up on the home feed from one of the girls on the freshman team! *Hashtag Micro Machine Explo* or whatever the hell with all these abbreviated words! The ones of you being cuffed and placed in the back of the cop's car were just fabulous! What am I supposed to tell the athletic department? The team? That little wheel-chair-bound child who never misses a race because she looks up to you? For Chrisssake, Kinsley!"

"You already said that. You *keep* saying that. You know I hate it when you take the Lord's name in vain. And that little girl's mother wouldn't allow her on social media. You think I'm not reeling that my nemesis decided to make a cameo back in my life? I admit, my language could've been better, but if the little girl sees it, then use it as an anti-bullying tool."

"*You* are the bully in the video, Kinsley! Micro Machine throws cop's daughter to floor for touching her boyfriend, obliterates her Miss Florida hopes. Forget the charges, hell, she could sue you! You'll be lucky if the school doesn't require you to craft some sort of speech about the negative effects of social media! You're the poster child now!"

"If the school requires it, I'll do it. And if the cop's daughter thinks of suing me, I'll out Miss Florida Hopeful for being drunk and high in a club! And use those videos as proof!"

"That's another thing. You've been walking around colored all over, now Micro Machine's caught in a trashy club with a boy from a band who has a notorious rep for banging everyone in his audience! What's next? Because I'd have expected pregnancy before I ever expected this, so why not?"

"Hey! You don't know me," Jase protested, but I held my hand to stop him.

"I may not know you, but your reputation precedes you, son."

"You call me son when you're, what? Five years older than me?"

"Well, if you're gonna act like a child—"

"Stop it, both of you. I'm not pregnant. I haven't slept with him, by the way, so thanks for the high opinion of both of us. Look, Coach, you're mad, you're saying everything that comes to mind."

"Yeah, you're one to reason with us on speech in the heat of anger, Kinsley Hayes."

"Okay," I admitted. "I screwed up, but when it comes to her, I'd do it again."

"Well, God help us if she ever attends a meet!" He cursed again and ran his hand over his hair.

"Walton, just tell me if my career on your team is over. Quit dragging it out. I'm already in enough pain, let's get this over with."

"Get this over with? Like you've not worked your ass off for years on your record? *We* worked our asses off for you to be where you are. For *years*! And you just throw it away? Who the hell are you and what have you done with my star? I can't stand this."

He sat down like a man defeated and smashed his hat between his balled fists.

"Kinsley, the athletic director owes me a couple favors, and this might be big enough I'll have to phone them both in to keep you on the team, but you're suspended from participation for the next two meets. That much I can tell you on the spot. If you think your handicapped ass is hiding in bed to recover from this, think again. You're going to sit on the bench where everyone can see the consequences of your actions, because they're gonna need proof that you're being punished. There will be shit rolling down on me for fighting for you to remain on the team. Who knows what you've done to your reputation?"

I sighed and closed my eyes, but commotion pried them wide open.

"Mrs. Walton? Ma'am? You can't go back there without signing in. Are you Mrs. Walton? Sir! Who are you? I'll be forced to call security if you don't—"

"Oh, shut up! No, my name is Mrs. *Hayes*. This is Mister *Hayes* and that girl is Kinsley *Hayes*! Did you not learn how to spell or read in medical school, but you're working on my daughter?"

The curtain ripped aside for a vicious ginger glaring at the doctor on her heels. My father loomed over her shoulder and shoved past everyone to kneel by my bedside with my hand scooped inside his. He gasped at the dried blood.

"Kinsley, baby, what happened?" my father begged and started interrogating the doctor as he scooped hair away from my injuries.

The poor, poor doctor. He refused to answer questions until everyone in the room identified themselves. My mother didn't like that. Walton began explaining to my dad what the doctor refused to say. Daddy spoke to him like I'd vanished, then asked why I'd called Coach and not him.

"Enough!" I shouted through their bickering. "Doc, this man is my trainer and track coach, Ian Walton, who claims to be my step-father in medical emergencies. The Hayes's are married and my biological parents. I called none of these people, though right now I consent for my medical information to be shared with each of them.

"My friend, here, drove me to the E.R. after I lost my temper on someone who'd long-since passed my point of tolerance. I exploded. It's all over the internet, my life is apparently ruined. I'm now the poster child for what happens when you fail at humanity in public while living in the land of Insta and every platform under our modern sun. Now, would you please give them the run-down and knock my collar bone back in place so I can finish these fluids and leave?"

The doctor appeared pleased to take point. He ordered everyone to the waiting room while he took me for imaging and repositioning the clavicle. Upstairs in the blessed quiet, he left me to another doctor who'd heard the commotion with my parents and requested me by name.

"Well, Ms. Hayes, if you'd have told me you were visiting, I'd have come down to the emergency room sooner." Delia's father shut the door to the private room. "You don't need anymore imaging. What you really need is rest. Plenty of fluids. You could stand another intravenous bag, but I won't force you. Need me to write a prescription for alone time to de-stress?"

"Is it that obvious?"

"Your family cares. Can't hold that against them, but the whole emergency room could hear your conundrum. You ready for this?"

His kind eyes held empathy when he positioned his hands along my shoulder, ran his fingers experimentally over the bone, then braced me for the maneuver. He counted to three, but on two, snapped the bone back into place. My head tilted back. I stared at the fluorescent lights while tears dripped down my cheeks. Pain, but relief.

"Thank God that's over."

"Not quite. We've got work to do on your face. I need to get this cleaned up to determine if this contusion on your left cheekbone needs a few stitches. Not to fear, though. I've a mostly steady hand. Only flinches every so often. After the stroke they revoked my surgical rights and tossed me into the E.R. with all the residents." He chuckled at my panic. "Just playing. I don't think you'll need more than liquid stitches or butterflies. I may have dabbled in plastics for celebrities for years, hence the mondo condo, so you're in excellent hands, young lady. You think I've got this head of white hair for nothing? Earned every one. Now, let's see ...."

The stool he sat upon rolled toward the counter as he steered himself for the cleansing pads. I closed my eyes and endured the dabbing with his mini lecture.

"Alcohol thins the blood. Makes you bleed too much. That's why it's everywhere, but this spot is proving difficult. Hang in there," he told me. "If you weren't drunk, I could give you something for the pain."

"Am I hearing an incentive to quit drinking?" I grinned, and immediately proved his point with my regret. Thump. Thump. Thump in my opened lip.

"Funny, we have another patient with similar injuries. Car accident, my bottom. There's something to be said for your honesty. I don't envy your generation recording every misstep and posting it for judgment. I'm grateful the mishap you had earlier in the week was at my house with no phones allowed. Not sure I'd be where I am today if the sins of my youth were recorded. She's worse, the other girl. Stitches in several places, but she doesn't have that nice little dot on her ribs from high heels the way you do."

"What?" I gasped and raised my gown. While I bunched the material, grateful I was wearing panties— *stupid, drunk Kinsley! Think before you act!* — he pointed to an angry red spot.

"E.R. doc briefed me. This mark is from a high heel. Lucky you weren't impaled. And see this?" He traced an outlined triangle. "Matches the tip of the shoe near the ball of her foot. Might hurt for a while. Expect these ribs to go through the colors of the rainbow in the coming week or so."

"Is this going to keep me from sprinting?"

He smiled. "If this hurts when you aren't moving, imagine the pain when you do. You can power through the pain if you so choose but apply cold compress to the ribs immediately afterward. This whole thing is a sad mess of affairs. Hell, when I was young, when we got into brawls, we slept it off at our buddies' houses and let the feud carry on for the fun of brawling again. Now-a-days, you say something someone doesn't like, you're in court for a hate crime. Are you in big trouble, young lady?"

I told him a bit of our sordid history leading up to my lashing out. All the while he traded sterile bandages for creams. Long Q-tips came away with blood stained results. I winced every so often as he tended the wounds and scratches, applying ointments and butterflies or Band-aids.

"Her father is the Sheriff. He interviewed me. Says they aren't pressing charges, but this is my one warning. I've never been so afraid in all my life. Look at this pretty face, doc. You think I'd fare well in jail?"

My joke worked. He laughed.

"I'm no lawyer but sounds to me like some of the statutes on her threats, especially with the scissors as those count as a weapon, may not yet be expired. Sheriff may be watching her back and calling it even. Seeing the other girl, I'd be afraid to be in jail with the likes of you. Who knew Delia acquired a miniature bodyguard in you?" He apologized for making me smile. "These will heal. Cold compress to reduce the swelling. I'm writing a prescription for pain—"

"No, please. There was a reason I didn't report what happened to me at your house, Dr. Duncan. The last thing I need is some gossip girl getting receipts of me at the drug store to start a rumor I'm addicted to pain meds. This is why I don't get online."

"Very well. Alternate acetaminophen and ibuprofen. Change the bandages out regularly. Fresh ointment to prevent scarring on this one below the eye. Hate to tell you, but it's gonna turn black over the next day. Be aware that new bruises may reveal themselves over the coming days. Tomorrow you'll feel pretty stiff. Get up and walk it off every so often, but if you're tired, sleep when you get the chance. Your body needs the boost for recovery. Good news is your nose is untouched. I hope her father keeps his word, but it's a good sign when no one came in to snap photos of your hands and injuries. Skirted past the urinalysis as well. Just worry about mending."

If only.

12 | ♀

DOCTOR DUNCAN COMPLETED HIS **work,** then handed me a stack of discharge papers with instructions. I signed in a couple places, he wished me luck and left me to redress. The moment I grabbed the shirt, my heart clenched at the cologne and the memory of Klive's skin beneath my cheek. The more I sobered, the less I wanted to think of him, because the more I thought of him, the more I knew something wasn't right. And I should want what's right.

Thank God there weren't mirrors in exam rooms. I avoided the shiny paper towel holder as I jerked several to dry my face. *Crap! Had I just undone all the doctor's work drying my stupid eyes?!*

I trashed the paper towels and gripped the small slab of Formica. *Breathe in ... two ... three ... out ... two ... three ....*

No more thinking for now. Man up!

My shoulders pulled back. Despite the pain in my clavicle, I lifted my chin determined not to wilt beneath the mounting mess I'd made.

When I walked into the waiting room, my mother chucked her phone in her purse. The men jumped to their feet. Daddy's first words were: "Kinsley Fallon, what are you wearing?"

"I loaned her a spare shirt from my car," Jase lied. "Her shirt was damaged in the mayhem and I didn't want her exposed."

"Mmhmm ...." My mother stared me down in that shit-calling way of hers which meant someone posted pics of me beside a shirtless

Klive. Guess her Micro Machine Insta account was now ruined. All those pure pictures of perseverance, dedication, quotes of devotion with my photo in the blurred background ... all destroyed by this trashy wasted slut standing before her wearing a man's clothes.

She rose and crossed her arms over her chest. "Jeannine came in with some story about Angela getting into a car accident and breaking her nose. The Sheriff said it was a shame she was gonna miss out on the next pageant."

"Wow. Ironic we should be here at the same time. True shame about that pageant," I said, deadpan. "Can I go now, please? I need sleep."

"Yes," Daddy rushed. "You need to go home and sleep this off, Kinsley. I can help you with your bandages and make sure you eat—"

"No, Daddy. I'm sorry. I need some space and Jase lives on acres of breathing room. I can't handle all this pressure from everyone. Please, if Jase doesn't mind, I'd like to ride home to his place and borrow Tyndall's room. At least for a few days. The only good news in all this is that I'm on Spring Break. The bruises should at least fade by the time school starts."

"A few days? But your mother and I will be on vacation by then. I don't think we should go, Claire—"

"Andrew, hush," my mom snapped.

Coach spoke up. "She has a point. She's drawn a lot of negative attention. With her hiding out for a few days, the gossip moves on almost by the hour. We can hope she might be a passing trend by the next meet."

Jase nodded and pulled his keys from his pocket. He extended his hand to Walton, then my father. They both shook his hand even if they had a warning in their eyes. He promised them both he'd behave with me, then my mother told him he'd better or else she'd call his mother.

"And you don't want me getting Bianca involved in this, boy. I want grand babies, but not under these circumstances. Are we clear?" She pointed a stern finger in his face.

"Yes, ma'am."

"Don't call me ma'am like I'm old."

"Yes, ma'am," Jase said like a scolded child, grinning eyes darting my way before glancing back at my mom.

I took his hand, bid them goodnight, and we walked into the lot to wait for the valet to bring his car around. He lifted my hand in his and kissed the back.

"I see that!" Mom shouted from somewhere behind us. "You owe me a co-pay, Kinsley Fallon." She marched up to me while I almost cowered against Jase's side. Her voice and expression softened as her arm came around my shoulders to pull me into a hug. "My baby girl. My poor baby girl. Oh, if I'd been there .... That vile, two-faced girl never deserved a single crown for her fake smile ...." One hand stroked the top of my head.

I whined when she squeezed me too hard. "Ribs, Mom. Look." I showed her the high heel mark. She and Jase winced. Mom was ready to throw one of her heels in Angela's face.

"Best you stay with Jase and don't show me anymore. I'm not sure I can keep my integrity. Kinsley, this is so hard for me. My tiny baby. So strong. You always were a fighter." Her eyes filled as I sighed.

"Okay, Mom. Daddy, please take her home before she melts on the sidewalk. I love you guys. I'll be okay." I kissed my father's cheek while I overheard Walton threatening Jase to keep his private parts to himself or else because his star was coming back, and she'd better not be knocked up when she did.

Fortunately, the valet rolled up, and Coach silenced to gawk at Jase's Charger. Funny how men could behave one way, tuck that subject into a file, place the folder in a box in their brains, and move onto the next subject.

"You can ask car questions when I'm not a bloody pulp, okay?"

Also funny was how I'd lusted over this car only days earlier and now I dreaded the drive home as sobriety smothered shock, adrenaline and the last-remaining buzz from my system. The exhaust droned as we left the nosy onlookers in the hospital parking lot.

After several minutes of heavy silence, Jase said, "Here." He produced a silver flask. "It's for emergencies. I keep this tucked inside a hidden pocket inside my seat. Whiskey kills germs and pain in case of accidents. If I'm honest, sometimes I need to take the edge off bcforc I go onstage. You could stand to take the edge off."

"Doc said I'm still drunk. Too drunk to even have pain meds," I said.

"All the more reason to kill the pain the only way you can." He offered the flask again.

I paused for thoughtful seconds to consider the consequences, then decided I was done thinking. "You know what? Fuck it."

Jase took a double take with a dumbstruck smile.

"Yeah, I said it. Fuck it! FUCK IT!" I shouted out the window. I'd fucked everything up, so why not toss a couple healthy swigs down my throat to numb the shame? "Jase, isn't it crazy how you can work for years and do amazing, then somehow undo all of it in the span of five minutes? How messed up, right? Because my reputation wasn't already shot to hell."

After I downed another long dose of Crown Royal, I sucked my teeth and shuddered, hating the taste of liquor.

"Tell me about it," Jase agreed and shifted to thunder onto the highway. Something dark and frustrated erased the nice friend from Jase's face. He looked like a mixture of the guy who'd smashed the biker's face across the stucco and my seductive singer.

"You okay?" I asked. The cap of the flask twisted tight beneath my fingers, but I couldn't stop staring at him to figure his mood.

"No, Kinsley. I'm *not* okay. *You're* not okay. Look what that bitch did to you. I'm sorry. I promise I wasn't flirting with her," he insisted. "She's trash. I have a bad rep, but hers is worse and I don't want to be associated with anything to do with her. And, me with you? What am I doing?" He touched his radio. Nickelback's *Animals* picked up over his car's sound system. He increased the volume to drown my questions on what he meant about him with me.

What the hell?

He also laid his foot heavier on the accelerator, and the emptier the highway, the more he pressed his luck with his speed. Jase was blowing off steam. Rather than tense the way my sober self may have, I stewed instead about the words he'd asked himself. *What was he doing with me? Because I was ugly and bloody now? What didn't I know about Angela's reputation?*

The more I stewed and listened to his heavy metal, the angrier I grew in my questions. No way would he even hear me shout the way he was driving, singing, ignoring me. *Did he not care whether this made me uncomfortable or hurt my head? Maybe he didn't want me to spend the night at his house after the problems I'd caused? Who the hell could know?!*

I glared at him like I could telepathically send these questions to him, but he pretended not to feel my eyes. Eyes that seemed to almost blur as the whiskey slammed my system far more powerfully than I was used to.

How did he handle drinking straight from a flask? How did he question our being together? How did he lose himself and turn off all his thoughts to be with whoever whenever? Was that how he numbed the problems in his life?

Shut up Kinsley brain! Not everything has enormous meaning! Not everything has to be significant!

I closed my eyes in an effort to shut my mind's mouth. I don't want to think anymore. I want to be like my friends and not care, to be freed of my rules, the continuous conscience.

I want to be numb too!

I opened my eyes on Jase once more. *If I did what he did, would I shut the thoughts up the way he seemed to? Did he even think very much? Ugh!*

I unbuckled my seatbelt, assessed the space between our seats, the shifter, climbed onto his lap and straddled him from my knees. His thighs felt firm though his jeans as I sat.

"Holy shit, baby. This is dangerous." Jase's arm came around me. His palm pressed me close to keep clear his view of the road. My whiskey-numbed lips found the skin beneath his ear as my hands ran into his hair. His hand pressed harder while he uttered a sound I somehow heard over this chaotic driving and music.

He tasted of salt like the ocean and smelled of body wash. His wavy hair tickled my nose as I freed myself to answer every question I'd forbidden my mind to ask. They always filtered through anyway. *What did Jase's muscles feel like beneath my fingernails?*

Good, that's what. His mouth was delicious. Something flavored his breath that I couldn't peg.

"Kins," he mumbled through kisses to my battered lips like he could care less if they opened and bled. "Damn ... I don't know if I can keep driving this way."

"So, pull over," I said between changing angles and deepening the kiss. Chills broke over my skin when I felt him down shifting and slowing as we exited the highway.

"Here," he managed and tapped his neck.

"Aha! A sweet spot?" I pulled back and grinned. He licked his lips and bit the lower one.

"Be still while I get us through these last couple miles."

My head tossed on an evil plan laugh. "Not a chance. Let's test these skills of yours, Mr. Taylor, because I'm tired of wondering." The bad girl I didn't know reached between my legs to his belt and began unbuckling. I loved every wince in his face, the way his mouth dropped open on his heavy breaths that could be felt from my proximity as I watched.

"That's a bad idea, baby. I don't know if you're ready. You're really drunk." His free hand grabbed for mine to still them, but I slapped his, then popped his cheek. "Son of a bitch, Kinsley. If you keep it up, you're gonna get exactly what you're demanding."

"Promise, player? I'm tired of everyone telling me what I want and don't want. Right now, I know I'm so tired of pretending you don't drive me insane with every flip of your hair." I gripped his hair for emphasis. "Every muscle beneath your shirt." Fingers trailed over his pecs. "The way your lips sing into the mic." I leaned forward to taste his lips, softer this time, slower, and licked his lower lip. "The way the whores at the bar brag about the way you use them."

"I can't use you."

"I won't let you."

"Fuck me. I promised your coach, your father, man, this sucks so much!"

"Was that an order, or ...?"

The car finished puttering over potholes in his driveway. He shifted into park, pulled the brake, killed the ignition.

"Baby, you sure this is—"

"Shut up, Jase."

111

13 | ♀

JASE NODDED AND SAID, "**Fair 'nuff.** Let's get you inside and out of these clothes."

I pursed my lips as I looked down at Klive's shirt. He had a point and I was certain Klive's cologne wasn't exactly the aphrodisiac for him the way the scent intoxicated me. *Was this loopy haze partially due to the way my brain fogged when breathing Klive's air?*

"Hey, baby, where you at in that head of yours?" Jase interrupted my thoughts before his warm lips pried mine apart one, final urgent time. His tongue stroked mine until I moaned and unconsciously rubbed my body against his. Rough fingertips gripped my hips. Suddenly I landed in the passenger seat while Jase yanked his key, rushed out of his side and slammed the door. The silent sound of night replaced the loud rock music. Jase trudged to my door, opening and extending a hand. When I stood, my body teetered and fell back against the car. Nausea gripped my gut and flooded my mouth with sour dread.

"Oh, I don't feel so good," I whimpered.

"I know." Jase took my feet from under me. I started crying as he carried me into the house. I remember a flash of my knees on cold white tiles, pain in my lurching ribs, porcelain beneath my fingers as I gripped his toilet seat. Hot tears and hoarse apologies. A wet washcloth dabbed my face as I was tucked beneath a comforter.

Rustin knelt to inspect my injuries in dim lighting. Jase admitted he almost broke his first promise.

"Night, baby. If you feel sick again, I'm putting this waste basket beside the bed." His voice instructed Rustin's help with packing pillows against my back to keep me on my side.

"I'll take first shift," Rustin said. "I've already showered. You need one. You smell like King. We should've taken that shirt off her."

"Nah, man. Her ribs were hurt before, so I'm betting they're on fire now. Those pants were already hard enough to peel away without losing her panties. I can handle a few more hours of his shirt on her if it means she doesn't add any more pain. After what she's been through, she needs to rest. I'll shower, then it's bedtime."

"Any idea what set her off? I mean, what're you gonna do if she is jealous of your fan girls?"

"Rusty, there's bad blood between them. I don't know what it is, but her mom was pissed at her for giving in. Something about crowns. My point is, I don't think this was about a fan girl. She handled those all night and did a good job."

"Or, you *think* she did a good job while each fan girl she held back for caused her to lose her temper with tonight's lucky winner," Rustin reasoned.

"Hate. That. Bitch," I grumbled through pained lips. "Trying sleep...."

"Sorry, baby. Get some rest."

Jase's lips and facial hair brushed my forehead, then the lights went out with my consciousness.

When I awakened, the room was still dark. My eyes adjusted with the moonlight seeping between the slats in the blinds behind the headboard. I blinked several times as the snoring form on the armchair in the corner became Jase's beneath a blanket. I smiled then winced. Dammit.

I managed to push myself to sit against the pillows, testing the pain breaking over my body. A sheen of cool sweat followed. Tears pooled in my eyes.

Move, Kinsley. Man-up and move!

Jase was in such heavy slumber, I did my best to shimmy out of bed without waking him, darted into the hallway to use the guest restroom. The night-light revealed several small scratches marring my shins. Coach was right. Looked like I'd picked a fight with a hyena. How did she even claw up my legs? Had she clawed me elsewhere?

I filed the paperwork, washed my hands, then reached for the light switch in debate. Did I even want to see?

Another hand covered mine over the toggle.

"What the—?"

"You don't want to do that," Rustin's voice said from the dark hallway outside the door. "Give yourself more time to recover."

"Damn, Rustin. You scared the hell out of me," I hissed in a whisper. "So much for privacy."

"I figured you didn't care about privacy since you left the door wide open."

Nice. I huffed. "What are you doing awake?"

"I just got off shift," he said. His hand wrapped around my fingers. I followed him into the sprawling living area. Through the two-story wall of windows at either side of the floor-to-ceiling fireplace, large trees swayed in the wind, the moss flying like flags from the branches. Light rain pattered the glass and the paved patio beyond.

"Oh, no. Is it supposed to storm?"

"The worst of the line already came through. Sit down." Rustin urged me to the large couch and tucked a blanket over my legs.

"I'm not cold. Just hellish sore. I really pray it's been long enough to get some meds in my system. I should eat first, though." My stomach growled in agreement.

"A light cool front blew in. I'm chilled and damp after pulling traffic stops in the rain, so I guess I'm trying to warm you up for the both of us. As for whether you can take meds now? Twenty hours of sleep will do the trick. Although I one hundred percent agree about feeding you. With a temper like yours, the last thing we need is to let you get hangry."

I gaped. "*Twenty hours?* Straight? What time is it, you brat?"

He pulled his wrist and lit his watch. "Twelve-thirty-three."

"Wow. I missed an entire day? What a waste of time."

"What else did you have to do? Jase told me your coach grounded you from the next two meets, you're off for Spring Break. Marcus ungrounded you from the bar but hasn't put you back on the schedule yet." He straightened as he unclipped the gun from the holster on his belt. "Seems you picked a great time to get into a fight." The pistol placed on the coffee table. Velcro sounds came next.

"I didn't choose or plan this," I said, "but I guess when you put it that way, I'm lucky it happened during this time."

"That your first fight?" he asked. His heavy belt with all manner of clipped pockets came next, a heavy vest over the uniform, then a deep sigh of relief.

"Yes. First and hopefully last."

"Well, if that's how you fight as a novice, just imagine how lethal you'd be if you let us teach you some tricks." Rustin grinned.

"I dated a boxer for a year in undergrad. He fights in underground rings. One night he rescued me from unwanted advances, beat them up, then taught me how to defend myself if it ever happened again." While lost in wondering what Nathan would have thought of my fight, recalling the night I'd met Klive after deploying those skills to get out of unwanted advances at Gasparilla, I found myself staring at Rustin in his uniform, unable to help my awed curiosity for how he seemed to throw his authority on and off with this costume.

116

He chuckled when he caught me watching. He quirked his brows as he unbuttoned the shirt. "Should I put on some music to do it right? Maybe roll the hips? Deploy some of your magic moves to light you up as revenge?"

I laughed, but immediately grabbed my ribs and mouth, a pained whine smothered into the pillow I threw my face into to handle the pain that followed. *Stupid! Stupid! Stupid! Was that bitch worth all this?*

"Hey, Kins, I was playing. You okay?" Rustin knelt to lift my face from the pillow with the gentlest touch.

"Don't look at me. I hate when people see me cry. I can handle the pain. Just not ... I dunno how to explain it." I sniffled and blinked to clear the rain from my eyes, averting them from his watching me now.

"You hate the consequences," he mused, those electric irises so full of concern. "I'm sorry I made you laugh. I should've known better. You stay here and I'll get you a snack and an ice pack." He pushed up and strode to the refrigerator. "You like yogurt?"

"Yup. If pain meds are crushed inside it," I joked and enjoyed his chuckle, even if I couldn't join. My eyes and head weren't buying the twenty-ish hours I must've slept, because they hung heavy with renewed exhaustion.

I listened to him rifle through cabinets and drawers for silverware and a cup. Heard the water on the refrigerator.

"Your wish is my command, Mizz Hayes." Rustin delivered the yogurt. "Two acetaminophen, one ibuprofen. Your pain tolerance seems high. We'll start with this and go from there. Sound good?" He passed a glass of water. I downed them in one grateful swallow.

"Thank you, Rusty. I'm sorry for everything. And I like Rusty better than Rus. That okay with you?"

He chuckled again and shook his head. "I like it better, too, so that's fine, but, girl, you're *not* sorry for everything. You enjoyed committing the crime, just hate the idea of jail."

"Why do you mention jail? Did the Sheriff change his mind about charges?" Everything tensed in dread.

"Sheriff didn't change his mind. He's pissed, but I think more at her for some reason. Weird, huh? I don't know what it's like to be a father, but I imagine if anyone laid a finger on my little girl, I'd be a nightmare for that person."

"I know my father was freaking out," I said, zoning in remembrance of Daddy's near hysteria at my bedside. I shook my head to clear the disturbing image of him in pain because of my foolishness. "Not every father is a good father, though. No offense to Mr. Ansley, but if he was a good father maybe his daughter wouldn't be such a—" I cut myself off. "Forgive me, Lord," I said to the ceiling in legit shame at the venom she inspired in my spirit.

"You make a fair point," he said. "She's been more than kind to me, though. I guess other women make her feel inferior. Daddy issues fit the bill. At least your fight bought me some time before I have to eat dinner with her and her family again. After Friday night, they invited me back. Considering my new boss is mad at me, I'm not too keen on spending a whole evening at their house, especially if Angela decides to flirt in front of him."

I shook my head while devouring the yogurt. For some reason the idea of him with her family nettled. Rustin was a promiscuous flirt, but he was too good for Angela's tainted trash.

"Well, for him being mad at you, I am sorry. Have you felt repercussions?"

"I came in like a drowned cat, didn't I?" Rustin went to the kitchen, then placed another yogurt in front of me. The ice pack laid on the table, but a chill seemed to permeate the air in the house. I left the sweating plastic there. The cold yogurt added goosebumps to the flesh of my arms. Rustin didn't miss much, because he grabbed the remote for the fireplace, ignited the flames a second later.

"Rustin, I could've sworn I heard somewhere that daddy issues are a specialty of yours and Jase's." As soon as the words came out, I wished I could take them back. I opened that door. Guess I should own up and walk through while I had the chance. "Also, pretty sure I was labeled as having daddy issues. How do I have anything in common with *her*, and which is your favorite type to conquer exactly, Deputy Keane?"

He sat on the edge of the coffee table, looking straight into my eyes with that assessment.

"Kinsley, you want me to pretend I'm not attracted to you? That I don't want to grab the kitchen shears and cut you out of King's shirt? Maybe fuck you with it on just to enjoy the dominance over someone he wants so badly?"

I gasped at his candor. The F-bomb sounded so harsh when I was sober. Did I use that word the other night? *Damn, that was last night. How insane!* One moment I thought I'd missed only a few hours, now I felt I'd missed more like a week. I wasn't sure how to digest his words and how he never looked away. No shame. Just blunt.

"Is that why you guys are into me? Because of some pissing match you have going with Klive? Makes sense with Jase's sudden interest. It's not about me after all, it's all about him and some stake. The game you both play with girls who have daddy issues." I felt sick to my stomach with grief, like I'd fallen into the ultimate trap. The predictability of the cliché and how easily I'd let my guard down. Sad thing was, I'd eavesdropped and been warned. So, in a way I deserved this.

"That's not true."

I jolted out of my skin at the sound of Jase's voice behind me. Rustin didn't flinch. How long had Jase been standing in the shadows listening to us? Why wasn't Rustin afraid of Jase's overhearing those words?

"Rusty, grab the kitchen shears. Come on, Kinsley," Jase said and walked around the couch. I took his hand without a thought because the authority in his presence commanded respect. Something was different about him, about all of this. Jase tugged me gently from the cushions and guided me back to his bedroom. The bathroom. The shower turned on, but the lights in the bathroom stayed off so all I saw was a shadowed version of my reflection in the mirror. Rustin walked in to hand Jase the requested shears. My lower lip trembled in the dim glow coming from a single lamp in Jase's bedroom.

"Stay still for me," Jase ordered.

The hem of Klive's shirt tugged between the fingers of Jase's right hand. His left took the scissors and began slicing the cotton from my body. I hated the destruction of this souvenir, hated my traitorous sadness.

"I could've just pulled it over my head like a normal person," I said as low as the lighting.

"No, I don't want you raising your arms yet. Not until we get you under the warm water, baby."

Was this okay? My fists balled, fingernails biting the flesh of my palms as the heat of my body seeped through the expanding slit Jase cut up my middle until his body blocked my reflection. Klive's shirt opened in the front like a backward hospital gown. Jase ran the sleeves off my shoulders and down my arms, let the scrap fall to the floor. He looked down at my blood-spattered bra and red panties.

"Rustin, throw that shirt in the fire, will ya? Kinsley, stay still."

Rustin grabbed the shirt and vanished. The bedroom door closed behind him. Jase set the shears on the vanity. His eyes lingered on my face and trailed over my bra. Adam's apple bobbed. Tongue wet his lips.

"I'm not a promise-breaker, I have no interest in making our parents grandparents, but my mom always taught me that if you get a chance to do something, do it, because you may never get it again, Kinsley."

I gasped when Jase's arms wrapped around me. His fingers unclasped my bra in a deft second. My instinct to reach for my breasts and hide them had me trembling at both his touch and the fight to remain still and let this happen. Sensation and trepidation overwhelmed my entire body with desires, inadequacies, fear of the things I'd surmised in the living room swimming through my mind.

"You're so sexy, baby. Like an MMA fighter. No stakes or pissing matches. No daddy issued conquest. You aren't a trophy. You're the trophy-winner. Let me be your groupie?" His mouth tilted in that lopsided grin. I bit the corner of my lip that wasn't injured, trying to prevent a smile. Jase eased the straps off my shoulders. My chest rose and fell faster than before, the breath hissing through my lips at the feel of his fingernails dragging down my arms. The bra fell away from my breasts, their weight unsupported and vulnerable. My nipples and skin prickled. Jase lowered with the bra. His fingers dragged the straps past my nails to toss the cups to the floor. When he kissed my belly beneath my navel, I moaned in pure weakness. How could I think of pain, feel anything other than his nose running down the front of my panties before he gripped the satin at my hips and pulled? The smell of lust mixed with the thick steam from the shower when the panties dragged to my ankles, but Jase never moved his face. His lips kissed my thighs at either side of my apex. His palms captured my hips when my knees gave. I grabbed his shoulders for stability, my nails digging into his skin as his left fingers pushed between my legs that squeezed shut of their own volition. Didn't take too much coaxing of the most sensitively exquisite place before I released the hold my brain had over my body and opened my legs for him to do whatever he did best. Nothing but pure ecstasy clouded my mind. No one else. Nothing else. No pain. Not even when my mouth opened on a full cry when his fingers pushed inside me at the same time his tongue stroked where his fingers had previously been.

"I can't! Too much! So much!" I cried incoherently. Sense fled as my body wept pleasure so intense, I could barely hold on. He nudged me back into the shower until my back met the tiles. I barely noticed the cold contrast because Jase crawled after me with the most wicked grin until he pulled the shower door closed.

My arms wrapped around his head as he remained on his knees and placed my thighs on his shoulders. His calloused hands held my thighs to stabilize me. I was prisoner to his mouth, a very, *very* talented tongue. One second, I was bent over his head, the next my body bowed back against the tile as tremors quaked and melted every receptor. His name echoed off the shower walls. His hands ran over my waist up to my breasts, groping and stroking. Now, all I wanted was that talented tongue to replace his hands, but something else would need to replace his magic mouth. My head rested against the tile. Jase's hair gripped in my fists as I shoved him harder against me.

How could this be? How did I feel nothing but pleasure in the place of pain?

He groaned and deepened everything. His hot tongue massaging, lips pulling, sucking like making out in the hungriest of ways. I no longer cared about scandal. Something about Jase's obvious enjoyment coaxed greater release of my inhibitions to increase the sounds I wanted more, more, *more* of now!

I heard my voice, my cries, tasted the metallic flavor of copper mixing with water from the shower. My hair soaked beneath the water, the ends resting on top of my thighs and his fingers.

"Mmmm ...." Jase hummed as he pulled away and licked his swollen lips. He eased my thighs off his shoulders in order to stand.

He lathered the bar of soap between his palms and aimed to wash my breasts first. At that moment, I had a coherent realization of how bad I was being, but Jase tugged my chin to plant my own flavor inside my mouth with his tongue while his soapy hands massaged areas of my body that reacted in pain that somehow wasn't the previous agony, but an additive to this forbidden. The apex between my thighs ached worse than my injuries without his previous touch. Somehow, I never realized Jase was nude, until the unforgettable pressure pressed against my closed thighs to be let in just as I'd opened before. He lifted me, pain ripped through my ribs, but so did the burn of him sliding inside me.

"Ohhhhh!" I shouted and clawed the flesh of Jase's back, my legs wrapping naturally around his waist.

"Sonuvabitch, you're tight, sweet Kins," Jase's lips breathed heavy, his voice hoarse against my lips as he held still like he needed to cope first. "Your body feels amazing."

"So does yours." I moaned long and loud when he moved inside me. My teeth found his shoulder, bit slightly to compensate. Tears of pleasured pain masked in the stream of water. I was too drunk on Jase's filling me, the taste of his skin beneath my tongue and the grunts he uttered, to care about how I'd feel beyond this moment. *This was happening!* Not a dream. His tattoo was really beneath my lips, his fingers holding my back as he impaled me at a rate too slow not to torment, asking me about the burn, speaking to me between breaths he sucked. His lips and tongue sometimes pulled at mine. I knew the corner of my mouth was bleeding, but he didn't flinch at the flavor or avoid kissing me.

"Jase, more, please. Harder," I gasped.

"No, you're gonna feel the pain you've kept me in for ten years. This can't end so fast. I've waited too long to be inside you."

"Ohhh ... promise?" I managed. Every time I tried to force him deeper or faster, he gripped me and controlled the pace like he enjoyed and relished the torment the way his wonderful forbidden words increased this drag.

"I promise. You're the reason I survived the war. Always living another day to fight for the moment I'd be inside you, hear you say my name the way you're saying it now. Say it again, sweet Kins. Say it."

I did. Again, and again until I was hoarse, depleted, resplendent with afterglow. Dressed in one of his shirts and tucked beneath his sheets once more. His body spooned against mine, lips caressed my shoulder with tiny kisses until we both slept like the dead.

14 | ♀

I WASN'T SURE HOW **my body needed so much sleep,** but I wondered if Dr. Duncan was right about my not resting easy very often. I'd never thought of rest quality until I woke to the sun setting on Monday evening. Jase wasn't in his bed anymore. His scent was like he'd spritzed his cologne all over the place to get rid of Klive's. As if he'd need to do that after marking his territory on my body in the shower last night ... I smiled and stretched but winced at the pain in my clavicle and ribs. Parts of my body ached worse now than when I woke the night before, but other parts were more relaxed than they'd ever been.

My hands ran over my tummy when a harsh growl invaded the silence. Jase had his phone to his ear as he walked into the room. Well, damn, look at the light in his eyes and face! Talk about afterglow! *I made that look in this man?* I sighed when he bent to peck my lips and offer his hand. I pulled hard against his palm to sit upright.

"Hey, Pop, can I call you back? Kins is awake ... yeah ... you got me. You better not tell Mom, cuz she'll tell Kinsley's mom, she'll tell her dad, and you'll need to design my headstone." Jase chuckled full-bodied with a radiant grin glued on his face at something his father must've said. I held to Jase's forearms as I shoved myself to stand and move my stiff limbs. My neck popped about five times when I tilted my head.

"Yeah, we're still on for next week. Tyndall flies in Friday or Saturday. She hasn't chosen yet. Oh— Sunday? Okay. Kins will be thrilled for the company, I'm sure. If she's not worried about any awkwardness, I won't be. If she is, we will address that when the time comes. I love you, too. Alright. Talk to you later. Nite." Jase stole his forearm from me to pull his phone from between his ear and shoulder. He tossed the device to the bed. "Morning, beautiful."

"Morning, Jase. Or, should I say evening because the sun looks like it's on the wrong side of the house."

"You'd be right." His palm cupped my face, thumb brushed the sore spots with feather-light assessment. "Your black eye is fading. This is good. You hungry?"

"Yes, but shouldn't you be in the middle of a blues set with Rock-N-Awe?" I adjusted to his guidance as he helped me get my footing before releasing me to use the restroom for a moment. He waited outside the door and asked to hold my hand after I reappeared.

"Constance and Rustin will lead tonight. I took the night to help you."

"That's so sweet, Jase. Thank you. For everything. Last night was ... *real*, right?"

"What do you mean? How you slept for over twenty-four hours?"

My whole face fell into despair. *Curse my lucid dreaming and sleepwalking issues!* I couldn't believe I'd dreamed of him inside me when he'd felt so real! The pain in my body was so real. In that moment I understood where my feelings on sleeping with Jase were. Had that been real, I'd not be sorry.

We walked into the living area near the kitchen. He paused by the back door. My stomach growled louder when Jase grabbed the same picnic basket he had last time. His foot tapped a pair of what I guessed were Rustin's cowboy boots. He wore boots, too. That's when I looked down at myself. I wore a large shirt with the word NAVY emblazoned across the chest and a pair of over-sized sweatpants with the same gold lettering down the leg. At what point had he redressed me?

"You changed my clothing," I said.

"Yeah, after our shower you needed something to wear. I don't need my PT gear anytime soon, so you can use it. Keep it if you want."

I gasped in relieved awe and happiness. "That was real."

"Yes indeed. Let's get you something to eat before I'm tempted to eat something else. You are very tasty and responsive."

I gasped as his expression heated and lit my body like a slow burning candle, areas melting in remembrance. His Adam's apple bobbed as he swallowed. "Here." He toed the boots with his own combat style boots. "You're gonna need these."

My nose shriveled at the feel of wearing someone else's shoes. Jase chuckled as I tromped out the back door behind him feeling like a kid in her father's shoes. They clunked all over the pavers till I was seated at the little outdoor table. A citronella candle burned in the center although the whole area was screened in to prevent mosquito invasions. He supplied a large bowl of something white with bits of lime and cilantro mixed with mango and onions.

"I really hope you like fish. I didn't want you having anything too heavy just yet."

"Omigosh, Jase, is this your mom's *ceviche*? Please say yes!"

"No."

My face fell into a playful pout while he chuckled.

"It's not my mom's because I made it. I mean, it's her recipe, but I had to do all the work, thank you very much, sweet Kins."

I clapped with excitement. "I'm not much for fish, but I love your family's *ceviche*. Remember, your mom made it several times when I spent the night. That with some whit—"

"White rice," he said as he pulled the bowl.

"This is awesome, Jase. Thank you." I leaned over to kiss him, but something far hungrier growled throughout my reawakened body. I pulled away in alarm at the intensity of what had previously been our kisses seeming so much more profound now that I knew exactly what they led to. I cleared my throat and gestured he continue. His lips twitched. I didn't miss the side glances he gave as though looking for changes in my body's reactions with him.

He made our plates and handed me cutlery. On my napkin, he laid pain medicine. He passed me a water bottle to take my meds with. I chugged the whole bottle realizing how thirsty I was. He passed me his. We ate as the darkness fell over the patio with the only light being from the candle. No lights on in the house, no porch lights, only moonlight on the large pasture of grass and the pond in the far-off distance. A million stars glittered across the sky.

"It's so beautiful. I could never get tired of star-gazing out here."

"Mmhmm." He hummed through chewing, then swallowed. "Mars is mighty bright tonight." He winked.

I grinned with girly awe that he remembered the line he'd used on me. Although the way he gazed at me, the fuzzy fondness, made me wonder if he'd not been running a line past me, but cared as much as he'd let on during his serenade. He'd been the one to tell me men thought with the wrong head, first, heart last. I had a hard time imagining horny high school Jase thinking with the heart so soon into mine and Tyndall's friendship back then. He'd only known me for about a month and half at that point. I re-imagined that boy lying on the leaves beside me, the smile as he held his hands in a box above us to show Mars. He did look the same now, just a harder edge to his features. No more innocent hope for the future. That bothered me. I wanted to draw that hope back out.

"Maybe she shines brighter tonight because the clouds have cleared away," I offered. His eyebrows rose, lips twitching at the corner while he chewed. I took another bite.

"You saying a certain cleansing renewed your mind, sweet Kins?"

I covered my laugh, not wincing with the stretch of my lips as easily anymore. "No way, couldn't be that, Jase." The more I ate, the stronger and more revived I became. "I'm saying maybe Coach was right about me getting enough rest. Even though I'm sore as a mother, my mind is so clear the more hunger disappears, and hydration takes effect."

"Always driving a hard bargain, eh, baby?" He leaned across to kiss my lips, careful around the healing corner.

"I'm playing, you're both right. Sexual depletion after a six year fast, more sleep in one period than I've gotten in my life, food, hydration, yeah. But, don't you dare tell Coach Walton I said he was right."

Jase swallowed and a laugh came from his throat. "Damn. Six years?" He wiped his mouth. "I greatly underestimated your pain threshold. *And* your capacity for self-discipline. I wasn't sure if you were a virgin until last night. Lemme guess, the little punk who shattered your heart?"

"Jack Carter, yes. I don't want to be in a bad mood. After the last one I was in, I'm surprised you aren't afraid to tick me off," I teased to try and make him smile. I needed him off this subject. I didn't want to taint this moment with Jase by talking about my high school boyfriend.

He did change the subject. "Your secret from your coach is safe with me. I don't know how I will be able to come to any of your meets without him shooting me mean looks. That guy doesn't like me."

"He doesn't like anyone but his good buddy, Mr. Miller, the professor teaching Intro to Color Theory." I took another blissful bite and complimented him before I asked about Tyndall. "You said she's coming at the end of the week? For how long?"

His head tilted in confusion. "You haven't talked about this with her? I thought y'all stayed in touch on the regular, baby." Crap. I couldn't let on that she'd been in her own world with her boyfriend. I cleared my throat.

"We did before I became involved with her brother." I chewed my cheek as this was a real concern. "Maybe I need to get in touch so she doesn't have an extra reason not to want us together."

He swallowed another bite and a drink of water as he peered at me for thoughtful moments. "You saying *you* want to be together, too, sweet Kins ...?"

"Jase, if you want mc to pretend I don't want to be together again in every sense, I can't. I won't. Your pain relief works way better than these tablets." I grinned. He was surprised by my openness, but did he not deserve some after I'd pushed him so hard?

"Damn. Did Kinsley Hayes just come on to me and admit to being wooed into submission by my body?" His lips lifted at the corner.

"I believe *Sweet Kins* just admitted to being wooed by more than your body, sir. You went to jail for me. You shredded an Inferno asshole's face for me. Rumor has it, you've done a lot to keep me safe over time. Misbehaving drunks. Inappropriate advances. Maybe my ears are open to the rumors as being more than that."

"Rumor has it, Jase Taylor asked Kinsley Hayes to be his official girlfriend." His finger tapped his chin, eyes narrowed playfully. "What did those rumors say about her response?"

I snickered and drank some of my water. "Well, if we're going off rumors? She's a bisexual Bible-thumper with daddy issues who is sleeping with two men, not one. Not sure I've heard anything about her response."

He winced as his humor vanished. "Bisexual?"

"Yeah. I guess being a tomboy makes me 'butch'." I did air quotes.

"That's bullshit. You may have a tough streak in you, and you can be mean as all get out, but you are feminine in every facet you choose to be. Round hips, delicate bone structure. Full boobs. Gorgeous legs. Your butch features are tying me in knots right now."

"That's really sweet. Thank you, sir."

"You're welcome. Wanna go for a ride?" He laughed when I gasped at what I thought was innuendo. "On the four-wheeler, baby. I gotta feed the animals."

"Animals? You don't have any pets."

"I feed the neighbor's cows while he's away at some beef meeting in the Capitol. We can talk about other rides later when our chores are done, though. Sound good?"

15 | ♀

JASE OPENED THE SMALL **side door** of the outdoorsy golf cart with mud tires and four-wheel drive. I tromped through the grass on the side of the house and let him assist me through the sore spots of getting seated.

"You're not bothered by us leaving our stuff on the patio for now?" I'd have thought his OCD would've kicked in at our mess.

"Nah. We can clean up when we get back. Here, you take the flashlight." He placed a large spotlight in my hands and closed the door. On his side, he started the vehicle and shifted into gear. I squealed as he floored the gas. We barreled across the pasture toward the edge of the forest.

"Thank God for the plexiglass windshield otherwise I'm positive I'd have grasshoppers in my teeth!" I shouted over the motor.

"I'd still kiss you and enjoy the snack!" he shouted back with a beautiful happiness about him. Maybe this inevitable thing with Jase should start now? How could I not relish the ability to make this man look so clearly happy?

"Oooh!" I grabbed hold of the oh-shit-handle as we hit a pothole and I flew up from my seat. He hit the brakes.

"Are you okay, Kins? Did I hurt you? I'm sorry, I got lost in the fun and forgot."

I gave a feeble smile. "I'm okay. I'd rather have fun than not. Think of it as tenderizing."

133

He held to the steering wheel and shifter as he stared at me like he did math in his head again. I glanced at the path ahead. Thick woods lined either side with the headlights as the only visibility. Small insects flew through the high beams. Darkness closed in everywhere else.

"What?" I finally asked.

"Kinsley, do you like pain?"

"What? No!" My chin lifted on laughter. He didn't flinch but stared like he'd stumbled upon a piece of that treasure he'd been prying for. "Stop looking at me like that, sir. I do not enjoy pain."

"You *do*. I get it. Explains a lot of what drives you to the point of pain for the wins."

Several cows mooed in the distance like they knew Jase was on his way. He took his gaze from my face and shifted us into gear again.

"Kind of scary out here. I don't think you guys ever brought me out this far when I came over."

"Nah. I cleared this path a few years back. If you're used to being around streetlights, I can see how the darkness might bother you."

"You're not bothered?"

"I worked night ops. I lost my fear of the darkness long ago. I have some Night Vision Goggles if you'd like to see the cows?"

"I'd love to play with those *and* see the cows! Do I get to pet them?"

He smiled. "Yeah, I'll put some food in your hands. Can you handle the tongue? They're really long."

"Oh, I don't even care I'm so excited! This is the perfect distraction! You're so lucky to live like this. If I lived here—" I cut myself off. I didn't want to pull my own tie too tight with life plans my fuzzy head fell in love with.

"You'd do what Tyndall wanted and fill our pasture with cow pies and flies galore, sweet Kins?" He squeezed my knee to loosen my tension and make me laugh. His hand went back to the shifter as he slowed, though I didn't see the cows yet.

"Why're we stopping?"

"Dead animal." He climbed out of the four-wheeler. From the tiny bed, he grabbed a shovel from on top of a tarp. "NVGs." He passed me a case to unzip the Night Vision Goggles. When he fitted them over my face, he paused long enough to turn off the headlights. Everything went way too dark until he pressed a button that made everything green.

"This is awesome!" I gushed. "Your eyes are creepy though. I see that look, sir. Behave."

"You want to help?"

"With what exactly?"

"There's a dead raccoon over there. Coyotes ate some of it, but I don't like leaving animals to linger and attract other predators. I collect the carcasses to feed the gator in the pond."

"Um ... what was I saying about if I lived here?" I cringed. He blew me an air kiss before turning toward the woods. Amazing how he didn't need any light to see what he was doing or where he was going! I turned the night vision the other direction as my heart broke at seeing a dead animal, even if the circle of life was necessary. No thanks. I felt the four-wheeler jolt at Jase dropping the body in the back. The tarp crinkled when he covered the mauled fur. "Guess I'd make a wretched country girl, dammit."

"Tyndall hates this too. She thinks we should just leave everything alone. She hates the gator too, but I think they're cool. Mine has never harmed anything, and he keeps the snake population down."

"Isn't it illegal to feed wild gators?"

"You gonna tell on me? If you do, I'll sing your gag-ordered secrets to the rafters. We can go to jail together. You'd be sexy behind bars," he teased. "He's not exactly wild. I brought him with me from Texas. Dad got me a baby gator when we lived there. He was tiny. I used to hold him in my hands. When we moved back to Florida, Dad told me if I kept it secret, we could put it in the pond at the house he'd built. That was about twenty years ago. So, you see, he's my only pet. No one outside of family knows about him. He manages well enough on his own when I'm deployed, but he looks forward to my treats when I'm home."

"He's gonna get fat now you're back, huh?"

"He's already fat and lazy. Let's turn these NVGs off till we get to the cows, baby. Don't want you going blind in addition to all these other injuries. This doesn't hurt your cheek and eye?"

"I guess I was too excited to notice," I said. True story.

"What was I saying about you liking pain?" He took the goggles and put them back in their case. We wove all over the woods. I couldn't help leaning closer toward him as the trees and darkness became too dense to see beyond a few feet at either side. Then, without warning, the trees ended. We spit out into another field heading toward a long fence with a broad gate. He drove over the cattle guard after entering a code into a little box. The gate swung wide, he waited till the metal closed behind us.

"Oh my gosh! They're chasing us!" I shouted as the cows galloped with the four-wheeler while he floored the gas. "Ew!"

"Yup! Smells good, huh? You wanted cows in my pasture, Farmer Jane?"

"I changed my mind, Farmer Jase!" We grinned together as grasshoppers flew from the grass in front of us. Even if the cow patties reeked and made our tires skid for a few seconds with every one we ran over, I loved and hated the cows stampeding with us. I loved the barn, the smell of hay, the sound of grain pouring into buckets we hauled to a large trough. Well, *he* hauled them while I watched with impressed reverie for how strong Jase really was. The chords he stroked on his guitar during performances had nothing on the cords of muscle lifting brimming five-gallon buckets. He scooped grain into my palms and grinned as I giggled at the fuzzy noses, cringed when the tongues came.

"I never realized how large even calves are!" I gushed as I fed the babies. They were almost as tall as me and only a week old. Gosh, they were super cute, though. My hands were thoroughly filthy by the time we climbed back into the four-wheeler to head across the pasture without a stampede on our tracks this time. The gate closed behind us and the woods enveloped our headlights.

"I swear if Sasquatch comes out of here, I'm pushing you out to contend with him while I leave you in the dust!" I joked.

He laughed. "Nice to see you love me, too, baby. Hold on to the handle. Sharp left coming up!" I grabbed the handle and squealed as we fishtailed on mud and moss when we entered a different trail. Large tire tracks created huge divots and bumps for the four-wheeler tires to contend with. My brow creased.

"You bring your truck out here?"

"Yeah, sometimes when I feel like mudding. Look! See the pond up ahead? I betcha Torro is waiting for his evening snack."

I couldn't help tensing. "Torro? Is that your alligator's name?"

"Yeah. AlligaTOR? I was fascinated by bull fighters when I was a kid. I decided to play on the word."

Okay, I guess I could understand why Jase pried for buried treasure. These little nuggets of insight into his childhood before I'd known him or Tyndall were pretty endearing. Even if I was tense at the idea of meeting Torro, I loved knowing about him because Jase shared a piece of himself that the war hadn't stolen.

A few minutes later we stopped in the clearing with the large pond. He killed the four-wheeler and the lights. Cicadas thundered throughout the silent night. The house loomed dark in the distance. Jase replaced the NVGs on my head and the flashlight in my hand. The house's details came into view. The tarp crinkled. I heard a distant growl. A shudder went all through me as I chose to stand close to Jase despite wanting to cry for the poor raccoon.

"Baby, he's already dead. Even if you wanted to resurrect him somehow, you'd be looking at *Pet Cemetery* terror. Half his face is gone."

"TMI, Jase. Thanks."

"No sense crying over something you can't change is all I'm saying. You see Torro yet?"

I looked at the pond. Eyes shined above the water's surface in the goggles. I gulped. "Yeah. He's swimming toward the dock."

"I'm gonna turn off the goggles so we can turn on the flashlight. I need to see what I'm doing. You don't have to look if you can't handle it."

Ugh. *Handle* was a trigger word of mine. How much did Micro Machine really need to handle? I mean, wasn't the pulp on my face enough to handle for the time being?

He laid the tarp onto the wooden planks we walked onto. "Hey Torro, buddy, I brought you somethin'. Also, you need to meet your new mom. I need you to see so you won't eat this one."

Jase grabbed my hips to rock me, pretended he was going to push me in. My scream silenced the cicadas. Jase's laughter filled the quiet immediately after.

"Asshole!" I shouted. "You do that again, Torro's gonna have another snack and become an orphan!"

He clicked on the flashlight, revealing a huge smile. I couldn't be mad at him when the gator came into view below. I watched in awe as the gator's mouth opened wide. Before I even had the chance to turn away, Jase rolled the racoon out of the tarp into Torro's mouth that snapped closed. Torro thrashed for just a second like he needed to kill the dead animal. I felt the tail slap one of the beams for the dock. My hands shot out for balance. A foolish turtle swam up as though curious, but Torro left him alone. To see the tiny animal stare up at me wondering where his own treat was helped to calm the chaos in my heartbeat.

"You okay, baby?" Jase leaned on the railing just like he did when watching the waves at the beach. I stood in the middle holding to nothing like the wood beneath us would collapse any second.

"I'm a little miffed."

"There's an app for that," Jase said. He took my hand with the stuff in his other and led us back to the four-wheeler.

"What do you mean?" I asked as I got in my seat. He didn't answer, just started the four-wheeler, punched the gas so I jerked back against the seat. The trek over all those tire tracks was a damn mess as he spun out and caked us in mud on purpose.

My arms blocked my face. "What in the world, Jase!"

"Have a little fun, woman! Quit being so uptight. Play in the mud and the rain!"

"It's not raining!" I blocked my eyes from a large splash.

"You were saying?" He shot me a vindicated smile. "Guess who needs another shower?"

16 | ♀

BY THE TIME WE parked the four-wheeler back on the side of the house, Jase said he wasn't letting us walk through the house this muddy. "You do look fun to mud wrestle with if you weren't already recovering from your last fight. Damn, what I wouldn't have given to see a replay in mud. Sexy."

"Jase, are you trying to provoke a fight you won't think is sexy?" I asked. He turned on the water hose.

"Kinsley, you want me to pretend two chicks fighting in mud isn't hot? Especially two hot chicks? She's a beauty queen. If I said she wasn't pretty you'd be able to call me a liar and doubt everything else I say to you. Thing is, you're hotter to me. Two women fighting is hot. Two hot women fighting ... well ...." He sprayed his boots. "Rustin said you told him your ex taught you how to fight, that he was some underground boxer?" Jase sprayed my boots, well Rustin's boots, clean.

"That's correct."

"What's his name?"

"Why, so you can have a problem with him too?"

"Why would I have a problem with a guy who taught you to kick ass and couldn't hold onto you? I want to know because maybe I've played around in the underground myself in spare times. Maybe I've already kicked his ass."

I peered up at his shadowed face. "No way you know each other. He's not military."

"That you knew of."

"I'd have known."

Jase snorted to himself. "You think so? Some men hide exactly who they are in plain sight women seem blind to."

"What's that supposed to mean?"

He shook his head. "What's his name, Kins?"

"Nathan Knox."

Jase gave an impressed whistle. "I know Nate. Two years older than me. Delta force. Went to school after being forcibly removed from the field for a knee injury. He had surgery, but they wouldn't put him back on mission because of the vulnerability. He went to underground fighting. He ever let you come watch?"

"No. He always told me it would make him weak and distracted. Told me I could kiss the bruises afterward."

Jase ignored my irritated dig. "I've not gone against him before, but he's not a bad guy to learn from, Kins. You had no idea the master you were taught under, did you? Marcus hated him because he beat the shit out of several guys he'd trained. Lost bets."

"What the hell?" I didn't know what to say.

"Bet you didn't know Marcus is co-owner of a gym, did you?"

"No." I also didn't know how to feel about the secrets Nathan must've kept throughout our relationship. I felt betrayed all over again.

"Where do you think Marcus found Gustav and Jarrell? Every bouncer the bar has ever had since coming under new ownership was one of his students first. You didn't know your world was so small, or that Nightshade sometimes poaches Marcus's boxers. They even tried to get Nate to join, but he up and left the lifestyle and the area. Married a sweet woman, has a kid. He's in Pensacola now, close to family, some gravy job on base running boats."

"Nathan left because of Nightshade?"

"He'd never become someone so dishonest. Good man. Better than me."

"What are you saying, Jase? Has Nightshade tried to recruit *you*? If so, we'd better throw the brakes on our relationship right now, because I'm a good woman. How old is his kid?" I dared ask what I shouldn't.

"I dunno, I think like two or three. Why?"

"No!" My chest heaved under emotional overload. "If Nate was such a good man, he wouldn't have abandoned me at Gasparilla or dumped me without a word."

"Nate *dumped* you? *Abandoned* you? When? He would've never done that. Something must've happened, Kins."

"Yeah, apparently another woman happened." I couldn't breathe. I wished Klive was in front of me infusing calm with his gray eyes alone. "If Nathan could keep the rest of his world secret, then he must've kept another woman secret, too." When I looked at Jase, the worst was that he didn't contradict my words with his expression. "Or, maybe he kept *me* secret from another woman ...."

"I shouldn't have brought this up. I had no way of knowing he was dating you."

"I'm so glad I never slept with that cheating son-of-a-bitch! I wish his boxing ass were here so I could nail him in the knee and re-injure his old wound to know what this feels like!"

Jase sprayed the hose over my body while I sputtered through tears I hated shedding over someone who'd used me. *This was humiliating!* Having a wound opened by someone who knew more about my own relationship than I had!

I replayed Gasparilla. *Oh, Nathan, I want to be with you the way you say you want to be together, but I promised to wait till marriage. If you think you're ready to commit to me that way, I'll do something out of my comfort zone in honor of you doing something out of yours.*

I hate Gasparilla, but for you, I'll go. Wear a stupid costume. Meet by the Bay at four. If you show, we spend the night in a room, seal the promise of being together. If you don't show, I'll know, and we won't waste any more time battling against our sexual desires. Fair?

I should've known as soon as he'd kissed me with as much desperate fervor as a man staring at a swimming pool mirage in the desert. The dream of us vanished the same the very next night when instead of his hands on my body, those fraternity brothers had taken liberty with what Nathan had thrown away for someone else.

I guess I let some of my pain leak, because Jase grabbed my wet torso and pulled me to his.

"Hey, calm down. I don't think he meant to hurt you."

"Don't defend him. I knew, dammit. Deep down I just knew something had to be wrong if a man was able to be with me without pressuring me to have sex all the time. Did this other woman and I go to school together? Was she part of my haters club? Laughing at me all the while as she banged my boyfriend because I wouldn't?" I buried my face into Jase's wet chest. "Sometimes people are shitty, period."

"Tell me about it!" Rustin said as he rounded the side of the house. "I've been looking for y'all. Where'd you go? Your truck and Charger are both here."

"We went to feed the cows and Torro. What's wrong? Don't tell me I have two pissy roomies to deal with tonight," Jase said. "You're back early. Did something happen with Rock-N-Awe?"

"She's shivering. You guys should get into dry clothes while I dig into your leftovers, or did you eat it all? You left the stuff all over the table. I cleaned it up since you didn't. Man, those are my snake skins! You got them wet!"

"Damn, Rustin!" Jase said. He ran a hand over my hair, then pulled back to turn off the water. "I'm gonna need you to ease up on the attitude. Are you blind or just insensitive? Can't you see she's dealing with some shit? They're cowboy boots, *cowboy*. They were made to be outside in rugged environments. Come on, Kins."

Jase cupped my shoulders on our way to the back door. Rustin's abnormal attitude problem stole from mine. I didn't like seeing him in a bad mood.

"I'm sorry," I told Rustin as I slipped out of the boots inside the house. He sighed, deflated. His finger hooked my chin.

"It's not your fault. It's *his*."

Funny, that's exactly how I felt about effin Nathan right now.

My eyes flared at the way Rustin glared at Jase. Jase shook his head. I expected Jase to bitch about the droplets we trailed over the carpet as we trekked to his room, but he didn't. He also didn't take me to the shower again. He helped me out of the clothing in the bright light of the bathroom. My hand cupped my gasp as I saw my body for the first time, my ugly face! Tears welled at the huge welt on my left cheekbone. The coloring all over the bruises marring my body and face.

"How can you stand to look at me?" My tears spilled over.

"Because as ugly as you think you are, I think you're beautiful, baby. No tears. You've cried enough. Leave Nate in the past. The bruises he left and the ones on your body will heal with time. If you'd ended up with him, you'd have to worry about being a stepmom. Consider yourself lucky. We'd never have had a chance together. Now, I need you to gather your emotions so I can focus on Rusty's. I haven't seen him this way in years. Can you dry those eyes for me?"

"After we get my fresh shirt on?" I managed. "I might cry again just lifting my arms."

"When we go into the living room, you're holding an ice pack to those ribs. You hear me? I may need it close by to cool my jets if he pisses me off."

I cringed at his irritation and my pain while my hands entered the sleeves of the dry shirt. He didn't make me step into pants. He jerked a pair of jeans up his legs and buttoned the low-slung waist. Something unfurled inside me. I leaned forward to run my fingers along his happy trail and the cuts of his hip bones showing just above the pants. These areas drove every straight woman at the bar insane with longing.

"I'll use the ice pack to cool my own jets if you go without a shirt," I dared. My eyes filled with a different emotion. He was right. Had Nate not cheated, I would've never experienced Jase. That was enough to shove Mr. Knox to the dark, dusty, disorganized files in the back of my mind. I did look forward to one of those bonfire breakup rituals to burn his photo when Tyndall came to visit, though.

Jase licked his lips, bit his lower as I watched him consider whether to leave Rustin to his own issues in favor of handling mine now.

"Bros before hos?" I teased but jerked his hips with my hand holding the button of his jeans.

His hand ran over his mouth. "You're not a ho, so do I have to put the bro before you, baby?"

"Put him before me and I might become one to reward you for good behavior." I winked.

He cursed. "Just so you know, I don't think Rustin would turn you down to help me. It's sweet you think of him, but don't mistake him for as good a boy as he looks."

"And how does that work, Jase? You okay with that?"

"Last time I had a problem with something to do with another man, you put me in my place."

"Aw, how sad you give up so easily." I turned away and walked out of the room.

146

Rustin had a fork in the main bowl of the ceviche, eating directly on purpose, like he wanted his OCD best friend to be pissed.

Jase strode into the kitchen to grab a bag of frozen peas and an ice pack. He bumped the door closed with his bottom. Rustin stared through me, but his eyes stuck to the hem of Jase's shirt at my thighs. *What had that man so ruffled? If the Inferno dicks at the bar hadn't made him look so mad, what the hell?*

I walked into the kitchen. Rustin hadn't taken his eyes from the spot I'd been standing. Despite the pain, I pushed myself onto the counter beside his meal. My hand waved before his eyes. Jase stole my hand to slap the bag of peas into my palm.

"Those are for the cheek. The ice pack is for the ribs," Jase told me. A flicker of compassion lit Rustin's electric blue irises when I winced. He looked beyond me to Jase who leaned against the counter at my left so he could apply the ice pack to my ribs while I held the peas against my cheek.

"Do I need to hold you both back?" I asked with a look between them. Jase didn't look bothered. Rustin was frustrated. "Enough of the hundred-yard-stare, cowboy. Out with it."

Rustin shook his head. "One of us has to break from Rock-N-Awe. It should be me. That would give me more time to devote to kissing ass on the force."

"Who?" Jase asked. "Me or you? Or you and someone else?" His free hand laid on my thigh like he knew I needed the heat.

"Me or someone else. Not me and you. You think I'd tell you to leave your own band? Shit. Who do you take me for? Maybe I should ask Kins."

"What do you mean, Rustin?" I asked.

His frustrated look fell on my face. I saw he had a hard time being irritated with me when he hated the bruises on my skin. I felt insecure and ugly under his assessment. Now, I wished his attention was back on Jase.

"Why do girls do shit where they know better but push anyway?" Rustin asked, resentment all over him. I shivered. His hand matched Jase's on my other thigh like their joined heat would dispel the chill. In a way sure, but only because this was inappropriate as hell. My alarmed gaze shot to Jase, but he was indifferent. Whatever. I wasn't going to be a jerk to Rustin by slapping his hand from my thigh right now.

"What girl was supposed to know better?" I asked. "And what issue did she push that she shouldn't have?"

Rustin's grip tightened a fraction. I swallowed.

"Constance. She knew exactly what she was getting into when we fell into bed together, because I told her straight, I'm not the guy you take home to mom. I'm the one that makes a good girl bad for the night. Goes back to good in the morning. We go back to normal like nothing happened. We had an agreement."

My breathing shallowed in thought of one of my best friends being hurt by him. "What happened, Rustin? Did she press you for more? That's not her style. She's the girl telling the boys not to fall in love because she doesn't have time or room for love."

"You're right. But she was a dismissive bitch tonight. When I asked her what was wrong, she had the gall to get pissed at my sleeping with someone else."

"If she got pissed it wasn't the fact that you did it with someone else, it's whoever you did it with," I reasoned. "Is it someone she knows or has to see all the time? Did you throw her in the awkward middle the way you did Jase?"

He looked taken aback, a sour frown studying Jase.

"Rustin," I said, "don't look at him that way. Constance is his co-lead. You talked her panties off. Now he's gotta deal with drama in the band."

"Oh really?" Rustin asked, displeased. "*She* talked *my* jeans off, Mizz Hayes. Get your facts straight. I slept with Angela after dinner with her parents. Had I realized what a bitch she was, I would've saved myself the loss of reputation points. Guess nearly everyone at the station's had a go with her at least once. Including two married guys. Constance didn't even give a shit that I was already sorry on my own."

My nose shriveled in disgust. "I know exactly why she's mad. Because I matter to her and she doesn't want that bitch to have anything to do with me. She's protective of me. Trust me, if Constance was into you, she's not now. You don't have to back off Rock-N-Awe. If she gave you shit tonight, that's the one and only time she's wasting her breath on it."

I looked at his hand on my thigh. He saw. His eyebrow arched. "Oh, that's right. The queen of morality is untouchable for promiscuous trash like me, but I guess not for Jase anymore."

I gaped and my palm whipped his cheek before he snatched my wrist. His other hand gripped my thigh even tighter.

"Rustin, how dare you behave like I've ever treated you as if you were beneath me. Just because I never invited you into my panties doesn't mean I've been condescending to you. In fact, I thought you were a nice guy, but you've just shown your true colors, and they're as bruising as the ones on my skin over the very bitch you tainted yourself with. I warned you!"

Jase lifted the ice pack from my ribs and set the cold pack on the counter. "Baby, don't be pissed at him. He's mad at me. Not because of Constance. He's mad because whether he'll admit it or not, he didn't want me tainting who he labeled as the queen of morality." Jase pulled my lips with his very soft ones. "Climbing her tower to touch her all over with my promiscuity." More kisses. "Because he thinks you should be with a nice guy. But a nice guy doesn't know how to handle you." Jase's tongue melted against my own. Tension fled my body in place of warm desire caused by his hand running up my thigh at the same pace Rustin's did like one person with too

149

many hands. My mind fogged as my body seemed to come alive with new desires with a huge hunger for more lascivious feeding like Jase had given last night. The nerve endings beneath my skin sang like never before, and the louder they cried to be touched, the quieter the argument in my brain against the impropriety.

"I can't," I breathed as my head fell back when both hands came together at the top of my thighs. The peas I'd held to my cheek fell to my lap on top of their hands. I winced for so many reasons. "I shouldn't ... this is wrong."

"You sure?" Jase whispered against my neck. My eyes closed on a long moan when Rustin's mouth brushed the other side. I could hardly breathe. Every coherent scrap of thought ripped to shreds. *Is this what Constance, Bayleigh, Tyndall all enjoyed regularly? Was this what they caved into to melt their morals?*

"You aren't in a relationship," Rustin whispered. Yeah, I understood Constance a little better. Too much sensation sang beneath his tongue on my skin.

"You're in the woods with no prying eyes," Jase whispered. His lips trailed over my ear lobe. "The only male you fear having a problem with this is right here."

Not true. *Klive! Klive! Klive!*

But, Klive had this opportunity and didn't take me. These men wanted me. Both of them. *Oh Klive ... gray eyes smiling, telling me he'd love me forever while I sat in the bathroom at Delia's.*

I smiled and Jase hummed like I was heading in the right direction. My mind went back to Delia's guest room. Klive's lips against my neck, his hands caressing and pressing places these hands now revived. Klive bending over me in St. Augustine to lick the custard from the cone I held. Klive holding my ankle in the shoe store.

"No one has to know if you take a walk on the promiscuous side your friends live on," Rustin said. His lips trailed along my jaw. Klive's nose had run the same course when he had me on Delia's balcony near the banister. He'd breathed against my neck while I couldn't suck enough wind to keep my knees from turning to rubber.

"Don't you want distraction from your pain?" Jase tempted. *Yes!* I wanted distraction from Klive, the source of my agony, the pirate in the elevator, the man on the motorcycle prodding me to be a bitch, gifting me a rose before shoving me away in public hours later as he'd made me feel like a trashy girl.

I was being trashy now. Klive was right to shove me away. Just like he had in the parking garage while looking pained and conflicted. As Jase's and Rustin's mouths worked in tandem on my skin, Klive's gaze in my memory looked down at me anew as though I were causing him more pain now.

Jase's mouth opened on mine. I kissed him back with the same abandon I'd kissed with Klive before the hallucinations had started in the bathroom at Delia's. *Show me who was fucking with you,* Klive's accent said from my memory.

They are. You are.

I couldn't form words to fight the lusty ones the guys spoke into the forbidden chemistry. "Oh, gosh," I hissed before Rustin's mouth stole the hot air I gasped for after Jase's hot kiss. I moaned when Jase tugged my chin and mouth loose from Rustin's to taste me again.

"Nuh, uh," Rustin mumbled at my cheek as he stole me back.

This was wrong! I wasn't a bad girl! Not the girl they spoke of! I was good. Maybe Klive still wants me! Or maybe he'll want me someday! Pull away! Flee temptation! You can do all things—

A gag shoved into the mouth of the angel shouting on my shoulder as she fought against the chains the devil on the other threw around her swinging arms. The devil tossed the angel's bound and gagged morality into solitary confinement then tangled with two of her own kind at once.

17 | ♀

WHEN I WOKE UP, I was disoriented. Several minutes passed before I figured out where I was, why I was tender all over.

"Morning, beautiful. How you feeling?"

I winced as something ice cold touched my eye. My elbow jerked up to block, but pain in my ribs sliced through my whole side. I whined and put my arm back down.

"Jase, how do you think I feel?" I barked. Sun streamed through the room so bright I had to squint from the rays stabbing my brain.

"She'll be fine. I don't know who ever labeled you sweet, but apparently they had everyone mistaken." Effing Rustin. "No afterglow for Attitudy Judy over here."

I struggled onto my side to face away from them, but no matter how I shifted, new pain kissed me good morning. I huffed an annoyed breath.

"Ew, someone needs a toothbrush for their morning after breath as well."

I cracked my eyes open. "Please, do me a solid and shut the hell up, Rustin." Momentary anger gave me enough strength to throw a pillow at him. He pulled the silver pillowcase down and grinned all toothpaste fabulous. No injuries. No bruises. No bad breath, stiff joints, aching muscles. In fact, if anyone had an afterglow, Rustin radiated enough relief I should've felt some for myself. Instead, shame silently told me I deserved every stabbing sensation. *I'd slept with this guy.* What a sad thing to be able to say now. *How was this possible?*

"Easy there, Rocky," Jase said. "You need to be still. Here, these will help." Jase held out his fist, pried my palm open, dropped multiple tablets. He offered a glass of water. I struggled to sit up. Stupid Rustin sat behind me to help prop me up against my will. I took the meds, chugged all the water. Rustin kissed my temple and eased me back down. He fluffed the pillow I'd thrown and replaced the cushion beneath my good cheek. Jase tucked the comforter around my legs. His lips brushed my forehead. "I have to go to work. If you need anything, Rustin is here. Sweet dreams, baby."

I fell back to sleep.

When I awoke again, the room was black with night. *Wow! How long had I been out for?* Whatever Jase had given me was more than pain meds. The sedative he'd used had better not show up in my system. *What day or time was this?*

Aw! Jase laid out on top of the covers beside me. He must've fallen asleep waiting for me to wake up because he held a thawed bag of what were frozen peas in his left hand. His light snoring droned like white noise tempting me back to sleep. Too bad my empty stomach and full bladder had other ideas. I eased out of bed as best I could with the pain in my ribs and crept down the hall to the guest restroom. This time, I braved the mirror beneath harsh florescent light as I washed my hands. I no longer had a black eye, but a deep red bruise colored my right temple, a green bruise under my left cheek bone with a healing scab the doctor had closed. My top lip swelled in the right corner, scalp still a tad tender, ribs hurt when I put my hands up to my hair to twist the mass into a messy bun. I left a long chunk out in order to wrap the hair around the bun to secure the tangled mess without a hair tie. After a couple seconds of recovery, I lifted the long T-shirt the guys had put on me. In the reflection, the triangle and dot of Angela's heel marks bruised just under my birthmark. Scabbed scratches slashed the skin of my arms.

Finally, I braved the look in my eyes, into my bruised soul for the foul play I'd participated in. The hard look stared back like Micro Machine protected Sweet Kins from condemnation. I shook my head in disappointment with myself, knowing the shame would slam like a wrecking ball against the walls I built around my conscience.

In the living room, the television flickered silent light over Rustin snoring on the couch. He'd been watching *Forensic Files*. That narrator always put me to sleep, too.

I stole a container of strawberries from the fridge and found the yogurts Rustin had given me the other night. My hands shook as I peeled the foil off the top of my yogurt and rinsed about five strawberries. I winced with closed eyes as I held a cold berry against the now stinging split in my lip. This blew. Then I pictured the foggy memory of Angela's blood caked mouth and broken nose. *Could be worse*, I told myself.

"That's not gonna cut it. You need something stronger." Rustin walked into the kitchen with a big yawn.

"I didn't mean to wake you," I said in a muted tone. "I don't want anything stronger just yet. Whatever y'all gave me was strong enough to knock me out for what feels like another day."

Rustin grabbed another bag of frozen veggies out of the freezer and stepped behind where I stood at the sink. He took the strawberry from my hand and pressed the bag to that entire side of my face.

I sucked my teeth. "Ow! That freakin' hurts, Rustin!" Iced pain shot through my jaw up to my temple.

"Trust me, it will be worth it when that spot on your temple isn't bigger tomorrow and your lip goes down tonight. You've already improved a lot while we've iced your swelling when you slept. Here, take it."

I hated doing what he said.

He shuffled through cabinets behind me, then he was at my back again as he ran water into a glass. Rustin held more pain pills to me.

"Are you deaf? I just told you I wasn't excited about taking anymore sedatives."

"Plain ol' OTC Tylenol," he said. I sighed and took them, gulped all the water. He grabbed the cup to refill, but I jerked the glass from him to turn on the water myself.

"I'm not helpless, Rustin. I think I can get my own damn water."

"Damn, girl, why you being so mean to me?" He turned me to face him, hoisted me onto the counter so he could pull the veggies from my face and give me some relief before putting them back on like he wanted a bit of revenge on my attitude.

I was annoyed.

"Rustin, you know good and well what's going on. Don't pretend to be so dense."

He nodded. "You're mad at me again because I had the audacity to taint you."

My jaw clenched. "Stop treating me like you think I'm a snob. Is that what happened? You wanted to corrupt me so you could take me down multiple notches on some scale you've created in your head?"

"Kinsley, if you want me to apologize, I'm not sorry. I enjoyed every naughty moment of watching you release yourself of every knot you tie yourself in. You relaxed and let us give you a much-needed night of surrender. Doesn't it get tiring walking around with all that moral obligation? I know I get tired of pretending injustice doesn't make me want to take the fast lane with my own hands. Sometimes you just want to lose control. At least I do."

My shoulders slumped. Rustin placed a spoon into my yogurt. I ate several chilly bites while he was kind enough to cut the leaves off the berries.

"Open wide." He grinned. A berry went into my reluctant smile. Both our smiles faded while I chewed. "Was it so awful, Kins? Did you not enjoy yourself, because you seemed pretty sated when we were finished. You slept for twelve hours, no sedatives necessary."

"Hold up. You're saying you didn't give me anything to help me sleep earlier?"

"Nope. Well, nothing in a pill bottle. Just the tools the good Lord gave men. Guess you could call it a homeopathic solution—"

"Rustin." I held my hand in a stop sign. "The good Lord is why I feel convicted while my friends don't. I can't believe you have the audacity to bring Him into this."

He shrugged. "Bible says to confess your sins to others. Tell me how you really feel, maybe it'll make you treat me like a human instead of a demon. After all, no one forced your cooperation, Mizz Hayes."

My tongue traveled my cheek. "Do you just want to hear me say I loved the debauchery of such sin? Every time I recount the overwhelming moments of too much stimulation, I'm begging God for forgiveness because I crave the release all over again. I work on the mystery of being blind folded and not knowing who was who, which of you did what. Even now, I know my breathing has changed the way your eyes have just listening. How do I reconcile everything inside?"

Rustin pulled my thighs apart to stand between my legs. I swallowed when he leaned in close. I froze as I panted without thinking.

"If I kiss you again, maybe you'll remember the difference between me and Jase."

"If I let you kiss me again without Jase, I'll be cheating on him, and I cannot keep stooping lower and lower until I don't recognize myself."

"How can you cheat on someone you aren't in a relationship with?" Jase walked into the kitchen, tugged the fridge open. I jerked to shove Rustin away, but he held me in place. "Eat the rest of your yogurt, baby. Your stomach is growling." To my ultimate shock, Jase lifted the milk jug directly to his lips. His Adam's apple bobbed with every loud gulp until the jug was empty. He grinned and ran a forearm across his smile. The jug hit the trash can. "Rustin's lactose intolerant. Guess I need to buy more yogurts since you aren't. How you feeling?" Jase asked. He kissed my good temple.

"Scandalized, if you must know."

"But loose and pliant like a good workout?"

"Not at all. I'm stiff and sore everywhere like a day after a good workout, thank you very much."

Jase chuckled at my retort. Rustin left my thighs and turned the lights on in the kitchen. He set about making eggs and bacon like the sun should've been cresting the horizon any second rather than having set only a couple hours ago. Jase peeled, cubed and fried potatoes. He tossed homemade tortillas onto a griddle. I sat on the counter and watched them work around each other in their undies. Oh, if I were a slut with no moral obligations, this would be quite the cohesive fantasy come true. Rustin wore boxers with hearts all over. Jase wore skin-tight microfiber boxer briefs. Neither of them bothered with their hair. Rustin's normally spiked and gelled toe-head blond laid softly in a classic good boy cut with a side part and all. Jase's unruly hair fell into his face until I asked to be excused and came back with a hair tie from my things. Rustin laughed as I forced Jase to be still so I could create a tiny bun on the top of his head. Rustin's Tylenol must've taken effect. Even though the pain to reach up was harsh, the knife stabs tamed to a dull gouge.

"There, sir. Think of this as my way of keeping your hair outta my food." I kissed his petulant frown.

"Who said I was making *you* anything to eat, sweet Kins? This is all for me and Rusty. Gotta replenish from the life you sucked outta us last night."

I chuckled and noted the pain in my mouth didn't sting quite as bad as before. "Didn't you guys go to work? You gonna tell me you didn't eat today?"

"I went to the beach and pulled a double. Could stand for you to rub me down with some aloe gel. I'm a tad pink. Check this tan line, though," Jase said and pulled his undies off his hip. I whistled. He nodded and quirked his brows. I bit my lip at the flash of scarring on the tiny bit of butt cheek he'd flashed. He didn't notice because he scooped fried potatoes into a colander to drain grease. He fed me a piece. Rustin fed me a piece of bacon as he grabbed a plate to dry the strips on a stack of paper towels.

"Y'all auditioning for polygamy?" I grinned.

"We are kinda a packaged deal for as long as—" Jase cut himself off. Rustin shot him a look filled with pure venom.

"As long as what?" I demanded at their sudden shift.

"As long as you'll allow," Jase said. *Hmm* ....

"No, what was that?" I asked.

Jase and Rustin shared another look before Jase sighed and rubbed my biceps, a little kiss to my head. "Rustin thinks you should have freedom of choice without pressure. To choose me or him, both, or none."

My eyes narrowed as I stared at Jase like I could read more. While the explanation had a grain of truth, I sensed Jase also knew the best lies come with truth. Though I wanted to press because I knew there had to be more, I relaxed my demeanor and played along for now. Whatever was hiding would come out at some point.

"So," I said. "You, Rustin, both or none, huh? Is this Rustin's multiple-choice offer or yours, Jase?"

Rustin dangled a whole slice of bacon in a way that had me fighting a grin. Like he was tempting me to choose him based on food alone. Jase scoffed and pulled a fresh tortilla off the griddle.

"She likes my mom's tortillas as much as Tyndall does," Jase told Rustin.

"Ah, but I also love your mom's tortillas with bacon," I told Jase. Rustin cheesed at his bestie. I snapped in Rustin's face to dispel his perceived victory. "But what if I want more than tortillas and bacon? Say, maybe eggs, cheese, potatoes?"

Jase and Rustin both stared in dawning.

"Hold up, are you asking what I think you're asking?" Rustin asked.

"Well, do I only choose from what you have to offer here, or am I free to choose for myself whatever I put in my body, gentlemen?"

Jase whistled and turned to pack a tortilla with all the ingredients I mentioned. He wrapped the food, held the burrito in offering, but took a big bite instead. I gaped and his chewing lips lifted in the corner. With his bun and full cheek, smile, he was mighty adorable. If you could adore Adonis.

Rustin filled another tortilla with everything, wrapped the burrito, but handed me the plate he laid one of my favorite foods on. When I smiled in gratitude, Rustin held the plate before relinquishing.

"Mizz Hayes, you're a free woman. You make your own decisions. Just know sometimes things look delicious but have hidden jalapeno or habanero peppers without the grace of a warning or choice. You may not like their particular sting. Then again, you may have a taste for spicy things, but isn't it nice when the courtesy of knowing is there?"

My brow furrowed, but Rustin released the plate to my grasp and turned to make his own breakfast burrito. All three of us ate in pregnant silence. *Was he warning me about Klive having some sort of hidden sting? Was that from the same underlying impression I got of Klive, or did Rustin know something more he couldn't tell? Ugh.* I didn't want to think about Klive right now because that was the worst part about what I'd done with both men. The claim they'd staked on me last night didn't feel right when the only one I felt unfaithful to wasn't Jase at all, but the man who'd told me I was worth waiting for.

My throat filled with grief that made more than half the burrito too hard to choke down. While my belly growled in protest, I shoved the plate to the counter. They watched me like I was more interesting than the muted show on the TV beyond. Like my brain had a closed caption feature printed on my forehead.

"Do you have any juice?" I asked. Jase nodded, swallowed, turned to the fridge. Rustin grabbed a glass from a cabinet. The two worked together as if necessary. Maybe they wanted relief from the truth of my thoughts as well? Couldn't be easy to see my loyalty to another man, my hidden conflict with feeling that they'd stolen what belonged to Klive, not them. I didn't like watching their silent justification either, so I changed the subject.

"Jase what caused those scars on your beautiful bottom, mister?"

His brows rose in surprise as I thanked him for the glass of orange juice.

"That's classified, baby."

"Oh, come on. Can't you give me like a declassified modified version of the truth?" I think Jase read that I knew he'd lied to me with a modicum of truth minutes ago. He had a knowing light to his eyes like someone who realized I wasn't as dumb as he may have thought. Nice. Still, he played like I was. He licked his lips, tugged his undies down on one side.

"I can't tell you where I was or why. Let's just say, you should never underestimate a blind banana farmer with a shotgun filled with pebbles."

My hand cupped an involuntary giggle, my eyes huge with guilt for finding that funny. Jase chuckled, too. He ran his hands over the backs of his legs.

"You look close, I have divots all over my legs, too. Just can't see because of the hair."

Rustin leaned back on the opposite counter near the stove, looking on with an amused light in his blue eyes. Jase shook his head. "While we're sharing war stories, maybe Rusty should tell you how your God saved his ass from being blown up."

Rustin tossed his plate on the granite and pointed right at Jase with a stern look. "That is also classified."

"It's legendary, Kins. So much better than mine. No scars other than the one to his ego and call sign."

"Oh, come on, Rusty ... I shared my body with you ... you can at least share this with me ...." I sang, kicked my feet back and forth like an innocent girl.

"Dammit. I was on high-dose antibiotics. Couldn't help it," Rustin said to Jase, more venom in his tone. He held his hips, but the severity was somewhat lost with the heart-printed boxers. I giggled while Jase's head tossed with a full laugh that warmed the room.

"If you don't tell her, I'm going to. It's gotta be my all-time favorite. At least if you tell it, you have a chance to redeem yourself."

"Saved many asses, thank you very much. Not just my own. But I hate to admit God has a wicked sense-of-humor," Rustin said. He shook his head. "I had malaria, was on the most high-powered antibiotics no one should even leave the house on. I was on mission once I could walk again. One night we were being fired upon. Know what an awful side effect of those meds are, Kins?"

"No ...." But I nodded and bit my lip, nervous where this was going.

"Yeah, my team teases I had a bout of nerves, but that medicine gave me the shits like no body's business. I ran to the only wall I saw, team ran with me, all shooting to cover me as I dropped trou to paint the blocks brown. But the moment my team followed me to cover for my shitty moment, the area we'd been standing in exploded. We lived to fight another day because I had diarrhea."

"He painted that wall like a Wagner sprayer. Ever since, he earned the call sign, Wags or Wagner." Jase beamed with pride and slapped a hand to Rustin's shoulder. Rustin shot a glare at him while I pursed my big smile.

"Are you shitting me?" I asked Jase. Rustin's frown deepened while Jase's grin expanded.

"I shit you not, sweet Kins." We shared pure glee comparable to when he'd first taken me for a ride in his car. "You banged a living legend last night."

"Alright, that's it!" Rustin nailed Jase's bicep while Jase busted out laughing.

18 | ♀

WE SAT ON THE couch together after eating and cleaning our messes in the kitchen. I'd never considered unconventional relationships being anything I'd define myself as being in, but Jase rested my head in his lap and played with my hair while he watched a recorded game. Rustin sat at my feet and pulled them into his hands. I was pretty ticklish and laughed at first until I whined about my ribs hurting the more he kept making me laugh. Somehow, he knew how to grip without tickling so my tension melted into the heat of his massaging palms.

I dozed off until they both shouted at the screen at once. Jase cursed when his phone chimed. "Someone just pulled into the driveway," he said to Rustin. Jase stood and went for the door while Rustin leaned toward the coffee table to grab his gun from beneath his folded uniform. Alarm shot through my veins. Rustin tapped his lips and told me to calm myself.

"It might be nothing, but people don't just come out to the country, Kins. Always handy to keep a gun within reach when someone comes knocking after midnight in the sticks," he said. His voice was very low to hear. "Lie down until I say." I had no problem following his orders now, that's for sure. He stood with the gun behind his leg as he went around the couch and vanished from view. I muted the game to hear Jase speaking to someone.

"I came to see Kins," a female said. "Heard she got into a fight. You guys are normally just ending your set at the bar when you sing so I figured you were still up. I don't have your numbers and Kinsley's phone doesn't seem to get service out here. I tried. Now, may I please see her?"

Rustin came around the couch and tucked his gun back beneath the clothing. "You have a visitor," he told me. Sara followed Jase into my view. She smiled then gasped and cupped her mouth at my appearance. I noticed she held a tackle box. She saw me noticing and lifted the handle wrapped in her fingers.

"Figured I'd offer my expertise in covering bruises," she said, a bashful glance at the guys. Jase cleared his throat and told me we were free to hang in his room.

"The mirror in that bathroom has the most lighting and counter space in case you need to spread out the tools," he told her. "Rusty and I were just catching the game we recorded. Y'all take your time."

"Thanks," Sara said to try and stop Jase's nervous rambling. Seemed he was trying not to make me seem as ugly as I was while also trying to imply whatever she had to teach might take time. Poor guy. He sat. I kissed his cheek before leading Sara down the hallway to Jase's room. "Oh gosh," I whispered. The scene of sin had after-notes of sex in the bunched-up sheets, clothing scattered on the floor. A deep blush consumed what felt my entire body as I saw the bottle of chocolate on the nightstand, the lid still open.

I risked a glance at her while she chuckled to herself and surveyed the room. "Looks like a good time was had. Hopefully by all?"

My blush deepened as if she had X-ray vision. She gasped, tossed her box on the mattress and snatched my chin. My eyes traveled up to hers. They filled as the wrecking ball broke loose on the wall protecting my conscience. Neither Rustin's funny story or his and Jase's copacetic dynamic from earlier could stop the tears of remorse. For any other girl, maybe, but I wasn't them. I was me and wished I wasn't right now.

Sara pulled away to shut and lock the door, then walked to the bed to quasi-remake the mess, trying to cover over what shamed me so.

"Kins, just so we're clear, when I say a good time was had by all, I meant that I hope you enjoyed it as much as Jase probably did after lusting for you for years. Must've been quite the release, but I'm not getting that vibe from you. Please talk to me. I promise whatever you say will not leave this room."

Ironic that the bartender needed another bartender's unbiased ear to unload her burdens, but could I say a word without a drink?

A half-empty bottle of vodka and shot glasses sat near the chocolate. Sara's eyes followed mine before she strode over and took up the post I needed most. In a flash, a shot glass was between my fingers, the fluid burning my esophagus. "Another?"

Her eyebrows shot up, but she complied. I tossed the vodka, then swiped my mouth with my forearm. "I'm a whore. I slept with both of them. I'm also a terrible friend because Constance is into him." The confession tumbled from my lips, numb from the alcohol and foreign concept coming from me in particular. Sara was a champ, because while I knew she had to be stunned, she stayed perfectly neutral and nodded like nothing phased her. "At the *same* time." I melted. Her arm went over my shoulders as she coaxed me to sit on the bed. She tucked me against her like she might do with her son.

"Is that all?" she asked as she rocked side-to-side.

I choked on a sob and ripped away from her like she was absurd for not chastising me. "*Is that all?* What do you mean is that all? I saved myself, kept myself celibate for six years, and I— I—"

"When you say you slept with both of them, I'm assuming you mean Rustin and Jase and not—"

I lifted my palm to silence her at the searing betrayal I felt at the mere thought that haunted me almost as bad as defiling myself.

"Don't say his name. I can't bear it, and yes, Rustin, not ... *him*."

"And does *he* have anything to do with why you're in such a bad state? I thought he'd been good to you. Did he hurt you and make you vulnerable enough to do this to yourself?"

"He has been good to me. As much as I'd love to point fingers like this was someone else's fault, I am responsible for myself. How could I be so weak? I feel ..." I trailed off in search of words.

"You feel ...?" she coaxed.

"Like I *cheated* on someone I barely know. Sara, how does that happen? How does that make sense? And, I know there's something wrong with him. I sense it, but in a way, that makes me want him more. Because he looks so perfect, but he isn't. He's haunted and there's so much there, but he seemed like he didn't want to be seen together. I was pissed at him for that, but we had a moment. He gave me his shirt to cover me after my fight.

"I can't even be mad at Jase and Rustin for this because as much as I wish it was only a weak moment. Brutally honest?" I paused to look at her and take the offered tissue she pulled and passed. "I overheard their locker talk weeks ago. Jase and Rustin talked about sharing me. I knew better, yet walked into this. I deserve the shame. I don't deserve Moonlight. He refused to compromise my morals when I begged him to touch me. He made me feel special. Said I'm worth waiting for. I'm not worth *anything* anymore! I'm *ruined*!"

"Oh, Kinsley, don't say you are ruined. If you are, what chance do any of us have?" She pulled me close again. We sat while she rocked until I slowed to sniffles. "Kins, I owe you the truth. You've been so honest with me tonight. First of all, never call yourself a whore. You call yourself a Christian which means you're flawed but forgiven."

I shook my head in bitter sorrow. "That's who I should be feeling like I cheated the most. I made a promise to remain pure until marriage. An oath of secondary virginity when I went to a youth conference after graduating high school. I broke my promise with not one man, but in an orgy. Sexual immorality 101."

"Kinsley, when the Pharisees brought the adulterous woman to Jesus, do you know what he did before instructing those without sin to throw the first stone?"

"What? I can't remember without it right in front of me for the moment. My brain is overloaded." *And stunned at her going holy-roller.*

"Jesus was drawing in the dirt. Ignoring them. He looked at her like she was beautiful not defiled. He told her to go and sin no more."

"Simple as that, eh? Seems too good to be true right now."

"Too good to be true? Isn't this the very foundation of your faith? Don't let this stupid mistake upend everything you believe in."

Her evident disappointment stung. She cleared her throat and took a kinder tone. "If right now you find forgiveness hard to accept, do you have any idea what a big deal that is for a true whore being paid for sex? Not just someone who sinned once feeling like a whore in a momentary lapse of judgment?"

I searched her face. "I sin all the time. My language isn't what it should be. I've lied to my parents. Hell, I've done so much I never would've. You have no idea, Sara."

"Did you doubt your forgiveness before this?" she demanded.

"I guess not." I hated this nose in your own pile of shit feeling.

"Well, you've always seemed so certain that no matter how screwed up you were, it was going to be okay because Jesus loves you. You said he loves me too. Do I doubt that now because you're doubting?"

"No, I—"

"Because *I'm* a whore, Kins." Her hands cupped to her chest while mine cupped my mouth. She seemed angry, defensive and pleading at once. "My son is in private school because I turned myself into a high-dollar escort working the Clearwater scene versus the cheap strip clubs along the Industrial complex. When Marcus found me, I was a stripper there. All those dirty men and drifters, truckers, bikers, dealers. Now I hook up with rich tourists and older snowbirds. Noah lives with my parents. I visit him once a month. I didn't want Patrick finding him, so I separated myself from my family.

"Kinsley. Please forgive me. I wasn't the innocent I told you I was. I really didn't grow up with drugs and a traumatic childhood or anything. I had a good life. My parents were great. I wasn't. I knew everything, they knew nothing, and I was going to show them that I could become a model and make it. I'd make them pay for their words of love and wisdom that I resented at the time."

What to say? Nothing. Be still and listen. Unbiased bartender.

"Jesus set that whore free when he told her to sin no more. He was giving her permission *not* to do it and stopped her punishment. If anyone has stumbled and fallen back off the path, it's me. Marcus hooked me up with support, but I met Patrick. The rest is history, but Marcus never turned his back on me for my choices because I never went back to whoring while working the bar. How can I be sad about leaving when I'm not poor anymore? I've never gotten my hair done in a salon, never had a massage, a manicure or pedicure. Now, I go to the salon and get the works. I buy myself real clothing that doesn't come from resale shops. I smell good like you. I feel pretty like you. I'm treated pretty like you, Kins. I understand you so much better. Now, what do you say you give yourself some slack and be grateful you choose who you sleep with."

Holy shit. Constance was right! How could I tell her when I dreaded facing her in my sinful mutiny?

"Enough with the heavy. I'm taking off the mom cap. Let's get you pretty again."

We went into Jase's bathroom. I watched in a numb state as Sara scattered various products across the vanity. Years had passed since I'd allowed a maternal redhead to apply primer and various foundations and concealers to my face. Just like then, I transformed from blemished to flawless, but felt caked and baked. At least I didn't have teenaged acne issues to cover anymore. I found myself wanting my mother so bad; a person that stayed the same, that I knew, that knew most of me, but loved me. Funny, now her words at the beach made me feel homesick for her instead of Daddy for the very first time since I was little. Maybe I was a little homesick for myself, too. Like if I went home, I'd fit back into my life and pretend none of my dirty deeds had ever been done. I wanted to believe the guys' words about no one knowing what happened while I was in the woods, that what I did would remain here with the girl I'd been when this happened. If only.

Sara set a gold tube on the vanity and told me to keep that since the tone matched my skin better than hers.

"I still haven't gotten your skin tone down," she said more to herself. I looked at her face without fog in my eyes. She was too engrossed in working on the red bruise on my temple to notice my inner alarm bells. "I called the bar to find out when your next shift is. I was gonna come up there to see you and check on you there. Marcus said you're back on Friday night. What if I made a deal with you?"

"What do you mean? What kind of deal?"

"This makeup hides the bruises well enough to go in public without questions, but I feel like I owe you for my dishonesty, Kins. I'd like to repay your kindness and ask you for a huge favor. You can say no."

"Okay?" *What kindness?* I dug through my mind.

"You helped me kick the carb habit and lose weight. You came to my rescue every time I needed shifts covered to attend Noah's

171

school events. You came by to visit me after Patrick died, and what a fool you were. Coming straight to me after being attacked like you were worried more about me than yourself."

"Of course I came to check on you. Are you saying no one else has?" *What a sad idea!*

"I don't have many friends. Not that I've gone out of my way to make any. Which brings me to my favor. Patrick's funeral is tomorrow. My parents refuse to bring Noah or attend since they never liked him. That means I'll be alone."

"You don't even have to ask. I'll be there. Tell me when and where." I wasn't thrilled with the prospect, but no way I'd let her suffer alone.

"Really?" She threw her arms around me in a tighter hug than I could handle. "Thank you so much, Kins. So, so, *so* much!" She released me and our eyes met in the mirror. "Let me take your shift Friday night as a thank you. I'm sure Marcus has a spare uniform I could borrow."

She looked at me looking at her in the reflection. *I looked like her.* Too much makeup covered every character trait. I liked the few stray freckles beneath my right eye that I inherited from my mom. The larger freckle on the left cheek. Right now, I was a blank canvas, which was better than a Christmas-colored battered wife look-alike. I guess without eye makeup I just seemed too monochromatic. I smiled to myself in thought of Mr. Miller being pleased I'd learned something other than our shared love of science fiction movies. She smiled back. I let her believe she'd caused the happiness. Why not? She'd done a good job even if I didn't feel like myself. Mom would be impressed.

"If you are comfortable taking my shift, I'm gonna say yes, because raising my arm still aches like a bitch, but my pride is too strong to admit that to Marcus," I told her. We chuckled. "I have a spare uniform in my locker. Marcus got me a blank name tag, so just throw whatever name you want on it, and I'll keep my stupid shirt with the embroidered name since he was kind enough to let me buy a bigger pair of shorts."

"Wow! He caved?"

"Yeah. After my being drugged at Delia's party got back to him, he didn't want me looking for new jobs anymore."

"That was so messed up. I've been there with a way worse ending, but that's a tale for a different time. We've already discussed heavy burdens. As it stands, I bow to the queen. Marcus is a hard nut to crack. Don't tell him what I told you, please? He'd be so disappointed in me, though I kind of suspect he already knows. I think that's why he was fighting so hard for me to keep up with my shifts even if they'd gotten dangerous. If he presses me too hard to come back regularly, I'll come clean, but I'm not coming back. Only for you, Little Red."

"Why won't you come back? It's safe now, right?"

"Probably, but I make too much doing what I'm doing. I control my own schedule. What jobs I take and which I don't. Some pretty hot guys in town for Spring Break and the summer months. Makes me like the tourist season far more than snowbird season, that's for sure."

I couldn't help shriveling my nose. She did the same and nodded.

"Gives me time to save up for the winter so I can hibernate versus taking the gross geezers. I only come out for the uber-rich ones. Sometimes score free trips and clothes."

"How do you do it? Share your body so freely?"

She shrugged. "I dunno. It's just ... I detached from myself long ago when I rode the pole. When Pat started putting me through the ringer, I went back to that habit. He could hurt my body, but I kept my mind. My body didn't matter to me anymore. I guess now I just look at it as a pretty product but I'm still just me in my mind. I'm not my body."

I struggled to understand but couldn't relate. I knew abuse did things like that, but so much of my existence depended upon my body's performance ability. In a way, my body controlled my mind. In that moment, I hated the realization since I'd always been so gung-ho mind-over-matter like I'd been in control all along.

19 ♀

I WAVED WHEN SARA **got into her car** with her kit. Jase stood behind me, his hand on my waist like he sensed I needed soothing. Or, did he sense I was upset about what he'd led me into?

"How did she know where you lived, Jase? Has she been to your house before?" I asked, a little too testy. Some of what Sara said rankled with the remark I remembered Constance making about Jase maybe sleeping with her. *If he had, would he be honest? Had Sara tailored herself to look like me?* What a sick thought.

"She's never been here," Jase said. "I'm not sure who told her my address or how she even managed to find it since the GPS devices lose signal a mile before reaching my driveway." Jase shut the front door and led me back to the couch. "Hey, Rustin, did you tell Sara where I live?"

"Nah, man. Why would I?" he asked, stared at the game in-progress.

I piped up. "Because you brought Constance back here when she'd never been, either."

They both took their eyes from the game. Jase hit pause to assess my expression instead.

"Oh, yeah. Girls talk, too," I said.

I headed back into the bedroom. Jase followed, then Rustin. Both watched me snap the lid closed on the chocolate sauce. I frowned, downed a shot, screwed the lid tight on the vodka before collecting the glasses in my arm.

"Patrick's funeral is tomorrow. She asked me to come. I said yes so she wouldn't be alone."

"Have you lost your damn mind?" Rustin demanded.

I bypassed him and his attitude while I carried everything into the kitchen.

"The sheets need washing," I said. The hot water in the sink burned my hands as I scrubbed the glasses clean like they'd had something other than clear liquor in them.

"I'm sorry. I never brought her back here," Rustin said with a timid tone. "I didn't tell her where we lived. I've never slept with her. Constance happened before I knew Jase's rules."

"Any other rules of Jase's I need to be aware of? Are his rules why you talk to me like you have some right?" I slammed a shot glass face down onto the dish towel and crossed my arms over my chest.

"Baby, it's not like that," Jase said. "He's just worried about your safety. It's not a good idea to go to the funeral."

"I'm not leaving a friend alone to suffer. If that were me, would you allow me to suffer alone? No. I already know you wouldn't. Just like neither one of you will allow me to go alone to support her."

"I have work tomorrow," they said in unison.

"Then maybe I should call someone else to come along and keep an eye on me."

Neither said anything for a long thirty seconds as the tension amplified between our triangle.

"Both of you want to act like you're my boyfriends, make demands, decisions, but what about *my* rules? *My* life? *My* choices?" I demanded. "I hope you enjoyed your fill, gentlemen, because it's not happening again. We are *not* in a relationship. One night of release isn't worth the way I feel now. My insides are damaged far worse than anything you see on the outside. However you resent my convictions, you should respect them. Neither of you cared about how much my body and boundaries mean to me. I could've said no. I didn't; that's on me. I can't change what happened, but I *can* say never again right now. So, there you have it. What happened isn't happening again."

Jase swallowed, but nodded without argument. I hated that look on him, hated the pain I'd caused, but I needed to hate the pain *he'd* caused me more.

While this pain festered, I decided to get all sources of pain out of the way and ask what I didn't want to. *How else would Sara know Jase's longing for me if they weren't close?*

"Jase, what about you? Ever partaken of Sara's services, or did you screw her for free because she didn't want you to pay?"

His whole face flushed. I nodded and swiped at tears that fell against my pride's will.

"No wonder she feels like she owes me," I muttered.

"What the hell did she say to you?" All Jase's sorrow morphed to anger. "Kinsley, it's not like I have feelings for her, or we had some long-standing arrangement. I was caught up in *you*. I didn't sleep with her. I let her give me head because then I could hold her red hair and pretend it was you." He averted his eyes, shook his head. "Dammit. This is humiliating."

"Tell me about it. Rustin, will you please give me a ride home? I need space. My own things."

"I think you should stay and work this out, Kins," Rustin said. "What does running home to your parents do?"

"I'm not running home to my parents, dammit. I'm going home to *my* apartment! *Mine.* Where I live!"

"No. I'm not gonna let you leave my best friend because of past mistakes he made before you ever gave him a second look. You don't know him, so you don't get to insult him. Men are physical, Kinsley.

If he wanted to pretend with a slut for five minutes so he could keep respecting you, I say you forgive him."

"You would say that because what does any of this shit matter to you? You don't give a damn who touches you!"

Rustin stepped forward like a cop toward someone armed and dangerous. I narrowed my eyes.

"You don't know shit about me, Kinsley." He took another step.

I stepped back. "That's exactly why I would *never* allow you to sleep with me if I were thinking clearly. I don't even date strangers, why would I ever sleep with one?" I found myself assessing soft targets on Rustin the way Nate had taught me. That bastard.

"Why does anyone sleep with strangers, Kinsley?" Rustin asked, stepped.

I shook my head like I didn't know but was also warning him not to come any closer. "I don't know, Rustin, you tell me since you make such a sport of it. Jase, you too," I said without taking my eyes off Rustin.

"That's it," Rustin said. In one quick motion, he dodged my swift kick to his groin and grabbed my wrist to spin me away from him. He bent me over the kitchen counter like I was under arrest, grabbed my other hand before I could punch him in the balls. "You have the right to remain silent, Miss Hayes. Now, if you change your attitude, I'll let you off with a warning." He shifted when my heel nailed his shin. Both his feet came to the sides of mine and trapped them together. "If you continue to assault me, I'm gonna pull the hand hold you hated so much at the club. Do I need to do that?"

"Jase! What the hell are you doing just standing by letting him do this to me?!" I demanded. My cheek pressed against the cold slab of the counter facing the dark kitchen windows overlooking the back yard. Jase stood on my opposite side. Rustin gripped my hands like he meant his threat about the hold I hated. He bent his weight over my back. I swallowed.

"Yeah, you feel this? You had no problem with this position last time I was behind you. In fact, you begged for more. You weren't under the influence of anything but your own desires. Neither of us forced you. We gave you exactly what you demanded, obedient to your commands, Mizz Hayes. Truth hurts."

I closed my eyes, ashamed of the conflicting desire that shot through my body at his contact, words, the truth he told. *I had begged, demanded, commanded, hadn't I?* But that was then. This was now.

"You are such a little hypocrite," he said. "Busting Jase's chops over another woman in the past when you presently fill your free time and dreams with another man."

"Don't flatter yourself, Rustin," I spat in rage, struggled with no results.

Jase stepped into my view, tapped his chin, a smug expression in his eyes as he scanned my helpless predicament. "I don't think he's talking about himself, baby."

I gaped. "You're not going to force him off me? Where's your attitude problem now, Jase? All the shit you normally give any man who flirts with me? Where is it?"

Jase shrugged, leaned against the counter. "I'm thinking of retiring the attitude problem I've had over you. Where does it get me to defend you, Kins? Looks like you do pretty well solving your own problems."

"You sonuvabitch!"

"Rustin does make a point about your hypocrisy, does he not, sweet Kins? I only had that woman's head in my lap for about five minutes while she fulfilled my thoughts of punishing you for tormenting me with those damn shorts Marcus makes you wear, the wedges you lace up your legs, the way you toss your hair before you set orders down, slap men's arms when you laugh, hold to them to make them feel like the only man who exists for that moment in time. At one point, I accidentally made her choke on it, but she moaned. Ruined it. Sweet Kins would never moan if I did something she didn't like. That's how you tell the difference between the porn star and the real girl."

I wasn't sure whether I wanted to cry or scream in anger at the images he created, the ugliness in Sara's profession and behavior, my broken heart at no one being who I thought they were. So many conflicting emotions.

"There's the real girl. The one who'd be disgusted if she ever knew the real me." Jase inhaled and stood tall.

"Don't do that. Say that. I'm not disgusted by the real you. I'm disgusted by the real her. By your use of her. By everyone's masks. That you hate me even as you claim to love me."

"I don't hate you. I hate the entrapment I feel when I don't know what you want. Who you want. How dirty you make me feel in the wrong way. Not the same dirty you made me feel when I graciously allowed *you* to fuck my best friend under my roof, in *my* bed."

I balked, tried to wriggle free, but Rustin being the predictable dick had the nerve to grind against me like I needed a physical reminder. Jase watched from where he stood. I flushed, closed my eyes so I wouldn't have to look at him.

"Don't close your eyes, baby. Did I not say that I allowed it to happen? You know that I gave him permission, and you know that you had to consent. You keep admitting you gave consent, but I'm not sure you believe that or take responsibility for your part. But, hey, no harm, no foul, here."

He tapped my nose. I opened my eyes to see his honey eyes hot with desire rather than the disgust and disapproval I expected.

"Is that all, Jase?" Rustin said at my ear without looking up at Jase. "What else? You know there's more on trial here. Don't go so easy on her."

"Hmmm ... Rustin has a point."

"No, he doesn't!"

"Let's continue, shall we?" Jase looked up like he was thinking, a sarcastic smirk on his face, tapped his chin again. He put his hands behind his back and began pacing behind us with his list of my transgressions. "Well, you have *no* reservations about shamelessly flirting with other men, letting them believe they have a chance with you ...."

"That's not fair, that's my job!"

"No, you do not get to speak right now. We will hear your defense after I am done presenting my case," Jase said. "You've become rather feisty as of late. A little spoiled. Demanding. Entitled to throw your whims wherever while those of us locked in your prison have to endure the torment of watching and wishing for our turn."

"That's disgusting. I am not doing anything like that on purpose."

"Does that make it alright? Because I didn't mean to purposely hurt you by sleeping with other girls before I ever asked you out. Guess I should've sought a psychic to tell me you'd one day give me a shot."

"That's not—"

"There's the matter of you seducing Alpha Beta Asshat, Chad and the man whose name you beg in your sleep."

I felt red to my toes.

"I never *seduced* any of them!" *How awful that he'd heard anyone's name in my sleep. That they knew secrets about me.* I was so humiliated, and I also hated that maybe in that moment I could understand how Jase said he'd felt humiliated revealing the shit about Sara; something he'd meant to remain secret.

"I'm sorry for whatever perception any of them may have gotten. I'm just living my life, dammit."

Jase tsked. He looked at Rustin, back to me.

"You okay there, Miss Hayes?" Jase asked. "You look a little nervous."

"The *guilty* usually do." Rustin snickered. I gasped, but quickly snapped my mouth shut before I said anything foolish. "Damn, so close to a confession."

"What else do you think you have on me?" I asked Jase. "Might as well air out all the crap you think you have against me."

"Pft. As if you don't know. Nice attempt at swaying the jury, baby. Deputy, will you please loosen the accused's hands? She may not be as dangerous as she was. Keep your eye on her, though. She can be unpredictable."

Rustin released the initial hold on my hands but intertwined his fingers through mine, still holding, but in an affectionate manner.

"Continue with the charges, please," I said and rolled my eyes.

Jase resumed. "Not only did you seduce them, but you let another man seduce *you*. Should I pull witnesses, Miss Hayes?"

I grit my teeth to keep my mouth shut.

"No? Do you deny, Miss Hayes, that you allowed another man to grind against you on the dance floor?"

"I do deny it!" I said.

"Hmmm ... maybe I should have you arrested on grounds of perjury. I have a personal witness who saw the deputy, here, pull you right up against him while you encouraged him by meeting his moves. Were you aware of these facts, Miss Hayes? Do you deny your involvement?"

Well hell. I thought he'd been talking about Klive since that's who I knew I must've talked about in my sleep. No way in hell I'd said Rustin's name.

I cleared my throat. "I object! I was drunk. He took advantage of my inebriation. I didn't set out to seduce him."

"Doesn't mean you didn't. You left yourself open."

"Oh, hell no! You left me open by letting me get too drunk while you chattered away with all your little military buddies like I didn't exist. Then I watched you check out every waitress who walked past. Guess the only one who wasn't seduced was *you*. Did you need someone else to look at while you let your best friend take your place?"

Rustin whistled and squeezed my hand before lifting up and stepping away. I stood, glared at Jase. Jase's eyes held intrigue. Rustin cleared his throat and stepped between us, pushed us apart.

"All right, love birds." Rustin crossed his arms over his chest with authority. "Before this becomes a domestic call, I'm gonna do what the lady asked and give her a ride home to clear her head. We can continue this trial at another time."

"But—"

"Nope. Jase, you heard her. She heard you. Both of you have some thinking to do about your relationship. Kinsley go get dressed. Jase, go feed the cows."

This time I protested. "I love the cows ...." I almost pouted, but I knew part of me pouted at leaving Jase with that look on his face again. The way he viewed me festered beneath my skin. *How did he love me if he had such a problem with me?* Maybe Rustin was right. Because I was starting to wonder if I loved Jase while holding back because of his own behavior we'd hashed tonight. We stood in silence for a full minute assessing one another's seriousness.

"Go get changed, Kins. I'll meet you by the front door in ten," Rustin said. I nodded and watched Jase shake his head, stare out through the dark windows.

20 | ♀

RUSTIN WALKED OUT OF **the kitchen** and jogged upstairs. Tyndall's door shut behind him.

"Hey." Jase broke his own silence. "Don't listen to him. Come feed the cows with me, baby. Just us in the moonlight. Animals always make things better. You can force my face into a cow pie ..." he trailed in sadness. The legit ache in his face broke my anger into fragments I swept under an imaginary rug. "You can even wear Rustin's boots again. Maybe step in cow shit to get vengeance. What do ya say?"

"Hmm ... that's mighty tempting ...." I looked upstairs to be sure Rustin was still behind the closed door. "Yeah. Let's go feed the cows."

Jase kicked Rustin's boots away from the back door, looked up at the balcony too. "Hurry."

I couldn't help giggling as I shoved my feet back inside Rustin's big snakeskin kicks and clopped behind Jase as quiet as I could before we got into the four-wheeler. Jase placed the night vision goggles in my lap before throwing the vehicle in gear. We barreled over all the divots and dips the same as we had last time, only this time he wasn't gentle. I gripped the 'oh shit' handle and his goggles case while the seat bucked me multiple times, but we both smiled with the adventure. My bruises didn't ache as bad. My emotions tenderized along with my flesh with every little beating of the trail through the woods beneath our tires.

At the gate, the cattle trotted back and forth before we entered, then they galloped while we followed some of them. The stench made us share gross expressions, but I couldn't resist smiling even bigger at the animals stampeding all around us like we got to be part of their herd for a moment.

"Can I try one of the buckets?" I asked as we filled them once inside the barn. The cows mooed like crazy behind their fencing.

"I only have one pair of gloves," he said, "so you can take the lighter one. Feed the babies again." He dumped the feed into the bucket for me. I fought the pain in my ribs and lifted the heavy ass bucket, penguin walking toward the calves flicking their tails.

"Okay, I confess. I need your assistance to pour the feed into the trough. Don't let that go to your head, though, sir."

Jase's lips lifted at the corner as he took the bucket and did for me what I couldn't. Damn, I hated weakness. Admitting weakness was worse. I took the empty bucket he passed me and headed back to the barn, but he stole my hand to stop me.

"You want to play with them? Pet them while they eat?" he asked. I noticed he held the barbed wire apart with his hand and boot. He tugged me gently toward the hole he made, then followed me through. The fence bounced back into place. The calf's fur was soft and coarse at the same time beneath my fingers. Her tail whipped back and forth like my time was borrowed before she might call her mom to stop me from interrupting her dinner.

"Okay, I'd better let them be," I said with a sigh. When I turned to climb back through the fence, I slipped and caught myself in a disgusting cow pie! "Oh, come on!" I whined. "Is it on my ass, too? Tell me I'm sitting in mud!"

Jase's hearty laughter carried over the mooing chorus I'd caused with my squeal. "I wish I could tell you what you want to hear, baby. Gimme your good hand. I'll help you."

I gave him my good hand, but when he gripped, I cupped my poopy hand over his arm and watched him balk and gag. Now I laughed as he pulled me to standing.

"You can't be mad because you told me I could rub your face in that. Think of the arm as my way of going easy on you. See? I can be forgiving."

Jase shook his head, a stupid smile on his face. He held the barbed wire with one hand and held my other so I didn't slip as I climbed back through.

"Water hose is over here." Jase led the way to the opposite side of the barn. Over here, an expansive pasture with no animals seemed to extend for a hundred acres. So beautiful under the shine of the moon, like God's flashlight showing me something pretty after the ugliness Sara revealed.

Jase hosed Rustin's boots clean but told me to step out of them onto the grass. I did as he said while staring at an old windmill with a large basin at the bottom.

"Does that work? Like it's real?" I asked.

Jase snickered. "Yeah, it's like real, suburban girl. Pumps water. The farmer puts his cows into that pasture when the grass grows tall, so they have plenty to graze on while he lets the one they're in now grow again. Back and forth. The other windmill is further back in their current pasture."

I rinsed my hands beneath the stream, but my ass was toast.

"Guess this means you're gonna have to strip it down, baby. Wanna go skinny dipping?"

I gasped and looked around.

Jase chuckled. "Farmer's gone. Remember? The farm hands come in the early morning and leave in the afternoon. That basin beats the hell outta skinny dipping in the pond with Torro."

I cheesed like he was crazy and loved the way he laughed at my animated panic. I loved Jase laughing far more than the sting I'd sent through him earlier.

"You win, sir." My thumbs hooked in my borrowed boxers. I smiled at my country version of Jase as I stood in my panties before all play fell from my face. Nervousness at public nudity engulfed me.

"If you want those panties hosed off, you're gonna have to lose 'em, sweet Kins. Besides, I've seen and tasted everything down there. You got nothing to be embarrassed about."

Oh my!

Jase sprayed the boxers clean, dropped the running hose and pulled his shirt over his head. The button on his jeans came open beneath his fingers, but he watched like a man bent on righting wrongs while I pulled my panties down. His look dried my mouth and made other areas too fluid and ready to be touched. He bent for my undies to rinse them clean but ran his lips up my bare thigh before he straightened with the most wicked smile in the dark. Yeah. I was ready to go. I stared as he turned off the hose. While he hung my clothes over the barbed wire, I pulled my shirt over my head, tiny wince at the pain. I *needed* him to right the wrongs I couldn't reconcile; needed him to be the last one to touch me. Alone. Two hands, not four. Two bodies in the water we dipped into.

"Omigosh, Jase! What a feeling! I've never done this before! I feel so ...." I trailed at a loss for words at the freedom of air and water, nothing else. "I dunno ... close to God, I guess? Like the way He intended when He made the Garden of Eden." I laid back to float on top of the water unable to help loving the feel of my bare skin in the moonlight.

Dammit.

I didn't want to think of Klive. Something *was* different about being with Jase alone, though. Like I wasn't an unclean cheater. Right now, I felt like a normal woman with a dilemma between two men the way I'd been before Rustin had taken advantage of my weakness. Even if I'd ceased celibacy for Jase, Jase was worth the wait, too. He'd waited for me for years, even if he'd shared his body with others, his heart was with me. Klive told me to be with Jase, even accused me of being a cheater in his own way when I wasn't with Jase. He'd never told me to be with Rustin. I was my own woman, but the thought made me feel as dirty as the way he'd said those very words to me before shoving me away from him at the bar.

I closed my eyes to the stars so I wouldn't cry and ruin this moment. I felt like Klive might shove me away in worse disgust if he found out I'd tainted myself by being with both men at once, let alone allowing Rustin to touch me. Damn, I needed Jase to make this right, to help my anguished soul feel special again.

My throat grew thick with emotion when I looked over at Jase. He wasn't checking out my boobs like I'd expected. He laid on top of the water, too. I didn't look at his nudity. I saw something simple in his eyes. Like the guy who'd told me I was like Mars. He seemed far away, too.

I rested my knees on the galvanized floor of the large basin. My hands formed a box I placed over Jase's stare up at the millions of stars. He grinned.

"It does feel ... closer to something," he said. "I bet Eve was as special as you, baby. That's why Adam ate that fruit, because he'd follow her down into a curse, he loved her so much," Jase said. He went to his knees, too. "Come here. I need to feel closer to you."

Was I giving off a contagious angst?

His arms wrapped around my waist. Our naked wet bodies melted together in the chill of gentle breeze brushing our damp skin above the water while what was below should've made the everything boil as we came together. I lost my breath at the pressure inside. My head fell back while Jase gasped and found a rhythm. His mouth stole my moans while I wrapped my legs around his waist.

"I didn't bring anything, Kins. I'm all natural, baby," he said through slow pants. "This is dangerous."

"I don't care. What's dangerous if we both want the same things?" I asked in drunken pleasure, in love with the view of the stars, the windmill breaking the patterns of constellations, Mars glowing pink in the sky; as pink and warm as his motion made my whole body feel. Jase's sounds further intoxicated my fuzzy brain. His hands gripped my back as he held me so I had to do nothing but experience him before God with no shame. *Is this what God intended sex to be when he'd created the garden? Was it supposed to be this simple? Take care of animals and plants, make love in the open air, treasure the bodies we were given and the feel of them together, use them to plant seeds that would fertilize into a new life?*

"Jase, will you be sad if you plant your child inside my body on this night before God?" I asked, half moaned, kissed his lips with mine tingling.

"Right now, that's all nature is telling me to do."

"Then do it."

"What if you wake to change your mind the way you did with ...." He didn't want to mention Rustin. I didn't want him to, either.

"I'm coherent. I'm not going to be mad about something I ran for first. Did you not follow me into this water?"

"I'd follow you into a curse, just don't curse me later when your belly is big, and my baby is ready to make an introduction."

My brief giggle morphed into a long moan. Soon, small whimpering sounds seemed to utter from another person as I released myself to Jase's talent. Oh, but the best was knowing this was no Floridian fling. I knew inside that he didn't give other girls the weakness or fervor he did me now. The water that had been so peaceful when we'd floated and watched the stars now rocked over the edge, splashed onto the ground.

My nails dug into his muscled shoulders while I held for dear life as we let go of all fear of creating such when we released every tension and boundary between us. I held to his hair as I kissed his loose lips, loved the sound of his grunts, harsh breathing, pants of my name on helpless whispers.

"Be my girlfriend, baby."

"Okay."

"Hell, yes!" He shouted to the sky as he gripped my hips and stilled while the most erotic praise reached the stars.

I grinned in pure victory as I appreciated the view of his teeth biting into his lip, eyes closed, hair tanged and damp, every sexy detail in his muscles, the stubble along his chin and throat. My arms wrapped around his neck and I bent my face to run my lips along his ear. The weakest wonderful sound breathed from his husky voice. Jase remembered himself as the last shudders of release ceased.

"That's the best. Tough guy gone weak."

"Oh, you like that, huh?" he asked. An almost drunk smile shaped his lips. He remained inside me while he hugged me against him.

"I like that, yes, sir. You made me lose sensation in my face for a bit there. Never knew things could actually be that intense."

"Me either, sweet Kins. Girlfriend Kins. I have a girlfriend."

"You have a girlfriend. I have a boyfriend."

"Guess we better get used to acting like it. This means I get to grab a boob whenever I want, right?"

My head tossed on a cackle while he grabbed a breast and squeezed. All play fell away under the scrub of his thumb over the most sensitive flesh. He built back inside me, and we sloshed more water from the basin while we sealed our new status.

21 | ♀

THE NEXT MORNING RUSTIN was a bit of a crab cake as he got ready for work. Cabinets shut harder than necessary. The contents of the refrigerator jostled when the door closed under his hand. Frozen foods rearranged into chaos as he dug around for unhealthy lunch options. Jase stood in front of the kitchen sink with a mug of coffee cupped in his hands, the smile on his face as warm and steamy. I couldn't help but smile back over the rim of my own coffee cup.

"You could've at least let me know you weren't going home until today," Rustin bitched. He tried to keep his tone low enough like he muttered to himself but kept lapsing into a louder lecture. "Yeah, y'all keep smiling. It's so funny. I was waiting on you. Got worried when I didn't know what happened. Hell, for all I knew you called Sara back and hitched a ride with her. I mean, why not? While you're busy lumping yourself in a dangerous packaged deal with the funeral, you could've just stayed the night with her while she paints away everything that makes you distinctive while she turns you into her replica."

Jase's smoldering smile became smug as he held my eyes like Rustin said everything he bit his own tongue about. I quirked my brows and shook my head. He wasn't getting under my skin or changing my mind. Patrick was dead. Klive seemed to indicate Pat Connor wasn't going to be a problem.

"Why cover the bruises anymore?" Rustin continued. "At least when I look at the bruises, I can remember why it's worth the pain the Sheriff is making my job. They're fading fast, you don't need that shit. Look at you. I can't see *you*." He finally tossed a Hot Pocket onto the counter, his free hand gesturing to my face. Electric blue irises finally met my green ones. I sighed and hopped off my stool to round the bar into the kitchen.

"Rustin, I'm sorry." I wrapped my arms around his waist and held to his back. He scoffed.

"Who do you take me for? King? Jase? You think you're just gonna wrap your arms around me and I'll be wrapped around those vile fingers of yours? I'm not that easy."

My lips pursed in a smile I hid as I rested my head against his chest. Jase's eyes lit with a huge smile while his lips remained neutral. I flared my eyes that he behaved so I could keep from laughing. My eyes closed while I inhaled Obsession and felt his name plate dig into my temple from his uniform. True to his word, he wasn't easy. Funny how easy he was to sleep with but when aggravated he wasn't going to be affectionate if he could hold to his pride. His hands held his hips instead of hugging me back. Ha! Sara thought Marcus was a hard nut to crack!

I ran my nails up and down his back, opened my eyes to see Jase watching Rustin like they were silently communicating above my head. My fingers kept their rhythm as I pulled back to look up at Rustin with the same look that melts my father.

"I didn't mean to cause you trouble with Ansley at work. I'm still not sorry about Angela but thank you for taking extra hours tonight and tomorrow to be here with me today."

Rustin's tongue bubbled his lower lip like a hick with tobacco stuffed in his mouth. He tapped his cheek as he lifted his chin like he didn't believe whether I meant what I said. He fought a smile while I cracked a big one and grabbed his face to plant the softest kiss on his cheek.

"You've earned a little reprieve, but not forgiveness, Mizz James. Now, I'm gonna tell you one more time, go get your stuff and meet me at the door. We're gonna take you home to change and get ready. If you stand me up again, I'm not bending over backward again. I'll bend over and tell you to kiss my ass instead."

I pinched his chin to tug his eyes to mine again. "Rusty, you know you'd love if I kissed your ass in every manner of speaking. I'll be at the door like a good girl. Thank you."

"Mmhmm."

When I walked away, Rustin popped my ass with a towel. I jumped and rubbed the painful spot.

My mother popped the exact same spot when I got out of Jase's truck forty minutes later. "Kinsley Fallon, you are so lucky your daddy is at work. He didn't expect to be apart this long." She looked at the guys. "Y'all go inside the main house. I need a moment alone with my daughter."

"Yes ma'am," Jase said. His worried eyes met my own. Ha! I wondered if he was afraid that whatever upset my mom also upset his and he'd have to battle Bianca's temper?

Rustin shot my mom a gorgeous, wholesome grin. "Purple is beautiful with your skin, Mrs. Hayes."

She chuckled like he didn't have her fooled. He smiled at me behind her back. Yup. Rustin wanted me to be in trouble.

"Come on, Kins. Let's go up to your place. I want you to see what I've had to put up there and give you a chance to put some away before Jase can see in case any of it belongs to a certain gentleman."

"Huh?" I asked as I followed her up the stairs of my garage apartment. She used her key to unlock my place. I went inside before her and gasped while she closed and locked the door behind us. "What the hell is all this?"

Several stuffed animals, cards and a few shedding flower bouquets littered my kitchen island. A small black and silver damask box sat off to the side with a card on top. She saw me looking. "That's the one that made me nervous. Seems larger than a jewelry box but can't be too sure. I didn't open it."

"Yeah, but why is this here? Where did it come from? Why?"

She snorted a bitter laugh. Shook her head. "The same reason your social media accounts are now brimming with friend requests, followers and message requests. Seems your stunt with Angela earned you far more fanfare and attention than your sprint ever has. I had to weed through hate mail, but this is all good. People are sick. They fixate on anyone in the spotlight, however short a span that light lasts. I'm glad you were with the guys. Did you behave yourself?"

I couldn't help myself. After longing for her last night during Sara's primping, I could fight my longing no more. Mom gasped when I rushed her with a tight hug. Her arms immediately wrapped me tight. The pain in my ribs wasn't worth ruining the soothing quality of her embrace. When her fingers came to my hair to do the mom stroke, tears fell.

"I missed you."

"What? Did I just hear you correctly?" she asked, tried to push me away to look at me, but I squeezed her harder until she relaxed and just did what I needed.

"Don't make a big deal of it. My friend lost her husband. She asked me to come to the funeral today to help her cope."

"Oh, Kins. That's awful. I'm sorry. How old is she?"

"Thirty-six, I think. They have a son. She did my makeup last night and I thought of you doing my makeup instead. I missed you. Let it be. I'm trying to equip myself to be strong for her. If I cry now, I can do that."

"Ah, so I'm being used, is that it?" she teased. I chuckled and sniffled.

"You didn't think I was gonna just dive into my mom's arms like a soft girl for no reason, did you?" I joked.

"Never. I'm proud of you for helping her through this. Need any help picking what to wear?"

"Nah. I already know. Gonna wear the full length black maxi dress. No frills."

"Wear kitten heels. I'll pin your hair for you. It's a big mess without your hair products, isn't it?" She ran both hands through my tangled mass. I chewed my cheek. My hair wouldn't have been such a mess if I'd washed and conditioned after Jase and I spent more time with the cows than I'd thought. We'd both gotten back to his house and fallen into bed together. More love, then sleep, but my hair dried in a tangled mass.

"Yes, that would be nice. Thank you," I told her. We pulled apart and she left me to get ready so she wouldn't fawn over me, but I saw the emotion on her face at my affection. That tugged my heart strings until I clipped them to be retied at a more opportune time. Today I needed to toughen up. The hell I was going to this and braving anyone with an appreciation for Patrick Scott with tears in my eyes. That asshole.

I leaned against the island to smell each of the bouquets. My whole apartment smelled of flowers, but those carnations would have to go. I'd take them to the funeral they reminded me of.

My fingers traced my handwritten name on the envelope sitting atop the damask box. I knew that writing. He had a beautiful scrolling K. *Would the signature be* Complicated *this time or his real name? How did this come?* There was no postage. *Surely Klive hadn't been bold enough to hand this to my father?*

I ripped the envelope and pulled out a black and silver damask card matching the box.

For the beautiful boxer beating bloody beauty queens.
Don't lose your fight.
X - K.K.

Even though I smiled at his alliteration and him calling me beautiful, I found myself sad and longing for more than such a brief sentiment. But, hey, at least he signed his initials this time. That had to be an improvement.

I lifted the lid off the small box, pulled back tissue and caught a wonderful whiff of his cologne. "Holy crap!" I gushed when I lifted the box. "He sprayed the tissue for me!" I girly sighed realizing he could've gifted me the spritzed tissue paper alone and I'd have been delighted. "How tormentingly thoughtful, Mr. King. Ha! Nice!" A pair of fingerless pink kick boxing gloves.

I allowed myself one long inhale as I carried these into the bedroom, through the bathroom, into the closet. The break-up box with Nate's cheating photo and Jack's abandoning ass came down from the top shelf. In a way, I felt guilty at hiding Klive's note and box with tissue inside like I already knew the end was inevitable. My throat choked tight with emotion. Right now, I was a cheater of a different kind. New shame colored the pink clouds in my brain grayer than Klive's eyes. He belonged in this box because I had a boyfriend now. Jase was my boyfriend. Shit. Jase was possibly a life-giver inside my body now. *Did I regret last night?*

No.

NO! I didn't. Wouldn't! Jase was the right choice. He was a great guy even if he was complicated in his own right. The things I'd said to Sara last night about sensing Klive wasn't normal hadn't changed. Nor had they come from a misguided place. They came from the right place I wanted to ignore when doing wrong with him was so exciting, like the rush of riding on the back of his bike, kissing in bed, running in St. Augustine.

"Oh, Klive King ... what you've done to me ...." I whispered, traced the damask patterns on the box, his handwriting on the envelope, then closed everything up and tucked the break-up box back on the shelf. Below, I rifled through hangers until I tugged the black dress I needed.

By the time I placed black studded earrings in my earlobes, I sauntered into Mom's kitchen where the guys were eating everything she put in front of them. The newspaper sat folded on the table in my daddy's vacant spot. Damn, I hoped they hadn't published anything about Patrick Scott's funeral in there. Mom and Daddy would put things together on their own.

Mom poured me a cup of coffee and set the cup beside Daddy's paper like she knew I'd want his spot just to be near him somehow.

"Thanks, Mama."

"You're welcome. Ready for me to pin your hair?"

"Yup."

"I was just telling the guys it was a shame they didn't have longer to stay or else I could break out the photo albums." She smiled like an evil fool while I panicked. "I didn't say I did, but I might if I ever get another chance. You got lucky this morning."

My shoulders sagged with relief.

"Jase might like to see baby pictures to decide if he wants a child who looks like you," she joked while I freaked for a different reason. When my whole face flushed, Mom gaped and jerked her shock at Jase. He pursed his lips before sighing and holding his hands up in surrender.

"Do your worst, Mrs. Hayes. I'm not sorry. What man would be? You have a wonderful daughter."

When Mom turned her head toward me, but didn't seem to pull her gaze from Jase, he cleared his throat.

"You gonna put my mom on me? She'll just whip my ass then hug me and thank me since she loves Kins almost more than she loves me."

"Jase Taylor, you are a brave fool."

"So I've been told, Mrs. Hayes."

"Kinsley Fallon, let's go pin your hair."

"Do I have to go upstairs with you? Why can't we do the hair down here with witnesses and a cop present?" I begged. She emitted another evil laugh. What to make of her humor, I had no idea. She seemed so mad at Jase, but also not mad at all. Almost victorious.

"Don't be a coward, Kinsley. Get your bottom up to my room *now*."

"Yes, Mama." I shot Jase a mean look over my shoulder. Jase blew me an air kiss, quirked his brows like a pleased player before I mounted the stairs off the kitchen toward her bedroom. Yeah, he could be cocky. Boys never had enough consequences. Funny, I was so caught up in the Garden of Eden feel last night I forgot the curse Jase spoke of. The burden of a woman, starting with what I expected was to be quite the blistering from my mother.

She pulled my hair into one large ponytail she started brushing tangles from. The grin on her face in the mirror showed no signs of evil anger at all.

"Mom, where's your lecture on sex and what boys want? No one's gonna want to buy the truck if I give the ice cream away for free? Abstinence?"

"Ha! I already told you. You're not fifteen anymore. That man downstairs doesn't look like he had an easy time catching you, but he looks like he had the time of his life once he caught you. He's glowing. He loves you. If you made me a baby, congratulations. Hope you had a memorable experience." She pinned various places as she created a sophisticated twisted knot. "Judging by the blush in your cheeks I'd venture to say you did."

"Nope. I'm not having sex talk with my mother. I have no desire to know anything about my father and that's what that leads to. I will just say Jase is good at being very bad. Fair?"

Her lips curled, eyebrows rose, as she bent and cupped my shoulders. Her cheek pressed against mine. The freckles beneath her eyes made my lack of freckles under this mask of makeup more obvious. She noticed.

"Let's add some color and waterproof mascara. You look remarkably improved, though. How's the shoe print on your ribs?"

"Ribs are sore, marks are a different color but fading. Nothing I can't power through if Coach ever thaws toward me."

"Did you see his card? He came by the house to see you yesterday. Several from the team came with him. He had that handsome art professor with him I think to reduce risk of impropriety."

"Wow. No, I didn't really look through anything. Did Coach seem any different than Saturday night?" I asked. "It's awesome that the others came. I'm guessing relay team?"

"Two from the relay team. Lucy came. She's so worried about you. She also offered to assist with your social media accounts or anything really."

"That's a bad idea."

"Oh? Why? Because she annoys you?" Mom handed me her waterproof mascara while she dabbed pink lip gloss to the apples of my cheeks and smoothed the color into my skin with her ginger touch.

"Anyone with too much information is a liability or a threat, Mom. *Micro Machine Manager Tells All.*" I gave air quotes around the headline, then applied the mascara to my lashes where I sat.

"She's an ally. Anyone who's willing to be bullied over who they believe in means they're willing to suffer for what they think is right. She suffers for you. I say you give her more of you, young lady. After all, didn't you suffer through high school defending others from your bully? Should we accuse you of being fake or somehow brown-nosing?"

Yikes! "Jeez, Mama, okay. I'll try. While I hate your point, you make a good one. But, if this bites me in the butt and I'm right, you'd better be ready to say you were wrong. To stand by my side through the fall-out. Deal?"

"Deal," she said. "Ian was calmer." *Coach Ian Walton.* "He showed me another video compilation that some pageant contestants put out under anonymity, of course. Testimonies on bullying endured by Little Miss Ansley behind the scenes. It's a nasty world, but Jeannine Ansley is probably ashamed to walk into public for what's come to light about her baby girl. The deputy in my kitchen said the Sheriff has been quite the crab. They're feeling the heat, especially with Sheriff Ansley being an authority figure responsible for justice when he overlooks everything for his daughter. You've caused quite the stir, but I'm proud to be on your team, honey."

I put my hand over hers on my shoulder and met her eyes in the mirror. "That means the world. Thank you. Now, I don't know what to expect from Sara today. I hate funerals, so please pray for me to be graceful in the face of death."

22 | ♂

JOEY STUDIED ME. "KLIVE, why are we doing this?" he asked.

I twisted the key inside the padlock on a roll-up door of a trashy self-storage shed. Perimeter cameras were for appearances only and hadn't worked in over a decade. The chain-linked fencing protecting the storage buildings had various human-sized holes cut for easy access from the dilapidated former businesses at either side. Joey, Eric and I walked into the shed and pulled the door closed. Eric hit the lights on our makeshift hideout and staging area. Various disguises and replacement clothing hung inside a wardrobe against the left wall. A vanity with mirror, makeup, prosthetics, wigs, contact lenses, eyeglasses, temporary tattoos all lined the back wall. To the right, an old washer and dryer combo for the used clothing. A Nightshade cleaner came to remove stains or incinerate items.

"Joey, you are under no obligation other than securing your charge. Nightshade needs to have a presence at the bloody funeral because Taylor says Kinsley was begged by Sara Scott to be there for support. Seems the whore is ready to play the role of sad widow while she displays the prettier, younger version of who she's tried to be in front of Inferno and anyone thinking of paying Patrick's debts with her. Ray would be a fool to choose Sara over Kinsley for business."

"After the message you sent with Pat Connor, you think Ray would be so dumb as to fuck with Kinsley? Especially since he's under the impression *you're* fucking her?"

"Face it, she might be more valuable a commodity because they think I've fucked her. I should've known better but lost my head in the middle of acute rage." I hated admitting I'd made a mistake. "If the whores at The Deep are more sought after once I've used them, why wouldn't the same apply to Kinsley? If Inferno thinks she's valuable to me, how much does her value skyrocket? He'd get a premium for her whether he sold her into slavery or kept her for regular use."

I disrobed and pulled the ugliest suit from the wardrobe.

"Nah," Joey said. He took the hanger from me and traded for a tacky suit. "I'm assuming you're going with the shaggy wig character. The one you used at the track meet?"

"Yeah."

"He's younger, frugal, but he's not without style, Klive. I know right now you have disdain for every suit in this closet, but you must think like a college kid. They pull shit like this just because they can." He handed me a leisure suit.

"You've lost your damn marbles, Joe. I'm *not* wearing that. It's ridiculous. Whoever shopped this suit should be fired and ousted from Nightshade this instant."

"Good thing I'm not Nightshade." Joey grinned like a dumb ass.

"Go with the seventies porn star mustache, too," Eric joked. "Or, no 'stache and opt for the Jim Morrison wig. Waltz into that church like *Riders on the Storm*."

Even if I stewed about the points I'd made to Joey over Kinsley's value, Eric made me smile. I pointed a finger in Joey's space. "Joe, I'll wear the shirt and blazer, but I'm *not* wearing those pants. *No damn way*. I'll wear jeans."

Joey snapped his fingers. "And I would've gotten away with it, too, if it weren't for you dumb kids and your style points."

Eric laughed to himself. "Hey, how come Taylor called you into this? Isn't *he* her boyfriend now?"

I pulled the clothing on knowing the cleaner had disinfected everything to my liking but still feeling dingy and gross.

"Eric, he's a candidate. He needs to know if Nightshade has his back," I reasoned. "If she's finally his girlfriend, good on him. About time he quits pussy-footing around and shows some courage."

Joey scoffed with bitter doubt. "Oh, yeah, real courageous to finally nail down the girl you've wanted for years while she's a refugee at your house in the middle of nowhere. He doesn't deserve her."

"And I do?" I asked. The wig adjusted under my fingers and over the liner as I fit the shaggy brown hair on my head. Tresses fell over one eye. Thick brows adhered over my groomed eyebrows to match the color of the wig. I pulled my eyelid open to cover my gray eyes with one blue contact lens. In the other I put a solid contact lens to make the eye appear damaged or blind. While I blinked those in place, the prosthetic slash across the damaged eye came next. I dabbed makeup around the edges to sell the scar, even if I planned to wear sunglasses the whole time. Three teardrop tattoos dotted the area beneath the scarred eye. Any similarity to Klive King would be diminished by the jarring appearance of the eye, especially since the hair fell over my good eye.

Mousse formed a swirl in the palm of my hand like ice cream. *Frozen custard in St. Augustine. Kinsley humming into my pineapple vanilla flavored mouth.*

I smashed the swirl in both hands and organized the shaggy hair into something respectable for the occasion. Even if this disguise was unruly in nature, thugs had a decorum in grief, too. Inferno was sure to look polished and kind without their vests, just like they wore their good-guy disguises when putting out fires for civilians while, in darkness, they created fires of a different sort; like the one that brought us together today.

"Klive, you know my standing on this," Joey said. "Why you let Jase take her is beyond me. The videos of her fight and the aftermath have gone viral. Short clips have been created with you taking your shirt off and putting it on her. Photos of you shirtless and holding her against you are all over social media with opinion polls on whether you're a couple like this is all some game. Locals are going nuts for this, but it's everywhere. Why hide your chemistry like some forbidden secret? There's no way Cheatham hasn't seen it, but at the same time, there's also no way that anyone he tries to hire hasn't. Your loyalty is like royalty ...."

"Boss, I'm with Joe on this," Eric said. "Klive, she's *your* girl. No one fucks around with my girl because Nightshade's got my girl's back. Inferno wouldn't be able to just sell off a girl that belongs to Nightshade."

"Which comes back to why Nightshade needs to have Jase Taylor's back and *his* girl's."

"Why does she have to be *his* girl, though? Did you see the video replays? Kinsley Hayes looks sweet, but damn she's got what it takes to be with *you*, Klive. She matches."

"I did. You think I'm honorable enough not to screen shot clips of her shirt ripped open?" No sense hiding. This locker talk would never get out of these walls and I didn't feel so guilty now that I knew she was Jase's girlfriend, although I knew I should feel guilty for that reason alone. No use masking my envy and vindictive enjoyment of the footage with us together while she touched my lips. Her gaze had been enamored. She'd stood by *his* car while longing for *me*. She looked so sexy in my arms. If I didn't kill these thoughts, I'd be ready to blow and clouded when I needed to focus.

Eric grinned and waggled his brows. "That blood on her bra and cleavage? A sick kind of sexy. Like Uma Thurman *Kill Bill* hot. Even my girl was impressed. She's the one that said you match, especially when I told her Angela was high on cocaine beforehand. Unbelievable. Kinsley ripped into someone who had superhuman strength and a good eight-to-ten inches on her."

Joey nodded his emphatic agreement. "Wonder who taught her to fight? Like a friggin' razorback in the woods. Ray isn't only a fool if he fucks with her because of you. How epic would it be to see her unleash that unexpected fury on Inferno's leader and beat *him* to a bloody pulp before he has to skulk back to his band of firefighting bikers?"

"Yeah, if he was a fair fighter, she'd whip his ass, but that guy plays fair with no one," I said. "He's dirty. If she unleashed on him, he'd see it as pure foreplay before returning the favor and breaking her in for the gang to use. No way he's shopping her to pay some debt. I'll never buy it. I think this started with an unknowing Patrick Scott thinking to trade a virgin for a debt to spare his wife, then Pat Connor caught on to my bloody personal attraction to her and saw something a hundred times more valuable. Pat Connor opened a box with my name on it, now Ray can't shut it for the same greedy reason." I licked the back of the temporary tattoo for the emblem on the inside of this character's left wrist. "Anyone heard anything out of Pat Connor since I castrated him?"

"Nah. In fact, it's been too quiet," Eric said. He dressed in a designer suit while I took the damn blazer Joey handed me.

"You're far too happy about this, Joe."

"You look like a college professor from the nineties. Of course, I'm happy."

"Did you get this from your brother's closet then?" I asked.

He chuckled. "Adrian may be stuck in the nineties, but there's no way in hell he'd wear something so awful. No offense. With your character complete, you look the part of the arrogant idiot too stupid not to pull off whatever hideous find he wants. Unless you remove the sunglasses, then you're just scary and I don't care what you're wearing."

"Don't patronize me."

"I still say you shouldn't go in disguise, boss," Eric said. "You can throw your designer suit on and straight up make a stand. If he tried to sell her with the underground knowing that girl was yours, Ray's rep would be flushed and challenged."

"No." I grabbed the shoes for this guy. "Cops are going to be there in plain clothes. If I'm spied, there's room for speculation. They're still looking to find Patrick Scott's killer. I'm not giving them any room to look at me."

"Oh, but this guy is better?" Eric gestured toward me like I was crazy. "At least people wear sunglasses at funerals, so you won't look weird. What the hell do you want me to call you while we're there? I never thought we'd be using our characters for social settings. Are you supposed to be Nightshade? I don't really hang with anyone outside the syndicate."

"I'll wear a Nightshade ring."

"You can't wear your leadership ring."

"I know that, dammit! Who do you think you're talking to? I'll wear the one I'm holding for Jase Taylor should he make the damn cut."

"Easy, Klive. Not trying to press you or piss you off. Just trying to say what if the cops have a file on this character? The wrist tattoo maybe caught in camera footage after a body was dropped or some shit?"

"That was the whole point of wearing the tattoo in the first place. If they catch on, you think they're gonna arrest me at a funeral?" I double checked everything in the mirror. "They're already treading on dangerous ground attending an Inferno event. They're not going to be making any moves. Just watching."

"Klive, I'm with Eric. Go as yourself. Who gives a shit what the cops speculate?" Joe asked with genuine concern in his previously humorous face. "Taylor's already screwing her up. If she was a virgin, she's not anymore. What's worse, he allowed his cop friend to get in on the action. This wouldn't have happened if you'd—"

I spun so fast the blazer fanned away from my body as I ripped the glasses off my face and pinned a glare on his. "If I'd *what*, Joey?! Tell me!"

Eric eased in between us, but Joey shoved him aside and faced me with anger all over him now. "If *you'd* quit being a coward and take who you love!"

"Who I *love*? That's a big word, mate. You're getting ahead of yourself now."

"Just calling it like I see it. If I'm tired of bullshit, I can't imagine what it's like to be her every day. Men really are pigs. The advances she's gotten just while I've been listening; sexual harassment, touching, blatant staring. *Now this?* It's enough to make me lose faith in men and become a lesbian."

Eric tried his damnedest not to laugh while I fought a smile. How did Joey maintain a sense-of-humor amid an angry rant? The disarming bastard.

My jaw clenched as I held to my hips. "You're saying not only did Taylor shag her, but now Rustin Keane has, too?" I asked. "How do you know this, Joey?"

"How do I know anything? Their phones. I've tapped their speakers so I can hear the conversations in the room. Been listening to what I can when there's service. Spotty signal, but not hard to figure out what's going on. Bedroom has better signal than the kitchen as far as I can tell. Taylor left his phone in his room last night when Sara Scott dropped by his house to chat with Kinsley. Sara admitted that she's a prostitute because Kinsley was crying that she felt like a whore who'd cheated on *you*. She also confessed to Sara that she knows something is wrong with you, but that she almost feels drawn to that because you aren't as perfect as you look. She calls you Moonlight to Sara though. She's never said your name."

"I've heard enough! This shit is too personal. In this, maybe you ought to stick with the rules and keep your surveillance to yourself. I have to stay focused so I don't lose my head."

My palms itched to beat the ever-living shit out of Jase as my guns slipped into their holsters at my ankle and back. I made sure the cuffs of my pants concealed my weapon, then placed a knife in my blazer pocket.

"Klive."

"Don't. Bloody. Speak."

We left the storage shed and pulled the door back down. Locked up. Joey shook his head and went one way while we went another. I'd been celibate for far too long. Now that I'd heard this bullshit, I was thinking about revenge fucking a whore or two at once to honor what Kinsley had done with *both* men! *How could she defile herself that way? How could she look at me with stars in her eyes and beg me to touch her, kiss me the way she did, tell me I was the dream, then give herself away?*

Eric cleared his throat, afraid to speak.

"What?" I demanded as we arrived at the fencing.

"You never answered my question about what to call you," Eric said as we dipped through one of the holes leading to the back lot.

"Maybe we should go separately and pretend we aren't affiliated?" I suggested.

"Nah, if you wear the ring, we know one another, and you have the syndicate's loyalty."

We walked through an abandoned parking lot with overgrown weed patches. He gave me the keys to his car since that's what I'd driven the last time I'd publicly worn this character. "Gotta love a guy who dresses like a pauper while driving a Porsche. Having no name would be suspicious. Even if you do look like a young hit man."

"Exactly. Like a free agent."

"You forgot the ring. Did you do that for this reason?"

"I didn't forget the ring. It's right here." I displayed my hand and slid the ring onto my left ring finger. Six years had passed since I'd worn a regular Nightshade ring. I didn't miss the experience, but right now I couldn't imagine being married to anything or *anyone* else since she'd given herself away so carelessly. I was in the mood to fuck around with the little woman. *Screw Klive King's chivalrous bullshit!* I looked Eric in the eye, enjoyed his evident discomfort in meeting my eyes with the scar. "Call me Henley."

"*Henley?* Isn't that the name Kinsley called you by accident that night at the bar?"

I tapped my smirking lips, slid the shades over my eyes and unlocked the gleaming Porsche.

23 | ♀

JASE WHISTLED WHEN **I came back downstairs** with my mother. "Y'all did a great job. Can't even tell she's got battle scars, Mrs. Hayes. She's almost as pretty as her mama again."

We both laughed and slapped one of his arms in an accidental mirror of one another. "Thank you, Jase," we said in unison. I cleared my throat while Mom narrowed her eyes like a vindicated brat.

"You're welcome, ladies. We about ready?" he asked me.

"She's not leaving until she eats and gets some coffee in her system."

While I sipped coffee, I watched Mom chop strawberries and pour them with a handful of blueberries into plain Greek yogurt. I was getting burnt out on yogurt. No way I was gonna complain about her making me food, though.

As she pushed the bowl and Monk fruit sweetener my way, I realized she and my father shouldn't have been here at all.

"Mom, why is Daddy at work? Y'all are supposed to be leaving for vacation."

She sat at the table with the guys. I ate my yogurt at the counter.

"Do you think *anything* would drag your father away from Tampa without seeing his baby girl is okay?" she asked. I caught a little resentment in there, but I knew she loved how he loved me. "Not to mention, he's never left without saying goodbye to you, honey. You know better."

"You guys have had this planned for months. Please tell me I haven't ruined your time together."

"On the contrary, your father has enjoyed a lot of stress relief while you were off-premises." She winked.

Jase and Rustin clapped hands in a high-five across the table while I almost gagged on a berry. Mom smiled, shrugged her shoulders.

"Why do you think I feel it's time for you to grow up and move on?" she asked.

"Alright, I can't eat another bite. I'm done." I gave her my half-full bowl. When I bent to kiss her cheek, I held my phone up in front of us for a selfie and snapped a gorgeous smile just for my father.

Go on your vacation, I texted. *Your baby girl is fine, Daddy. I love and miss you!* I sent the photo.

Daddy: *Yay! Both my beauties in one place! You look so pretty! Way better than the Ansley girl ;). #proudpapa. Not leaving till you have dinner with us to reassure me. Saturday night. My treat. Bring your boyfriend, whichever one you want. :P*

Me: *You need to behave sir! Deal. Love you.*

Daddy: *Love you too Kins.*

"Okay, I'm ready," I told the guys. "Mom, you'll get your vacation only if I have dinner with you two on Saturday to appease Daddy. Guess he needs to physically see that I'm okay."

"Excellent!" she gushed. "Wonder where he wants to take us? It's been too long since the three of us went out."

"Mom, weren't you just complaining about me not leaving the nest? You're bipolar."

"You're gonna get your little butt paddled if you keep it up. I don't care if you are bruised, young lady." She swatted my bottom while I laughed and jogged to the front door.

"Here, boys! Let's go in the car!" I called them like dogs, did the little kissy lips for effect.

"Bye, Mrs. Hayes. Always a pleasure," Jase told her, winked. She shook her head and shoved him out the door. Rustin shook her hand and thanked her for breakfast.

"Did she feed you?" I asked.

"No. I was thanking her for feeding *you*, so we don't deal with any mood swings."

"Asshole!" I slapped Rustin's belly.

"Language!" Mom shouted with a wave of her finger. I cringed and waved my whole hand before we got into Jase's truck for the dreaded drive to the church.

Sara stood on the sidewalk wringing her hands then made a clumsy dash down the steps in her heels. She reminded me of Constance's observation about women in heels. *Constance. My dear sweet friend.* This week was so isolated from reality I felt weird stepping out of the truck and into Sara's arms.

"Oh, thank God. I was so afraid you'd change your mind. I mean, who wants to do something like this, but you told me if I needed someone to crumble with ..." Her speech was rushed. I caught the scent of booze on her breath. Understandable. Not gonna condemn those in pain. After all, Jesus said to leave the wine to those who need the wine. She smelled more like whiskey, though.

"Here." I extended the bouquet of carnations.

"Thank you," she said. "Now that you're here, I'll put them with the others. The casket is in the church already. It's closed, of course, but I can't be in there alone. Ever feel like someone can see you from beyond the grave?"

"Um ... I guess." I peered over my shoulder at Jase and Rustin following behind us while Sara tugged me toward the church. Jase almost looked like he knew the feeling she spoke of. Like he was afraid to enter. Rustin glanced at his friend, placed a soothing hand to his shoulder.

"The service starts in about an hour. I wanted to be here before anyone else. Oh—" She stopped short. I bumped into her as we paused in the foyer. Beyond, inside the sanctuary, at the front was the casket flanked by flowers and photos of Patrick Scott as the smiling father of a newborn Noah. Another photo of him in his firefighting gear looking like the quintessential first responding hero.

A man in a brown blazer stood before the sleek white coffin, his hand resting atop.

"Do you know him?" I whispered.

"No," she said. I felt the tension in her hand as she squeezed without realizing. This sucked. I understood now that every stranger could be Patrick's killer drug dealer seeking revenge.

An hour later, I stood at the doors to the church handing out fliers in memory of Patrick Scott with a nice little obituary printed inside. Talk about irony. Maybe I could understand the feeling of a ghost peeking over my shoulder after all. Then again, the guy over my shoulder was my behemoth boyfriend standing at my back like a bodyguard after several came through the doors who gave pleasantly surprised smiles at seeing me. When they greeted me by name, Jase had shifted from standing across the aisle to stand right behind me. I knew he was probably mean mugging anyone with bad intentions. Quite a nice perk when I didn't have to look at his mean expression while assholes did.

Sara stood near me as if she could leech off Jase's protection.

"Hi, I'm so sorry for your loss," I said over and over, handed out a flier, shook hands while faces blurred. Sara thanked each of them for coming. The scent of whiskey was so much stronger, she could give someone a contact buzz if they got too close. The pastor came to get Sara. The church was packed; shocking since such an array of personality types lined the pews.

"I bet half these people didn't even know him," Jase muttered. "They just want to watch the same way people file into a courtroom to watch drama they overheard on the news."

"The bonus that she's here is like a cherry on their sundaes," a gruff voice said. My eyes ripped away from the sanctuary toward a man in sunglasses, shaggy hair, brown blazer. *The jockstrap Bieber wannabe from my track meet! The guy who couldn't name his own cologne! What was he doing here? Using words like Pat Connor had used on me!*

He waited while I remembered myself.

"I'm sorry for your loss," he said like he was calling my shit. "I saw your video. Glad to see you've healed well. Impressive skills and recovery. Hope to catch you at another meet soon. May I have one of those programs?" he asked. I nodded and watched him use his left hand to take the flier I gave. The blazer pulled enough to give a peek at the tattoo I remembered seeing at the track. He thanked me and walked into the sanctuary.

"Who was that guy, Kins?"

"A fan from my last meet." *Had he known Patrick Scott? If so, what the hell did that mean about my meet in Tallahassee? Was he there spying on me for Inferno? Why use those same words like he knew? Oh, gosh, I wished Klive were here!*

"Seems familiar. You know his name?" Jase asked. I swallowed my fear so Jase wouldn't put his dog on the hunt too soon. No need to rile him until the threat was certain.

"I don't, but I've never asked. He does seem like an itch at the back of the brain, right? But I'd remember that tattoo on his wrist if I'd ever officially met him. Is he suddenly a threat for being my fan?" I teased over my shoulder before greeting another person and expressing my condolences.

Jase didn't dignify my question with an answer, he tickled my sore ribs by mistake instead.

"Omigosh!" I gushed and rushed to throw my arms around Bayleigh when she and the crew from the bar walked inside. Marcus, Jarrell, Gustav, Garrett, Bitch Server and even Constance. *Oh, thank you, Lord!*

"Kinsley, girl, I've missed you!" Bayleigh said. She squeezed me until I winced. Constance hugged me next. I expected guilt to engulf me, but in this setting, guilt could wait. Besides, Constance was too busy checking me over. Her eyes studied mine, assessed my face, looked over my head at Jase. She nodded and gave a soft smile.

"You finally did it," she observed. "Y'all together now?"

We nodded. Marcus grinned like a proud parent and clapped a big hand to Jase's bicep. I looked over my shoulder to see the most adorable expression on Jase's face.

"Glad to see you, Little Red," Marcus said in a low tone. "The whole bar's been asking about you. A lot more fans after your fight video."

"Yay," I muttered. We shut the main doors and walked into the sanctuary minutes before the service started. Sara ran into Marcus's arms when he came toward the front pew to express his condolences.

"Thank you so much for being here, Marcus. All of you," she said with a look at the whole group. They each gave her a hug, though Garrett's was reserved. He also had a cautious eye as he studied her with me like he didn't trust us together. Interesting. He saw me noticing and gave a smile that didn't reach his eyes. Odd to see him in regular clothing with no Steampunk character traits, no eyeliner, suspenders, top hat. He wore a button-down shirt and black slacks, combed hair. This seemed more like a boring character than the guy I was used to making drinks with.

"We're gonna go find somewhere to sit, but we'll see you after the service," Marcus told Sara.

"No, you guys are the closest thing to family I've had outside my own," Sara said with tone jabbed at the elderly couple who must've been Patrick's parents. "You guys please sit up here with us."

We didn't argue because that would've been rude. Though the couple watched us like contagious lepers, we filled the front pew and did our best to keep space from them. The woman made no secret of shooting sneers at Sara, though. *Yeesh, name one thing that makes your ex-husband's funeral more miserable for five hundred. I'll take the evil mother-in-law and pray I never have one of my own!*

Jase's mom, Bianca, was a bitch when pissed, but she loved me. I couldn't see her ever being a nightmare like this, well, unless she thought I had something to do with Jase's untimely death. That's exactly what this woman implied when the pastor finished the standard lines told to grieving people who'd never cared a day for God. Patrick's mother stood at the podium with a sobbing story about what a good boy her son was until he'd gotten mixed up with Sara, that the only good thing that came of her tricking her baby boy into marriage was their grandson, who by the way, she never saw because Sara refused to let him know his dad's side of the family.

Jase squeezed my hand when this woman sneered at me, too, like I somehow supported or participated in causing all her miseries. I squeezed in return as I bit back the tirade I wanted to unleash about how *I* remembered Patrick Scott, dammit.

Patrick's father tried to tone down the damage his wife had just inflicted on grieving Sara. The tears arrived. Sara was a weeping mess. She scooted up against me and gripped my free hand. Good thing I wasn't crying, or else I'd have no way to dry my eyes. Marcus sat beside Sara and held her after supplying extra tissues. I was starting to wonder if Patrick's parents were racist as well. Why not?

Marcus didn't handle Sara like they were a couple, but I hated the way Patrick's parents looked at our mixed group with evident disdain. I found myself praying to keep my mouth shut more than I prayed for Patrick's soul. *Not in good Christian mode today. Forgive me, please, Father.*

After an hour of memories recounted by firefighters who watched Sara, me, or both too often, Sara's eyes had to feel like sandpaper. Mine did and I hadn't shed a tear.

Well, hell.

That probably looked awful. *How could I cry about something that didn't upset me?* I started thinking about every instance in recent memory Patrick Scott had come into the bar. He wasn't the Rusty Nail, Pat Connor was. That meant Patrick Scott was the guy who gave Jase shit about playing with his instrument. The guy tapping his cheek, so I'd know where to hit him. The guy who beat the hell out of the woman beside me. Of course, he'd get off on showing me where to hit him. He'd been trying to provoke a problem longer than I could recall. *How long had Jase kept him away from me before I'd known to worry?*

That realization did bring tears to my eyes. I glanced at my new boyfriend who'd been doing boyfriend things for me behind the scenes for a while.

Jase's eyes were glassy as he kissed my temple. Our moment dashed when I heard a voice take to the podium that had Jase removing his hand to place his arm protectively across my shoulders. He pressed me to his side as close as possible. Tears of anger flooded my eyes and spilled onto my cheeks.

A shudder went down my spine as I felt Klive's eyes from somewhere. I only hoped he watched the bastard standing before the church.

"You'll have to forgive me." Pat Connor cleared his throat. "I'm not too good at public speaking, but if I can't go out of my way to honor a friend, what kind of friend was I ever?" Pat Connor's gravelly voice grated my nerves the same as Jase had grated his face just under two weeks ago. His skin healed but scabbed in places. I noticed Gustav and Jarrell both sat forward with their hands clenched between their knees. Constance between them shot me a look like she worried about their shift.

"Pat was a good man. Loyal husband. Devoted father. Never a hesitation about running into a burning building to save a life. I'm sure he'd have climbed a tree to save a cat if any calls had come in." He and the audience chuckled, sniffling sounded throughout. My bullshit meter was off the charts.

"I'm Pat, too. We became fast friends because we sought each other out to clear up the confusion over two Patricks. He chose to go by Patrick, I chose Pat, but old habits work back in. We got to the point where we didn't mind taking care of business for the other when someone confused us for the other. We put out many fires together. Enjoyed the open road on our hogs. Love our kids and wives. Watched out for each other's families to keep them safe." *What the eff?* "You know how they say those with unfinished business become ghosts? I know the Pastor told us that we rest with God when we pass, but Pat lost his life. Someone *stole* it from him. He didn't die in his sleep an old man the way we all hope to go one day. He left so much unfinished business I can't help hoping he either haunts those he left, or someone brings him peace beyond the grave by finishing his last work."

Gustav and Jase inhaled loud enough to hear while Sara gasped. I glared at the bastard as I couldn't tell whether he looked at me or Sara.

24 | ♀

THE CHURCH CLAPPED FOR Pat Connor's colossal bullshit speech. *Yeah, let's all be haunted. Who claps for that?* I was so pissed off I hadn't realized I'd squeezed Sara's hand too hard until she whispered, "Don't let him get to you, Kins. That's what he wants. It's what they all want, all the time. They lost. Of course, they're gonna be pissed."

They lost. Odd phrasing.

I nodded and went with the flow of people lining up to leave the church. My eyes searched the space and mass of people for Klive, but he wasn't who I found staring at me. The Bieber guy was. At least I thought he was. He never removed the sunglasses.

"Kins, let's go," Jase said. For some dumb dawning reason, I just realized Rustin hadn't been with us.

"Where's Rustin?"

"Back of the church. Watching. Observing," Jase said. "We need to be walking with everyone else. Don't let that asshole see he rattled your cage, baby."

"I agree with Taylor," Gustav said, the bass of his low voice felt in my chest. "We got your backs. Nothing to fear, Little Red."

He meant that in a way that made me wonder if they'd come for the sole purpose of keeping me safe, because while Sara glued herself to my side and cried her heart out at the graveside, Gus and Jarrell stood in ways that blocked us off from anyone expressing condolences. Jase held my hand when he could, but there were times that I had to hold Sara up with both arms around her.

Okay, Patrick Scott busted their son's nose. She'd broken a crystal vase over his head to save them both. He'd harassed her and threatened her for months, sold their family out for a drug fix. *I couldn't cry for a guy like that. How was she?* I had no empathy thought I tried. I was shitty at fake.

Pat Connor stood on the other side of the grave watching me and my bodyguards with the meanest resentment on his face. His look condemned me for the death of Patrick Scott. In a way, I felt we stood out in this group while we shared a staring contest like I could threaten him just the same with my eyes alone. In my head, I recalled his fear that something might happen to him because of a call I'd make. No idea who I'd call to make that happen, but Pat didn't need to know that I didn't know. My glare dared him to do something. *Try me, asshole.*

Sara lifted her face from my shoulder, wiped her eyes, peered at what I was. Pat Connor winked at us before turning with the crowds who left the cemetery for the food at Patrick Scott's parents' house.

"Do we have to go to this?" I asked when I was safely inside Jase's truck. My attitude pissy, I was ready to shank Pat in the knee to give him a permanent limp like a warning of worse to come if he tried to harm me ever again.

"We have to go, but I was the one against this from the start, Kins," Jase said.

"This is the final lap before the finish line. Hang in there," Rustin said from the backseat. Before Jase put the truck into drive, Constance opened the back door and slid inside beside Rustin.

"Let's get the hell out of here," Constance said. "Tell me I'm not the only one who saw that asshole staring *Kinsley*, not Sara, down the whole time."

"Yeah," Rustin said, "we saw, but Kins didn't help herself by staring back." He shook his head. "Constance, you still mad at me? I can't handle any extra drama while she's busy creating a mountain for me to deal with."

Constance chuckled while I stared out the window to hide any guilt. I was too angry at Pat Connor anyway.

"Boy, you give yourself too much credit. As long as I'm not written in your history book as a cliffs note, we're good. I gave you at least a paragraph in mine," she joked. I expected her to be upset or vindictive, but she was more dismissive; ready to relax after their tension boiled over on Monday. "Not only that," she said, "but I don't like covering for the band by myself. I'm never sleeping with anyone I work with again. Gives me way too big a load to deal with on my own."

Jase and Rustin laughed. Rustin spoke up. "I feel stiffed since I gave you two paragraphs in my history book."

I turned and smiled, but like a total fool who wanted to die, Rustin said, "Don't worry, Red, I'll give you two as well. No need to be jealous."

Constance and I gasped. Our eyes met as she shook her head. Tears filled her eyes. Jase's head tilted back as he groaned in aggravation and punched the steering wheel.

"Dammit, Rustin," Jase said. "I thought you already had a mountain of drama on your hands. Now, it's volcanic, you dumb ass. 'Cuz this day wasn't shitty enough."

"You *slept* with him?!" Constance demanded of me. Disappointment stung her face. Any tears I'd fought came raining down. *She'd never been disappointed in me before!*

"It wasn't like that, Constance," Jase argued. "We banged, then I let Rustin get in on our action the next day. Kins didn't say no. She said yes quite a few times. Shouted, actually."

"Jase Taylor!" Constance shouted. "I'm gonna show you shouting if you keep talking!" Constance slapped the hell out of the back of his head. He sat up but I threw a finger his way with an order to focus on the road. "What kind of inconsiderate fool are you?" she asked. "Kinsley was almost a *virgin* and you tainted her with a three-way like one of your slutty groupie redheads you screw in her honor! You call yourself her *boyfriend*? She shouldn't even call you her *friend* after this shit! Who does that to someone they *love*?" Her rage turned on Rustin. "Who does that with the girl their best friend *loves*?! Rustin Keane, I'm gonna slap the shit out of you and you aren't going to argue with me or stop me because you deserve *so* much worse, do you understand me?"

Whoa! I'd never heard that tone, but Constance Marie Laveau seemed ready to spout a voodoo curse on both of them. *Dear, God, please spare me this wrath!*

"Yes, ma'am," Rustin said, lifted his chin and faced her so she'd have enough leverage to create a thunderclap through the truck with her hand against his face. "Shit!" Rustin cursed and held his cheek.

"You be lucky it wasn't a right hook," she said.

"Am I next?" I asked. Her eyes were angry at me, but she shook her head.

"Why would you be? Although you deserve your ass beat. Did you agree to be his girlfriend before or after this happened?"

I shook my head in shame. What a sobering awful realization of how far I'd fallen.

She shook her head too. "I thought you had more self-esteem than that." *Ouch!*

"Hey, ease up, Constance, damn!" Jase broke his pissed silence.

"No! Why should I? Because ever other girl tells you everything you want to hear, Jase? Must be so hard for you having a real woman telling you how it is, yeah? Let's play a game of compare and contrast. Klive King kept her pure for you while you desecrated the girl he treasures. Clearly Klive has more respect for her and you, Jase, than you have for either of them.

"Kins, I hope you can see the clear difference between a real man and a horny boy masquerading as a man." She stared at him in his rearview mirror, snapped her fingers, bobbed her head while I covered my lips and swallowed the ugly truths pouring from her mouth. "Oh, by the way, I quit Rock-N-Awe. I knew I worked for a womanizer but made an exception because of your musical reputation. I can't work for you in good conscience anymore. I'm done."

"Dammit, Constance! Our sex life is none of your business. What we do behind closed doors with full consent from each participant is our *own* business!" Jase shouted. "We have a set tonight. You can't quit without notice. I'm sorry I let you both down, but why does the girl always get a pass while the man is *always* the bad guy?"

"The man *isn't* always the bad guy. I just spelled out what an honorable guy Klive was. I only labeled you two the bad guys for being womanizers. Get your facts straight. You can lead your own band with your sidekick since you don't do *anything* without each other. Kinsley, you're coming home with me instead of him since you're still hiding from public. If you're smart, you'll break up with him now before he screws anyone else with his best friend."

Holy shit! Thank God Jase's GPS gave the final instructions for our arrival.

Constance jumped out of the truck and slammed the door too hard. Jase got out and grabbed her hand before she could storm away. She jerked free and slapped the absolute shit out of him, spit in his face, then her knee met his nuts.

Rustin winced. "I thought I had it bad with the slap."

"I tried to warn you not to screw up."

"I screwed you, but I didn't know in doing so I'd screw her over."

She walked around the truck and pulled me out like the men were the dangerous ones rather than the Inferno biker gang inside the house.

Sara stood on the stoop gnawing her lip and chewing her cheek. She held to the column on the far end of the two-story home, staring at the sky. My blood froze with my pace when I caught sight of Pat Connor walking up to her. He placed his hand on Sara's back, caressed up and down the way I'd wanted to do to Klive in St. Augustine but didn't feel permission. *That was a permissible gesture. Intimate.* Sara didn't flinch, which made this worse.

Constance froze at the same sight and jerked me to the side of the house where we could eavesdrop without being seen.

"Think of your son, Sara. We can protect you both. Inferno looks out for each other like I said in my speech. I just don't want anything to happen to you because of King's little princess prancing all over town looking just like you."

I gasped in offense. Constance clapped a hand over my mouth and held me still. *King's little princess?! WTF?!*

"I knew I hated that bitch," Constance whispered even though Pat was talking.

"I don't need you to protect me," Sara said. "I can protect myself."

"Really? Bet you didn't know you banged two Infernos last week, did ya?"

"What the hell?" Sara demanded.

"No need to get upset. They said you were pretty talented. Worth keeping around."

Ugh. Constance and I shared disgusted expressions. As angry as I was, I felt sorry for Sara.

"Pssst!" Someone grabbed our attention toward the back yard. The Bieber wannabe held a cigarette and took a long drag. His reflective glasses showed a mirror of the gray clouds covering the sky today as he exhaled. The invitation was exactly what Constance needed. She towed me behind her as I caught a glimpse of Jase and Rustin heading toward the front of the house. *Would they see or disrupt Pat's little interlude with Sara?*

"Can I bum a smoke?" Constance begged the guy. He nodded and held the pack out to her. As I looked up at him, I caught the lower portion of a green teardrop from his eye. *Yikes! Prison tattoos!*

Constance lit the smoke and sucked as if through a straw. I wished I could suck from a straw inside of a mixed drink. Hell, I'd take shots at this point, even if they'd make me sick. In a way I envied smokers for having something to soothe themselves with while everything festered inside me.

"Thank you." She finally breathed as she released the cloud from her lungs. His lips tilted. He offered the pack to me, but I shriveled my nose and said no thanks. He shrugged and pulled another, lit the stick between pretty lips. Like Klive's lips. *Oh, Klive. I wish you were here.*

"You're not wearing your cologne today," I said.

Those lips formed a full smile, though he didn't open his mouth. A dimple creased his left cheek. *Like Klive.* Damn if Klive wasn't on my heart and brain because of Constance's freaking rant.

"I ran out," he said. "Since I couldn't remember the name, I'm kinda screwed. That's what happens when you bum free samples."

"Guess it smelled good if my girl remembered you by your scent," Constance said. She watched me with cautious eyes needing to protect me from all men. "Say, killer, you part of Inferno?" she asked.

"Killer?"

"Yeah. I see the bottom of a teardrop under your glasses."

He smirked before releasing a plume of smoke toward the sky. "I'm not Inferno." He wiggled his left fingers holding his cigarette, flashed a ring.

Nightshade.

"Why do you ask?" he asked. "Is Inferno why you two were hiding on the side of the house instead of going inside? That one guy was watching Micro Machine pretty hard at the graveside."

"Yeah, we overheard something that makes me think the one staring her down is up to something. What's Nightshade doing here?" Constance asked in almost a whisper, a quick look around.

"Someone in high places wants eyes on the situation." His chin dipped as his head gestured at me. My jaw fell in awe.

"Yeah?" Constance blew smoke. She tipped my lips closed, then turned to face him while she leaned against the house. Oh, hell. That was her interested posture. Maybe Tyndall wasn't the only one into bad boys. "Would that someone have a British accent and gray eyes?" she tested.

He smiled again, the dimple creasing his cheek. "You know I can't tell secrets. Just know while I'm here, she's safe."

"Ooh lala! What if a fight broke out in the middle of all those Infernos inside? One guy gonna take on the whole group?"

I couldn't believe I was watching Constance come onto this guy and press him for information! *Had Klive put protection on me? Not just any protection, but Nightshade protection? Was this what Constance meant by rich men buying dangerous friends?* When I'd served him at the bar the first time, Klive had been sitting with Eric, who openly bragged about what a badass you have to be to earn a Nightshade ring. *Oh, Klive King, you have thickened the plot in my life.*

"I don't have to take the whole syndicate down. I'm not alone and you know it. She'd better get inside before her boyfriend comes looking for her."

"Her boyfriend's not here. He hired you guys to be here in his place," Constance said as she stubbed her cigarette out on the stucco wall.

"Oh? This the gray-eyed British guy you were talking about?" he asked. "He the same guy who gave you a rose at your meet?"

I rolled my eyes. "That's who she's talking about, yes, but he's not my boyfriend. The guy I'm with today *is* my boyfriend. She'd just rather the Brit was because she's mad at my boyfriend."

"Damn right, I'm mad. If the Brit had been your boyfriend, he'd be here by your side, and if you'd banged *him*, you'd be even brighter than the night you fooled around."

"Constance!" I hissed. My eyes shot toward the guy in alarm, cheeks hot with embarrassment. "Don't say things like that in public."

"Kinsley Hayes, I'll say whatever the hell I want. It's the truth. Look at your eyes. They were glowing when he put his hands on you. They're dim and it's partly the Brit's fault for letting Jase have you. That asshole."

Okay, Jase had a point about men being blamed. *I* could've said no. I should've spoken up to tell her but left her alone to keep her from doling the fury she'd unleashed on the guys already.

"He's not even your boyfriend and wants eyes on you?" the guy asked, stubbed his cigarette out. "Kind of possessive, don't you think?"

I studied his ugly brown blazer and floral silk shirt beneath. The hot guy who buys tacky clothing to repel people from being attracted to him. Nice bone structure. Facial hair a tad darker than the hair on his head. Still had no idea what his eyes looked like though. *Did handsome men fare well in prison? Had he? Maybe not faring so well in prison was why he was in Nightshade now?*

Constance shook her head and rolled her eyes. "Boy, you don't know possessive. Keeping someone from talking to other men, that's possessive. This British guy, he's *protective*. There's a difference."

"I see. What if we weren't hired but *ordered*?" he asked like a test.

Wow. I narrowed my eyes as I mulled the idea. *Would I be surprised to learn Klive might be a shot-caller?*

Constance shrugged. "Did the British guy order you to be here?"

He shrugged like her. Not a yes. Not a no. Interesting.

"Look, killer." She moved closer. "I wouldn't care if he'd ordered a damn thing. Even bad boys have good sides, huh?" One of her flashy nails traced an ugly yellow flower on his chest. He seemed mildly amused, but unaffected. Oh, boy. That was Constance catnip. She didn't back down from a good challenge because she never really had to work for anyone she wanted. Funny. She had a lot more in common with Jase than she realized. "If he's somehow in the upper echelon ordering men like you around, Kinsley's safer than I knew. I'd sleep better at night because I trust him. If he chose *you* to watch her, that says a lot about you."

"And you, Ms. Hayes?" His reflective glasses displayed my image as he took his attention from her advances. The confident reflection in Jase's glasses when we'd cruised in his Charger now displayed fear in her eyes and no flush in her cheeks. "I've heard you have high morals," he said. "Your outstanding reputation on the track speaks for itself. Does it bother you that someone from Nightshade has me watching you?"

I swallowed, still contemplating the enormity of the implication, the view of Klive changing, my own views shifting like a puzzle piece settling into a place I should've seen sooner.

"Well, I guess I should be bothered in a way, but given today's surroundings, I'm gonna say thank you. I'd be a fool to be offended by the protection. However, without anything to defend me from, you're just a stalker. I'm curious where you truly fall in?"

"No offense, Ms. Hayes, but if I had time for stalking, I'd be doing other things with my freedom."

"None taken. If you were at my meet, does that mean I'm in danger outside of today?"

"I just told you you're safe if I'm here. You were safe when I was there as well."

"And if you're not here or there?" I arched an eyebrow.

He arched one of his own, lips twitching as he shook his head. Like Klive. *Dammit Klive King, what have you done to me when you are possibly on the wrong side of the law???* This meant I definitely needed to cut him out of my picture. *How could I when apparently he had this guy protecting me? Good grief. How much did Jase know?*

"You ever met the head of Inferno?" the guy asked as he led us toward the back door.

"Not that I know of," I told him. Several people gathered in the back yard for breathing room watched us emerge from the side of the house.

"Well," he said, "if you charmed the British hard ass, maybe you can make friends with Inferno's leader? Then he's no longer an enemy and I won't be needed?"

"Sounds dangerous," I said. "I didn't charm the British hard ass. Since you call him that, means you know him. I've been a bitch to the Brit from day one. Should I plan to be a bitch to Inferno's leader and think it will land me anywhere but chained to someone's bed?"

Constance cursed and shot him a nervous look. She and I walked through the sliding glass door he pulled for us.

"Dangerous, perhaps," the guy agreed, "but danger had no problem toying with you in the church and graveside."

Constance and I leaned back to look at him like he'd lost his mind.

"Are you saying what I think you are?"

"I'm saying you may as well walk right up to the face of danger and know your enemy while you have ample protection. Who knows when you'll get another shot? Ray doesn't come to Inferno gatherings for just anything. I think he wants to meet you in person."

Holy shit! Was I brave enough for this?

25 | ♂

KINSLEY'S PULSE JUMPED IN her neck while she looked up at me like she might siphon courage from another who didn't fear Raymond Castille.

"Damn, baby, there you are," Jase said as he rounded a corner. Worry etched every faint line in his face like he aged with each passing second in the presence of Inferno. Not because he was nervous, but Kinsley was a moth surrounded by flames desperate to consume the girl provoking a war. "Who's this?" He asked with suspicion.

"He's with me," Constance said and grabbed my hand. "You gonna have a problem with guys I talk to being around Kinsley as well? Guess she'd better get used to having no more friends since guys are nicer to her than women."

"Hey, Constance, ease up, alright? I'm sorry for everything."

"Not me you should be apologizing to," she said. "Have you apologized to Kins for defiling her?"

I arched an eyebrow. Jase shot me an attitude before refocusing on his girl who didn't appear to disagree with Constance.

"Kins, I'm sorry for defiling you." Jase at least seemed genuine even if brief.

"I forgive you, Jase. Constance, now that he's apologized, you'll say no more on the matter," Kinsley commanded in a sudden personality shift. *My words. My tone. My solidarity.* "You need to remember yourself as my friend. This is my boyfriend now. I need you to respect him for me if you can't do it on your own."

Two years ago, I'd watched the fearful girl morph into an empowered woman after I'd riled her enough. Just as she had then, she'd shifted now, and I wondered if she sensed my true identity.

"Where's Ray?" she asked Jase.

"*Ray?*" Jase asked like she'd lost her mind. "As in *Raymond Castille?*"

"Yeah."

"Hell no. We didn't come for Ray. We came for Sara."

"I'm sure he did, too. But if he really came for me, I'm not cowering in a corner. You can either take my hand and stand with me or stand down and see yourself out."

"Damn," Constance whispered with reverence in her friend. She looked up at me like I possessed some magical power. I pretended not to notice, kept my eyes glued to Kinsley and our surroundings.

Kinsley closed her eyes and released a shaky breath. While we watched, she shook her whole body loose, stretched her arms, popped her neck same as she did before the beach obstacle course or before walking onto a track.

"Let's do this shit." Her expression hardened, shoulders pulled back, chin lifted, and she walked out of the room. I released Constance in order to fall in behind Kinsley. Jase took her hand, but she told him to instead place that hand on her back. The way I would've. The way I wanted to.

Constance stood close behind me in new fear for the situation Kinsley was thrust into. "Hell, no," Constance said under her breath when Sara grabbed Kinsley in a big hug.

"Where were you? I was worried," Sara said, checked Kinsley's expression. "What's wrong?"

"What's right, Sara?" Kinsley asked.

"Good point. Silly me," Sara said. Her nervous eyes inspected Jase and me. She gave Constance a polite, if not tense, smile. "If you'll follow me, food is in here. There's beer, liquor, water, tea, soda. Patrick's parents are upstairs. Patrick's mother's been sedated. His father is lying down with her so we shouldn't have anymore drama. She thinks you're my sister. Sorry for the mean looks she gave you." Sara led us toward the kitchen with a huge island full of catered food.

"Did she think Kins was your sister because you told her she was?" Constance asked. Jase and I exchanged a look over Kinsley's head as Sara stopped short to assess Kins, then Constance.

"Why would you think that? No. I never said anything. Same ol' shit that used to get us mixed up at the bar. We look alike, Constance."

Constance snorted like she wished to call bullshit. Kinsley glanced at Constance, then diverted when she saw the large dining room full of Inferno vests and rough men. They mixed with nicely dressed Inferno members. *Here goes nothing.*

All silenced when Kinsley interrupted their conversation with an, "Excuse me, gentlemen."

Gustav, Jarrell, Marcus, Joey and Eric joined Jase and me around Kinsley like she really was the *Queen Bee* I'd code-named her. Sara shoved through our huddle to pinch in between Constance and me to see Kinsley. Jase stood on Kinsley's right, but glanced at me like he didn't want Sara near her. I agreed but bad form to treat her as a threat in front of the current audience.

"Ray Castille," Kinsley said with dawning. She apparently knew his face. "Fire Marshal. You warned me about capacity and threatened to call the cops about me potentially serving under-aged drinkers last year," Kinsley said to the man sitting on the opposite end of the table. "On a separate occasion, you also told me *I* was too young to be drinking before you bought me a drink. Still sore I refused?"

Ray chuckled.

"A true pleasure to hold a place in your memory, Kinsley Hayes. Glad you took my warning seriously, but you do still look too young to be drinking." He smiled at the beautiful girl with balls of steel. "Please, sit. Pat. Give her your place. You," he snapped at another, "make her a plate. What's your fancy?"

"I'm not hungry. Thank you." She clutched Jase's hand as she watched Pat Connor rise from his chair with mere inches between them. Her chin lifted with his person as she held his glare. He took in her entourage.

"Guess you could say I remembered my big bad bodyguards this time, eh, Pat?"

Good girl.

"Don't you worry your pretty little head about Pat anymore, Ms. Hayes. He's now wearing dentures and been castrated for laying hands on you," Ray said.

Kinsley gasped and cupped her mouth. Without a bloody thought, the damn woman placed her hand to Pat's arm! He flinched in real fear.

"What'd I tell you?" he asked her in almost a whisper.

She shook her head. "I didn't call anyone."

"You didn't have to," Ray's voice rose over their private conversation. "You gonna tell him you're sorry for his loss?"

All the men laughed, but Kinsley had tears in her eyes. The little fool felt bad for a man who would've raped her! She had no idea the evil that would've befallen her.

"Pat, leave us." Ray waved his hand. Pat's cold eyes looked me over. I smirked and tilted my head like I was able to see his empty scrotum through his pants. *Perhaps he sensed my true identity as well?*

"Please, Ms. Hayes, be seated."

Kinsley took Pat's vacated space across the long table from Ray like two royals of different kingdoms discussing foreign policy. The rest of us in the room were now spectators to their meeting.

"Did you castrate him?" Kinsley asked with the tone of a disapproving diplomat.

"If I did, how I discipline my men is none of your business, Ms. Hayes."

"Do you discipline your men, Mr. Castille?"

"If they need it, yes, but if they're following orders, there's nothing to discipline them for."

"Have you ordered your men to harass me and my friend, Sara?" she demanded.

Sara placed a hand to Kinsley's shoulder, leaned close. "Kinsley, don't. It's not safe."

Kinsley placed her hand on Sara's but squared a look on Ray before inspecting his men. "I see some familiar faces. Some heroes. Men I've admired. Some I've served. I know half your drinks by heart."

"We're not all bad because a few bad apples spoiled the whole bunch for you," Ray said. "These heroes are just a group of fire fighters who love our bikes and the open road as reprieve from stressful jobs. In fact, we rather admire *you*. Some of us attend your meets. We enjoy watching you run. Get the article." He ushered one of his guys to lay a newspaper in front of Kinsley. A marker came next. Ray laced his fingers on top of the mahogany. "Would you do me the honor of autographing your photo?"

Kinsley pulled the cap from the marker with her teeth, scrawled *Sorry for your loss* over her photo. I held my smile to the best of my ability at my feminist bitch implying herself as their loss. *Very good girl!*

Eric cleared his throat in silent communication. *He was right. She matched.*

Ray thanked her when she passed the paper back. I watched him grin at her writing as he understood her private message. *Oh, to see Kinsley buck Cheatham the way she did this man.* Ray was enjoying her spirit, but *would he enjoy her enough to allow her to live in peace? Would he see the clear message that she was Nightshade's girl to be left alone or else?*

"I have a proposition for you, Ms. Hayes. Seems you've endured some accidental fallout from my men mistaking you for the wife of our fallen hero. When they were supposed to be keeping an eye on her, they lost focus when you entered the frame. How about I call Pat off you permanently in exchange for you attending our next fundraiser for the fire department?"

"Call Pat off me? Confirmation you had him on me. You call *all* of them off me." Kinsley's brows rose. "What's the catch about the fundraiser?"

"There's been a lot of scuttlebutt about your fight with Sheriff Ansley's daughter. You have a great many fans, not just of your running. I speak for every one of us when I say we admire your skills. King teach his girl to fight?"

Kinsley's chin snapped up. *Shit! Shit! Shit! How was she to respond?*

Jase cleared his throat. "The girl is *mine*, not King's. I taught her."

Ray assessed Jase. "Guess that means you're Nightshade now. Congrats. Means you've got more balls than Patrick Scott ever gave you credit for. God rest him. We also know this girl of yours has more balls than Pat does now, too."

The group of men chuckled.

Kinsley didn't see the humor. She stared without giving away any shock she may have felt. *Would she give her boyfriend the same pass she appeared ready to give me outside when I'd tested her tolerance?*

"I am," Jase said. "Which makes her Nightshade property. Your guys mess with her, well, they lose their balls."

Kinsley clenched her hands together beneath the table as her only tell. I was glad for reflective glasses hiding my eyes. No one saw my noticing her attempt to remain unflinching.

"Guess we know who took Pat's jewels now, Ms. Hayes," Ray said. He didn't mind. Maybe I'd been right about Pat going rogue and making calls which jeopardized Inferno's good standing with Nightshade. "As I was saying, I'd like to invite you to our fundraiser. Micro Machine would bring in quite the crowd. We could raise a lot of money for our fire department."

"Does your feud with the police have anything do with my being there?" she asked. "Seeing as how I beat the Sheriff's daughter to a pulp, you wanting to use me to give you a one-up? Puts me at a disadvantage with the Sheriff if I say yes. I'm not sure your offer is fair."

"Great point," Ray said. Kinsley wasn't a fool, but I saw her considering the prospect in the name of peace.

I looked over at Jase. He watched me shake my head in the smallest possible way. He bent down to Kinsley's ear. While he spoke inaudibly, Ray looked at me with more interest.

"You. I see a Nightshade ring, but I don't recall meeting you in passing."

"You're right. You haven't," I said.

"Why the glasses? Who are you to be interfering in this deal I'm working with her?"

Eric shook his head at Ray. "Nightshade doesn't answer to you."

"I know who Nightshade answers to, Eric. Ms. Hayes, would you mind asking your guard to remove his glasses?"

"I'm not his boss, Mr. Castille."

"You sure about that?" Ray dared. "Maybe I should ask your boyfriend who his boss is."

She shook her head. "He keeps his glasses on. Here are my terms. While I'm thinking your offer over, I'd appreciate you demonstrating your leadership skills by leashing your dogs and leaving Sara and me alone. Once you prove your ability, I'll let you know. Deal?"

Ray's eyes narrowed a fraction as she rose to stand tall for such a petite woman. Her hands pressed to the table like she dared him to press the issue. He stood to his six-foot-six height, placed his hands on the table to return the threat. Kinsley held her stance like his height had no bearing on her courage.

"You've got a deal, Ms. Hayes," Ray said.

"Thank you." She assessed the crowd, met each set of eyes. "I really am sorry for your loss, gentlemen. Now, if you'll excuse me."

"Certainly." Ray gestured his men clear the way for her.

Kinsley grabbed Sara's hand in a show of solidarity, even though I saw she wasn't pleased with Sara.

"Oh, and Kinsley," Ray called after her, "tell King he's got quite the pretty pet. I look forward to the day he forbids you from playing with the new members and puts you into submission."

Bloody hell.

Kinsley froze, turned ever so slowly, venomous eyes hot with a poisonous glare. "I'd rather be the submissive queen of an honorable king than the ruler of a crumbling kingdom."

Fuck. Fuck. Fuck! All kindness vanished from Ray's face as he saw her as a direct threat. *How did one tiny person make such a mess with a few powerful words? How did such a young person have so sharp a tongue or wisdom to spout such? How was Cheatham not about to be all over Nightshade's shit?*

Kinsley turned her back on a new enemy. "Time to leave. I'm done paying my respects to disrespectful humans." She marched out of the dining room of riled rabid dogs ready to rip her apart. Nightshade surrounded Kinsley like she *was* their queen, but the craziest of this was how she held herself like she really was. For someone who claimed to be a shitty pretender, she was doing a marvelous job of playing a role I'd never wanted for her.

She'd spoken to him like a queen who had inner knowledge. *How would she know Inferno might be a crumbling mess? So many unanswered questions! The damage control! Cheatham was going to order a number on her.* Shit just got real.

"Holy shit, Kinsley Hayes, you damn fool!" Sara trotted beside Kinsley's strong pace toward the front door. She gripped Kinsley's hand like she might jerk her before whipping her ass. "You have no idea how stupid that was."

Kinsley came to an abrupt halt, her hot eyes on Sara daring her to have anything more to say. Sara dropped her hand like the look might've radiated through Kinsley's skin.

"Someone had to do it, Sara. The hell if I'm gonna let you become Inferno's whore on my watch. If you choose to do so on your own, just do me the courtesy of letting me know so I don't endanger myself fighting for you."

"You just did!" Sara rushed, looked around at the massive men guarding Kinsley.

"I'm no one's willing victim," Kinsley fired. "I didn't ask for this. He admitted they lost focus on you to focus on me instead. It is what it is. Stay safe, Sara. I hope we both can. Go enjoy your son."

Shame colored Sara's cheeks as she watched Kinsley leave her. By the time we got out to the vehicles, Kinsley wiped tears from her cheeks in a belated fashion.

"Holy shit, baby, I can't believe what just happened." Jase looked down at his girlfriend with reverence. "You okay?"

She whirred around and shoved him back. "No. You're a liar. At least Eric told me the truth from the start. Sara wasn't the only one who involved me in shit I shouldn't be. This isn't the place to reveal my hand. Right now, I look like I'm grieving same as everyone else. We can discuss your lying bullshit after I've had some space."

Jase nodded without argument. Kinsley grabbed Constance's hand, her lower lip trembling as she looked at the staff from the bar like everyone was a liar. The bouncers weren't sure how to help her with digesting the truth she'd failed to see all along.

Marcus remained calm and neutral. "We need to get you out of here, Little Red."

Gustav dangled his keys. "Let's go," he said.

He placed a hand to each of the women's backs and directed them toward his heavily tinted black Escalade. Jarrell moved Kinsley to one side, Gustav led Constance toward the other. I gave Eric his keys and jogged toward the Cadillac. Jarrell assisted Kinsley inside. I got into the back seat and forced her to sit center. Constance scooted in at her other side. The bouncers got into the front seats.

"Kinsley, head down," Jarrell said. I placed my palm to the back of Kinsley's head and forced her to lie on my lap. If I weren't busy anticipating the actions of the enemy, I may have relished the feeling. She placed her hands beneath her cheek, though one gripped my thigh while tears fell over her nose onto my pants. I had a hard time stilling my hands when nature would rather I soothe her, caress her hair, wipe the tears I should've been angry about. This damn woman. *Why her?* As I looked down at her, I also asked myself, *why not this damn woman?* She had spirit, tenacity, foolish bravery beyond backing up on her own. Giving power to a young person could be as dangerous as giving one a million dollars. However foolish her courage, she didn't deploy her words in the careless foolishness her peers may have. Ray was under her skin. She was under his and he wanted to watch a young person bring Nightshade down through rash actions. *What else could be his motivation for provoking her?*

Once we were on the highway headed back toward Tampa, Jarrell broke the silence filled with only Kinsley's sniffles. "Kins, we're in the clear. You can sit up now."

She sat up and apologized for the makeup smudge and black dots on my pants. "I hate wearing foundation. See what happens? I can't believe the mascara ran. I wore waterproof and everything."

"I've had worse stains on my pants," I told her. She cringed and faced forward.

"You okay, baby girl?" Jarrell asked.

"No. I asked you once, Jarrell, why are men so mean?" She scrubbed tears from her cheeks.

"Jase isn't mean," Constance said. "He loves you, Kins. *Really* loves you. I shouldn't have given him so much shit. I'm sorry. I need to go in later and fix this. I was too hard on him."

I cleared my throat. "Jase isn't Nightshade, Kinsley. He was bluffing back there for you."

"Thank God." She sighed and leaned against my shoulder. "Is Klive?"

Always asking what she shouldn't.

"Let's just say Klive has a powerful influence and leave it at that."

26 | ♀

WHEN WE TURNED INTO **the parking lot** of Constance's apartment complex, Jarrell and Gustav got out of the Escalade while we were told to stay inside.

"They're going to check the grounds. I'm going to see you up to the apartment and inspect the inside to be sure no one from Inferno goes back on their word," my apparent bodyguard said.

Constance nodded where she leaned against the window like she was as drained as I was.

"Say, killer, what's your name?" she asked.

"Henley."

I gasped and leaned so far away from him, I bumped into Constance.

"Whoa, what's wrong, Kins?" she asked.

Henley's thick brows dipped below the glasses.

"I want you to remove the glasses now, please," I said.

He shook his head. "Not till we are inside the apartment."

"You gonna say no more on the matter, too, like Klive would?" I tested.

"You gonna accidentally call Klive by *my* name again because my face came and went without a second thought while his looks caught you and held you?" he asked.

Shame lit my cheeks, but before I could craft a retort, Jarrell opened the door. Henley exited and offered his hand. I took his offering and scooted out of the vehicle. Jarrell put his body close to mine, tucked me under his arm and walked me inside the building. We entered the stairwell rather than taking the elevator. Henley jogged past us. I couldn't help recalling Klive in the stairwell of my father's building. How I longed for that same commanding presence to grab the chaos churning inside me and quiet the meltdown the way he had then.

Ray was tame enough back at the house with everyone watching, but if Pat Connor took orders from that man, what did that say about the true darkness lurking under the cordial character? When I'd bucked up at the end, hc hadn't an ounce of kindness left in his appearance. Ray seemed barely restrained and ready to show me who was boss and why. Pat might have scared me, hurt me, but Ray ... he was a dangerous predator who appeared to be the safe one to ask directions from. Then again, Klive had that same friendly appearance, but held himself with a calm authority that said you may regret questioning such.

I swallowed as I looked up at Henley holding the door when we came to the third floor. Gustav unlocked the apartment. All three men escorted us inside Constance's humble abode. She beelined for the pack of smokes on her coffee table. She slapped the pack against her palm, pulled a cigarette, lit up and walked out onto the balcony. Her head tilted back in evident ecstasy. Lucky. I wished to relieve myself that way. The only thing that made me tilt my head back that way was Jase.

Even if I was confused and irritated with my boyfriend, my body craved his calloused hands and rough love. He'd work this amplified tension from my back and shoulders by bending me to his will while I wasn't allowed to run.

Ray said they liked watching me run.

"Place is all clear," Henley said as he came back into the living area.

I stood with my hands on the counter in the kitchen, zoned out on the faux granite patterns and veins. He walked close. My eyes closed as he felt so much like Klive I could imagine turning and hiding my face against Klive's chest. I hated that I had no outlet for everything compounding. Hated that I had no idea what Klive was doing, who he was, what powerful influence he had and why.

"You guys should be safe. Eric's got eyes on Inferno. He said they stayed put after we left."

I turned to see Henley leaning back against the opposite counter near the coffee pot. Coffee. Yes, please.

He removed the glasses. I flinched at the jarring sight of a jagged scar slashed over his left eye. Three teardrop tattoos dripped from the edge of the scar.

"Happy now?" he asked.

"You're blind in one eye."

"I am."

"You've killed more than three."

"I have," he said. "I won't hesitate to add another if you're in danger or harmed."

"Henley, I'm really sorry if you've introduced yourself to me before and I didn't remember. You have no idea how many people come through the bar, even ones with scars, but don't think I forgot you. I can see why I mistakenly called Klive by your name. You have similar bone structure, jaw lines. Are you related?"

"No comment. I need to go back to my job, Ms. Hayes. My work here is done."

"You're leaving?" Constance asked. "Come have a smoke with me before you go." She stood in the frame of the sliding door. He nodded. I watched him go outside with Constance. Her hand went to his temple, but he caught her wrist and calmly pulled her hand down. She lit his cigarette, leaned almost close enough to brush his chest with her breasts. He remained indifferent.

Henley. How in the hell had I forgotten his scar? Had our paths crossed before the track? Gosh, what an oblivious bitch I could be. My poor friends and family. I needed to do better by them.

I found myself watching him with intrigue. Body language always fascinated me. I loved people-watching and guessing their life situations.

She smiled up at something he said. He smiled down at her. My head tilted at how much that profile, that smile, the body type reminded me of Klive. That man was haunting my every thought the way my bad boyfriend should've been.

Who was I kidding?

Jase haunted me to the point that I didn't want to think of him for fear I'd be a goner for the same boy who'd stolen my attention when I was a teen. Klive was a nice distraction to ponder in place of mulling the mysteries surrounding Jase's life. Was I afraid to be let inside his sore spots? Part of me feared I'd damage him beyond repair if he allowed me to know those vulnerabilities. I was a bad girlfriend. He needed a healthy woman, someone whose pride wouldn't tear him apart in vindictive anger when and if he pissed her off. He needed patience and kindness. Damn, he was so good in bed, though! He wanted me. I wanted him to want me, wanted to be Jase's object of affection.

Henley pulled the sliding door. Constance followed him inside. Both reeked of smoke. I shriveled my nose.

"You can sleep on the couch," Constance was saying. "Or you can sleep in the bed with me while Kinsley takes the couch."

Henley shook his head in disapproval, though he seemed amused. He hadn't put his glasses back on. His good blue eye looked me over. He had dark lashes like Klive's. They had to be related.

"I'll be seeing you around, ladies. Stay safe." He paused. "Shit. Constance, I left my lighter on your patio. Would you mind checking?"

"Sure," she said. He watched her go.

"Kinsley." He took my hand and tucked a card inside. "Behave."

"Okay, jeez." I tucked the card into my bra before Constance came running back.

"Here you go." She slapped the lighter into his palm.

"Thanks," he said.

"No, thank *you*," she said. "I appreciate what you're doing. Give my best to Klive and tell him she misses him."

I slapped Constance in the belly, even if I giggled. Henley's lips curled.

"Henley," I said, "how about you tell that pain in the ass that if he has anything to say to me, he can say it himself. No messengers."

"If I were a messenger, perhaps I'd deliver your request," he said.

"Perhaps if you were a messenger, I'd tell you to tell him I'm going to murder him next time I see him. Unless you'd rather commit mutiny and kill him for me."

Henley whistled, but I made him smile, so there was that.

"Maybe I'm protecting the wrong person," Henley joked.

Constance shook her head. "All right, killer. Be safe out there."

"Thanks for everything," I called. The door closed behind him and Constance locked up. Her shoulder leaned against the wall.

"He told me I don't need to go anywhere for the rest of the night. To let Jase and Rock-N-Awe suffer the consequences. I tell ya, that one is as hard to get as Klive. Wonder if Klive makes his guys abide by his personal set of standards."

"Assuming Klive is involved in Nightshade at all. I'm glad you're not going into work, but I can't believe you're so capricious about Nightshade." I followed her into the kitchen where we set about cooking dinner together.

"Why would I have an issue with Nightshade if my cousin is involved? Gustav's an added layer of protection. Like Jase said, any girl that's with someone from Nightshade belongs to Nightshade whether they know it or not. I'm related, so I'm protected. Interesting how Ray Castille referred to you as Klive's girl. That bit at the end was badass, Kins. Do you know something I don't?"

"What is this? The sixties? Being called someone's girl is so antiquated. No, I don't know anything. I just wanted to knock Ray off his arrogant throne. Seems I succeeded."

"Ugh. Guess those college cronies been convincing you all men are evil and being labeled someone's girl diminishes your feminine equality. We're not talking about being called just *anyone's* girl, Kins. There's something so sexy about being labeled as a bad-ass's girl. Can you imagine if Klive is who we are thinking? How cool it is that he's claiming you? That makes you the HBIC! And it explains why Ray dared you to prove who was in charge. What if *you* are Jase's boss? I think if anyone could make you submit, Klive would be the only one. I'd be glad to get on my knees for him, that's for sure."

"Constance Marie!"

"I'm sorry, is this pissing you off because that's *your* man? You gonna give me the same shit about respecting him that you did about Jase? Cuz you don't have to tell me to respect Klive. It's a given."

"I'm gonna kill you."

"Since queens don't get their own hands dirty, which one you gonna order to do it? Please pick Henley. There's something so sexy about a guy who's hot but altered. Wonder how he got that scar."

"You've lost your damn mind. Henley said Jase wasn't Nightshade. He probably got that scar from being shanked in prison. I'm not anyone's queen or the head bitch in charge of anything illegal! I'm Kinsley Hayes, track runner, future Diabetic counselor. I feel like I don't know anyone or anything anymore."

"Including yourself, apparently."

"Constance, shut it."

Rather than take my colossal hint to leave shit alone, she laughed at my anger. "You gonna also tell me you'll say no more on the matter like your King?"

"I'm gonna call my damn father to pick me up if you don't stop."

That got her to shut up. How she overlooked Henley's tear drops and the crimes blew my mind. I found I had a hard time looking at her as we scooped our food onto plates and sat down in front of the TV.

"Kins, don't be mad."

I didn't say anything. She lifted the remote while I lifted my fork faster than any lady would've. I was starving! *When was the last time I ate?* While I choked down dinner, we played *Jeopardy* with the contestants, then watched recorded episodes of dating shows.

"Boo!" We threw popcorn at the screen for the stupid decisions the foolish women made.

"What an idiot! He was totally hot." I shoved a handful of popcorn into my mouth. My cheeks filled.

"Your mother would be so proud," Constance teased. "What kind of idiot turns down the hottest guy who loves cats?" She stuffed her face, too.

"Maybe it's when she heard he loves cats that she called bullshit and picked the other guy. A hot kiss-ass is still a kiss-ass."

"True." She pulled a few pieces of popcorn from her cleavage and chowed. "I need a shower."

"Me too." I checked my cleavage and remembered the card tucked in my bra. "You mind if I go first?"

"Not at all. The hot water heater is so much better in this place than the last one."

"Hot water heater? If the water's already hot, why do you need a heater?" We went into her bedroom.

"Aren't you funny," she said with a look over her shoulder. She produced a sexy silk pair of pajamas that looked more like lingerie.

"Whoa, girl, don't you think that's a little risqué considering we aren't lovers?"

"You'd make a great wife, *cher*, I just know it," she teased. "You're so old-fashioned. You ever worn lingerie? Because you're gonna need to in order to be a good little wife, although I guess feminists from on anything that makes men want them. Wear pants to bed instead."

"Bitch." I sighed in annoyance. "I've had a long day. A long week, actually, so it's great you feel the need to mock me. I'm not a feminist, okay? It's hard to be tied down though. I'm used to being solo."

"Maybe you're with the wrong guy if you feel you're tied down. Has Jase tied you down?" She waggled her brows.

I slapped her stomach while I gaped. "No. He's not tied me down in the physical sense, but I'm not sorry I slept with him. He's an *amazing* lover." A blush warmed my cheeks." I *am* sorry I slept with Rustin. Please forgive me. It was a spur-of-the-moment temptation. You want me to say that you, Bayleigh and Tyndall haven't made me wonder about what it's like to just be with whoever whenever the mood strikes? I've discovered I must be defective in the world of modern females because I enjoyed the moment but felt like total shit after. Automatically cancels me out in the world of feminists."

"Hey, come here. I'm sorry. I shouldn't have screwed with you." She tucked me into her arms and gave a hug even though she hated hugs. I took what she gave and relished her offering as a Constance hug meant a lot. "I forgive you, Kins. Rustin's not someone *I* want to tie down for anything other than corporal punishment."

We shared a smile while I relaxed some.

"Kins, you're more traditional than you'd like to credit. I don't want you feeling ashamed of your values or personality because it doesn't match with someone else's dogma, that's all. Don't base your relationships off your friends. Do any of us have a relationship you envy outside of sex?"

"No."

"Exactly. You probably don't have many friends in college who have long-term relationships. Don't look at your peers. Do what you do. Pray. Be yourself. Have faith in who you were made to be."

"Thank you, Constance. I really needed this."

"I doubt Mr. Right will be a perfect guy, Kins. You don't want a perfect guy. They seem perfect because they're good at hiding ugliness. I'm not talking about looks. I'm talking about the ones who seem too wholesome, kind, Christian. Demons get comfy in church too. Jus' say'n." She held the sexy PJs. "These are for me. If Henley has to watch you, I'm gonna prance around in my favorite set to show him what he's missing. You can have my big Hooters shirt."

"Yay." I shook my head.

"Just kidding. I have something extra special just for you." My head tilted as she dug inside her closet. "Remember this?" She came up with a white linen button-down. I sighed in too much happiness to hide. "Yup. Sorry, I don't have any of your real boyfriend's shirts for you to sleep in instead. This'll just have to do."

I took Klive's shirt I'd slept in at Delia's and tested the scent. She nodded with a sad smile.

"Still smells like him."

"You have a thing for fragrances," she observed. "You remembered Henley based on his scent."

I chewed my cheek. "Correction. I have a thing for *this* fragrance because Henley was wearing Klive's cologne the first time I remembered meeting him at the track."

She tilted her head this time. "I call bullshit on his free sample excuse. This means he's close enough to Klive to use his cologne for some reason. We need to take something of Klive's to the Emporium and see if those perfume girls can figure out what it is."

"I'd love you forever. I may not be able to be with him, but I can at least breathe him in."

"Yes, now you can have sweet dreams tucked back into his cologne. Your secret's safe with me."

"Constance, do you really think I need to break-up with Jase or were you just flipping your shit?"

She sighed and crossed her arms under her ample breasts. "Truth or ass-kissing?"

"Truth. Why would ask if I wanted ass-kissing?"

"I told you not to sleep with either of them until you were ready to commit. You slept with him and now it seems like you commit because you don't know how to be with a dude *physically* without commitment, which isn't bad. It's good, but it is working against you because now you've committed yourself to Jase while you are so into Klive. Thank God you aren't committing to Rustin, too. What a mess.

"Kins, in my opinion, I meant what I said. Klive kept you for Jase. Seems like a test of honor. Especially if Jase is a Nightshade candidate. I'm not sure Jase passed the test. Maybe that's the only reason he isn't Nightshade."

I nodded in sorrow. All of this was too heavy to continue talking about.

The spray of the shower against my skin felt wonderful, but I still had a hard time relaxing as I replayed the day over and over. Hindsight sucked. How in the world had I taken on the leader of Inferno? Where had I come up with that phrase on the spot? *I'd rather be the submissive queen to an honorable king than the ruler of a crumbling kingdom.*

Did I really feel that way about Klive?

Who was that? Certainly not me, Kinsley Hayes, Micro Machine, Diabetic counselor.

256

When I was done with my shower, I lifted the card to see a replica of the one I'd lost. Black, soft touch with a single puff of smoke. No markings even when I shifted the item in the light. *Did Klive figure out that I'd lost the one he'd given me outside Sara's condo? Was the card Klive's or Henley's?*

Was Klive just a rich guy with powerful influence with Henley being his personal favorite go-to for dirty deeds?

Sad enough, some of Klive's mystique and edge vanished with the idea of him only being a wealthy dude with people at his beck and call.

No. Klive was my knife-wielding psycho from the elevator in my father's building. I recalled his words in that elevator two years ago when he'd demanded to know who'd caused the marks on my arm: *maybe it should be the business of the one with the knife.*

Yeah, Klive was dangerous the way Henley was. Maybe more dangerous if he wasn't coming right out in the open the way he'd ordered Henley to do on my behalf. If a man like Ray asked whether King taught his girl to fight, what did that say about Klive's reputation? That he couldn't wait to see King put me into submission, implying all fell into submission sooner or later ....

Oh, Klive King .... I shuddered as everything Constance spoke of jogged laps across my brain.

I wiped the steam away from the mirror and wrapped a towel around my wet hair. My bruises were already fading. I'd always been a quick healer, but maybe if I'd let Henley see me with these marks, he'd feel a little better that I wasn't flawless? Then again, the sight of bruises might make him more vigilant or angry that I'd been hurt at all. Either way, as I inspected my reflection, I realized my views had shifted. Klive being in Nightshade should've bothered me the same way the thought of Jase being in Nightshade had, but now I realized I expected Jase to have higher morals than Klive. My honorable soldier was on a pedestal inside my mind. Jase may have been promiscuous, but even I knew only the tiniest numbers of our population had the fortitude and tenacity to become a Navy SEAL. Hell, some never even made the journey through training with their lives.

I admired Jase more than anyone for his strength, for surviving, and I couldn't fathom belonging to someone so accomplished. When I imagined the wives of great warriors, those women were warriors of their own sort. They weren't weak girls suffering from acute indecision who lived with their parents and ran away from life on the texture of a track while pretending to be strong and determined. What a spoiled existence. An illusion.

What the hell was the matter with Jase and Klive? Both of them were men's men. They made no freaking sense playing games with me.

As I buttoned Klive's shirt, I wanted to cry from inadequacy. The queen to an honorable king. Was there really anything honorable to the male whose clothing covered my skin? He'd refused me in St. Augustine for fear of not remaining honorable with me. He'd used that word.

The knife-wielding psycho had done a fabulous job of pretending to hold the high ground I felt buried beneath as I fell asleep on the couch. He was anything but perfect. Neither was Jase.

I was the most imperfect of them all.

27 | ♀

CONSTANCE SAT ON THE edge of the couch. "Morning, babes. You okay? Sounded like Klive pissed you off in your dreams. Your pillows are on the floor. Blanket is a mess."

"Guess I had a rough night. What are you doing up already?"

"I have to go to work. I'm helping open up."

"Oh, right. Real life still exists." I blinked back spots from bright sunlight streaming in through the open sliding glass door. She held a lit cigarette. Her boobs bubbled from a tight Hooters tank. She stood to give me a view of barely covered butt cheeks in the booty shorts she wore. I watched her tap the ash off the end of her smoke before stubbing the cherry in the ash tray. Her purse went over her shoulder. She tossed her long weave to her back. I reached for my cup of water on the coffee table.

"I know Henley already warned you, but I need you to keep the door locked. There are plenty of frozen meals in the fridge. Snacks in the pantry," she said. "When I get back, we'll go out to eat unless you want me to bring you crab legs?"

I sipped and looked up at her. "Constance, you trying to butter me up while you imprison me? At least at Jase's I could play in the big yard. What am I gonna do with myself here? Why can't I just go home?"

"Kins, you aren't a prisoner, you're a refugee. Completely different." I gave her a deadpan look. She gave me the remote.

"Watch the man-hater channel and eat some chocolate mug cake or something. We are already functioning like lesbians so your friends from track would be proud. Since I'm going to work like the man, I'm gonna need you to do my laundry and those dishes if you're not gonna put out. Can't be all one-sided."

I cracked a grin. "Get out of here, Constance. Behave. Go make that money, honey." She kissed my cheek and I pinched her butt. "You're already a terrible wife. Flashing your goodies all over town and there's none left for me when you get home. If this keeps up, I'm going straight."

She laughed. "Nuh, uh. I'll go work it to come home and spend it all on you, love," she imitated Klive's accent.

I growled, then mocked Klive's accent as well. "Now, you're really advertising for my going straight, my sweet." I winked.

"I wouldn't hold it against you if you cheated on me with that Brit. Jus' say'n. Have a good day, sweetie."

"Ta ta!" The door locks flipped behind her. After that, I did watch the man-hater network. The kitchen was a bust. My stomach growled and I found Toaster Strudels. This was really bad, but oh so good! "Julia! Dude's behind you! Kill him, dammit! Quit letting him live to hunt you another day!" I shouted at *Sleeping With the Enemy*. "Ugh. I've got to get out of here before *Snapped* comes on."

I opened the sliding glass door to look out over the parking lot and highway beyond. After counting airplanes and blue cars, reading a few pages of the memoire on Constance's coffee table, I was far too restless. *Wait!* I checked the time. *Almost lunch time!*

I tripped over my own feet as I dove for the bedroom and rifled through Constance's clothing until I walked out in a tank top and Capri leggings that fit me to the ankle. I used the shirt I'd slept in as an over-shirt, undid the buttons, tied a knot over the tank, rolled the cuffs up my arms, made sure the back covered my bottom. I did what I could with my makeup considering I had no foundation or concealer in my skin tone at her house. Mascara, eyeliner, shadow, some blush. Highlighter. Lip gloss. My hair helped hide the bruise on my temple and maybe accounted for the shadow under my cheek. Hell, if so many had seen my video, I was hiding nothing. Why bother?

The bright sunlight felt so good on my skin. *Oh, to be in town again! To walk among other pedestrians and come and go as I pleased!* The ten blocks were wonderful.

Was Henley somewhere watching? Yeesh, I hadn't thought of that. Screw hiding in fear. Effing Ray. Like Henley said, he wasn't afraid to kill again if I were harmed. I should feel guilty about the idea, but I hushed my conscience and strode into the high-rise Daddy worked in. The elevator was empty since I'd arrived about thirty minutes before the standard lunch break. Twenty-two floors zoomed by in under a minute. *What floor did Klive work on?*

"Kinsley! How nice to see you!" Amy, the receptionist, said. "Look at you. I can't believe how pretty you are after that video. Good stuff even if your language was dreadful." Oops. I cringed at the thought of her listening to me in that capacity. She was always so sweet, holy, wholesome. "The man in the end who put his shirt on you, that's a mighty tall drink of water, though he should be whiskey since he can make you dizzy and hot just walking by. Your father told everyone in the office to quit talking about him, that you aren't a thing, but the women have a little pool going to see if you are. So, are you, or aren't you?"

"Um ... I ... don't even know his name. He was just a good Samaritan who kept me from being exposed after my fight." *Holy crap! Did I just tell myself this woman was wholesome?*

"Uh, huh. Guess it will all flesh itself out. Maybe if it's supposed to be, fate will bring you back together." She winked like a naughty woman wanting to win a bet. "Your father is in his office. Want me to let him know?"

"Nah. Is it okay if I just walk back?"

"Absolutely. He'll be so happy to see you." She clapped her hands and held them like a peppy former cheerleader.

"I hope so," I said with a smile. When I knocked on the door frame, I peeked inside expecting him to be alone. A cold rush of nerves seized everything calm. No wonder Amy was such a dang fool back there. That wicked woman!

Klive and Ben sat together speaking to my father. Daddy looked up first.

"Kinsley Fallon, my gosh what a wonderful Friday surprise!" Okay, anytime my father was so evidently happy to see me, I could never pin back my best smile.

"I'm sorry. Amy said you weren't busy. I didn't mean to interrupt. I stayed the night with Constance. She's at work." I stepped inside the office. "I was bored and wanted to see if I could have lunch with you. She's got one-hundred-percent junk food in her place."

Daddy hugged me so tight I lost my breath. My back popped; ribs felt pain in new places. He pulled back but kept an arm around me. His other hand came to my hair and moved the sections away from my face to assess the damage.

"Well, you certainly look better than your opponent. Then again you always have." Daddy winked while I gave another full smile. "Ben invited his friend to have lunch with us while we discuss the same problematic doctor who's been giving Ben a hard time. I believe you've met Mr. King?"

We turned toward the men while his arm remained around my waist like he was afraid I'd disappear if he didn't hold to me. Poor guy.

"Yeah, Mr. King wouldn't forget her," Ben teased and elbowed Klive. "Especially after he gave her his shirt to keep her honor intact after the brutal beat down of her sexy nemesis." Ben looked to the heavens and whispered a praise to God. I chuckled while the most adorable bashful grin overwhelmed Klive's suave features.

Oh, Klive.... How on Earth could this *man be the possible shot-caller of a syndicate?* He was such a gentleman.

"I didn't forget him or his kind gesture, either, Ben. Thanks again, Mr. King. So glad you were in the right place at the right time. Who'd have thought such a refined man would be slumming it in the club with a bunch of kids half his age?"

When Klive chuckled and nodded, I felt more natural happiness than I had at my father's genuine greeting. The six days since I'd last seen him felt like a month. I sensed Ben and Daddy watching us. I cleared my throat and girly crap.

"Do you guys mind if I crash your lunch plans? I've been told I have a knack for difficult men, maybe I can help."

Klive's eyes smiled at my joke, but so did the others. "Not at all, love. Did you have anything in mind?" he asked. *Oh, happy day! One love. I'd said that to him, hadn't I?*

"Well, I should be asking you guys that question."

"We didn't plan anything yet," Ben said. "Since you've been without real food at your friend's house, you pick."

"Anywhere you want," Klive agreed.

I glanced at my father to be sure he was okay with this since he'd given me such a hard time about Klive. He nodded. A wicked grin spread across my face. No way I was going to have lunch with my dad and Klive at the same time without Constance having a front row.

"Hooters."

My dad choked on an absurd laugh. "You're kidding."

"I'm not. What can I say, I'm in the mood to get my fingers dirty." I cheesed at the guys. "I only go there for the wings."

Ben laughed and high-fived me. "Life's not fair. Why does the perfect woman have to be my boss's daughter?"

"Your mother is going to murder me, Kinsley Fallon."

"So, keep your eyes up here and don't traumatize me," I reasoned and pointed to my eyes.

"Challenge accepted," Klive said but quirked his brows at my father. Daddy smirked at Klive like he just realized a way to watch this man squirm. He gestured I go ahead and lead the way.

We took my father's car, but when I got into the front passenger side, Daddy told me to get in the back. "Kins, I need Ben's face when I'm talking to him. I'll get nothing if I don't have his eyes when you're around."

"Dad, you're gonna have your eyes on the road. How you gonna have Ben's eyes? Maybe I should drive while you and Ben sit in the back."

"Fine, but no grinding my gears, girl." Daddy meant what he said because he tossed his keys over the car. I winced as I caught them. "Oh, honey, I'm sorry. I wasn't thinking of your ribs. You okay?"

"Yeah, I need the pain. Gotta get back into the swing of things."

He looked like he didn't believe me.

"Seriously. I'm okay. Get in." I waved him on while I remained on the passenger side to open the door for Klive like a smart-ass.

"How kind of you," Klive said. I kept the door closed for a moment after my dad and Ben sat inside.

"What kind of feminist would I be if I didn't open the door for a man? Although, we are about to enter the public sector. Gonna be able to handle it, Mr. King? Wouldn't want people to speculate."

"Kinsley, my sweet, I undressed to give you my shirt in public before a hundred spectators with cameras. If *you* don't want to be seen with *me*, I can go back upstairs. Your call."

My eyes narrowed as I yanked the door open for him. He chuckled and got in. I closed his door like a gentleman, then bounded to the driver's side.

My fingers drummed in mischief over the steering wheel. "I'm so happy to drive again!" I gushed. True story. So happy, in fact, that I didn't care about Klive ruffling my feathers.

"You better behave with my car," Daddy said.

"Do I have to? Yours is so much faster than mine."

"Your mom has that dang monitoring device to track my speed. Plus, she can see me travel on her phone."

"Jeez, what's she afraid of?" I muttered as I backed out and drove outside the parking garage. "It's almost like she's afraid you're gonna skip work and go to Hooters for lunch like a perv." I snickered.

"She's got the same on you, too, Kins."

"Psh. She thinks. Mr. King, be a dear and unplug that little device under the dashboard, please?"

"Oh, no. This is what happens when this girl has been cooped up for too long," I heard Daddy say to Ben. "You thought she was the perfect woman, but she's got a lead foot and road rage."

"Wonder where I got that from!" I said as I shifted gears and shot across the lanes on the highway headed for Clearwater. "Oh, honestly, you don't need to hold onto that handle. You're such a backseat driver, Daddy. *You* taught me to drive. Go on, chat with Ben. I'll chat with Klive. So, Klive, are there many traffic tickets in your past?" I wanted to ask if he'd ever been arrested, gone to prison, committed a crime, led Nightshade, pretended to be a good guy while being a bad, bad boy. He was too beautiful to be so bad which made this much worse if he were as bad as Constance was thinking.

I caught Ben smiling at me in the rearview mirror like he knew I was into his friend. He cleared his throat and focused on Daddy.

"I have been told I have a lead foot, as well," Klive said, "but I've never had a ticket I couldn't charm my way out of."

Oh, I bet. "What a coincidence, me too!" I gushed. I loved the smile he gave.

"Perhaps you were right," Klive said. "Maybe we should hang out to deter women and speeding tickets." *Happy sigh* .... "I'm impressed. I always muse that manual transmissions are anti-theft devices for today's youth."

"Today's youth?" I asked. "That's right. Old man in young places. Daddy made me drive a standard through high school. I used to hate it until I traded for the Hybrid Honda I'm in now. I'm all about helping the emissions control and saving the environment, but the Civic doesn't get quite the same pick-up I had in the Mini Cooper. So, how old are you, Mr. King? Like fifty?"

"Ha! Brutal. I've been told I have an old soul. Any guesses?"

"Forty-seven?" I asked with a mischievous grin. He shook his head and smiled toward the window. His head tilted against the head rest as he looked back at me.

"Want to play hot and cold?"

If I wasn't driving, I'd have closed my eyes. Freaking Klive. *Was he bent on tormenting me? Making me think of how much he mattered, too?*

"Forty-two," I said.

"Ouch! Easy with those forties. Cold, so cold, Kinsley."

"So, I've been told." I winked, shifted lanes. "Thirty-six."

"You're hot."

I snickered. "I'm flattered."

Ben chuckled while Daddy tsked.

"Up or down?" I asked Klive.

"That's cheating."

"Fine. Thirty-four?"

"Target acquired," he said.

"Not yet," Ben said. "His birthday is next Friday. He's thirty-three for one more week."

"Wow, not so old after all," I said loud enough to grab my father's attention. *Now I knew Klive's birthday.*

"Not so old?" Klive asked. "To a co-ed the late twenties are ancient."

"Meh, I guess I'm also an old soul for my youthful age, sir. My parents are nearing fifty and still wild and crazy. A good many of my friends outside of campus are varying ages, decades apart, yet we converse easier than I do with my peers. Real humans aren't caught up in such small things as defining others by a list of restrictions or requirements to be friends. To me, you aren't old at all. Now, if you start talking about back pain or predicting the weather with arthritis, we might reevaluate."

"Very funny, young lady," Daddy said. The rest of us chuckled.

"What about you, Kinsley?" Klive asked. "How old are you?"

Did he really not know? I guess why would he?

"I'll be twenty-five in June."

"Not so young as I feared."

Klive was a bold SOB, was he not?

"Do you have plans for your birthday?" I asked so my father wouldn't have time to comment.

Did I want to know? Could I handle that? What was wrong with me?

I looked over my shoulder to be sure the lanes beside me were clear to exit while I down shifted.

Ben leaned between our seats. "There's this private party we go to every year where we will be celebrating his birthday," he said. "What are you doing next Friday?"

"Prepping for a track meet if I'm ungrounded from running."

"Well, young lady," Daddy said. "You're grounded when we get home because I'm now in trouble since your mother can see where we've parked."

"Better make it worth it, then, eh?" I bat my lashes and gave him Bambi eyes as I wrapped my fingers in his hand while we walked to the restaurant.

He fought a smile before putting me into a head lock to give my hair a noogie I wrestled my way out of.

Klive chuckled and made a comment about karaoke hair when I walked through the door he held for us. I smoothed the crazy and asked for a table for four in Constance's section. The brilliant blonde tossed her perfect hair away from her boobs. When she bent for menus the guys had a sumptuous view of her cleavage.

"This way."

"I'm gonna die. I'm gonna die. I'm gonna die," Daddy kept saying under his breath.

"Pretend she's me."

"I'd murder you," he said.

"I'd be a frequent flier," Ben joked.

"Do y'all hire men?" Daddy asked her. "Because this one's gonna need a job in about five minutes."

She giggled as we were seated and laid her hand on his arm. I shot her a venomous glare. Ben whistled and glanced at Klive like he could have me. *Ha!*

"Do you all know what you want to drink or need a few minutes?" she asked.

We ordered our drinks. Klive looked over my head at a past football game on the TV. I asked Ben to trade with me so I could see as well.

"Oooh, the Bengals and the Bears. Football was so much fun when touchdown dances were allowed. They've stripped the fun out of everything," I said. "The Ochocinco river dance? Yes, please. Watch, after this play."

My father leaned over to watch, a proud smile on his face. I kissed his cheek.

"I'm so lucky to have a daddy who spent time with me."

"*I'm* so lucky to have a daughter who wanted to spend time with *me*."

"I'm lucky if I have an appetite after all this cheesy sitcom love," Ben said.

Daddy and I chuckled while we watched Chad Johnson dance in the end zone.

"That's one fine football player," Constance said. Our attention transferred to her.

"Constance, how good to see you," Daddy said. He seemed pleasantly surprised, then disapproving like he was her father too.

"Good afternoon." She passed the drinks around. "Now, I see that look, Mr. Hayes. You aren't allowed to ground Kinsley from hanging out with me. Jesus loves me even in my Hooters uniform."

He fought a smile and shook his head. She walked around the table to hug him. When she stood straight, she asked if we were ready to order.

Klive shook his head. "I've no idea. Never been here before."

"Never?" she asked like I'd struck gold. "Well, let me tell you the specials." She cast Klive a gorgeous smile and extended the grin my way but with an edge like I was in trouble for leaving the house. She listed the specials then said, "Kinsley is a big fan of the crab legs and the hot wings."

"Those do sound good. How to choose ...." Klive mused while looking at the menu as she pointed at sauce flavors.

"If you want, I can put in an order for both wings and crab legs, sauces on the side, and you two can share? Kins can't finish an entire order of either one on her own."

"Does that sound good to you?" Klive asked me. "I mean, only if you wash your hands."

Ben dropped his menu with his jaw.

I grinned and nodded. "Constance, lots of wet wipes and a drop cloth, please?"

She chuckled "Yeah, you wouldn't want to get buffalo sauce on that white shirt, now would you?" Constance called me out. I blushed since I'd forgotten. "At least if you stain it, you can just take it off, but when it smells so good why would you want to?" Her eyes smiled at me. Constance may not have slapped me yesterday, but she always got her revenge.

28 | ♀

DADDY AND BEN ALSO **ordered wings.** I noticed my dad watched Klive like he understood I was testing Klive for both of us. If Klive could pass the Hooters test, maybe my dad would give him more credit?

When Constance walked away, Daddy looked at me, the shirt, in particular. "That Jase's shirt, honey? It's too big to be Constance's."

"Jase?" Ben asked. "Is that the guy you're seeing?"

"It is," my dad said.

Klive looked at me in his shirt like he was just realizing I'd kept his clothing. Great. After he'd just been a brat about giving me the last shirt after my fight. The man was practically gloating in private victory just as he had when he'd bought me that strapless dress and I couldn't wear a bra.

"He's a performer at the bar she tends. Pretty talented guy," Klive told Ben. "You ever watched him, Mr. Hayes?"

"Kinsley and I have an agreement that I don't go to her place of work for the same reasons I should also avoid Constance's," Daddy told him, then shot me a look. "Kinsley Fallon, your uniform had better cover more than hers or else I'll bend you over my knee here and now."

"I'd love to see that," Ben teased. I slapped his arm.

"Would that be a no, then?" Klive asked with a grin at my father.

"I've seen him sing with his father at family barbecues. They break out the guitars and harmonize. His sister is pretty talented, too."

"A singer?" Ben asked. "Come on. I thought you had better taste, Kins. What is it about guys in a band?"

I grinned as Klive chuckled.

"Well," Klive said, "he's got more going for him than that. He's also a Navy SEAL."

"That's it." Ben tossed his paper napkin on the table like he was gonna walk out. "You just killed my dreams in one blow. I swear, if you tell me he isn't ugly, I've got nothing going for me anymore."

"Aw, Ben, you work with doctors," I said. "And you drive a nice car. You're easy on the eyes. Not to mention, your boss is amazing."

"Easy on the eyes, eh? I'll take it, but there's *no* way he looks better than Klive," Ben said. That naughty man smiled with a challenge like he knew I was attracted to Klive, too.

"Speaking of killing dreams, it's not Jase's shirt," I said to my father in order to avoid complimenting Klive. "Constance had it lying around from an ex. It was either I sleep in this or her naughty lingerie."

Ben pulled his napkin back onto his lap while my father shook his head. Klive smirked and looked up at the game again.

"Ben, her boyfriend looks like your boss probably did twenty years ago," Klive said. "Maybe some daddy issues there."

"Oh, hell no you didn't, sir!"

My father laughed out loud while I deployed a butter knife and told Klive game on.

Lunch was kind of fun. I loved that Klive didn't insult Jase once. He spoke of him in a respectful way. However, Ben watched Klive the way other men watched the sports on the large flat screens. I tried not to do the same. Or at least held my interest back for the sake of trying to pretend I couldn't see Klive trying to stay clean while eating saucy wings.

"Just get dirty, Klive. Like this," I said and bit into a good-sized hot wing. Sauce lacquered my lips and fingers. "You can use that tongue for something more than speaking prettier than anyone else in the place."

Klive licked his lips like a cruel reminder of what else his tongue was good at.

"Kinsley, tame that flirtation down a bit," my dad said like a brat. He licked his fingertips before grabbing another wing.

"Thank you, Mr. Hayes," Klive said. "I can't even have a bloody meal without someone coming onto me the whole time."

I laughed through my bite. "Oh, Mr. King, did you think I was flirting with you? I was just trying to teach you how to eat like a man." I waved my chewed chicken bone.

Ben and my father chuckled.

Klive wiped his mouth with grace, no sauce on his face or fingers, prim and pretty as always. "I must say, your daughter has cheap taste in venues. Her boyfriend must be rather pleased."

"Ah, yes," I agreed. "She has cheap taste in venues, but impeccable manners." I cracked a crab leg open with my bare hands and nipped the meat free with my teeth.

"Why stare at breasts and thighs when this is the best view in the house?" Klive teased. "Pray tell, am I scoring better than your boyfriend? Did you put him through this test?"

"Well, I was going to, but he stares at my breasts and thighs too much for my father to participate and let him live, so there's that." I grinned. "If Jase can't even resist at church, how can I bring him to Hooters?"

Klive burst into unexpected laughter. Ben marveled at my ability, and I couldn't help feeling honored to make Klive laugh. He didn't have too many laugh lines. Poor Klive. He should laugh more. His smile was freaking amazing when he laughed. *He* could win pageants with that one.

They shifted into conversation about the problem doctor. Klive listened for a bit.

"Is there financial incentive for the doctor to prescribe surgical replacements?" Klive asked as he sat back. His air was different; in charge while being open-minded. The women walking around us weren't even on his radar. As he listened to Ben's frustration, my father's ideas, he focused on my father and Ben as though they were the only ones in front of him. My dad's lips ticked up when Klive requested more napkins and pushed them toward me while never losing his place in their conversation. "Well, there's your first problem," Klive observed. "He may enjoy the beautiful prescription pushers that sashay into his office, but I am certain the commission is what drives his pen over recommending a scalpel for a permanent solution. What you need is an incentive program. Maybe you give a referral bonus for the doctors? Money is more important than sex or the idea of sex. Money can buy sex if they don't have a source at home. Money is where you'll reach him."

My father sat back in the same way Klive had while I paused my feasting on the first protein I'd had in too long.

"I hope that doesn't offend," Klive said. "Not everyone has the same compass or integrity you possess, Mr. Hayes. Though I am glad you do, because your daughter possesses the same, even if she's lacking in the basic hand-to-mouth feeding skills."

"Oh, hell no, Mr. King. Just because you didn't enjoy your food doesn't mean you're stealing my joy in mine." I dipped my thumb in sauce and swiped his cheek. His eyes flared while his mouth dropped in shock. "Money also buys women who are willing to clean for you," I teased. "You know, in case you're worried about getting those pretty hands dirty, but it'll have to be someone else, because this woman can't be bought. High compass and integrity, that sort of thing."

"Kinsley Fallon, have you lost your head, young lady?" Daddy asked.

"Not at all. Mr. King has no fun. He should smile more. Admit it, you didn't invite him here for the pleasure of his company. He's here to work even if he doesn't work for you. Where's the fun in that, especially on his lunch break?"

Ben sat back and looked a tad guilty. "I'm the one who invited him, but my shit has officially been called. Klive, I'm sorry for shamelessly using you on your lunch break. You're probably scarred for life with all this anatomy overload. Now, Andy's daughter rubbing sauce in your wounds. I'm a wretched friend."

I tossed my head on a pleased laugh. Klive also smiled. My dad cleared his throat and thanked Klive for his willingness to talk shop on his lunch break.

"While I know my daughter was being a brat, she does make a fair point in your defense. Ben and I appreciate your insight. I also appreciate your frank honesty. Straight shooter."

Constance came to the table with a box for my leftovers. "Will I see you later, wifey?" she asked.

My eyes met hers with playful disapproval while Ben whistled like she'd created the best fantasy. "Is there room for a husband in this?"

"Benjamin! Shame on you!" I said and smacked his arm while I laughed.

"What? I'm just asking if there's a chance either of you are straight. No wonder she gets along with Klive so well. I never thought about it, but no wonder she's always turning me down, too."

"Ben, she really has a boyfriend, mate," Klive said. "You have to accept defeat. But that's also why we get along. She's not trying to jump in my lap. Good thing because she'd ruin my suit with all that sauce. Tis a wonder the shirt is spotless."

Constance and my father laughed. She left the check while I packed my food. Daddy insisted he pay since he was the one who let Ben and Klive crash our father-daughter date.

"This was the most interesting father-daughter date I never knew existed," Ben observed. "You two gonna craft an excuse together for where you were so Claire doesn't kill you? She's probably at the office tapping her designer heel right now."

Daddy cringed. I looked at him the same way. Ben and Klive looked on, amused.

"Daddy, any chance Amy might like a few hours off so I can ride home with you at the end of the day? I'd love to spend the night in my own bed," I said. "I'm so homesick." Constance came back on the tail end of my comment. Her lip popped out. I grabbed her and pulled her onto my lap just for Ben's torment. "Don't be mad. I left my dress on your bed. Now, I have a reason to call you back, love."

She grinned at my mocking Klive's beautiful accent. Constance looked at the corner with a faux simper.

"I guess, but only if you promise you're gonna call me."

"Only if you promise you're gonna buy some real food. That's what brought me out of hiding today. If we're gonna make this work, you have to remember I'm an athlete. Didn't anyone ever tell you the way to a man's heart is through his stomach? Looks aren't everything. Man cannot survive on Toaster Strudels alone."

"Deal. Now let me get back to work. You're as handsy as some of the pervs I serve. Honestly." She blew an air kiss over her shoulder as she walked away with my father's bank card.

"So, Daddy, what'dya say? Can I come be your receptionist for the rest of the day? Please, please, please? I can even assist with files ...."

"If you don't hire her, *I* will," Klive said with a wink. "Like I said, would be nice to have a woman around who isn't trying to climb in my lap."

Oh my gosh, I was gonna kill this man when I had the chance. His eyes glowed with that private smile that drove me crazy. No woman in a relationship should be so attracted to another man the way I was attracted to this one.

My father tsked with a playful wave of a finger at Klive, but he nodded at me. "Honey, you know I miss you too much. I'd love nothing more than to hire you. I'll take whatever temporary work you're willing to give. Amy will be thrilled to have some free time."

Ben and Klive placed cash tips on the table. Constance walked back up and handed my daddy his card, thanked us all for the pleasure of our company in her section. She kissed my cheek. I popped her bottom.

"Oh, and we still need to talk about you flashing your goodies to the whole town if we're gonna be together," I called after her while she laughed and waved. I shook my head like what a damn shame. "See why I can never be a lesbian, Daddy? She has no scruples. Aren't you relieved I turned out to be such a goodie-two-shoes?" I cheesed and bat my lashes.

"As evidenced by those faded bruises on your face, young lady."

"Ooo-kay. I walked into that one. Here, Daddy. You can drive. I've got food coma after so long without meat." I gave him the keys. He arched an eyebrow like I was up to no good. "What? I'm serious."

"Okay, Ben is sitting in the back with you, though."

"Really, Daddy? You want *Ben* in the backseat with your baby girl?"

"Fine. Behave."

"You telling him or me? I'm not sure who you're worried about," I said.

We got inside the car. Daddy made a pointed show of how long he had to wait for his seat to go back into position from how short I am.

"I had so much leg room back there," he whined. When Ben got into the backseat beside me, Dad told him to get up front where he could see both hands. "At least if Klive's been traumatized by my daughter I can trust him to keep his hands to himself."

Ben grinned at my dad. They both knew he'd never try anything physical with me, but Ben seemed delighted to watch Klive appear indifferent when he wasn't indifferent at all. We weren't touching. A good eighteen inches separated us. We each stared out of our own windows at the view, but my hand rested beside my thigh. His hand rested beside his, no ring. The invisible force of chemistry was stronger than distance. Seemed the more we ignored each other, the heavier the feeling, the more I felt my father checking his mirror to see if something was amiss. Ben turned around a couple of times, but nothing.

We were innocent but squished together when we boarded the elevator with others who clustered into the building in a rush to get back to business. Ben mashed against my left, Dad at my right, Klive at my back. I could barely breathe as I felt Klive's fingers against my upper leg. They trailed up in such a whisper of movement I questioned whether I really felt him or imagined what my wayward mind conjured at being in his cloud of cologne once more. No way my cheeks weren't on fire. Several looked back at me, then over my head at Klive so close. *What did his face look like? Did they see indifference? Did he ignore them? Look annoyed by my proximity and their attention? This was madness!*

Multiple prayers buzzed my brain as I felt conviction for lusting over another man. Jase deserved much better because in this moment I knew that if this elevator were empty, I'd use Klive's tie as a rope around his hands so he could no longer refuse me; slap the red button to halt all progress, get my hands on that belt around his waist for various reasons. Every intimate moment we'd had at Delia's massaged the wicked spots in my imagination like the physical touch of his fingertips tiptoeing over my bottom to the base of my spine. At least I wasn't the only one affected.

By the time the elevator opened on my father's floor, the free space between us hadn't mattered. I'd pressed myself against a far wall and watched the doors, but the damage was done. My father and Ben both knew I was into Klive. I hated that I could be categorized as a cliché in Klive's female fan club. That club was for weaker women who wilted over a handsome face, not someone like me! *Dammit.*

I rushed toward Amy to give her my proposition, but heard my father and Ben being polite enough to thank Klive for his suggestions. My rudeness stood out. I glanced over my shoulder just before the doors closed on Klive's knowing gray eyes filled with heat of his own.

"He's so handsome. Did you see the way he looked at you?" Amy asked when I refocused.

"Meh, he's okay," I joked. "My boyfriend is better."

"Boyfriend?" she asked like I'd just pushed her off the monkey bars.

"Yeah. Didn't my father tell you?"

"I thought he was just bluffing to force us to shut up about Mr. King. This is a disappointment."

When I gaped, she hurried and remembered her manners.

"I'm sorry. I'm gonna get out of here and let you take the reins, but next time I want to see a picture of your boyfriend." She gave me the brief overview and almost jogged into the elevator ten minutes later. Her eyes were bursting bright as she waved and wished me luck. "Don't worry, Fridays are never as busy as Mondays."

The doors closed while I lifted the phone for the first call and several after. The staff greeted me in passing, asked me for small favors; Ben asked me to say he was out of the office if a certain woman called. Fun.

"He's a goner, Kins," he told me while walking backward toward the hall of offices.

I smiled and answered the phone, spoke the name of the company, then, "This is Kinsley speaking. How many I direct your call?"

"Kinsley is who I was looking for. I wanted to see how you were doing today after the events that transpired yesterday."

"Who is this?" I asked.

"Don't play coy. You know who this is. You've been wondering about me, how much I know about a certain British guy, whether I'm wearing cologne."

"Henley." A little thrill rushed through me at how he somehow knew where I was. Creepy, but good since Klive had put him on my protection. *Oh, Klive.*

"Yes," he confirmed.

"Well, aren't you cocky? I'm in a way better mood today since I don't have a funeral to attend."

"You sound better. You look better today, too. Lunch looked enjoyable in many ways. Thanks for the eye-candy."

"You talking about the breasts and butt cheeks or how great I am at eating wings?"

He laughed while I grinned. "All of it."

"Well, yes, lunch was very enjoyable. I'm always happy when I'm with my father."

"And Mr. King had nothing to do with this?"

"Ha! You're barking up the wrong tree for damning information. You know good and well I have a boyfriend and enough drama. Mr. King is fun to tease, though. Speaking of teases, Constance was asking about you. She wants to know how you got that scar."

"But you don't? It's all her?"

"Well, I guessed it to be a prison injury. Am I warm?"

"Cold, so cold, Kinsley. Maybe I'll tell you another time. Try not to think of me too much. Have a good day. Stay safe."

Henley hung up. I gaped at his audacity, then answered another phone call. An hour later, I'd found Amy's crossword puzzle book and had most of the blocks filled on a movie-themed puzzle when I answered the phone to the most elegant accent.

"So, the rumors are true, and I hear it from the lips of the angel she now has a boyfriend at long last. How is everything, my sweet?" He typed in the background.

I glanced around myself to be sure no one was eavesdropping.

"I feel like a caged bird, Klive. Is that what you wanted to hear? But not because of Jase, because of my life situation." I sighed in frustration with how he tormented me. "Name a seven-letter word for a man on my mind who never lets me forget he wants me but doesn't want me all at once. Down. I'm stumped, but it appears to begin with an A and ends in an E."

Klive chuckled. "Asshole. That's a bit harsh don't you think, love?"

"I don't think it's harsh enough. Should've rubbed sauce in your eye so you walk around looking like the male you hired to watch me. I suppose I should say thank you."

"I've no idea what you're talking about," he said. The fact that Klive, of all men, didn't press for more on this man said everything. "Oh, pretty bird, would you like someone to open the door to your cage? You don't have to fly away. Just climb the bars outside for freedom while remaining tethered to your prison."

I could practically see that suave smile, gray eyes narrowing a fraction in the sexiest smolder.

"That's dangerous, sir. You shouldn't say such things. You were the one who labeled me a cheater when I didn't have a boyfriend. Now you blatantly tempt me while I do."

"You shouldn't admit to being tempted, for I might tempt you further to see how far I get. All I can think of is the way you licked the custard I gave you while you melted at the thought of my touching you."

"Klive King! You need to behave!"

Shit! Thank God no one was around.

"How do I behave, Kinsley?"

"Better than this."

"Does he know you wear my clothing while you belong to him? Do you know how you torment me with thoughts of the last time I saw you wearing that shirt; my hands on your body while your legs wrapped my waist and pressed me so hard against you as you begged in desperation for me to soothe the ache."

Sonuvabitch!

"Even now, I hear your breathing has changed. The sound of your moan is still fresh in my mind. The stairwell so close I could soothe the ache right now if only you stepped out for a break."

"I— I— um." My voice choked with my breath. "The stairwell? Are you in there?"

"Best you don't find out if you care to remain honest. Call me when you've a craving for open doors. Something tells me the innocence is lost. The morals are compromised. *Now*, Kinsley Hayes, I believe you *are* ready for me. I've been waiting too long to rekindle our battle, my sweet. Even longer for a worthy adversary until the day you pointed your pretty finger in my face and had the audacity to reject me. Keep those spikes on, run your ass off, because when *I* catch you, you won't want me to let go. You'll hold on so tight, your nails might have blood beneath them as you slip right through Taylor's fingers."

The line clicked as my eyes closed.

Bloody hell! What a cocky, cryptic, sexy, screwed-up warning!

29 | ♀

A WORTHY ADVERSARY. KLIVE'S words intrigued my thoughts. I mulled our conversation over and over, chewing on the possible meanings for hours between phone calls and tasks. Adversary - antagonist, opponent, opposition, resister.

The innocence lost, morals compromised, now I was ready for him. How so? Were we in some sort of battle? Had I missed something? I guess we were always in some type of bipolar battle, but to use that word: adversary.

Daddy made sure all offices were locked as I made a note for Amy on a sticky pad, then joined him for the trip down the empty elevator.

"Today was a good day," he said. I tucked beneath his arm and sighed with the happiest smile. Home. Daddy. Safety. Normalcy.

"I agree. Today was a very good day." After weeks of reservation and teasing, Klive King legit sexually harassed me and I loved every sinful second. I was definitely not a feminist, considering the thoughts I'd just had. I was also an awful girlfriend. Constance was right. I shouldn't have committed myself to anyone when I couldn't be faithful in my mind. I knew Jase knew this. Odd that he'd still wanted to take me off the market knowing I was torn in two.

We walked to the car in contented silence. Across the almost empty parking garage, I saw a bright white Tesla. *Was that Klive's?*

Did he always stay this late? What did he do when he left work? Nightshade? How?

Daddy opened the passenger door for me before he started the car on his side. He backed out of his space.

"Ben and I think we've figured out an incentive plan. At least a basic proposal for our CEO to read over and approve," Daddy said. "Maybe your older man's not the super snob I'd originally thought him to be. He still seems uppity, but he was attentive to you even when he seemed impartial. He asked for a refill on water every time you were low. Fresh napkins. Wet wipes. Reminds me of your mother when you were little. She'd know what you were about to need before you could fuss. She'd pull whatever from that diaper bag of tricks. You were content today just as you were then."

"Ha. You're saying he's like a mother hen keeping me content? That makes me the baby in this."

"I deserve more credit than that, young lady. You know what I'm saying."

"I do, but need I remind you I'm also in a legit relationship with Jase now, Daddy, so I'm not sure why you watched Klive in that regard today."

"Give me a break," he said as we aimed for Plant City. "You know exactly why I watched. I'm trying to apologize to you."

"I forgive you," I told him. He grabbed my hand over the console; held the way Klive had when we'd left St. Augustine. The way Jase did anytime I sat beside him in the truck.

"You were playful today, Kinsley. Made him smile and laugh a lot, which according to Ben is some sort of magical feat. *You* smiled and laughed a lot today, too. That's how I like my little girl. Right now, you're bothered. I feel responsible. Like I pushed you into a relationship I wanted that's made you miserable."

"Daddy, Jase makes me happy, even if he's good at pissing me off."

"Language." He said that like a substitute for the word *bullshit*. "Klive King just seems so serious I find it hard to imagine you being happy. That he can keep you smiling. I don't want you losing that silly spirit that pokes fun in the too serious people you're around. You may have developed a cynical side over the course of your college years, but you're still an idiot. Fitting for your generation, but—"

"I thought you were trying to apologize." I grinned. "Let's stop you there and recap while we bandage new wounds you've created by calling me an idiot. I mean, do you want me being a defective human the rest of my life?"

He chuckled and I loved his laugh.

"See what I mean? There's so much negativity in the world, a sense of humor is a treasure. But we tend to become who we're around for too long. Jase is strong, he's scarred, I won't pretend not to notice, but I know he's a good man. He also has a silly side, plays with you, loves you so much. He treasures what I treasure."

Funny. Didn't Constance say Klive treasured me yesterday?

"Kins, Mr. King specializes in money-making. Money isn't everything. He has a lot of it. Sure, it can buy you a boat to play on like those country songs talk about. Things. But, money plants greed inside a heart. It can also plant an incurable boredom and dissatisfaction."

"You're worried I'll become vain and selfish? Shrewd? Bored?"

"It's not just that. I'm worried that what looks like a good thing might be a bad thing. Like how he took care of what you needed. Sweet on the surface but could indicate control. Micromanagement. Possession. Mr. King doesn't laugh or smile easily, which means there's something that makes him miserable."

Nightshade perhaps?

"And you don't want that transitioning to me," I said. "I get it. Very insightful observations. I won't discredit you with some biased view on him. Just because I want someone to be perfect doesn't mean they are." I went ahead and told him about Jase knowing my ex, Nathan Knox, and that Nate has a kid. Daddy's lips became a thin frown. "Sucks, right?" I asked with an undeniable ache.

"Very much. I'm so sorry, Kins. I'm glad you told me because you also reminded *me* not to be too biased. Don't want to lose the correct view. I fought for Nate and you were right to let him leave your life. This tells me you have your own intuition I need to trust as well. Just know I'm trying to keep my mind and eyes open while love may goop yours."

"Don't close your eyes?" I asked as I laughed at his visual.

"Ah, she does listen to her father. Exactly."

Felt good to have porch swing type confession without having to be crying on the swing. Sometimes confessions were easier spilled when I could stare through the window instead of his face. *Should I tell him I might have made him a grandfather while I'd promised to behave at Jase's house?*

Nope. I'd wait for my dark passenger to make her monthly visit. If she didn't show her bloody face, I'd tell him if I'd tested positive on a pregnancy test. Subject change.

"What movie are we watching tonight as you and Mom make me gag on popcorn with your grotesque physicality?"

"That's quite a mouthful. None. There's a reason I didn't invite you to dinner tonight instead of tomorrow. We have plans with Bianca and Mike. Going to a concert later."

"No fair! Which one?" I pouted.

"The one our children aren't invited to. This way you're spared from seeing your parents get crazy."

I huffed in frustration. "Will you tell me about it tomorrow? The parts that don't scar me?"

"I'll bring you a t-shirt. You can unwrap it like a reveal."

"Nice. Are y'all coming back home tonight or staying at a hotel after?" I asked.

"Hotel. Why? You trying to get your parents out of the house to get in trouble with your boyfriend?" He winked at me. I shook my head.

"Daddy, my boyfriend has a house of his own. If we wanted to get in trouble, I don't need to get my parents out of the house."

I felt suddenly inadequate. I lived with my parents. Jase owned his own house. Constance had her own apartment. Did Bayleigh? Mel? Garrett? My track team lived in dorms and shared apartments. Even if I was normal with my peers, I didn't match up to the ones I valued most.

Daddy's thumb brushed my knuckles like he sensed my sudden sadness at this and being left out of their lives. What an odd middle I found myself in.

"Kins, this is hard for me, too. Your mom is calling this Project Band-aid. It's aptly ripping my heart out. Just know that you are loved. While we're rocking out, I'll be wishing you were there and glad you aren't all at once."

I grinned and kissed his cheek before we parked in the driveway. Mom came out of the house looking less like a lady and more like a Guns-N-Roses groupie.

"Day-um, Mom!" I held my fist over my smile as I checked her out like a dude.

Daddy got out on his side and did the same thing I had, poking fun at me. Mom and I gaped as he never cursed, but Mom's cheeks lit with a flattered blush. *Adorable.*

She giggled and thanked us. "I trust your dad already told you about the concert?"

"He did."

"He's gonna go grab a quick shower and change," Daddy told her, "but may need to use the cold setting to keep it clean."

"Daddy! Omigosh! My ears are bleeding!" I cried and cupped my ears. My parents laughed.

"You dropped the ball on teaching the facts of life, Claire." He kissed her cheek and jogged inside. Mom smirked in knowing.

"Did I?" she asked. "Guess you did a good job keeping naughty secrets today, which makes you better than him for not wanting to scar your poor father."

"Right, cuz I'm gonna tell my dad about sex with my boyfriend."

"You tell him everything else. Why not?" she asked while we went into the main house. "I left dinner on the kitchen counter. Remember to feed the cat and turn off all the lights except the lamp in the living room. Lock up before you head to bed. Mike and Bianca are already heading to the restaurant, and you're in trouble for that Hooters visit earlier."

"Ahhh," I said in dawning, a wicked grin on my lips. "No wonder you look so hot tonight. Hooters was my idea. Klive was gonna be there. How could I not put him through the Hooters test to be sure he wasn't a phony?"

She tossed her red spirals on a laugh. "I taught you better than I knew. Did he pass?"

"With flying colors," I said. "Daddy even ate crow on the way home this evening. *He* also passed with flying colors, by the way. He watched Klive more than anything else."

"He watched Klive with *you*."

"Yeah. Made me wonder if he's ever watched Jase with me," I said.

"That's not a bad idea. I don't know that he has. He knows a lot of Jase when he sees him with Mike or Bianca, but I don't think he's ever had the chance to observe you together. Should we invite Jase to dinner tomorrow night and make it a double date? Give him a fair chance since he's who you're in a relationship with? Andy did give him permission to marry his child, for goodness sakes."

"I'd love that. I need to open up. Let Jase in. Just scary, ya know?"

"More than you realize, honey."

She turned when her cat, Sphinx, came into the kitchen looking for food. The cat jumped on the table and cleaned himself. He watched her the same way I did as she made us both plates and set them down together like she had two children. I shook my head.

"For someone always on Daddy's case about babying me, have you ever noticed how guilty you are of the same? I can't believe you let Sphinxie eat at the table."

"Careful, you might lose perks you're not ready to just yet. I have to have someone eat at my table with me now that my baby is no longer a regular in my house."

She kissed my head. Daddy jogged down with damp hair glued to his forehead, towel around his neck. He was fully dressed in jeans and a black muscle shirt. He grabbed Mom's butt and jerked her toward him. The cat and I rushed into the living room before we barfed our beef stroganoff. When they were done being gross, I kissed them bye, told them to be safe and make good choices, waved them out the door. I peeked through the blinds to mock my father since he always did the same with me. He opened her car door and my heart ached as they drove away. I loved how he loved her and she him. There wasn't enough love in the world. Thank God for my little piece.

I walked outside to my apartment and unlocked, switched on the light, expected to go inside and collapse on the couch in relief as I had for so many years of tiring shifts or meets. Instead, I looked at the kitchen island filled with more fanfare I didn't deserve. This place just didn't feel like me right now. Was Constance right when she'd said I didn't even know myself?

What did I want?

I ripped open envelopes from people who'd gotten me *get well soon* cards. Several made me laugh as there were personal notes saying they never realized how cool Micro Machine was. Okay, this was nice. Like the year before my settlement with the school and the atheists against me; when peers could openly like me without being ridiculed for supporting me.

I carried a box into my room, grabbed Klive's pirate coat from my laundry area, removed Constance's leggings, untied Klive's shirt so the linen fell almost to my knees and pulled the coat over my shoulders. The box dumped onto the bed as I sat crisscross-applesauce on the comforter. Forty minutes later, I realized I couldn't concentrate on the mementos. I picked up my phone.

Whatchu doing? I thumbed to Jase.

Thinking about you, baby. Whatchu doin? He texted back.

YOU when you get to my apartment? I dared as I bit my lip at the sluttiest words I'd ever typed.

Perfect because I'm n area.

"Shit!" I ripped Klive's coat off my body, scooped all the cards back into the box I stuffed under the bed, shrugged out of Klive's shirt. There was no lingerie in my closet like Constance owned! Think. *What did Jase like about sweet Kins?*

Shorts and tank top across the hall while hanging with Tyndall at his house.

I yanked on a pair of track shorts to go with the tank I still donned from Constance's. Checked my bra to be sure I wasn't wearing a crappy one.

Jase knocked on my door a second after I finished applying fresh deodorant and spritzing places with my favorite body spray. I jogged around the room and the home office to disperse the smell that way I didn't seem lame or too fragrant.

"Hey," I said with a bright smile as I opened the door. He looked me over while one hand leaned on the door frame. His hair had no product. A pale blue shirt strained at his biceps and hung off his pecs. *This* was *my* boyfriend. *Good grief, he was sexy.*

"Do I get to come in or did you have plans to be an exhibitionist?" he asked.

"Ooh, big word. I like it, but we already did that. Come in." I grinned and stood aside, locked the door behind him. "What were you doing in the area?"

"I heard the parents were gonna be gone all night." He walked over to my Juliet balconies to pull the heavy curtains closed over the sheers hanging in front of my French doors. Heat hit my cheeks as I wondered if he'd been *really* close by. *Had he seen me through the French doors? Well, hell. I hadn't really considered peeping perverts before.*

"I can confirm you heard correctly," I said. "Jase where were you to get here so fast?"

"Watching."

I gasped and covered my mouth. "Why? What for? My gosh."

"My girl bucked up to Ray Castille yesterday. You have a personal bodyguard that we know about, probably others you don't, and that's not including your damn boyfriend. No way I'm not joining those ranks and letting everyone else do the hard stuff."

"Speaking of ranks ...."

He shook his head. The attitude problem surfaced as he licked his lips. Rather than argue, I wanted to lick his lips too, so I did. Jase caught me in his arms when I dove and knocked him back onto the couch with zero alcoholic influence driving my desire for him.

"Did you bring tools for the job?" I asked as I reached down to his jeans.

"Sure did," he mumbled against my mouth.

"I need you inside me."

"Coincidence, because I need to get inside you too." He rolled me beneath him but lifted me off the couch when he stood. My legs wrapped around his waist while he pinned me against his chest and walked us into my bedroom. "What's that?" he asked after dropping me onto the mattress. I looked at the pillow he stared at. A black card.

"I dunno, just a business card or something. I was going through fan mail from my *Fight Club* episode earlier. Guess I missed it. Come on!"

He didn't seem to pay attention to me lying on the bed ready and waiting anymore. Jase grabbed the card and held the puff of smoke to the light. Oh gosh. *That* card.

"Odd. How did that get here?"

"Get up. Get dressed. *Now!*"

I startled at his sudden severity. He rushed out of the room and checked the room across the hallway. I heard a small noise before went into the guest bath and jerked the shower curtain. The accordion doors on my laundry area creaked open then closed. I stood in wait somewhat dumbfounded.

"Hurry, dammit! We need to get out of here!" He threw his hand toward me. Damn. My flip flops were by the dresser. I stepped into them and grabbed my wallet.

"Do you always leave the window across the hall cracked open?"

"What? No. Why would I?"

"Shit. We need to leave." He checked the closet and pulled the big coat off the floor. *Crap!*

"What is this? A pirate coat?"

"It's an old coat from Gasparilla."

"I see that." He pulled the coat toward himself, smelled the crushed velvet. Jase looked at the floor while I pulled him to hurry and get us out like he'd said. When Jase didn't want to do something, he didn't. "This is a dude's shirt on the floor. What the hell, Kins? This coat smells like *Klive*! So does the shirt! Why are his clothes here?"

"Whoa! It's not what you think."

"Is that why you have perfume on? To try and cover his scent on you like I can't tell he's been with you? That why you cracked the window? To air things out?"

"Wha— wa— what?" I stammered. His eyes flickered into an inspection of my body, my face, a look I'd never seen before.

"Holy shit. I should've known you wouldn't just text me like some naughty girl. You don't do that. This is a *guilt* fuck to cover your tracks."

I didn't even know how to process everything. "No! No it's not! He has never been here! Those are things from a while ago."

"With body heat still in the sleeves? No wonder his card was on your bed."

Jase strode out of my bathroom, stormed through my bedroom like he was gonna find Klive hiding under my bed or under the covers he tossed to look for clues of an affair that wasn't. This shit stung like a bitch. I'd been mentally unfaithful but never physically. I knew I deserved the treatment he was giving for that, but I couldn't bear the thought of him thinking I'd just slept with someone else while we were together!

"The body heat is mine!" I followed him, trying to get him to stop. "Klive gave me his shirt to sleep in at Delia's party because I was uncomfortable in her dress. It was the middle of the night when I woke up from the sedatives they'd given me. I didn't really have many clothing options. I told you to your face about that night the very next morning. Constance kept his shirt without my realizing. She gave it to me to sleep in last night since I didn't want to sleep in her slutty lingerie."

Jase stopped at my front door. *Thank God.*

"I wore the shirt over a tank top today because none of her clothes fit me. I didn't have any of my own things. When I invited you over, I didn't want to be wearing a man's shirt. I tossed it on the floor. I'm sorry. I really did want to be naughty for you. I know I'm always, I dunno, too sweet in your eyes, I guess. That you hook-up with bad girls. I can't help that I wanted to feel that way for you. With you. This is so embarrassing to admit."

"I'm just vindictive enough to enjoy the irony of your embarrassment." He shook his head, chewed his lower lip. "The coat? You gonna tell me you were cold when it's eighty degrees outside?"

No way I was telling Jase about Gasparilla and meeting Klive. I wasn't going to lie to him either.

"It's soft and pretty."

"Whose is it, Kinsley?"

Complicated.

"A Gasparilla pirate gave it to me after Nate stood me up." *True story.* "I was over-exposed in my corset. The weather was chilly. I really do think it's pretty and soft. When Nate broke my heart that night, the coat became kind of a security blanket for vulnerable nights." I threw myself against the door to stop him from turning the knob, looked up at him so he'd have to look down at me. "Please, Jase. The person *I* want to be when I'm with you, for you, it's a vulnerable thing. I sat in the coat while I texted you to gain courage." I put my hands on his cheeks, desperate for him to look at me with something kind again.

"I don't like it, Kins. If you found a woman's clothes in my place, knowing they weren't Tyndall's, how would you feel? Especially if I kept them for security blankets?"

My face stung with my heart at this. A lump formed in my throat at the prospect of giving up the coat. He was right, but I couldn't handle this yet.

"Why did you flip out in my room when you found that card? Do we not need to get out of here now that you think I'm some cheating skank? Jase, you're my guy. Not to sound totally Biblical, but you planted seeds inside me. I didn't let you do that lightly. I also never opened my window, just so you know. My mom might've since she sometimes airs the house and my apartment out if she's been cleaning."

"Well, maybe she did do it and I'm overreacting, but for the record, I didn't do that inside you lightly. I've never done that with anyone before. I've never been with anyone I'd want to plant a seed inside of. You're it, Kins. Now, leave the lights on and let's get out of here."

30 | ♀

WE WALKED ONTO MY **balcony.** Jase checked our surroundings and waved me to hurry. My fingers fumbled with the key in the deadbolt as I buckled under pressure. Jase never showed fear. He wasn't now, but he batted my hands away to do what I was failing at. His phone started ringing in his pocket. He grabbed the device and answered while he locked the doorknob with the other.

"What?" he demanded in irritation. "Yeah, she's right here. Why? Shit. Okay. Why does she need to go— uh, huh. No. That's his problem. Why should I? This is bullshit and you know it, Rustin. Do you know—" His questions ceased while Rustin's tone went from garbled to bitching. "Okay! Okay! Find out and let me know."

Jase hung up and all but took my feet from under me to haul me to his Charger and throw me inside. The door slammed. He started up on his side a moment later. As we peeled out of my driveway, I managed to buckle my seatbelt.

"Rustin says you're wanted for questioning at the station."

"What?!" I exclaimed. "What for?!" I didn't even know how to fathom this.

"One of the bartenders was attacked tonight. He can't tell me anymore."

"Omigosh, Jase! Go to the bar. Not the station."

"No can do, baby."

"Jase Taylor you get your ass to the bar before you even think about taking me to station or else I'll sing my little heart out about you and Nightshade and—"

"And what? Sell me out? Klive, too? Besides, what're you gonna say, Kins? You don't even know anything."

"I know you weren't with me all night when Patrick Scott died! Please, as your girlfriend I'm begging you to take me there. My gosh, what if it's Bayleigh? I can't handle if something happened to her. Please, Jase, please! I'll go to the station afterward. I need to be there."

"If I take you there, what if it makes the situation worse?"

"Did Rustin say which bartender it was?" I asked, bounced my knee, checked his speed because I knew we could go much faster.

"He didn't know. He just arrived on the scene. They don't share much with deputies, only use them to keep loiters away from a scene. Rustin is being given a little room with the lead detective to try and make a name for himself, but after what happened with Angela, he's been pushing pencils as a desk jockey and making midnight traffic stops on rainy nights."

"Come on, Jase, hurry. Go faster. Why aren't you burning rubber tonight like you did when you took me out?"

"Dammit, Kins. Make up your mind. You said you didn't want me to take you to the station. Now you want a reason for them to railroad me and keep us? Any excuse to nail the boyfriend of the girl who beat the shit out of Ansley's daughter. We are both on thin ice."

"Fabulous. Ever consider maybe that's why they want me in for questioning? I'm not sure how I'd have anything to do with what happened tonight."

"Me either, but I don't like it, just like I don't like you out of my sight, Kins. Wherever we end up tonight, we stay together, you understand me? Don't even try to argue. I'm done taking your shit.

If I have a bad feeling about someone, you're gonna get over your attitude and fall in line or else I'll take it out on your fine ass in the bedroom in ways you might not like."

Whoa. Crazy how the stress combined with his attitude and dominance, naughty words, made me ready to climb on his lap. Much the same way I had last weekend when I'd been drunk. Why was there always some damn drama going on to get in the way?

When we turned down the main street where the bar was, lights flashed everywhere. The patrons crowded outside, apparently forced out of the bar. They loitered in the street behind yellow crime scene tape.

"Oh. My. Gosh. Jase," I said. My hand held my mouth.

Jase cursed, too. "This isn't just an attack." He voiced exactly what I feared the most. *Bayleigh! Bayleigh! Bayleigh!*

I wanted to jump out of the moving car to run beneath the tape and know what happened. Cops milled all over trying to control the panicked crowd. When we parked, Jase took my hand while we jogged up to the perimeter. Rustin cursed at Jase.

"What the hell? I told you to take her in, dammit!" he said. Zero kindness in his normal sunshine. Wow. "Jase, sometimes I tell you to do something for the good of everyone. She shouldn't be here. It's not safe."

"What happened?" I begged. As I looked around for any hints or clues, I saw Sheriff Ansley pacing while talking on the phone, his hand gesturing in an angry rant.

"Come on, baby," Jase said close to my ear. He tugged me behind him to keep me out of Ansley's sight. He also seemed to ignore Rustin's asshole-ish treatment.

"Oh my gosh, Kinsley! Thank God!" Delia tugged me from Jase's grasp. He almost saw her as a threat when he spun to find the source of our disconnection. Her arms wrapped me tight. She sniffled like she'd been sobbing. "I'm so relieved it wasn't you. Someone said it was you."

"No!" *No! No! No! NO!* "Jase! I can't breathe!" I cried. "Why would someone say that? I can't breathe! Help me breathe!"

"Shhh," he soothed. His big arm wrapped around my shoulders as he ushered me away from Delia while I gasped for any air. "We don't know what's happened yet, Kins. Rumors run rampant around a scene. We don't know why someone would say that. Stay calm and don't draw extra attention to us. Ansley's gonna see you."

I nodded and sucked wind like I was coming off a hard sprint. *Focus. Calm. In slow and deep. Out slow and long. Calm down. In ... two ... three ... four ....*

Patrons and regulars blurred in the masses I couldn't focus on. Concerned voices called out to me, but Jase told me to stay quiet, eyes straight ahead. He finally found Marcus standing off to the side by a police car.

"Dammit, Taylor, she shouldn't be here. She should be fifty miles away from here. What the hell is the matter with you?" Marcus bitched close to Jase's face so no one a few inches away could hear.

"Marcus, back up, man. Gimme the run down," Jase said.

Their voices should've been my focus, but I rushed to see who was in the back of the nearby police car. A deputy blocked me, but I heard a familiar voice give him a piece of her mind, so he let me through.

"Oh, Kinsley. *Kinsley.* Now I'm okay. I'm okay." Bayleigh wrapped her arms around me and cried. I held onto her, too, and I cried from relief that she was okay.

"Oh, Bayleigh Blue, thank God you're okay. Thank God."

Jase stood talking to Marcus while keeping me in his sights. Marcus had obviously been crying, though right now his eyes were just glassy. Jase scanned our surroundings with the same mean streak that scared the hell out of me with Pat Connor. I wasn't sure of his specialty in the SEALs, but his fists clenched with his arms crossed over his chest that way, his biceps bulged tense and ready, chin raised, feet apart, shoulders back, he appeared *very* intimidating while he watched the crowd like any one of them was the perpetrator. Was the perp still here? Watching?

Finally, Bayleigh pulled back. Her blue eyes rimmed black with runny mascara. I put my thumbs beneath her eyes and rubbed the makeup away for her as I gave her a questioning gaze, though I wasn't sure I wanted to know.

"Was it the bitch?" I asked.

Her lip trembled again as she shook her head. "No, Kinsley, it's *Sara.*"

"Sara?" Dread kicked me in the stomach. "Why would Sara be—" *Oh, hell.* "Is she alive?"

Bayleigh shook her head again.

"No." A sob wrenched from my chest. Without warning, bile shot straight up my throat. I cupped my mouth and turned away before I doubled over and threw up right onto my feet. Bayleigh jumped while Jase grabbed my hair. I threw up again at the sight and feel of my feet. I threw up until I was dry heaving. *Sara?!* Who'd just taught me to cover bruises and volunteered to cover my shift while I recovered. *How had I forgotten?* Sara, who'd confessed to whoring to make ends meet while hiding from her ex-husband. Sara, who'd called me a fool for daring to defend us from Ray Castille. *Did he do this? Was his ego so fragile as that?*

I couldn't breathe! I heaved some more, sobbed, panicked at my lack of desperately needed oxygen that had me gasping as I cried. Jase pulled the water hose we used to clean the sidewalk and hosed my feet clean. He ran his hand under the water, placed his palm to the back of my neck to keep my head between my legs while he shushed me. Bayleigh held my hand and sniffled by my side. Jase held the hose. She stood back while I rinsed my mouth then gulped water. I splashed my face, too. Bayleigh took the opportunity to try and clean hers a bit.

Sara. Who had looked so much like me from the back that we never liked working the same shift because we were continuously mistaken for one another. *Oh, no!*

Jase was just going to turn the water back off when I grabbed his arm again. I grabbed the hose and let the water run against my face for a few sobering moments before handing the flowing water back to him. He turned off the tap. I stood and looked at Bayleigh with dread. She gave me a solemn frown in knowing. Oh. My. Gosh. Baylcigh wasn't crying for Sara alone. She understood where my mind was.

Oh, Klive! Where are you? Did he know what happened? If he was friends with Marcus, babysat the bar on occasion, surely Marcus would've told him, right?

Suddenly, I just wanted my car. Wanted to grab Bayleigh and run. The men could have this. *I couldn't do this!* "I need the restroom," I said and snatched Bayleigh's arm. Police protests fell on deaf ears as I hauled us through the side door. "Bay!" I gasped for air and bent to hold my knees.

"Come on. Jase is coming," she ordered. We ran inside and flipped the lock, gripped hands and slid down the door to sit on the floor. She sighed; her head tilted back against the wood. "The cops are asking about you. They said they're bringing in all the staff for questioning. What for? We both know who the hell did this."

"Do we? Patrick Scott is dead. She was happy about that. Without him what motive would anyone have to hurt *her*?"

"I dunno. Unfinished business, maybe?" She turned and yanked me into her arms. "Kins, what if they would've gotten you instead? It could've been you! I'm so glad you weren't here tonight. I can't believe she came in. She wasn't my favorite person, but she definitely didn't deserve any of the shit she dealt with, least of all, this."

"Oh, Bayleigh. I'm a terrible person. It's my fault she came in."

"You can't blame yourself for this."

"That's what everyone says when there's nothing you can do to change an outcome. Her son is an orphan now, and it might be my fault in more ways than her coming to work in my place."

"Why would you say that? Because some douche bags from Inferno targeted you, sexually harassed you? Did that mean you somehow deserved the burden? Creeps don't give a shit about life. They just want to get their rocks off."

I wanted to tell her that I'd stood up to Inferno's number one yesterday while Sara was upset at me for doing so, but if they were pulling the whole staff in for questioning, I'd better stay quiet so she didn't have as much information as possible. I held tighter to her. *Could a motive for murder be so shallow?*

"Kinsley! Bayleigh!" Rustin shouted through the door before hammering the wood with his angry fist. "You are hereby ordered to vacate the premises or else you will both be forcibly removed by failure to comply with law enforcement. I'll have no choice but to put you both under arrest. You are compromising a crime scene."

Bayleigh's head tilted back against the door. Fresh tears spilled in a mirror of my own. I nodded at the questioning look she gave me.

"Anything you don't want me to talk about?" she whispered.

"Be honest. We will let the chips fall where they may. I've done nothing wrong. If we are innocent what are they gonna lock us up for beyond failure to comply right here, right now?"

She nodded. We stood and opened the door. Rustin shook his head, disapproval all over his furious face. Who was this man and where was the charming flirt who made Bayleigh think of rope and country songs? I slept with this guy? The morals were definitely compromised. He looked so disappointed in me.

A deputy escorted Bayleigh away and left Rustin to deal with me.

"Careful, officer," I said, "you look upset I wasn't the dead girl." He checked our surroundings. Finding them empty, he shoved me back inside the bathroom and flipped the locks.

"Careful, Ms. Hayes, you don't treat me like someone I'm not. What I'm not is happy anyone is harmed. What I'm not is unhappy to see you safe."

"Rustin, you make no damn sense right now. I can't decipher double negatives or whatever the hell this is."

His hands cupped my cheeks and his lips kissed mine one chaste time before he pulled me against his chest. "I'm so damn relieved you didn't come to work tonight. We don't know much about why this happened or who did it, but I do know that we need to get you in for questioning sooner than later. Sooner looks good on you. Can you just please go with Jase to the station so you can both be questioned and crossed off this list? I'd sleep a lot better later."

I opened my mouth to reply, but he covered my lips with a warm palm.

"No. I shouldn't have asked. Don't argue. Just go. Be good and for once, do what you're told. And don't call me officer again," he said. A glimmer of humor lit his electric eyes. Relief calmed the shaking in my limbs for a second.

We exited the bathroom and the bar through the side door I'd pulled Bayleigh through earlier. Ugh, I felt green all over again and was grateful there couldn't possibly be anything left in my stomach. Jase was scanning the crowd with his arms crossed over his chest. There was such a hard look in his face like a different person. As if I were looking at Jase's brother or something, if Jase had a brother, that is. His friendly facade had crumbled, and in his footprint stood a man ready to kill someone. When he saw me watching him, he gave me a concerned gaze, along with a glimpse of *my* Jase. I placed my hand in his.

"You ready to go now?" he asked.

I nodded. He nodded too. When I looked up at him, my Jase was gone again.

As we meandered back through the crowds, I gasped. "Jase!" He tugged me to his side and told me to keep quiet, keep my eyes straight ahead. The Fire Marshal and several other respected firemen and first responders stood along the edges of the caution tape. Ray Castille spoke to an emergency medical technician, but near to him, Pat Connor searched the crowds I blended into like he sensed my presence.

Jase picked up our pace, and we tore out of the parking lot three blocks away once we got back in the car. He was *very* angry now. The car roared down the street. We caught up to Rustin as he was pulling into the station. I didn't speak to Jase, nor had I realized Rustin was leaving the scene. My gut warned me to remain silent. The more time passed, the angrier Jase became. A stranger. I wanted to pull my Jase back out of this person.

When we got out, he fell into quick step with Rustin. "What the hell was that asshole doing at the bar? Did you *know*?"

"Jase, I spotted him right before I left. They just arrived. He is lucky or else I may have been arrested."

"Yeah, well, we aren't the only ones who spotted him." Jase gestured back to me while they walked. His voice shrank to the point I could no longer make out what he was saying. Rustin stopped in the parking lot before going up the steps.

"Just keep her calm and try to calm *yourself*, too." Rustin studied him. I noticed he hadn't lowered his own voice, clear to see Jase had confided something he didn't want me knowing. What the hell? Rustin held Jase's gaze and gave him a meaningful look. "Jase, focus. Come on, man. Stay with me," Rustin told him under his breath. He grabbed Jase's shoulders and squeezed. Jase stared at him and nodded, exhaling heavily. Rustin nodded and continued. "It won't do either of you any good for her to be extra nervous when she is under questioning. That's why I need you to calm down so you can help her. Jase, help her," he whispered. He pulled Jase to the side and walked back down the lot a bit. I could faintly make out what Rustin was saying to him. "Look, Jase, this is bad. With nothing conclusive, it's possible that someone has got something going against her. If the sheriff wasn't Angie's freaking father, I would be telling the detective to drag her ass in here for questioning. I still may ...."

Holy shit. Why hadn't I thought of that? Angela was a psycho bitch, but would she be that crazy? Maybe her dad was as loving as mine in his own hidden way?

Jase nodded. He'd been thinking the same thing. They both walked back over to me. Jase's gaze softened some as he inspected my expression. Rustin, too, glanced at me. A tender look crossed his face. He wanted to touch me, but right now wasn't a good time.

"Kins, if they think that I have any ties to you that may be too personal, I will be pulled off the case and left in the dark, stuck receiving second-hand information. I'm sorry," he said with a sad smile. I nodded and gulped through the pain in my throat. *Was this real? Can this just please be a horrible dream? Please?*

"I understand, Rustin. Should I be worried about these questions?"

"No, they are standard. Be honest. I will be in there with you the entire time. My partner and I are in charge of questioning for now. Garrett is already on his way in there, so I need to be going. You will be shown into a room shortly. For now, I will let you stay with Jase. Try and calm down some." He turned to jog up the stairs into the station. We made our way slowly to the steps.

Jase grabbed my hand and ran his thumb over mine. I read his eyes with nervous trepidation. I was no fool. This was bad, and I looked like someone who had possibly just escaped with her life by the skin of her teeth. The question was, *did I already know and set my replacement up to take the fall? Ugh.* Just because I knew I'd never do something so disgusting, didn't mean an investigator did. I struggled against the threatening tears as I thought about Sara's poor son. Now, her baby had a reason to hate me forever. I hoped that the cops never told her family they suspected she was killed in my place. 'Unconfirmed suspicion', that is. *Would Angie possibly be that low?* I didn't want to think anyone could be.

All in all, Ray Castille or even Pat Connor could've decided he'd had enough of Sara. After all, Pat Connor had harassed her first. I'd given Ray one job. Leash your dogs. Prove you could. In exchange for thinking of coming to their fundraiser, thereby making myself a stated enemy of Sheriff Ansley. Ray hadn't looked ready to play fair once I'd rebuffed the bait he'd laid for me. *If he was the one behind this crime, would he now be coming for me, too?*

31 | ♀

WE WALKED INTO THE **station** teeming with activity. I was ushered into a cold, cinder-blocked room with a two-way mirror. Hell. This was an interrogation room. *Did they question even innocent people in these?* I had nothing to be guilty of that they didn't already know about. I was glad that the fight the other night had been documented by police and witnesses. That didn't look good, but at least all was above board.

I sat bouncing my leg, chewed every fingernail to the burning quick, wiped away tears as I mourned the loss of my friend and co-worker. *What the hell was taking so long?*

Finally, the door opened. In walked Rustin with a man in plain clothing, gold shield hanging around his neck.

Fabulous.

I knew this type-A asshole. He had been to the bar many times. I hated serving his drinks. No nonsense and *no* sense-of-humor. Yes, there are some men who are just jerks no matter what. Will Bartlet was one of those cops you loved to hate. He nodded at me as he pulled his chair, permanent frown etching his impassive face.

"Evening, Ms. Hayes." He sat across from me. Bland gray eyes rivaled the walls in the room, just as cold and nondescript. Rustin sat beside him and studied me, colorful and bold by comparison even in his uniform. Rustin set a recording device onto the table. Will watched me with unwavering scrutiny that made me cry harder. I furiously wiped the tears out of my eyes because I knew they were only an annoyance to Will. As hard as I tried, I couldn't keep myself from grieving.

"Let's get this going, please," Will said. He sat back and crossed a foot over his knee.

"Yes, sir." My eyes darted to his, fearful of pissing him off.

Rustin's face held concern at first, then I watched his expression go neutral. "Ms. Hayes, I understand you've been through a lot tonight, but the sooner we get this over with, sooner you can leave," he told me.

Damn! I thought briefly of the way he'd looked at me before kissing me the first time. I was now a stranger who held no weight in this cop's world, no bearing on his future, no place in his imagination. *Is this what he looked like when he was done? Had he given Constance this look to make her feel like an afterthought?* I could see feeling that under this stare.

At least with Jase, I knew his emotional shift. From love and flirtation to angry at what he loved being threatened. Klive; I knew his cold side came from a place of pain for the feelings he didn't want to feel for me. Even Will exuded a contempt for bullshit which equated to an emotion. Rustin's previously electric eyes fell blank.

I trembled from a chill no one else felt. Was I not even worth good cop bad cop? Two bad cops on one innocent young woman? How to contend?

Will cleared his throat and hit a button on the device. "Please state your full name for the record."

"Kinsley Fallon Hayes."

"This session is being conducted by Detective William Bartlet and Deputy Rustin Keane." He finished running through his official crap about time and date, blah, blah, then cut to the chase.

"Ms. Hayes, what is your relation to Sara Scott?"

I sighed and sat up straight, determined to be respectful. "We are friends— oh gosh! Were friends." I choked on a sob. Will gave me a few moments to recompose, then asked me questions that filled in the blanks on how long I had known her, her training me into a bartender, how we filled in for one another when needed.

"So, you met her at the bar?"

"Yes."

"Did you know her beforehand?"

"No." Did he know about her sordid past as a hooker?

"Did she ever train you in anything else?"

I gaped in stunned silence, insulted to my very core at the idea. Will nodded, made a note. My tears turned to rage. He nodded again, took another note. What the eff?

"No."

"You sure took your time answering that one."

Jesus, please, help me not throw a chair or a punch at this guy.

I looked up at the mirror. Invisible eyes scrutinized my every word, but theirs weren't what made me pause. Just like the mirror in the dark bathroom when Angela and I were in middle school. She'd held me there and called upon Bloody Mary over and over, insisting Kinsley Hayes killed her baby. Did Sheriff Ansley call upon Inferno to do him a favor and kill the girl upsetting his baby? The enemy of my enemy is my friend. Was I looking into Sheriff Ansley's eyes right now?

"I'm not a whore, William Bartlet. In any capacity of the word," I said with a lifted chin and hard eyes. He nodded, made no note. Don't fall for his mind games.

"Ms. Hayes, I need to know why you were called to fill in for Sara so often," Will said.

"She was harassed by Inferno because of her ex-husband, Patrick Scott. I didn't know that was why I was being called in. She was running away while they came in asking for her. When she wasn't there, they harassed me instead. I figured they had a thing for redheads. Just assholes in a bar wanting to get a rise."

"Is this how you got those bruises? One of them rough you up in her place?"

My tears dried as I felt no mercy for anyone in that group of miscreants, the same as I felt no mercy for the bitch who'd bruised me.

"No. How I got my bruises is well documented by your precinct as well as on the internet." My eyes shifted nervously between Will and the mirror. He sensed my trepidation, nodded. No way I could spell out my fears or suspicions.

"What else can you tell me about the harassment you endured from Inferno concerning Sara?"

I told him about Sara's abuse at Patrick's hands, about the stalking.

"You witnessed this abuse, or this was second-hand information?" he asked.

"Sara told me herself."

He made a note. "She was being harassed. You were being harassed. Yet you still saw fit to go hang out at the bar in your off-time?"

"The bouncers keep an eye on us."

"Did you see where the bouncers went the night Patrick Scott was fed to the alligators outside Inferno's bar?"

I gasped and covered my mouth as he divulged what the news hadn't. His gray eyes held a spark like he relished my reaction. *Asshole*.

"Detective, why would I know what the bouncers were doing if I was gone?"

"You left? What time did you leave?"

"She left with me after I ordered her out of the bar," Rustin said. "I didn't like the way Patrick Scott and Pat Connor were treating her. I took her home for her own safety."

Will turned his scrutiny on the deputy, no different from the expression he'd given me. "Were you there on an official capacity?"

"I was there hanging out with her boyfriend, my best friend, and got her out of there before they could cause a fight. I was off-duty and made a conscious decision to deescalate the situation."

"Why didn't her boyfriend take her home?"

"He followed my truck. He wanted her with a cop in case Inferno pushed their luck. He said I had the ability to call for backup if I got in trouble."

I swallowed, the tremor coming back at the lie Rustin just told on record. *Had Jase followed?* Maybe Rustin was being honest. Just because Jase hadn't come straight back to the house didn't mean he hadn't followed us. *Whatever makes you feel better, kid.* Klive's accent beat through my brain and warned me not to mention him.

Will turned back to me like he'd heard my thoughts! I held to what I could of my anger at Patrick's wife-beating to still my nerves.

"So, Ms. Hayes, not only did you go back to the bar after being harassed, but after an off-duty deputy escorted you safely off-premises. Those must be some dangerous bouncers. These the same guys I saw around you at the funeral of Patrick Scott, the same biker who harassed you, who died soon after?"

Rustin's neutral expression shifted to concern, but I wondered if he worried about me or for what I might get myself into with my mouth.

I sighed and pulled Micro Machine off the track. Shoulders pulled back the way they had before I'd walked away from Klive at brunch. Screw playing shitty poker.

"Detective Bartlet, the bouncers are great, but my boyfriend was at the bar with me to hang out. My boyfriend is a Navy SEAL, so forgive me if I don't cower to assholes who threaten me over someone else's private business. Especially when the news said repeatedly that the very same threat was then dead and gone. Tell me, should I have been worried about him coming back from the grave? I loathed the idea of going to that funeral, but Sara begged me to be there for support to help her since she didn't have many friends. The whole regular staff from the bar was there. Not just the bouncers. Yes, same guys, but no sense singling them out."

Rustin swallowed. His electric eyes charged with an itsy smile. Will's pencil scrawled furious notes over his page.

"You have a lot of faith in your boyfriend's abilities. Please state his name for the record."

"No."

"No?" Will balked. Finally, the type-A asshole broke character.

"Am I going to be arrested for keeping my private business private, especially about a matter that has nothing to do with him or me? Besides, he was with me the whole night."

"I'd like you to state his name, so I know which of these men is the boyfriend you speak of."

Will produced a manila folder from his lap. He opened and dealt several still shots of me with Jase, Brayden, Chad, Klive and most shocking, *Henley*!

"What the hell?" I demanded. "Are you *following* me?!"

"Which of these is the boyfriend you speak of?"

"None," I said like a defiant bitch.

"Lying to a detective can open a world of trouble you don't want on your doorstep, Ms. Hayes. I'm not trying to incriminate you. I'm trying to rule out suspects. If you don't tell me who these men are, I will have the courts compel your cooperation."

My accusing glare shot to Rustin. He didn't look happy with me right now. I swallowed, trembled with offended rage. "Mr. Bartlet, you know what I *don't* see in these shots?" I asked.

Will angled his chin, the first glimmer of a cruel smile changed his expression. I read his joy for being able to rile me with that unwavering, uncaring, unblinking stare.

"What don't you see?" he asked.

Rustin's eyes narrowed a fraction like he could silently tell me to shut the hell up.

"I don't see Inferno. I don't see Sara. I don't see anything incriminating. I don't see any reason for me to be here anymore."

Will pulled more photos. Klive and me sitting across the brunch table from each other before I'd stood up and left him.

Jase and Klive sitting together at the club before my fight.

Klive leaning toward me when I'd stolen his fedora at the bar. His hand holding mine over his glass.

Pat Connor sitting at the same table with Klive and who I now knew as Eric, Jase beyond singing onstage, but looking down at all of us.

Henley at the grave site standing almost right behind me without my knowing. Henley holding the small of my back as he handed me off to Jarrell at Constance's yesterday.

I felt green. *These were taken yesterday!*

Klive at Hooters smiling at me while I smiled at him with a wing in my hand. *Today.*

My eyes filled. All my bravado and attitude fell apart when he next pulled photos of Sara and me sitting at the beach bar she'd worked in. We were chatting like we shared secrets. Klive and me in the same exact place and position, then one of me holding to him before we'd driven away on his Ducati. I almost crumbled when a sob escaped my throat at a photo of Klive and me in St. Augustine, the little bar, my friends and I holding up shot glasses with Klive before we'd drank.

St. Augustine our little secret. X- Complicated.

Nothing was secret. Nothing!

"Who took these?" I almost growled, tears flowing over my cheeks.

"We pulled these from a phone found at the scene of tonight's crime. Some were in the camera file, some inside text messages. How about you quit giving me a hard time and tell me why someone might be following you and your love interests? You aren't a suspect. You might be the *target*."

"Whoa! Are you trying to say someone may have killed Sara *instead* of *me*?!"

Ray. Sheriff Ansley. Pat. *The enemy of my enemy is my friend.*

Will didn't flinch or blink, just stared like he was waiting on me to get over my emotional bullshit so he could proceed.

"He's saying we have to keep an open mind until we have a definitive conclusion. We can't get to that conclusion until everything else has been ruled out," Rustin explained like he, too, was annoyed by my stalling. As if an emotional barrage was optional versus an overwhelming panic attack!

"I'll ask you again," Will said. "Why would someone be following you and these men you've been with?"

Chills broke out over my skin. "I don't know," I stammered as the world no longer made sense. "Why would someone do this?" I gave Will the most pleading expression I didn't mean to. Damn, I was all over the map, and that never looked good during interrogation, but the hell if I could script myself when I hadn't done anything to defend against. With that mirror there was no way I could tell the truth about who I was afraid of.

"Ms. Hayes, let's start by creating a timeline and a cast of characters." Will tapped the photo of Jase. "Who is this?"

"The SEAL. Jase Taylor," I answered. He thanked me. Tapped another and another until no one was a mystery, except Henley. I wasn't going to talk about him.

"You don't know this one's name, yet he walked you and your friend up to her place?"

"I also work with a bitchy bartender whose real name I've never known either. Been working with her for a year and I just call her bitch. I make drinks for hundreds of people per week, don't know their names but I could tell you at least half their drinks by heart. I've only seen him twice. No. I don't know him. After being around Inferno yesterday I was grateful for the added protection."

"Inferno is a fear for you."

Ugh. Duh! Did we really have to keep asking stupid questions like Captain Obvious didn't know how to put two and two together?

Next came the questions on dates, times, when and where I was in each, why. *Who could explain why, though?* I couldn't.

"I meant why were you in St. Augustine with Klive King?" Will tapped the drinking picture. He pulled another photo from the folder. "Does this have anything to do with why you were together?"

I gasped. Klive had me leaning over the balcony at Delia's. He held my waist while his nose nuzzled my throat as my head fell back. Intimate as hell.

I closed my eyes and counted to myself before opening them.

Rustin leaned back like a dude dating me and wanting an explanation. *Oh, now he acted like he had some right?* I felt like asking Rustin to leave. I mean, *why was he not featured in any of these photos if even Brayden and Chad were? Lord knew I'd been far more intimate with Rustin Keane than three out of five of the others .... How had someone taken that photo if no one could have a phone at Delia's party?*

I couldn't help glaring at Rustin. "These photos are unrelated. My relay team and I were celebrating victory and kicking off Spring Break in St. Augustine. My girls came to see me the night before while I was working. They met Klive when he and I stood together. They invited him to come celebrate with us because he's hot."

"That's it?" Will arched a skeptical eyebrow. "You two look mighty cozy in this other one. Looks like you were at this party together. Dressed fancy. This was a planned event."

I snorted and shook my head. "Detective Bartlet, will all due respect, you're talking about co-eds. Being hot is the only requirement for them to invite someone to party with us. The other photo, Klive and I just happened to be guests at the same party and sure, I think he's hot too. I had some drinks, we made-out. There's nothing more there."

"Why didn't they invite any of these other guys? You make-out with any of them?" he asked. "What about your boyfriend? You and Klive have something going on the side? I'd hate to be responsible for making trouble in paradise."

He'd sure lumped all those questions together like he was trying to confuse me into giving up something good. "Mr. Bartlet, I hate to disappoint, but I've never made-out with any of the others. Jase only became my boyfriend a couple days ago. He wasn't invited to St. Augustine because he was performing while my girlfriends were visiting me at work. Chad wasn't there. Brayden is just a frat boy with a crush on me. In fact, he's sleeping with one of the other girls on my team. Klive was in the right place right time for the invite, simple as that."

"Does that happen a lot?" Will asked. "Right place right time?"

My brows creased like he was crazy, but damn if ever he'd repeated my very own thoughts not too long ago! Rustin looked vindicated somehow.

"I can't say that Klive happens up any more often than Jase, Chad, even Deputy Keane, here. Sometimes our paths cross."

"Where were these men the night Patrick Scott was killed?" Rustin asked like he needed to. He pointed at Klive and Jase sitting together at the club like he wanted to divert attention away from my mention of him.

"Jase was with me all night. I slept at his place," I told him. *Inside I wanted to shout that he was there! What was his problem?* "Deputy Keane, why would I know where Klive was? At the time we were barely acquainted."

"Yet you rode off into the sunset together earlier the same day? After speaking in depth with Sara Scott about the abuses she endured and a potential that you would be harassed in her stead since you both have red hair, similarities? Where did you go after you had breakfast at the beach bar with Klive King?"

Will sat back once more, glad his counterpart finally contributed. I couldn't help feeling Rustin wanted Klive under more scrutiny than Jase, but something was there about Jase too. Like Rustin had some repressed frustration with his bestie pertaining to all of this.

"Klive took me to a festival at Hillsborough State Park. The actors were rehearsing for opening day of some reenactment of the Seminole War. Klive gave me a sneak peek at their performance, told me I had a right to defend myself against sexual harassment from Inferno. That he wanted me to see that sometimes people ended up in battles they didn't ask for, but that I didn't have to be a willing victim."

Rustin nodded, some of his attitude taking a back seat as this wasn't what he'd expected to hear. *Jerk.*

Will perked up. "So, you don't know where Klive was that night? After he told you not to put up with sexual harassment? Was this before or after the party where you made-out?"

"Before. William, I'm sorry, but are you implying that I should've put up with the sexual harassment and been a willing victim?"

He seemed satisfied by my defiance. Back and forth. "No, but I am curious what Klive might do about it were you to become a victim the very same evening after warning you. You had lunch with Klive King earlier today. Do you know where he was this evening?"

"He stayed late at work. I saw his car in the parking garage when I was leaving the building with my father. They work in the same building. I was filling in as receptionist for my dad which is why we had lunch together."

"About what time did you see his vehicle?"

"Six-ish? My father and I were the last to leave the offices on the twenty-second floor. We double checked the locks on the doors and stuff."

"Any defining features on Klive's car that made you certain it was his you saw?"

"No."

He nodded and made a note.

"*I* have a question," I said. "Is it true that there were multiple calls to authorities concerning Inferno misbehaving and even assaulting a bartender at my place of work before Patrick Scott was killed?"

"Yes," Will answered honestly.

"Is it true that the police did nothing to stop the problem?"

"We cannot stop what we can't prove," Will said.

"If you cannot stop what a victim cannot prove, how could it not escalate to this? Whether or not I'm dating around has no obvious bearing on tonight's tragedy, nor Patrick Scott's demise. You knew about the problem, meaning this may have been prevented if your precinct had taken action. Maybe quit wasting time on me and look into the domestic violence calls Sara made to you guys over the past year. You failed her. Not me. Not these men in my life. *You*. Clearly someone is stalking me, so is it fair to trust you to keep me safe? If you don't do your jobs, is it fair to be pissed if someone does it for you? Why did it take a body before any of this mattered?"

Always calm Will shook his head in a pissy attitude I couldn't help feeling pleased with. He gathered the photos, shut the folder like he wished to shut my mouth as fast. His gray eyes, so flat compared to Klive's pretty gray, studied me for a few beats.

"I think we're done for tonight. Don't leave town in case we have more questions as we continue through the files on this phone."

"I have track," I told him. "Out of town meets."

He scoffed. Of course, the only laughter I'd ever witnessed from him would be bitter. "While under suspension? Nah, you ain't running, Ms. Hayes," he told me. The cold look in his eyes conveyed his double meaning. *Under suspension? How could he know I was suspended from track unless I was already being looked into for some reason?*

32 | ♀

WILLIAM BARTLET HELD THE **door open** for me to walk through. Jase sat in a chair in the hallway like he'd already been through his own interrogation. He jerked to his feet the second he saw my face.

"Rustin, what the hell happened in there?" He cupped my face, smoothed my hair away from my eyes, gaze traveled between my irises for answers that may appear. "Baby, are you okay?"

I nodded. Jase did, too, but looked over my head. "Let me guess, Bartlet gave you a hard time because of me?"

"Why would I do that, Taylor?" Will asked from behind me. "I'm doing my job." Nice. *Why had Will made me name who Jase was in the photos if he'd known all along?*

"Looks like you did a number on an innocent girl the same night she lost a friend. Where's your sensitivity training?" Jase asked. "Come on, Kins. Let's get you home."

"Would you be talking about her family's home or your house, Taylor? Just so I know where to reach her."

Jase's arm encased my shoulders. I felt his fingers tighten. "Mine." He pushed the door open. Rustin followed us out to the parking lot. "What the hell was that, Rustin? This is bullshit."

Rustin ignored his friend. "Where you parked?"

Jase pointed around the side of the building. "No cameras over there. In case I need to pull a dirty detective aside for a lesson."

323

"You need to get a grip on your shit, Jase. I could arrest you on the spot for saying that."

"At the rate we're going, why not? Maybe some time in the think tank will do me some good," Jase said. "He can call her phone if he needs to reach her. He doesn't need to know where she is unless he's planning on making a visit."

I gasped and looked up at them in alarm. Rustin shook his head and looked down at me.

"Don't let him scare you. Will's job is to rattle cages and see what feathers knock loose. I promise he's more worried about you than looking at you for anything to do with this." Rustin met Jase's eyes. "I'll fill you in later at home, however long that will be. Things got tense when she got defensive over Will's questions."

"My friend just died, Rustin," I said. "I'm exhausted, overwhelmed, lost my dinner so I'm on an empty, queasy stomach. None of this seems real. I know law enforcement prefers to question when things are fresh, but I agree with Jase for once. Sensitivity would've been nice. Tell Will he can call me when he puts his gloves back on."

"May I have a moment?" Rustin asked Jase. I expected to leave them alone, but Rustin urged me around the corner outside the camera's view. He cupped my face. "I will be home as soon as I can, Kinsley. Stay with Jase at all times, do you understand me?"

"You were a bigger dick than him. If I'm the target, why did he talk to me like I'm responsible somehow? What's unclear is a motive in all this."

"I don't have time to answer your questions, but things are a lot more complex than that. Now, just answer me, please? I need to know you'll do what I said."

"Fine." I sighed. "But I'm not doing what you said because you said it. I'm doing it out of my own self-preservation."

"Thank you. I'm sorry for the interrogation." He wrapped his arms around me, kissed my hair. "I'm sorry for everything, Kins. For Sara. I promise I tried to nail them before it came to this."

All the tension dissolved into tears I cried against his uniform. "Can this not be real? Tell me I'll wake up and this will fade as some awful nightmare!" My voice muffled at his chest.

"Shhh ... I know." His hand stroked my head until he needed to go back inside. I straightened and wiped my face. To my shock, just beyond, Jase leaned against the brick wall with a lit cigarette between his lips. He watched us as he released a long cloud of smoke.

Oh, wow! What the hell?

I'd never seen Jase smoke before, but he wasn't coughing, nor was the smoke exiting his nose. I looked at Rustin to see he appeared worried at the sight. Jase took one more long drag off the cigarette and blew the smoke into a group of rings in front of him like he dared me to have a problem. Okay, definitely not new at this. Jase stubbed the cherry against the brick, flicked the filter into the trash can. He pushed off the wall, waiting for Rustin to bring me to him. Jase appeared odd to me.

"Rustin ...?" I whispered.

"Stay here," he told me. I leaned against the bricks as he approached Jase and put his arm over his shoulders. He looked back at me and motioned for me to get into the car and wait. So, I did. When they turned their backs, I eased the window down super slow to stay silent. I had enough of a crack to hear muffled talking, but not enough for them to notice.

"Keep your shit together, Jase. Adapt. Improvise."

"This wasn't part of the plan, dammit. We need to be honest."

"You're gonna flush everything if you say a word," Rustin said, almost whispered. From my periphery I saw him look back at me, so I pulled my phone from my pocket. A normal person would be texting right now, right?

Bayleigh had texted to ask how my questioning had gone.

Shitty, I texted back. *They treated me like I have something to do with all of this.*

B: *They asked me about Jase, Chad, Moonlight, some frat boy we served. I told them I knew enough about you to know that you were a good girl and if you were involved with anything, it was Sara's doing, not yours. I know you liked her Kins but I don't like where their angle is. They seem like Sara set you up somehow. Watch your ass. Maybe you should get the hell outta here till graduation!*

Me: *No can do, Bay. I'm w/Jase. He's watching my ass. We better stop talking about this in case they confiscate our phones. In five secs this message will self destruct. 5, 4, 3, 2 ....*

B: *1*

We deleted our conversation. A second later she texted me again because we knew if there weren't any chats between us that would be just as suspicious.

B: *Hay Bay*

A play on my last name, *Hay*es, and *Bay*leigh's name in case we needed to text for safety reasons. Sometimes she texted that from random numbers to create a record of who she was with last. In case we were ever victims. *Like Sara. Dammit!*

Me: *Hey Bae.* I texted back the correct form as I always did. Our way of being positive we had the right person. *Sorry 4 loss. Sux for bar. So grateful ur ok. Luv u grl*

B: *Luv u 2. Call n morn.*

Me: *K*

No doubt she was afraid for me, but everything I had spent six years working for was coming to a close. I needed to finish here. Afterward, if no one had been apprehended, I would go away for the summer. My parents already booked me a dream tour of Europe for my graduation present they'd made payments on for a year. I'd have to tell Bayleigh next time I saw her in person to give her at least a little relief. In the meantime, things might get tense.

Next up, Garrett's texts about pleading the fifth on anything that had to do with me. He was very pissed off at "Traitor Sara" as he called her. He struggled with grieving for her and hating her.

Me: *Garrett, you can't blame the victim. We don't know what happened. She has a son. She wouldn't just leave him.*

G: *Exactly, Kinsley. What better motive to set someone else up to take your fall for you? Make yourself look like a co-worker, act like her, insinuate yourself into her life? People will do anything for their kids. No offense, but don't tell me what to do. Not right now. I'm not in the mood. Stay safe Red Running Hood. Could've been you. I'm glad it wasn't.*

I was lost in thought and text when Jase got into the car looking like himself again. He smelled like cigarettes, though. My phone vibrated too many times. I flirted with the idea of an auto-reply saying I was alive and thanking anyone for concern, but to please pray for Sara Scott's family. I answered the important names before I felt exhaustion and sadness weighing my eyelids down. A headache threatened to obliterate any chances of genuine sleep in the near future.

"Hey, Jase, I'm here," I told him. My hand rested over his holding the billiards ball shifter while he drove. He probably couldn't help his aggressive driving. Even though the excessive speed was a bit scary, I made myself stay calm. Guess he wasn't really caring about getting pulled over and taken to the station anymore. I squeezed his hand to get him to look at me. Finally, he gave a sad smile, his eyes weary even as he kept checking his rearview mirror. He drove a couple of exits past ours just to be sure we weren't being followed.

We made our way through the twisty back roads to Jase's house. He barreled over the dirt potholes and divots of the driveway without care.

"Easy, Jase. You will regret this later," I cautioned.

"Baby, the only thing I regret is being so lenient with that stupid son of a bitch, Patrick!" he shot back. "This wasn't supposed to happen! He's *dead*!"

"Which Patrick? Patrick Scott?" My voice quivered on a shudder that shook the length of my body. I wrapped my arms over my chest and squeezed my biceps, suddenly way colder than I should've been in eighty-degree humidity.

"Yes, Sara's ex-husband. Kinsley, I haven't been honest with you. Ah, shit, I am so gonna get my ass handed to me if you leak this." He hesitated and stared with an intensity I wasn't used to. "You can't breathe a damn word to *anyone*, understand?"

"No." I pulled one hand away just enough to form a stop sign. "Plausible deniability is what I want. Whatever you're going to say, I can't. I just can't."

"No is not an option. Like it or not, I'm telling you because there may come a time when you need to know to keep *yourself* safe if Rustin or I cannot."

I nestled deeper against the leather as his tone conveyed like a veiled threat. Add in that he somehow refused to blink, my gut flamed like he'd offered a lit match and watched while he forced me to swallow the fire.

"Jase, I can't lie about what I don't know. Do you realize Rustin lied during that interview? He made it look so easy, but I'm not a good liar, even though I told Will you were with me all night when Patrick Scott was killed." I hushed myself up and swallowed, looking from his unblinking stare to the wild palms outside. Wasn't too often I wanted the dark, but right now I did. Wanted to rush into the maze of woods and scurry like an animal into some burrow to hide.

Shouldn't he need Visine by now? This was like Will all over again!

"Come on."

He got out of the car, slammed the door a second later. When he saw me do nothing, he crunched over the gravel to my side. His shadow hovered while I refused to move or look at him. He'd ruined my view of the woods. Now I stared at the vapor light in front of the house. I couldn't look at him, know he'd killed Patrick and be okay. Speculation was one thing; uncertain. If he confirmed and told me I had something to do with the reason ... that he set part of this in motion ....

"You want to play that game, Kinsley? Fine." Jase plucked me from the car faster than I could respond. When he set me on the ground, everything went haywire. Fight-or-flight rose within me. While he bent to manually roll up the window on the car, I bolted around the vehicle and ran into the dark woods Tyndall and I camped in as teens.

Pine needles broke beneath my shoes. My side burned from running cold with injured ribs. I wanted the pain, needed the stabbing stitch in my side like absolution for Sara. The foliage blurred in my haste to escape an encroaching and enraged SEAL pounding the ground behind me, but I didn't care. I ran faster, dodged branches and hurdled small shrubs, nicked my thighs, shins and ankles on twigs and thorny vines trying to trip my fluid motion.

I thought of Klive pretending to chase me in St. Augustine while we ran from bikers, him calling me a kid in the parking garage, breaking up with me when we didn't even have a relationship, the condescension, the needless shift in his behavior, telling me to stay away, that he was bad, and I was in danger. Thought of Henley conveying he'd been ordered by someone high up to keep eyes on the situation that was me. I knew whatever Jase had to say was about Klive, because deep down I'd always known my pirate was bad but wanted to believe in the good. I couldn't handle him telling me Klive had anything to do with this, with being in the right place at the right time all the time. Klive wasn't all bad, nor was he the only bad one in my life.

Jase was bad, too. Rustin was bad in his own way.

But, so was I.

I should've whipped Angela's ass over her touching Jase, but I knew I'd knocked her out because of how she'd looked at Klive, clung to Klive, wanted Klive.

Sara. Dabbing makeup over my bruises, what? Two days ago? Sara in my uniform. My name. Her number or mine? Whose had been up? Had she done what she did because she felt guilty for this? If she set me up, why go into work in my stead, wearing my name tag? My hair color, my shy factor ....

In a clearing just ahead sat a dark, dilapidated old shed Mike Taylor used for his yard tools and hunting rifles.

"Dammit, Kinsley! Stop!"

Something sharp sliced the front of my ankle, then the brunt of two-hundred-and fifty pounds of muscle pounded my one-hundred-seventeen pounds onto a slab of sticks and mud. At the same time, I heard a *ffffit* and a splintering of wood somewhere overhead. I tried to wriggle free, lift my head, but Jase shoved me harder into the ground like he wanted to bury me six feet under. I could barely breathe!

"No, dammit. Stay! You set off my traps. Now, we have to lie here and wait for them to finish and pray Rustin doesn't come looking for us just yet. Shit." He cursed as more soft noises echoed in the woods around us, around the shed, until at last, he lifted off.

"How am I not levitating?" I bitched and scrubbed tears from my eyes and face because I didn't want to cry in front of Jase right now. I didn't want to give him the satisfaction of what felt like a sprained wrist and re-injured ribs.

As I pushed slowly off the ground, I felt every tiny cut light up while I attempted to dust the caked mud and pine needles, leaves, twigs and dead bugs from my skin.

"You finished throwing a fit?" His voice wasn't behind me as I expected. He was somewhere else. I saw a beam of light and squinted. In this absurd moment, Mr. Anthony from Miller's Color Theory class popped into my head. Our debate about the strip of yellow on the black canvas. Jase's bulk came into the frame. Guess I could tell Mr. Anthony that I now knew that doorway went to bad places. That the light beyond held a back-lit shadow from a horror movie in an abandoned shed in the middle of the woods with killer booby traps awaiting the girl he'd just chased down.

Round two?

I spit some grit I licked from my lips and wearily hobbled to the shed. Jase stood aside to let me enter, staring down at me with a mix of anger and amusement; smug amusement, that is.

I glared at him with zero humor. "What? No chainsaw?" I popped off.

"It's right there." He gestured to a damn chainsaw leaning against a shelf.

"Asshole."

"But, am *I* really the asshole? Or is this the asshole?" His hands gripped my shoulders and turned me to face the wall. There, before me, in a serial killer collage, was everything I'd run from. Everything I couldn't unsee but wished I could. The trembling and tears came back.

"What the hell?" Nausea gripped my empty gut.

"So much for plausible deniability, baby."

Ignoring his bitter jab, I tunneled on the photo in the center. Me in the parking garage at my father's building. I leaned against the concrete wall. Klive stood over me, his hands on my cheeks while he gave me the talk. From this camera's lens, and maybe

Jase's point-of-view, the moment appeared intimate and tender. I stepped up to run my fingers over every matte still-shot surrounding our photo. This was way worse a betrayal than the photos in the interrogation that Will had forced me to see.

Bodies. Death.

I shuddered. "Did you arrange these? Follow me?"

"It's my job. Yes, I arranged them." His tone had a timid quality. My body roiled in something foreign, strong, disgusted, confused at the violation. The photos from the interrogation were taken by a stranger with no business following me, but these had been taken by the very man I'd allowed to take my body in the shower after holding out for six years! The man I'd allowed to plant seeds inside me and possibly create life! A budding future. All bullshit!

"Were you busy hauling ass to the beach after taking this photo in the parking garage?" I asked. I didn't really care for his answer.

"I went in at my normal time for lifeguard duty. I had no idea you were coming to see me. That was a coincidence."

"Who are they?" I asked as my chest heaved. My fingers branched around the rim of death outward to the living faces I recognized from the bar, some I didn't, some with huge bags of drugs, some shaking hands with more people I didn't know. Close-ups of the ring Bayleigh and I routinely looked for. None of the photos of Klive King pictured a ring on any of his fingers. Not one picture of damning evidence held a trace of Klive King. In fact, every single photo featuring Klive had to do with me, and me alone. Around each photo of us, splayed more photos of death; a series of black and whites with color pops of bluish purple flower petals scattered over corpses.

"Nightshade," I observed as Jase's voice stated the same in unison. "Jase, who are you? Do I even want to know?" I wondered aloud, overwhelmed, going numb. "A double-agent?"

"Double-agent?"

"Don't bring me here, shove my nose in this shit, then play dumb and pretend it doesn't smell. Nightshade. Are *you* Nightshade spying on other Nightshade members with plans to turn them in?"

He licked his lips. "No, I'm not Nightshade, but I'm trying to be. I'm with an acronym you've never heard of working to help the acronyms you have."

"FBI? CIA? DEA? WTF?"

"That's classified."

Nodding, I turned toward him. Through tired eyelids dry like sandpaper from crying, hanging low and heavy, I saw Jase in a new light. "What is this, Jase? Are you using me?"

His throat bobbed under a swallow. "No. Never. He is," he said, pointing to Klive King.

"Jase. A friend of mine died tonight. She's dead. D-E-A-D-*dead*. And you're telling me how I'm being played by a guy who comes into the bar and flirts with me? That he's apparently linked to Nightshade and these dead bodies even though none of these pictures prove it? Now, of all times, you're gonna show me this?"

"*Flirts* with you? Don't pretend it's not way more than that, Kinsley, for both of you. You admitted to being attracted to him, but baby, I know you only held out on me because you see yourself with him."

My jaw dropped with incredulous offense. "Saw myself with *him*? Seriously?!"

"You're damn right. You told me to prove shit. Actions over words. Kinsley, you stood me up to ride off to who knows where on his bike! You fooled around with him at Delia's. You spent the night shacked up in a hotel with him in St. Augustine! Do you have any idea what could've happened to you?"

"What's the matter with you? Have you lost all sense of decency? Seen too much combat? Become jaded to tragedy I've never experienced so you just dump it on me because you can handle it like these people weren't alive? Like Sara wasn't just alive hours ago borrowing my uniform after teaching me how to cover up bruises on a woman's face? You bitch at Will for lack of sensitivity, yet you're upset in this moment about me standing you up for someone who wasn't breathing down my neck while you came on too strong? Do you know why I went with him? Because I'd just found out what a wife-beating bastard Patrick was and got scared. I didn't want you to know I was upset and get involved with Inferno! What about men like that, Jase? The ones who beat women and children? The ones who kidnap them and trade them like slaves for sex? Why do millions of dollars of drugs matter more to law enforcement than domestic terrorists holding hostages in their own lives? Know what I see in these photos? Dead men with gang tattoos. Even I know the awful terroristic shit they pull to be inducted into the gang."

"So, you find out about Patrick, and King just happens to be in the right place at the right time to take you away? Maybe scoping places to kill you but wanted to have some fun first because you're just so cute. Decides to make it linger, draw it out because you let him fool around with you. Did you hold out on him in St. Augustine and accidentally save your life by keeping him hungry for the same flavor you've tormented me with?"

A sound smack cracked like a whip in the room. My lip quivered and my palm stung like the pink print I'd delivered to his face without thought. He snatched my sore wrist, pinched the flesh like the head of the snake that had struck him.

"I didn't sleep with him. He told me I was worth waiting for. *He* holds out on *me*, Jase," I said every word through gritted teeth.

"So, he *is* drawing this out. You think I wanted this?" he asked in a level tone with a river of anger dammed up threatening to break. "I'm in love with you, Kinsley. *I love you.* She's dead. She wore the name of the woman I love on her chest and a professional hit man is all over your shit. You feel me?"

"Don't say that. Don't! Not here, now, like this! I can't do this."

"Neither can I! Dammit, Kinsley! Pay attention and stop running from what you don't want to see like some crippled child who can't handle the truth and needs her pacifier of virtual reality. This is the world you live in and it just got ugly. I'm trying to fix it but can't do that until you choose to see it for what it is and accept the pain behind it. Baby, I'm here."

He tugged my wrist so my whole body followed. His arms wrapped me inside his heat while I shook. I hated his ugly words. Hated the feel of his arms right now. I pushed against him until at last I lost my cool and sagged so he had to hold me up as sob after sob wracked my torso.

"I'm here, Kins. I'm here. Shhh .... Just get it out."

33 | ♀

By the time Rustin's **boots crunched pine cones** through the woods, I hunched sobered on the tiny stoop of the shed.

"What the hell?" Rustin demanded of Jase in the darkness. The light was off for the time being to give my eyes some rest. "What is she doing here, Jase? And why is she smoking?"

He ripped the lit cigarette from my fingers. An inch of ash tumbled off the end and rolled down my shirt.

"She didn't smoke. She wanted to hold it. I didn't have anything else to soothe her with."

"Need me to?" Rustin's hand jostled my knee. I stared into the woods; his humor lost in this black hole. At my lack of response, he pinned Jase with a pissed-off glare. "I can't believe you told her."

"Rustin, I'm right here. I don't want your brand of soothing, or his, and I don't want to be talked about like I'm not in front of you. Now that I've been enlightened, I think it's best I go my own way and distance myself from all of you. At least until I grieve."

Rustin cursed. Jase took a final drag on the smoke between his fingers, the smoke Rustin had taken from me, then held his hands in surrender like a douche.

"All right," Rustin said. "We're doing this my way. Starting now. Get up and take a seat in this chair, Kinsley." Rustin gripped one of my hands and helped me back inside the shed. He turned on a dim

337

lamp and pulled the door closed, left Jase outside. "I'm going to ask you the questions I couldn't in the station. Off the record, okay?"

"Do I need to be Mirandized? Need my lawyer? I wasn't the one who lied to the cops tonight. I've never cheated. Not with you. Or him." My chin jerked to the photos on the wall.

Rustin knelt before my bitter bitch and wiped at mud caked to my temple, then seemed to notice the rest of the mess.

"I know that. So does Jase."

"Right. Because you followed me. What is this? I mean clearly I see what it is, but *what is this*? Me being pulled into a room and forced to see these things you insinuate about Klive with no proof? Jealousy? A way to kill off my kindness toward him? Why? You think I didn't pick up on the bodies around the pictures of us together so Jase can indicate death? A psychological hatred of me with other men while he hooks-up with women everywhere? Because I'm seen talking to someone—"

"Quiet, Kins. You're not thinking straight, and that's understandable, but this isn't about your relationship."

"We don't have a relationship."

"I wasn't talking about you and King."

"Neither was I."

"You have the right to remain silent. Please do so until I ask my questions, Ms. Hayes."

"Oh, so we're back to that again? Nice to see you, officer."

"You want proof?" He stood and pulled something from his back pocket. "Have you ever seen this before?" A Ziploc baggie unrolled before my eyes. Inside, a single black card tumbled with bluish purple flower petals.

I nodded, my breathing shallow, and pointed to the wall at the flower petals pictured. My anger toward Rustin dissolved.

"In person?" he asked.

Cold sweat broke over my skin. I nodded. "I've seen Nightshade flowers before."

"The flower petals aren't what's rattling your cage. You know what this is."

I shook my head because I really hadn't known what the card was for that Klive had given to me, that Henley gave me, that Jase found on my pillow. Technically, I wasn't lying.

"Where did you get that?" I rushed like my head had been held under water, the question like oxygen at the surface.

"How did your prints get on it?"

Hell, I wasn't sure which one he had.

"A patron left it at the bar. I get business cards all the time that I don't pay attention to." Again, not technically lying. "I'm almost positive it was in the mix of cards I looked at once, so where or how did you get it?"

Rustin squatted so that he was eye-level. Psychological gaming. Trying to play me.

"In addition to spying on me, were you two going through my things? Perhaps the night that you both stayed over at my apartment without asking permission first?" I accused.

He stared, unresponsive. I realized he was trying to make me nervous so I'd babble all my secrets away. I didn't have anything to hide from him because they'd taken what they wanted from me without permission. I was angry, but I wasn't stupid. I shook my head and stood up.

"If I'm not under arrest, I'm leaving. This is bullshit. You two are no better than the guys on that wall. Thanks for the enlightenment."

"Kinsley, it's his calling card. Klive King's. He gives it to his prey as a warning that he's coming for them. A single puff of smoke like the vapor off his barrel after a life has been extinguished. Like blowing out the flame of a candle. This was on Sara's body before the forensics unit showed up. The petals, too. Awful coincidence this was in your possession before it was with her while she wore your uniform to work. A place she hadn't shown her face in almost a month. Lost some weight before coming back. Your name on the schedule. Your name on the shirt. Low lighting ... see where I'm going with all this?"

"What are you saying?" I slowly turned to face him. The door opened behind me, but I was too rooted to care.

"He's saying that *you* are Klive's target." A woman's voice jarred the tense silence. I spun to see Jase and a Hispanic woman. Petite. Coral lipstick. Full hips and tiny waist. *The stacked helicopter pilot from the club!*

She walked inside and made the space feel crowded. Her hand extended my way. "Carmen Solis. I've been assigned as Jase's partner in this investigation. Glad to officially meet you. Sorry the circumstances aren't positive." She looked me up and down. "Girl, what happened to you? She's bleeding."

Jase sighed. "She set off the traps and cut her ankle. It was either I dive on top of her or she take an arrow to the throat. It'll all wash off. She's alive."

"And we need to keep you that way," Carmen said. "Sit back down. We need to cover some ground."

"No offense, but I can't handle much more right now. I'm wiped, depleted. I need sleep."

"Fun fact about Klive King," Carmen said, "he doesn't sleep more than about four hours per day, and not always in one frame. Cat naps work just fine for him. He's got a genius IQ, loves the thrill of the hunt and never misses a mark. You are an unusual circumstance. He's never left his prints before, but they're all over that card with your own. A very opportune mistake that could be the key to his undoing."

"So, I was right?" I looked up at Jase and Rustin with angry accusation. "You *do* want to use me. Maybe have been all along.

Guess Klive isn't the only one who wanted a little fun before finishing the job, eh? If he's never left prints before, how do you guys even know he has anything to do with these people? I don't see anything."

Carmen turned to peer up at the guys. "*Both* of you? Really? You both slept with the holy roller? You want to go to hell?"

"I'm in hell already," Jase told her with a snarky smirk. "Know what they say about misery loving company? Figured I'd drag Rustin down with me."

"I'm so glad sleeping with me is such a miserable game for you two. Game over." I crossed my arms over my chest and shook my head. "What did you do, Jase? Get too involved with me and need Rustin to bang me too so you could throw safe distance between us after all that talk of marriage and babies, life together?"

"You should stop talking for all the reasons you just named," Carmen said with a soothing hand on my thigh that wasn't soothing at all. I didn't like her. "It's like Will told you in his interrogation. You can know something and have no option to act because you can't prove it. We just know. This card is golden. Now, Kinsley, you're tired. Grieved. Shell-shocked. Let's get you inside, cleaned up, fed and maybe let you take a nap."

"It's like midnight. I'm in need of more than a nap and I don't want to go inside the house, I want to go home. I have no desire to sleep here in any of these beds ever again."

"Tough luck, babe. We need to secure your residence before we allow you to sleep there. King's been watching your apartment."

"Well, I know he's had me watched. Henley was there to protect me yesterday and implied he's watching me still."

"Henley? As in the name you must've called Klive that night at the bar?" Jase asked. "Is that the guy who was at the funeral yesterday?"

"Yes. He said we'd met before but that I'd been too enamored with Klive to notice him again after that. He said I called Klive by his name like he was right there with us. He has this awful scar across his eye. Blind in that one. Tear drops. A tattoo on his inner left wrist. Constance spoke to him yesterday at the house. He said he'd been ordered to keep eyes on the situation for someone in high places. Said he was Nightshade. He also told me you weren't, Jase."

Jase looked at Rustin and Carmen. "We got anything on this guy?"

"Not yet," Carmen said. "Now that she's given a good description shouldn't be too hard to find those features within Nightshade's syndicate."

I gasped and looked up at Jase. "My parents!"

"Remember, they're out with mine right now. Supposed to stay out all night. He's watching an empty house."

"Is this why you told me to get out of my apartment? You said you'd been watching, too, Jase."

"Yes. Why leave his calling card on your pillow, baby? Plans may have changed tonight when he thought you were at work."

I couldn't even wrap my mind around what he was implying.

34 | ♀

COULD THAT BE?

"Kins, your dad said they have vacation," Jase said. "When do they leave?"

"They're supposed to leave after I have dinner with them tomorrow, so Sunday morning. Jase, if they've heard about this, they're not going anywhere. Hell, my dad will probably make me go with them. Quit my job, quit everything to keep an eye on me."

Rustin nodded. "Let's get you packed up and presentable. Head to your place together. I'll take the couch. Carmen can pull surveillance. When your parents wake up, I'll be sure to let them know that what Sara got herself mixed up in had nothing to do with anyone but herself. Authorities aren't releasing the specifics of her death like the uniform bearing your name."

"Did she bring it on herself?" I asked him. "You said you'd let Jase know when you got back. Here we are."

"Oh, suddenly you've got your second wind?" Carmen asked me. I inhaled my irritation. She knew I didn't like her. She didn't care.

"Fine." I stood and asked for an escort like a bitchy smart ass. "Wouldn't want to take an accidental arrow to the throat or be tackled by Sasquatch before he needs to throw my body to his alligator."

Jase shook his head. I expected him to storm out of the shed with that shitty look on his face. Instead, he jerked me to him and threw me over his shoulder the way he was so fond of doing like he was deliberately trying to piss me off.

We stepped into the dark of night. My eyes had to adjust, but Jase trudged through the black shapes of trees and shrubs like he wore his night vision goggles.

I lifted my head to look at Rustin in the glow of the door frame with Carmen talking to him. They stayed put. Good. I wanted space.

"You can put me down, Jase."

"Nope. You'll run away from me like I'm the bad guy in your life. The one who wants to kill you. The one who somehow doesn't want to make a life with you or have babies with you because I gave you life-saving information about a man you almost slept with. What's it gonna take to drill the truth into your thick skull, Kinsley?"

"At least shift me to piggy-back because I've done so much crying my nose is burning. Hanging this way makes all the blood rush to my already pounding head. Please."

He stopped but didn't allow me to do the shifting myself. He maneuvered me in an awkward way I had to help with. This was ridiculous.

"Better?" he asked. Our pace resumed.

"Not really. Why are you doing this?"

"Personal reasons. It's not my chosen profession. I'd much rather be on mission with my guys."

"Is this a military operation?"

"No. I told you I'm done. They gave me an unfavorable discharge after I started a firestorm for dropping bodies who were stoning a woman to death. I couldn't sit and watch. Did time in Leavenworth before I got a visit from the acronym you've never heard of. They knew I was from Tampa, offered to reinstate me and clear my name if I helped take this guy down. They can't touch him because we can't prove a thing. We need proof, but we also don't know who King answers to. We're in new territory with you, Kinsley. He's *never* delayed gratification. *Never* left a link back to himself. Whoever ordered the hit has got to be floored King hasn't delivered yet. You don't call King unless you want the job done in a snap, no trace. You also don't get an audience with him unless you've gone through multiple Nightshade channels. The guys surrounding him are like barriers, the first few barriers treat you like you're crazy if you ask about him. As if King doesn't exist in Nightshade. Yet, you've been invited straight into the court with the ruler himself."

I gripped his neck and shoulders a little harder while he adjusted his hold on my thighs to tuck me closer as well. Like I was precious, and he couldn't stand letting me out of his sight or even his grasp. Shame washed over me for how I kept giving Jase a hard time where his feelings were concerned.

"What if this acronym hired the hit knowing I was a weakness for Klive?" I whispered.

Jase's pace faltered. "They wouldn't do that." He reached up to his ear like he had an itch, balled his fist a second later and hooked his arm back under my leg. "Anyone ever tell you how sharp you are when you're not busting balls, baby? That would've been a brilliant idea. Dirty, but brilliant. However, if they want my cooperation, hiring a hit on my girl would send me in the opposite direction. I'd rather go back to prison than help anyone who'd put my girl in the cross-hairs just to catch a killer."

"I can't believe any of this, Jase. I can't believe you have gone through so much without anyone knowing. I'm so sorry. That must've been awful. You're a good man for saving that woman's life. You don't belong in prison for anything."

"She still died. So did a couple others. I let everyone down when I broke orders. Like your gag order, I'm not allowed to discuss this. Just know Tyndall and my parents know the truth. So does Rustin. He is here on a favor as my handler to keep me on track. I had to pick someone willing to vouch for me. I screw this shit up, Rustin goes down with me."

Tears filled my eyes. As heavy as I'd thought my life-situation had gotten tonight, Jase's everyday burden was unbearable.

"If you are so tainted, why does the military community still respond so favorably toward you? I've seen the way the vets at the bar respect you and I've also seen the disdain they can have for someone who was dishonorable. Carmen's retired Commander at the club didn't look at you with disapproval. Neither did the groups you had gathered around you that night. Hell, they were *with* you when you were sitting with Klive at his table. None of this shit makes sense. I guess I just don't understand how this works. You told me yourself Klive bailed you out of jail. Mutual respect."

"The community talks. There are a lot of people who think my punishment was overkill since the others who'd died during that event were terrorists on our list. Targets. The CIA wanted them alive to follow for bigger gain. More than a few of us got sick of recon and letting these people live after the violent shit we saw them pull on innocent people, women and children included. The military trains you to kill, to suffer, to keep pushing. No one trains you to sit still and watch rape and murder. I snapped. Took the shots too many others wanted to make all along."

My eyes closed as my heart clenched for the things Jase had to live with. This poor man. No wonder the light was gone from his eyes.

"Kins, as far as Klive goes, he's like a double-sided coin. Double life. Popular. Big money buys clout and free drinks, and I don't know many in the military who turn down free drinks. Loyalty is very cheap if you know how to gauge someone's price. Klive has a *lot* of loyalty, holds damning secrets over big and small names alike.

"His favorite personality type is former military who've gone rogue. Soldiers of fortune. Another reason they approached me instead of someone else. I fit the bill. I'm trying to get invited in and I'm *so* close. Klive's vetting me, but the closer I get, the more often you're around and he's distracted. I won't lie to you, it's an unexpected bonus and curse in one. Whether it's because he's attracted to his target, debating whether to kill you, we just don't know what to think. We also don't know who wants you gone or why. Hell, someone may not have even hired him to kill you. I wouldn't put it past King to want you dead for the distraction and the shit he's had to deal with on Inferno's end.

"Nightshade has Inferno under their shoe. Klive controls Nightshade. I guarantee he's displeased about their boundary-testing. That shit you said to Ray Castille yesterday about being a queen to an honorable king over the ruler of a crumbling kingdom? That was some seriously messy shit you may have brought to Klive's doorstep."

I released a shaky breath against his neck. "I can't apologize for what I said to that asshole. He pissed me off. I am sorry if I somehow got Sara in deeper with my words. Jase, what if you guys are thinking too much into everything? Couldn't this really be about Sara? The way it started. Like whoever Patrick Scott stiffed wanting to finish the job and send the message?"

He nodded. "Indeed, it could. Garrett told police he thinks she set you up to take her fall. There's more there than anyone's letting on. Marcus is torn between caring about her and agreeing with Garrett. The more like you she tailored herself, the less I trusted her. Bayleigh told police she took you to the beach bar that day to make Sara own up to the things she was running from that put you at risk. Seems everyone at the bar agrees Sara was up to something nefarious. Coming to my house the other night was below the belt. Not sure how she got my address, but if she had it, found it, others she had dealings with probably do too."

Something scurried through the shrubs. I gasped and gripped Jase's neck too hard. He gave a choked sound and laughed when I loosened my grip.

"We're gonna have to work on your country girl skills, Kins." I heard his smile fade before he picked up in a more somber tone. "I need to test your self-defense, add to what Nate taught you." I closed my eyes at Nate's name, at all of this. The idea of needing to defend myself or die.

"Kins, I made some calls. His kid is four. Guess he left you when he learned he had a daughter. He didn't cheat, he did right by the mother. I just wanted you to know he wasn't a shit bag."

I kissed Jase's neck and left my lips against his skin. His hair tickled my nose. "Thank you, Jase. For everything."

"I love you, Kins."

"I know. I'm sorry for doubting you."

"I forgive you, baby."

We traveled in silence till I saw the vapor light in front of the house through the woods.

"Jase, Sara was a whore," I said. "She confessed to being one before she met Patrick. Said she picked it back up to make ends meet when she hid from Patrick. Do you think Klive killed her to keep her from getting me killed?"

Klive just seemed too interested to want me dead. Henley didn't feel threatening. Nightshade really did seem to treat me more like Klive's queen. So did Inferno if I thought of how Ray wanted me to order Henley and Jase around. This was big. Jarrell and Gustav were on Nightshade's side, hell Constance acted like they weren't nefarious characters, but criminals were just that. Was Jase keeping Constance close to use her for connections too?

"It's possible. But dead, Sara can't pay the debts Patrick didn't before he died."

"Meaning?" I wished I hadn't brought this up. Jase slid me down his body when we got to the back door. He faced me. His hands gripped my biceps, rubbed in a soothing manner.

"Meaning they're still coming for you, baby."

"They, being Inferno?" I asked as we walked inside.

"I think so." Jase led the way to his bedroom. I walked into his bathroom while he turned on the shower. We were both messy from the mud dive. I began pulling my clothing off while Jase did the same. My elbow and ankles had dried blood mixed with dirt and moss.

"According to your hunch, Klive controls Nightshade," I said, took off my shirt, barely felt my ribs. "Nightshade keeps a boot on Inferno's neck." Down came the shorts. "Inferno has been screwing with me because Sara set them up to." Panties tossed. "Klive seems hesitant to kill me to maintain the peace." I walked into the shower where the floor was already colored in the mud rinsing from Jase. "Is this a fair summary?" I ignored the sting of water cleansing the various cuts and scrapes marring my body. Now, Angela wasn't the only one who looked like she'd been in a car accident. I was a damn mess.

"If we're simplifying, yeah. Assuming we are going with the Inferno theory. Shampoo?" Jase held the bottle while I cupped my hands and wet my hair. We took turns beneath the water after sudsing our tresses. We shared conditioner.

"Jase." I ran body wash over his torso, tattoo, held to his shoulders while looking into his face. "I can't stand the idea of you ever going back to prison. *Ever.* I can't tell you that I'd ever want to see you reinstated and deployed into the misery you described, but it's not my place to judge what you honor; that duty you have to your men. If bad men are after me no matter what, let me help you get in to do what you must do. If I'm the key, use me. I ..." A lump of emotion filled my throat. "Jase, I love you."

Klive's voice on the phone today popped back in my mind. *A worthy adversary. Was this what he'd meant after all? That now I was somehow ready for him? Rekindling our battle?*

Tears blended into the splash of shower water on my cheeks. Jase sighed and wrapped his soapy arms around me. His arousal pressed against my bare belly, but he didn't try anything. Just hugged me. Held me beneath the water for a long while.

35 | ♀

WHEN WE WERE CLEAN, dry, dressed, I was ready to go back to my place if only to be back in something other than Jase's ginormous sweats in eighty degrees. Of course, I couldn't argue since he'd pointed out the pirate coat was too heavy for the same weather.

The ride home was lost to the cluttered mind map my conscience tip-toed through. Every internal path seemed riddled with unexpected land mines. When would the next explode and obliterate what I thought was true? I tried removing myself from the problem to see this from above or read the mess like a character in a book. Objectivity. What would I be screaming at the protagonist in the moment? I think I'd have put the book down and said a praise of thanks that this girl wasn't me.

How was this girl me? How was Klive so bad yet good at getting away with those deeds? Was my one misfortune running into him in that elevator two years ago? Klive didn't strike me as the type to be so calculating that he got away with this much yet targeted someone due to annoyance alone. Klive was a cunning strategist, that much I'd garnered through questions he'd asked at lunch with Ben and my father. Even if they'd been talking shop, I could replace the doctor's name in the scenario with any criminal element. The whole structure could work with the same simple precepts.

Jase said Klive didn't deal only in money, but knowledge, secrets. Hell, I found the more I wanted to stop thinking of Klive, the more he consumed my thoughts. I just couldn't do this; couldn't be hopping on the back of a killer's motorcycle, snuggling in a killer's coat for comfort, wearing a killer's clothing, be a killer's submissive queen. Maybe Klive wasn't the killer. What if Henley was used as a secret weapon and way of keeping his hands clean? If Jase and Carmen had never seen Henley before, though Klive deployed this man to keep me specifically in his sights, maybe Klive wasn't who I needed to fear. Ugh!

I sat in the truck while Jase checked inside my apartment. Rustin stayed outside after doing a perimeter check. Rustin was on my naughty list. *What the heck was up with him and Will coming at me that way during interrogation? How long had he been worming in close to me for my value with Klive? Jase said he wasn't using me, but Jase also had deep history with me. Rustin had no qualms about using anyone for their body so why would that somehow stop when a case was on the line, especially if Jase said Rustin was trying to make a name for himself here in Florida? Could I really fault him for pushing to make the progress that they needed to keep Jase a free man?*

Jase was in prison.

Talk about the worst part about the whole situation. Before I lost myself in the misery of my mistakes, I had to realize the reality Jase faced if I failed at this. The idea made me want to puke. *How could Tyndall not tell me about her brother being in prison? Had she gone to visit him? Was she ashamed?*

Jase jogged back down the stairs. I fought tears of grief at my valiant warrior behind bars for trying to save a woman from being stoned to death. *Oh, God, please let me do right by him.*

"Hey, you mind unlocking the main house for me?" he asked. I nodded and swiped my nose. He gave a tight, sympathetic smile that didn't reach his honey eyes. My house key slipped inside the locks before I opened the door for my boyfriend who went in like a Bloodhound looking for a scent. Sphinx meowed at us while he paused grooming in an unflattering position. Jase cracked a joke, but I couldn't smile. He nodded his understanding.

"Hey, Jase, will you text your dad for me and see how everything is going?" I asked. "What time he thinks they'll be back? You said he knows this stuff?"

"Yeah, no secrets from him." Jase took his phone out and texted as I wandered into the kitchen. "He says they don't plan to be back till tomorrow evening. I told him I needed your dad distracted. He's talking him into a day at Busch Gardens. We might get lucky and keep your dad away from all news for at least a day. Then, you can work your magic on him Sunday morning. They can leave, we can pick up my sister, all will be good."

"Wow. Well done," I said, half-listening. I thumbed through Mom's mail piled on the small business area she crafted for correspondence and invitations. She did Calligraphy and elegant handwritten lettering for weddings and parties. Stacks of events sat in even piles of pretty parchment. Her specialty pens and ink, embossing tools, pads, dyes, stored in a wall unit Daddy had built her. I tilted my head as I grabbed the invitations that had our own names on them. These weren't in her signature styling.

"What's that, baby?" Jase walked up behind me. He read the invitation aloud over my shoulder. "You going to some party on Friday? What's with the Old English?"

"I'm not sure, but my name is on this with my parents' and cousins', so probably something my eccentric Uncle Edwin has us going to."

"I'll have to get more information and see if we can get on the inside to keep an eye on you," he said.

"Yay. More spies," I said. "Guess I'd rather know than continue feeling eyes and telling myself I'm paranoid."

"I'm sorry, Kins. I just want to keep you safe."

"I know, Jase. I'm used to being my own person. Feels like there will be no alone time for the foreseeable future. I never really contemplated the luxury of going and coming as I want without anything but my parents to worry about."

"This too shall pass, right?"

I looked over my shoulder to assess his expression.

"Yeah," he said with a sheepish tone, "I told you I've read the words. Can I have that invitation for now?"

I nodded, passed the pretty card stock back to him. My empty hands rested on the counter. Maybe I could see how he was bitter about scripture. Faith was easy when things were good. To use those words for comfort with small time problems like passing an exam or winning a heat. This mountain before me held more than one peak but loomed like an entire range. I stood before the insurmountable like a newbie with bright white cross-trainers thinking I was going to climb sheer cliff-faces without help. What an idiot. A naïve, foolish idiot. My father used that word playfully, but this was no joke. *How would this pass? Would I live to see that?*

"Oh, Jase, how will I continue like everything is normal when nothing is? How do I go to school on Monday when Spring Break is over? Attempt track in the condition I'm in now? Pretend I can even handle a party on Friday?"

"You won't go it alone. You'll have Tyndall, remember? She will be an immensely helpful diversion from all this heaviness."

"Are those allowed? Diversions? You want me to play like all is well? Won't that piss these people off, whichever of them is the real enemy?"

"Baby, you'll go to school and track, resume your routines to prove you are unafraid of pissing off assholes and not guilty of a damn thing Will Bartlet is looking at you for."

Damn. Confirmation Jase felt the same about Will Bartlet.

"But Rustin said—"

"I don't care right now. This is us, Kins. You and me. My girl with her boyfriend. Rustin doesn't know Will's issues the way I do. Will earned his shield fair and square but earning it so young made him the same cocky dickwad he was in high school. Rustin was just shy of earning his as well before I asked him to help me with this. Gives them something to bond over, I'm sure. I don't want to tell Rustin I've muddied yet another aspect of this with my love life, but Will graduated high school a couple years ahead of me. He's still got a chip on his shoulder from when I banged Karen Teague. They'd been together before he'd graduated. He loved her. She'd been out of sight out of mind with him. In my eyes, I did him a favor. Better she cheated before he popped the question. He doesn't have the same point of view."

I shook my head, stared at nothing. *This was my boyfriend?* I was starting to question my taste in men. Between Jase and Klive, I wasn't too confident in my personal decisions. *Where had I gone wrong?*

"Can you just not remind me of the past?" I asked. *How was I building a successful future with the same man who carried so much baggage I might buckle beneath the weight on my shoulders? Was love enough?*

Yes. Love conquers all, right?

I was just exhausted. Thinking too deeply right now wasn't a good idea. Better to ponder everything with a clear head after some sleep.

"Hey, baby, look at me." He turned me and wrapped his hands around my waist. "You will come through this because you've made it through so much more. Remember when that asshole from high school left you a crying mess in your driveway? You didn't know how you'd ever live without him? You made it. You figured out a way to keep going. I have a feeling you're gonna do better at this than you know. You're so much stronger than you think. That's how you, sweet little Kinsley Hayes, stand in the face of someone like Ray

Castille and manage to put the fear of wrath upon him with a single line. He's scared. You may think you need to be afraid, and in some ways I need you to be for the health of your well-being and safety, but I promise, dude's got his tail tucked after what you said. Klive might be afraid, too, about what pressure you may have put on him through what you said to Ray. But your fight video went so viral, I wish them luck trying to pull anything on you until your infamy dies down."

"Well, hell. I'd forgotten about all that. I haven't watched, but I have all those gifts upstairs on the island in my kitchen. Maybe you're right about the attention it's drawn, but dammit, Jase, I don't want to think about Klive or Ray or *anything*. I'm so tired. All I want is for you to drive them out of my mind while you drive yourself into my body and deplete my brain of all thought."

"Mmmm ... see what I mean about how you slay a man with a single line? How could I not do as you ask?" His strong hands hoisted me onto the kitchen counter opposite my mom's workspace so we didn't mess anything up. Smart man. Before long, Jase's lip was between my teeth while we sucked each other's wind as he coaxed me into a relaxed state by forceful thrusts so rough, so raw, I loved the deferred pain too much to care if I desecrated my parents' house.

Who knows, maybe my mom would be crafting my own wedding invitations after I found out I was knocked up and we'd figured a way through these mountains?

No more thinking. No more pain. No more plotting, planning, pining. Just rough love.

While my stressors melted, Klive's accent in my head threatened to stifle the sounds of my cries against Jase's skin. Dammit!

If Klive King wanted to rekindle a battle we'd begun long ago, wanted to look at me as an adversary, he was right about one thing:

I'd be worthy because I wasn't going down without bringing him with me.

VOLUME 4 OF THE DON'T CLOSE YOUR EYES SERIES

SILVER FALCHION
FINALIST
2022

DANGEROUS GAMES

Lynessa Layne

USA Today Bestselling Author

1 | ♀ - Dangerous Games

JASE MADE MULTIPLE PHONE **calls** before we settled down in the upstairs makeshift media room of my parents' house. He felt we'd be safer where no one could see us. That Klive's eyes would be expecting the apartment. As I laid on the couch, in pure darkness, I stared up at the ceiling fan while my eyes adjusted. As a child I'd done the same thing many times when I was supposed to be napping. Like then, I wasn't sleepy, even if I felt ready to throw a tantrum. *How to sleep when the guy you ... well ... when a guy you know is looking good for the murder of a co-worker, who also looks like she set you up to be murdered in her place but in the end failed miserably?*

Jase snored at my back, his bear paw resting against my belly. According to the clock on my phone, I'd managed a two hour nap. This was one of those times I wished I soothed myself with social media like my friends. Bad idea, especially right now. I shifted. Jase's hand fell lower, gripped. Sex was a fun idea for coping, but the guilt of our romp in the kitchen roiled in my growling intestines. I moved his hand, desperate to be alone while feeling smothered in concern and body heat. He stirred, muttered an incoherent apology, scooted back into the cushions, tugged me closer.

"Close your eyes, baby. Go back to sleep." He kissed my temple.

"I can't sleep, Jase. You're too warm. I need space."

He lifted his hand to pat the wall for the light switch over the back of the couch. We both winced as light pierced the darkness. I stood up and rolled my shoulders, cracked my neck several times. His eyebrows rose over puffy eyes. A long yawn came before a nod of his head. His feet hit the carpet.

"Get dressed, Kins. No sense wasting energy while you've got it." He reached for his boots.

"What should I wear? You gonna let me go into my apartment because that's where my clothes are." I paced, hands wringing. "I need to workout."

"I know. I can see that. You think you're gonna be able to handle running while your ribs hurt?"

"Jase, I'm so amped, I think I could fight Angela all over again with these injured ribs and still come out on top." I waved him on for an answer. "Can I go to my apartment?"

He jumped up to slam a hand to the door I attempted to walk through. "Not without me. I know it's not your style, but you gotta allow someone to take charge."

"Ugh!" I growled. He snorted.

"Kins, give me my shirt."

"If I give you your shirt, what am I gonna wear?"

"You're gonna stay in here while I go to your apartment and pick clothes for you."

My mouth flat-lined. "I don't want you to pick my clothes. I'm particular."

"Too bad, Miss Independent. Give me a little credit. I've picked clothing for Tyndall many times. Stay here."

"But—"

"Stay." He left the room. I waited. Shame at my defiance mingled with fresh tears of grief for Sara brimming in my eyes. *Klive. Oh, Klive King ... did you do this? Why? When? How?*

Jase came back in about ten minutes later. To his credit, he'd retrieved one of my favorite sets of workout gear. I gasped at what rested on top. He told me he grabbed them because I'd need them.

"Where did you find these?" I asked about the pink fingerless kick-boxing gloves Klive had gifted me after my fight with Angela.

"The kitchen island in your apartment. Figured if you'd laid them out, you probably wanted to wear them to prevent more callouses on your hands from the rope climb and the net at the obstacle course. Go on, girl. You were the one with ants in your pants. You've ruined my hibernation. Get dressed. Sun comes up in about an hour." He clapped his hands while I hustled to the guest bathroom upstairs. The same bathroom that used to belong to me when I'd lived in this house. I locked the door behind me before I grabbed and held to the sink.

"Just breathe," I whispered to my reflection. *Should I tell Jase about these gloves? How I'd put them up in a box in my closet days ago? That they were from Klive?*

Who'd gone through my things to get them back out? I lifted the lid on the toilet to empty my stomach at the sickening thought that Klive may have come into my apartment! *Who was I dealing with here? Had he done that when the guys were keeping watch? What if I'd been inside when he'd come in? Would he have killed me?*

"Baby, you okay?" Jase asked through the door.

"Yep. Nerves," I said. True story. I flushed then cleaned my face, patted my cheeks with a wash cloth. My eyes were puffy, scratchy. My throat felt the same. I hoped I wasn't getting sick on top of this bullshit. I pulled Jase's big tee off my body and winced at the bruises on my ribs, the lingering shadows over my face without the cakey layers of makeup Sara put on me. *Dammit, Sara, did you get yourself killed in my place or did you set me up to die in your place only to have the plan backfire? Could she really be that awful?* Garrett certainly seemed to think so. *Did Bayleigh? Marcus?*

363

After struggling into the Lycra layers, ignoring the stabbing pain as I did, I opened the door to Jase holding socks and tennis shoes. He'd exchanged his jeans for basketball shorts. His boots were gone, replaced by flip flops. I took his offering with a harsh thanks.

"Beach time, baby. Don't forget your gloves."

"Right." *How could a gift that had given me flutters a couple days ago now make me so nauseous? How could a man I'd fallen into flurries over be a mortal enemy? Could Klive go through with something so heinous? Would he have Henley do the deed for him? Henley said as long as he was on me, I was safe. That was before I'd bucked up to Inferno's leader, Raymond Castille. But, if that had thrown everything out of whack, wouldn't Henley have reacted then rather than pretending I wasn't a problem? Ugh! Would I ever have a normal thought again?*

"Hey, baby, right here, right now. Don't get too lost in the maze inside that brain." Jase stroked my hand while he drove.

"How do you do that, Jase? I don't know how to stop thinking." I swallowed a big lump of emotion.

"I don't stop thinking. I'm always thinking, but I compartmentalize. Gotta keep focused on what I can do rather than the what-ifs. Those will pull you down to dark places. Ask me how I know."

My mind was already in dark places during the remainder of the drive. Darker than the ocean waves with no moonbeams shining on the surface.

We got out of his truck. Again, I rolled my shoulders, popped my neck, but added a jog to test my body's pain threshold. Delia's father, Dr. Duncan, warned that I'd be in pain but could still run. The choice was mine; *how much could I handle?*

Jase jogged across the empty street. I fell in beside him.

"I'm supposed to work the beach today. I may pull half a shift to keep from pissing my boss off with calling in so last minute."

I nodded, focused on breathing in ways that didn't slice new wounds inside my lungs so close to the ribs shouting in pain.

"You okay, Kins?"

"Yeah. Just jog. I don't like to talk when I'm running."

He grinned while I grimaced. *Did he like my annoyance? What the hell?*

"Good job bringing those gloves. We aren't using them for the obstacle course today, baby."

"Huh?"

He jerked to a stop, snatched my hand while my other flew automatically toward his nose. He ducked and kicked my legs out from under me. My back slammed onto the sand. Jase hovered over me, a gloating prick while I waited for oxygen to return to my lungs.

"Come on, Kins. Show me! I just attacked you! What if I was the asshole who caused you to twist your ankle a couple weeks ago? Would you lie there and let him—"

My fingertips thrust to his throat while my foot connected with his balls. I rolled to the side and shoved off the sand, spun for momentum to land a kick against his side while he cupped his jewels. He lunged, caught me, and I failed because I panicked rather than staying level-headed the way Nate taught me. Jase wrapped his arms tight around me. His mouth came to my ear.

"Shhh, I needed to test your reflexes. I need you to calm yourself. Breathe. It's me. Breathe. I won't hurt you."

Tears streamed down my cheeks while I gasped for air, sobs stealing any calm I had left while the injured ribs added to the angst. "I hate crying, Jase," my voice scraped over the raw lining of my throat. "I hate this! Hate my weakness! Jase, do it again."

"Maybe we should do the course to get you in gear."

"Don't coddle me while I cry, Jase! Do it again. You're right. If you were the asshole who'd caused me to twist my ankle a couple weeks back, my reflexes aren't good enough. If I cry during, so be it. Don't let me be this pussy. Train it out of me! Come on! Do it again!"

Jase chuckled without humor. "Careful what you ask for."

*Thank you for reading. If you enjoyed this book, please take a moment to share with the world in a review.

Acknowledgments

Thank you to my editor, TK Cassidy, for your devotion, patience and honesty. I couldn't do this without you and my associate editor and consultant, AJ Alford.

Thanks to AJ, I can get as nitty-gritty and/or raw in masculinity as I need without being unrealistic.

Thank you once more to my grandmother, Garlene, for consistently asking when these novels will be published in paperback.

Thank you to each reader who has reached out to me about these books, whether ebook or paperback queries. You drive me forward and bring joy to the rocky road of mistakes and learning the hard way. You also reinvigorate my love for this series, because I wrote these books for myself first when I couldn't find what I wanted to read.

A warm thank you to my friends at TWIG, including TK, and Suanne Shaefer from WFWA for constructive criticism and critique. I wouldn't be the writer I am today without that tough love.

About Lynessa Layne

Lynessa Layne is a native Texan from the small town of Plantersville. She's a fan of exploration, history, the beach (though she's photosensitive), Jesus, and America too (RIP Tom). Besides being an avid reader, she's obsessed with music of all types (hence her reference to Tom Petty). As a child, she created music videos in her mind and played Barbies perhaps a little longer than most with her little sister, not yet realizing she was writing and enacting stories all along.

Though she's put away the dolls, she now uses her novels as an updated, grown-up version of the same play.

Lynessa is also a certified copy editor and a member of Mystery Writers of America, with work featured by Writer's Digest and Mystery and Suspense Magazine. She has also graced the cover of GEMS (Godly Entrepreneurs & Marketers) Magazine and was a finalist for Killer Nashville's 2022 Silver Falchion Awards for Best Suspense and Reader's Choice.

For more visit lynessalayne.com and sign up for her newsletter, Lit with Lynnie and follow on social media:

https://www.facebook.com/authorlynessalayne

https://www.instagram.com/lynessalayne/

https://twitter.com/LynessaLayne

Writers like me depend on
readers like you.
Please leave a positive review.
Thanks
♡ - Lynessa

Made in the USA
Middletown, DE
27 July 2024